G.I. JOE

A REAL AMERICAN HERO

VOLUME 20

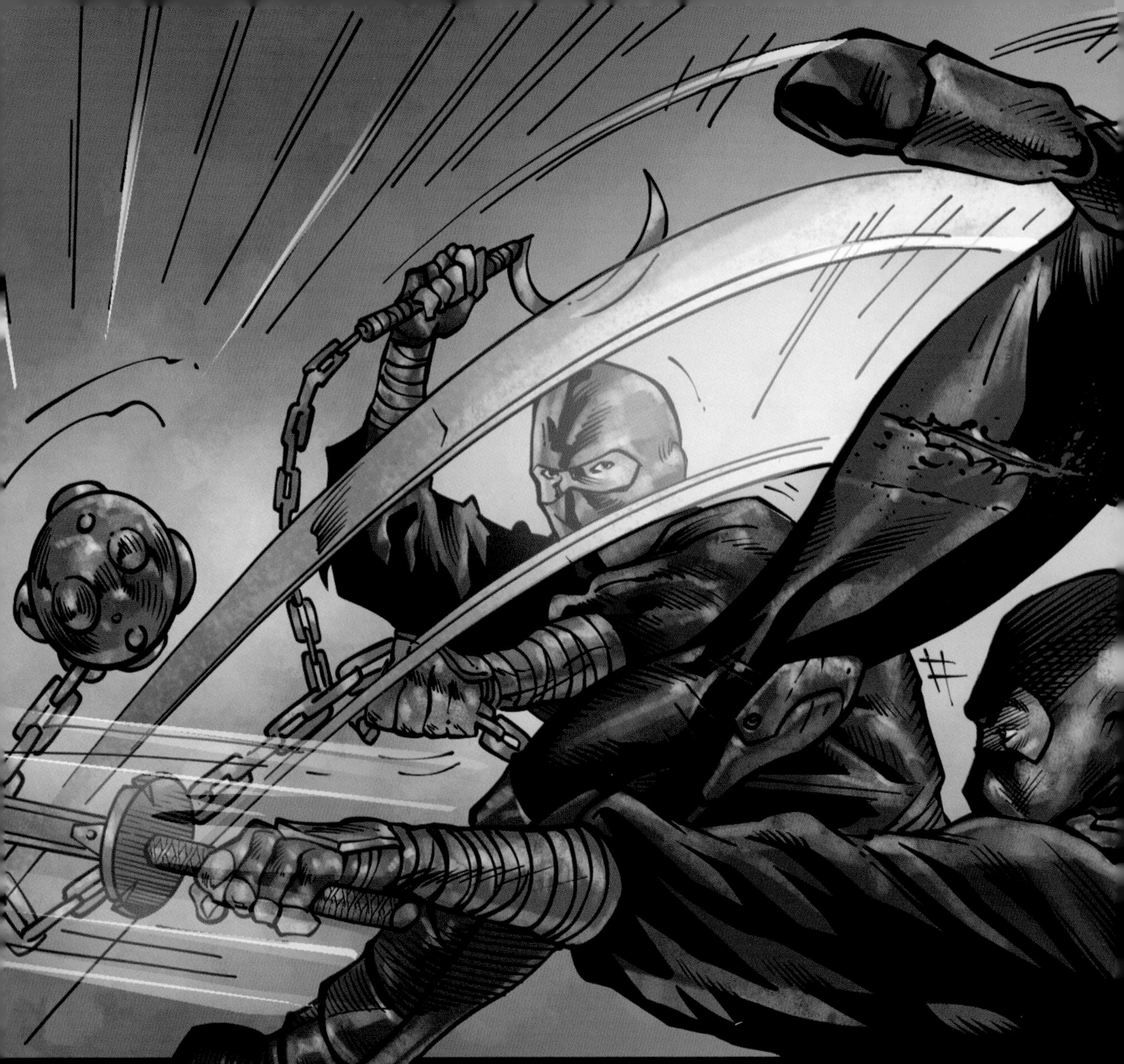

Licensed By:

Hasbro

IDW

Greg Goldstein, President & Publisher
Robbie Robbins, EVP & Sr. Art Director
Matthew Ruzicka, CPA, Chief Financial Officer
David Hedgecock, Associate Publisher
Laurie Windrow, Sr. VP of Sales & Marketing
Lorelei Bunjes, VP of Digital Services
Jerry Bennington, VP of New Product Development
Eric Moss, Sr. Director, Licensing & Business Development

Ted Adams, Founder & CEO of IDW Media Holdings

For international rights, please contact
licensing@idwpublishing.com

Special thanks to Hasbro's Derryl DePriest, Ed Lane, Beth Artale, and Michael Kelly for their invaluable assistance.

ISBN: 978-1-68405-257-8   21 20 19 18   1 2 3 4

Become our fan on Facebook facebook.com/idwpublishing
Follow us on Twitter @idwpublishing
Subscribe to us on YouTube youtube.com/idwpublishing
See what's new on Tumblr tumblr.idwpublishing.com

G.I. JOE: A REAL AMERICAN HERO, VOLUME 20. JULY 2018. FIRST PRINTING. IDW Publishing, a division of Idea and Design Works, LLC. Editorial offices: 2765 Truxtun Road, San Diego, CA 92106. Printed in Korea.

Originally published as G.I. JOE: A REAL AMERICAN HERO issues #246–250.

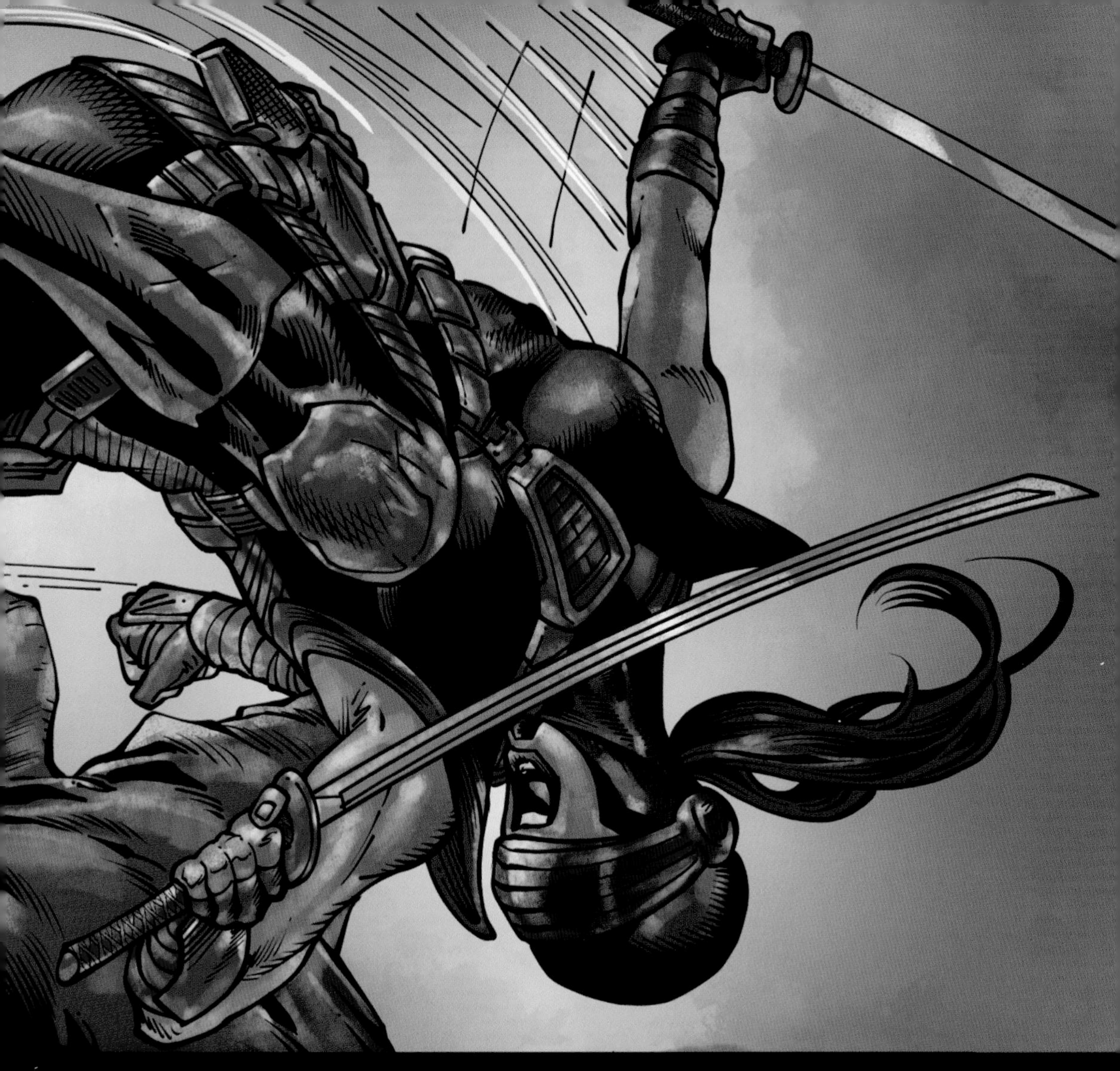

DAWN OF THE ARASHIKAGE

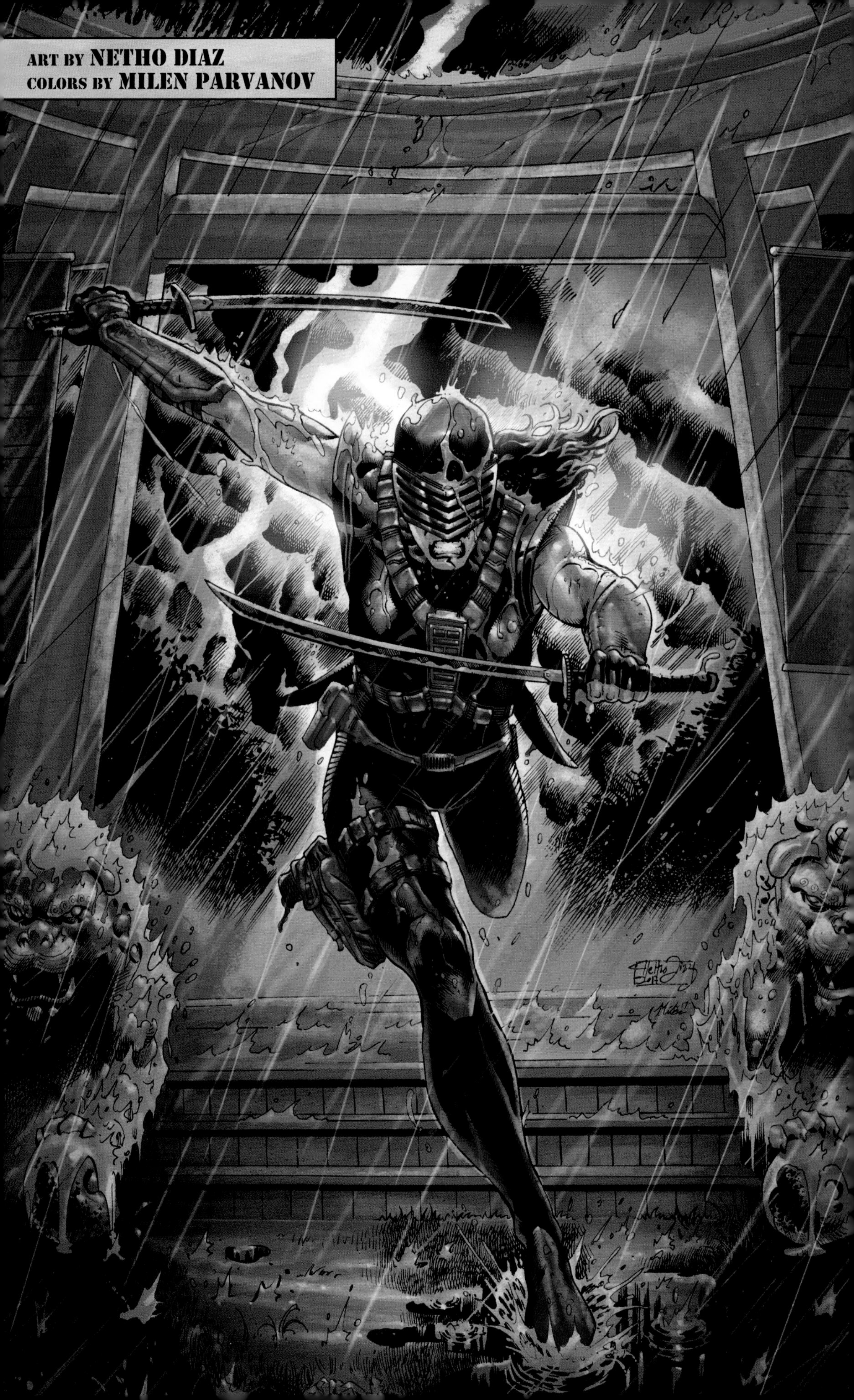

ART BY NETHO DIAZ
COLORS BY MILEN PARVANOV

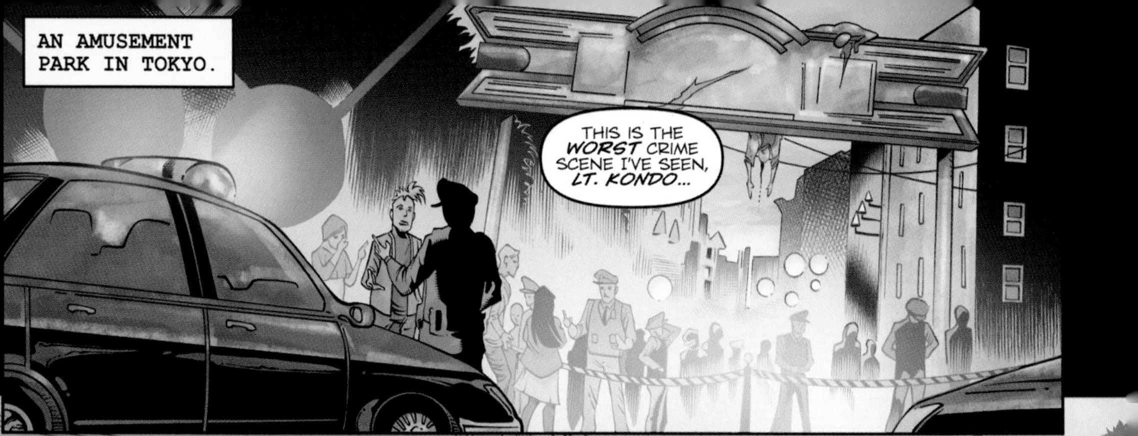
AN AMUSEMENT PARK IN TOKYO.
THIS IS THE WORST CRIME SCENE I'VE SEEN, LT. KONDO...

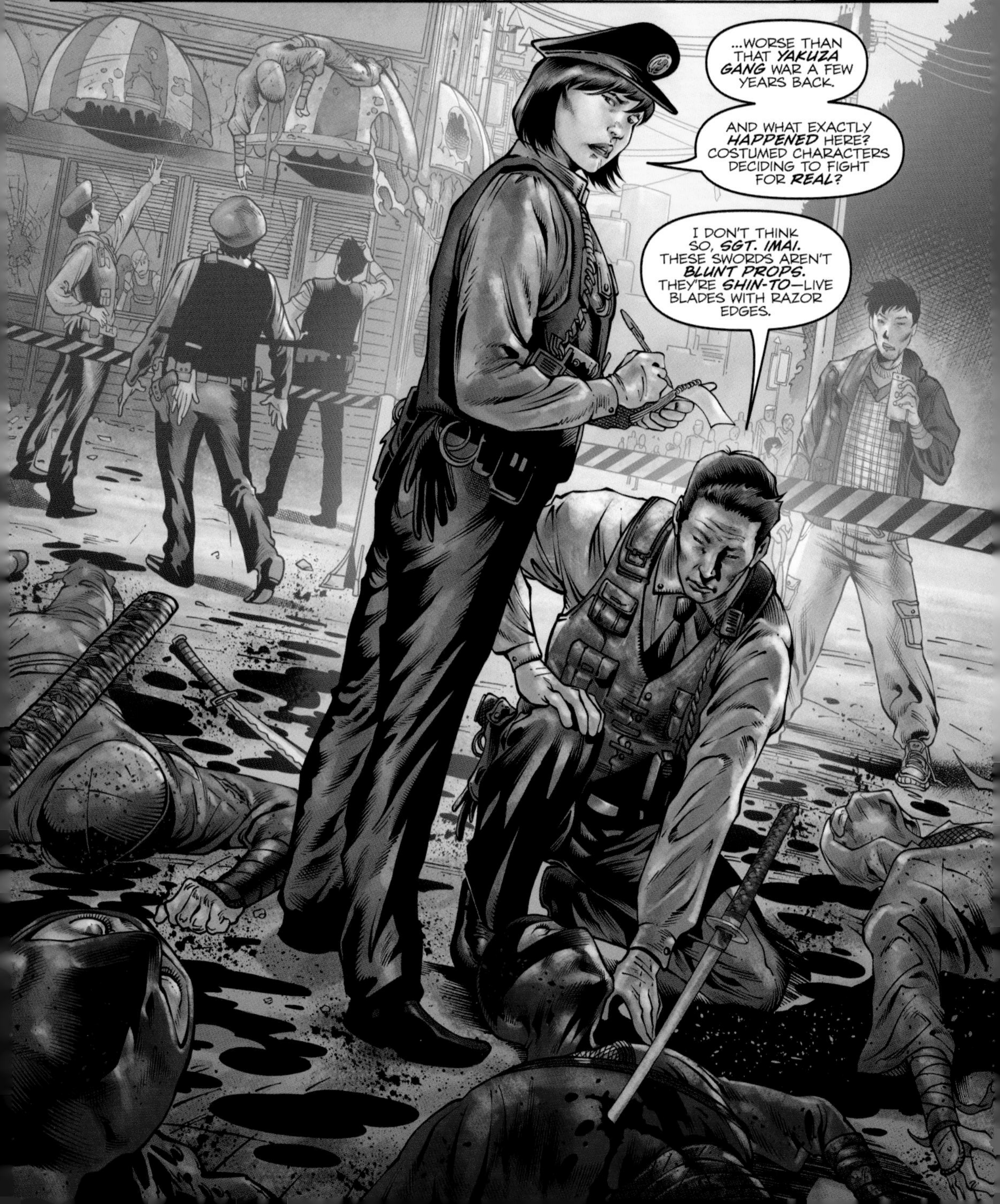
...WORSE THAN THAT YAKUZA GANG WAR A FEW YEARS BACK.
AND WHAT EXACTLY HAPPENED HERE? COSTUMED CHARACTERS DECIDING TO FIGHT FOR REAL?
I DON'T THINK SO, SGT. IMAI. THESE SWORDS AREN'T BLUNT PROPS. THEY'RE SHIN-TO—LIVE BLADES WITH RAZOR EDGES.

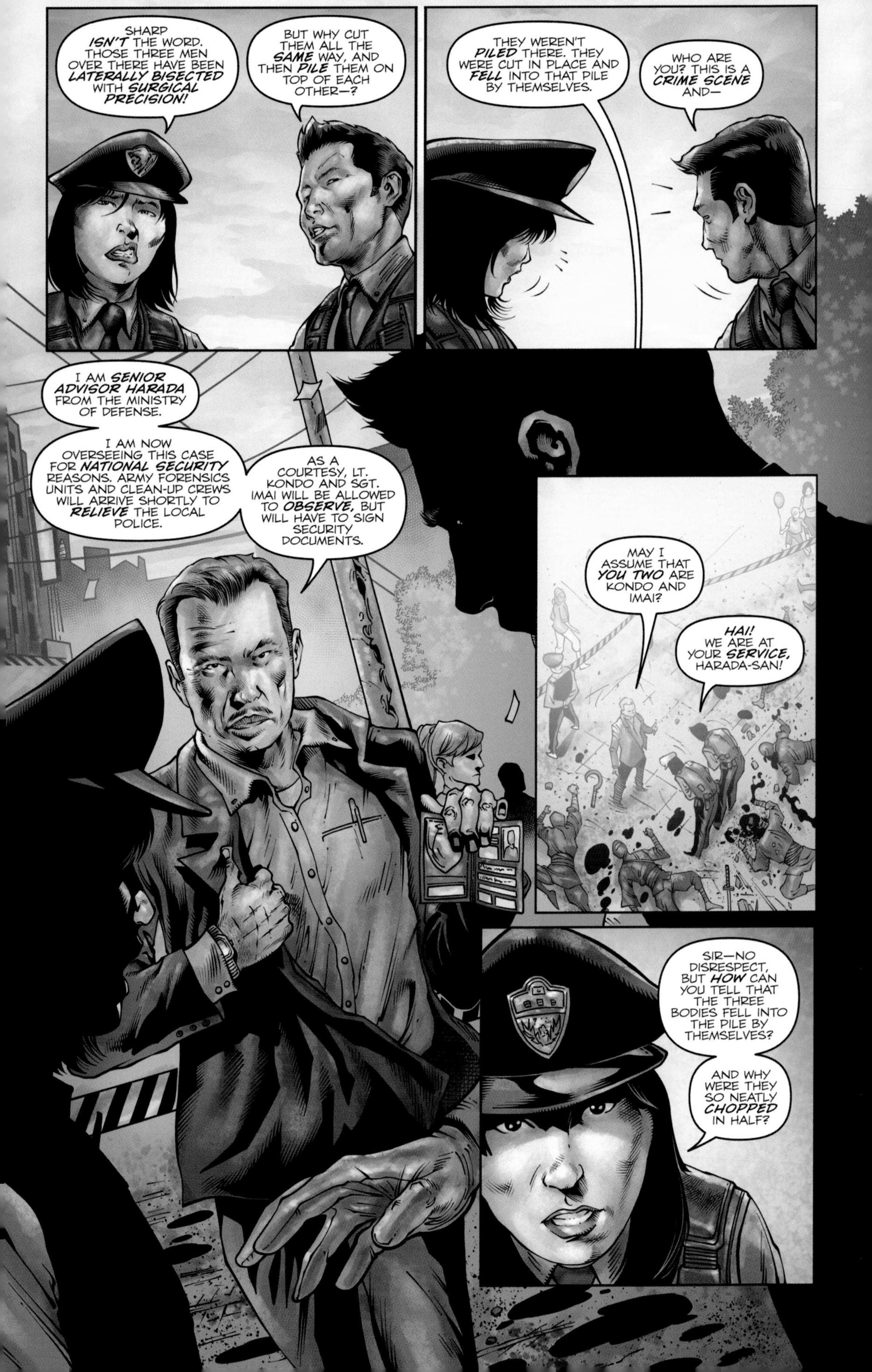

SHARP ISN'T THE WORD. THOSE THREE MEN OVER THERE HAVE BEEN LATERALLY BISECTED WITH SURGICAL PRECISION!
BUT WHY CUT THEM ALL THE SAME WAY, AND THEN PILE THEM ON TOP OF EACH OTHER—?
THEY WEREN'T PILED THERE. THEY WERE CUT IN PLACE AND FELL INTO THAT PILE BY THEMSELVES.
WHO ARE YOU? THIS IS A CRIME SCENE AND—
I AM SENIOR ADVISOR HARADA FROM THE MINISTRY OF DEFENSE.
I AM NOW OVERSEEING THIS CASE FOR NATIONAL SECURITY REASONS. ARMY FORENSICS UNITS AND CLEAN-UP CREWS WILL ARRIVE SHORTLY TO RELIEVE THE LOCAL POLICE.
AS A COURTESY, LT. KONDO AND SGT. IMAI WILL BE ALLOWED TO OBSERVE, BUT WILL HAVE TO SIGN SECURITY DOCUMENTS.
MAY I ASSUME THAT YOU TWO ARE KONDO AND IMAI?
HAI! WE ARE AT YOUR SERVICE, HARADA-SAN!
SIR—NO DISRESPECT, BUT HOW CAN YOU TELL THAT THE THREE BODIES FELL INTO THE PILE BY THEMSELVES?
AND WHY WERE THEY SO NEATLY CHOPPED IN HALF?

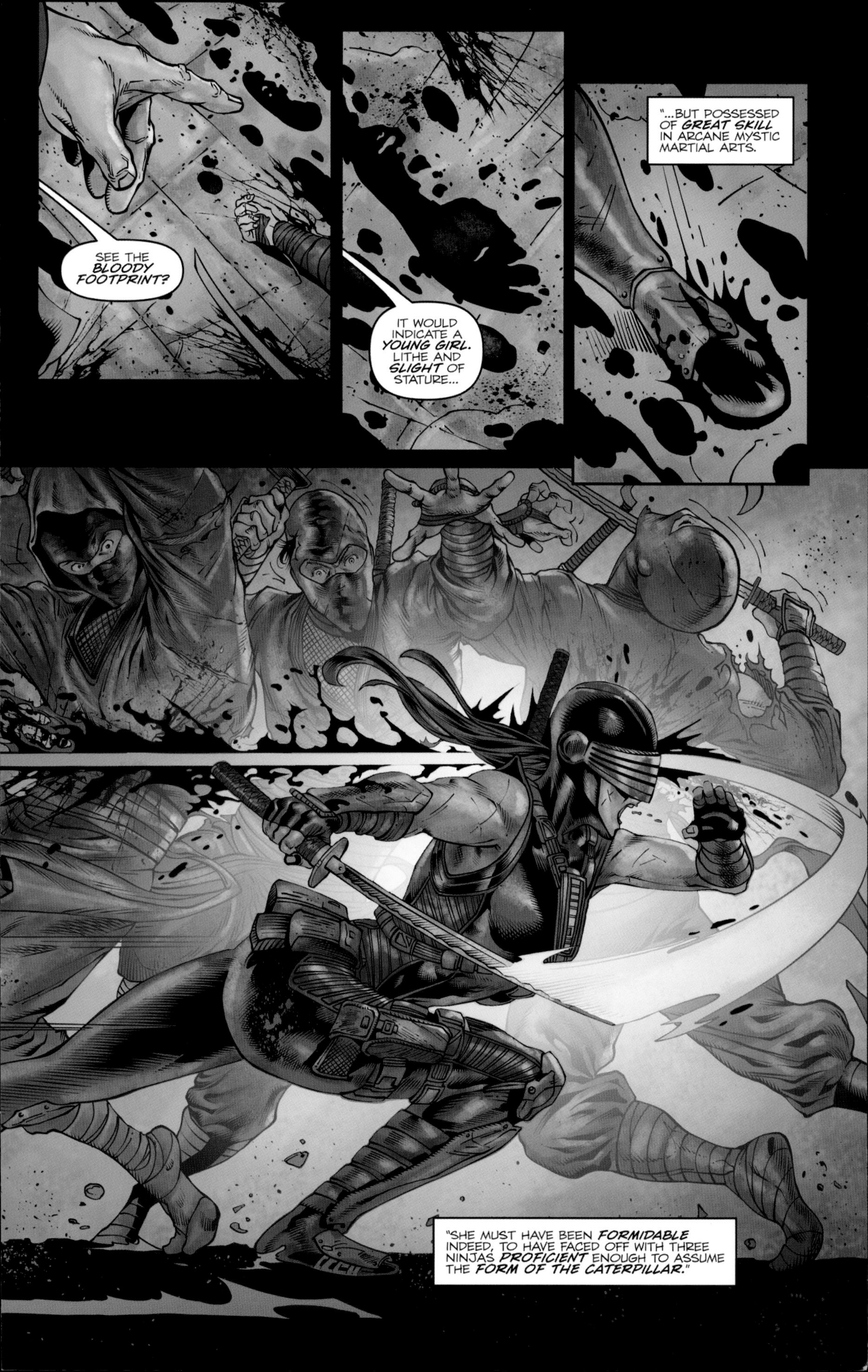

SEE THE *BLOODY FOOTPRINT?*
IT WOULD INDICATE A *YOUNG GIRL.* LITHE AND *SLIGHT* OF STATURE...
"...BUT POSSESSED OF *GREAT SKILL* IN ARCANE MYSTIC MARTIAL ARTS.
"SHE MUST HAVE BEEN *FORMIDABLE* INDEED, TO HAVE FACED OFF WITH THREE NINJAS *PROFICIENT* ENOUGH TO ASSUME THE *FORM OF THE CATERPILLAR.*"

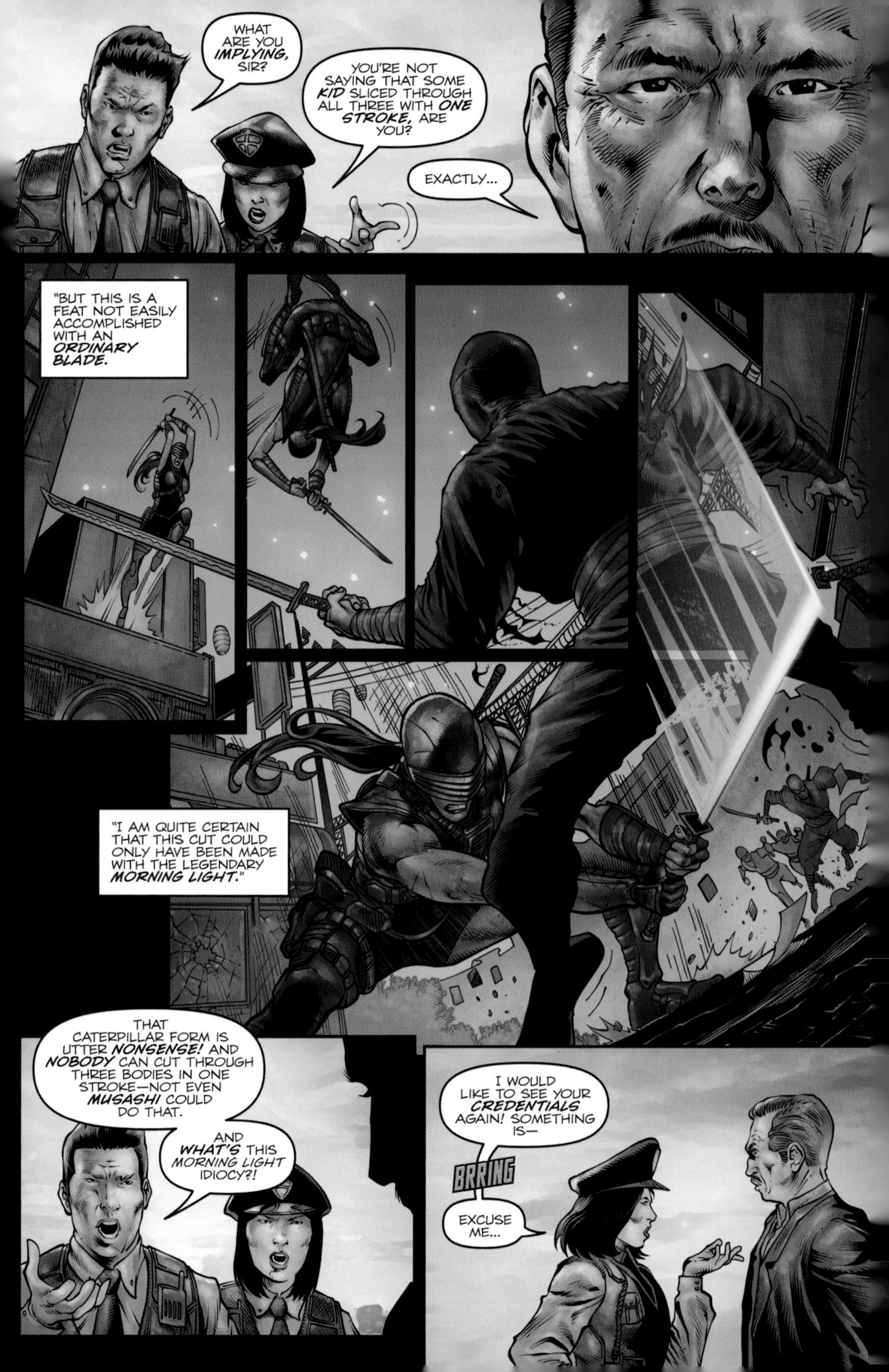
WHAT ARE YOU *IMPLYING*, SIR?
YOU'RE NOT SAYING THAT SOME *KID* SLICED THROUGH ALL THREE WITH *ONE STROKE*, ARE YOU?
EXACTLY...
"BUT THIS IS A FEAT NOT EASILY ACCOMPLISHED WITH AN *ORDINARY BLADE*.
"I AM QUITE CERTAIN THAT THIS CUT COULD ONLY HAVE BEEN MADE WITH THE LEGENDARY *MORNING LIGHT*."
THAT CATERPILLAR FORM IS UTTER *NONSENSE!* AND *NOBODY* CAN CUT THROUGH THREE BODIES IN ONE STROKE—NOT EVEN *MUSASHI* COULD DO THAT.
AND *WHAT'S* THIS *MORNING LIGHT* IDIOCY?!
I WOULD LIKE TO SEE YOUR *CREDENTIALS* AGAIN! SOMETHING IS—
BRRING
EXCUSE ME...

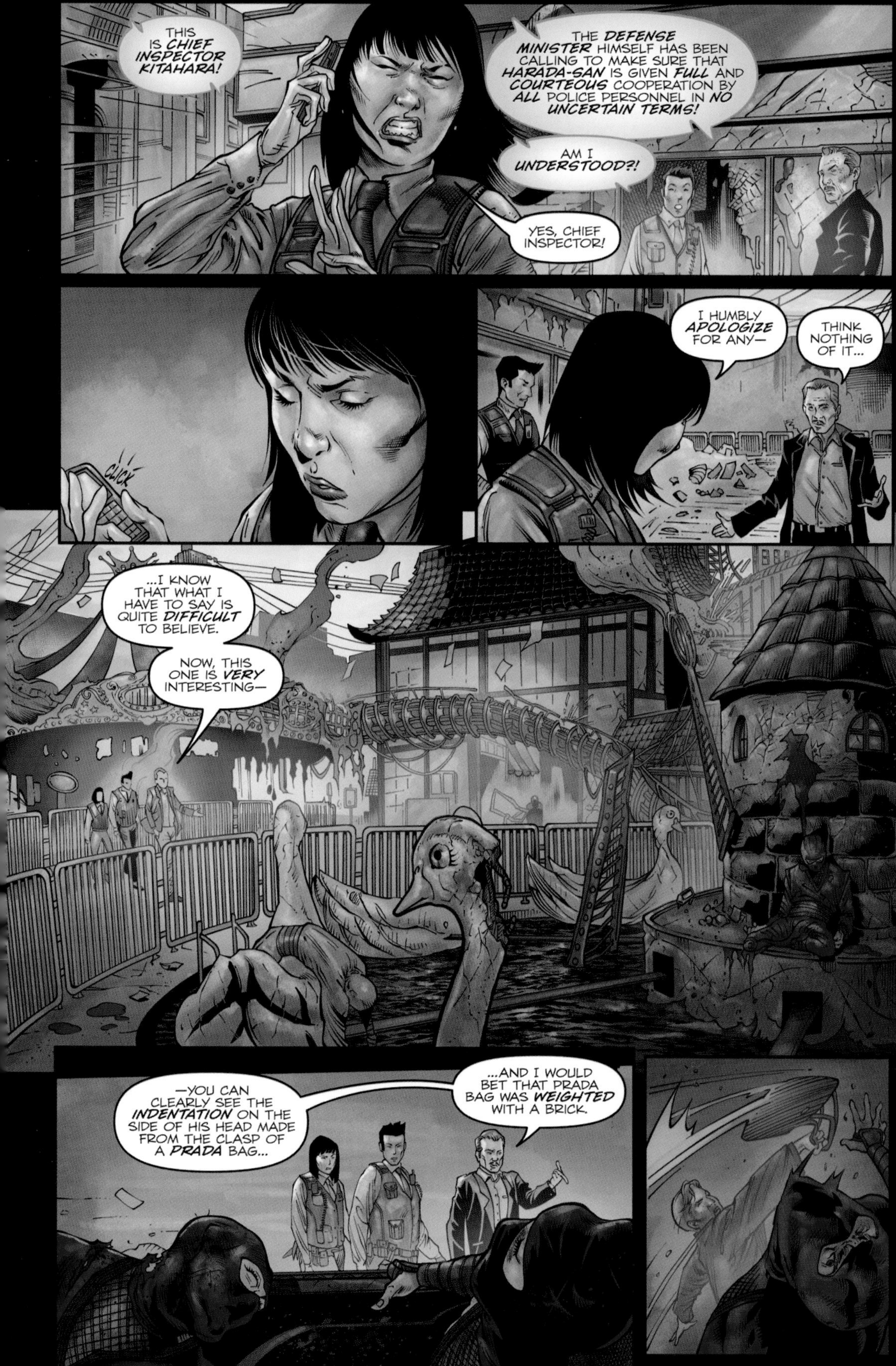
THIS IS CHIEF INSPECTOR KITAHARA!
THE DEFENSE MINISTER HIMSELF HAS BEEN CALLING TO MAKE SURE THAT HARADA-SAN IS GIVEN FULL AND COURTEOUS COOPERATION BY ALL POLICE PERSONNEL IN NO UNCERTAIN TERMS!
AM I UNDERSTOOD?!
YES, CHIEF INSPECTOR!
CLICK
I HUMBLY APOLOGIZE FOR ANY—
THINK NOTHING OF IT...
...I KNOW THAT WHAT I HAVE TO SAY IS QUITE DIFFICULT TO BELIEVE.
NOW, THIS ONE IS VERY INTERESTING—
—YOU CAN CLEARLY SEE THE INDENTATION ON THE SIDE OF HIS HEAD MADE FROM THE CLASP OF A PRADA BAG...
...AND I WOULD BET THAT PRADA BAG WAS WEIGHTED WITH A BRICK.

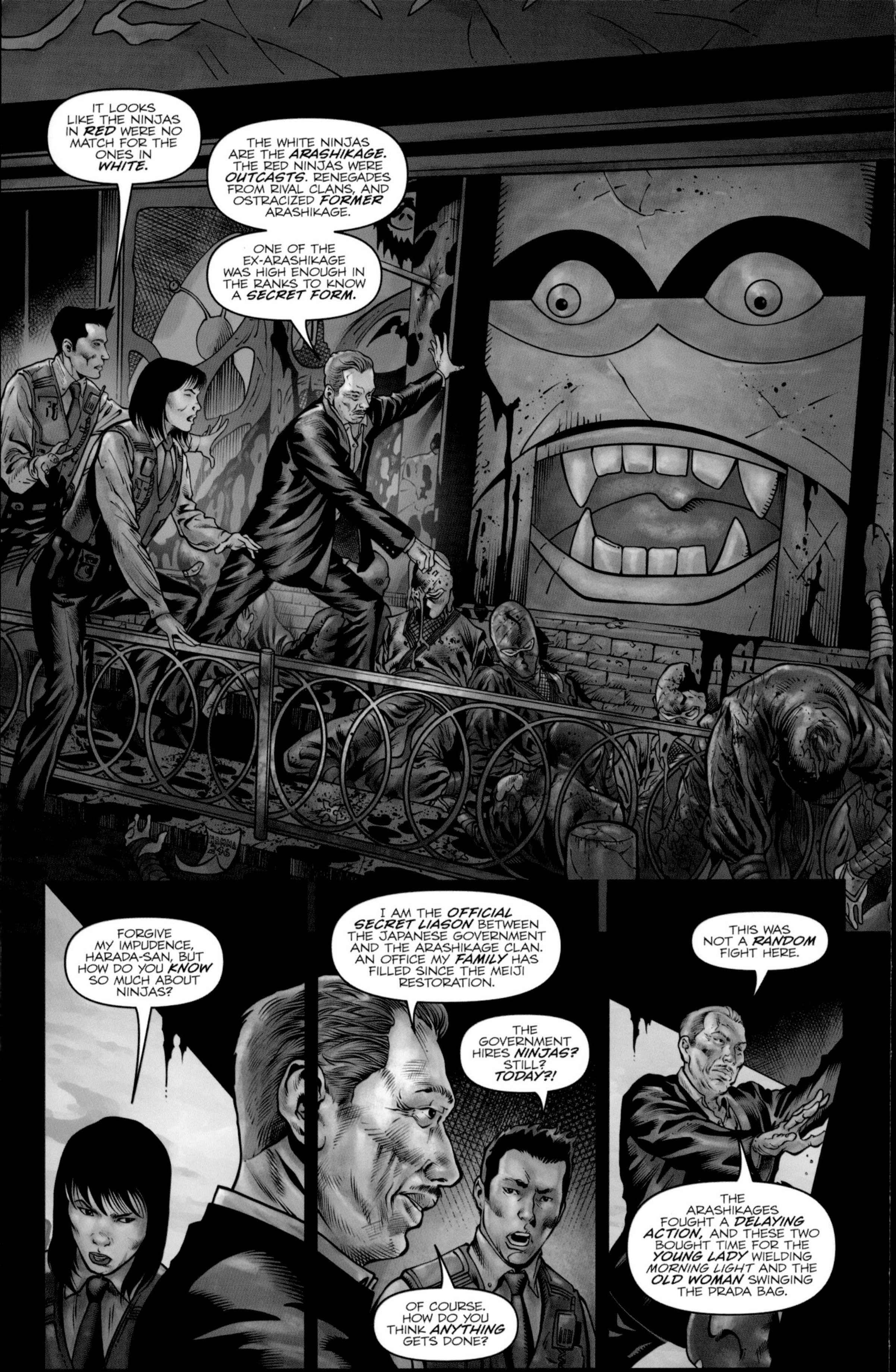
IT LOOKS LIKE THE NINJAS IN RED WERE NO MATCH FOR THE ONES IN WHITE.
THE WHITE NINJAS ARE THE ARASHIKAGE. THE RED NINJAS WERE OUTCASTS. RENEGADES FROM RIVAL CLANS, AND OSTRACIZED FORMER ARASHIKAGE.
ONE OF THE EX-ARASHIKAGE WAS HIGH ENOUGH IN THE RANKS TO KNOW A SECRET FORM.
FORGIVE MY IMPUDENCE, HARADA-SAN, BUT HOW DO YOU KNOW SO MUCH ABOUT NINJAS?
I AM THE OFFICIAL SECRET LIASON BETWEEN THE JAPANESE GOVERNMENT AND THE ARASHIKAGE CLAN. AN OFFICE MY FAMILY HAS FILLED SINCE THE MEIJI RESTORATION.
THE GOVERNMENT HIRES NINJAS? STILL? TODAY?!
OF COURSE. HOW DO YOU THINK ANYTHING GETS DONE?
THIS WAS NOT A RANDOM FIGHT HERE.
THE ARASHIKAGES FOUGHT A DELAYING ACTION, AND THESE TWO BOUGHT TIME FOR THE YOUNG LADY WIELDING MORNING LIGHT AND THE OLD WOMAN SWINGING THE PRADA BAG.

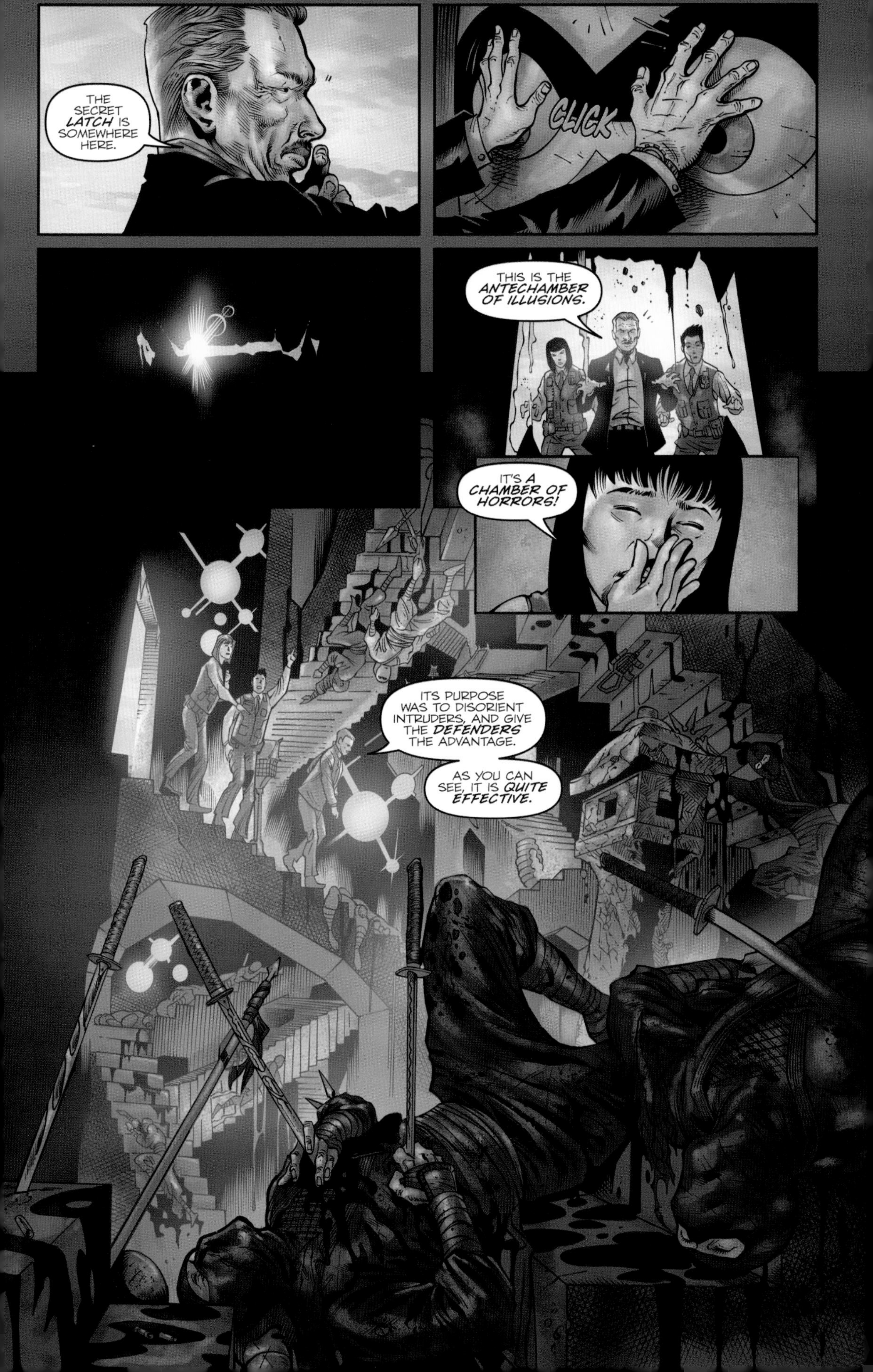
THE SECRET LATCH IS SOMEWHERE HERE.
CLICK
THIS IS THE ANTECHAMBER OF ILLUSIONS.
IT'S A CHAMBER OF HORRORS!
ITS PURPOSE WAS TO DISORIENT INTRUDERS, AND GIVE THE DEFENDERS THE ADVANTAGE.
AS YOU CAN SEE, IT IS QUITE EFFECTIVE.

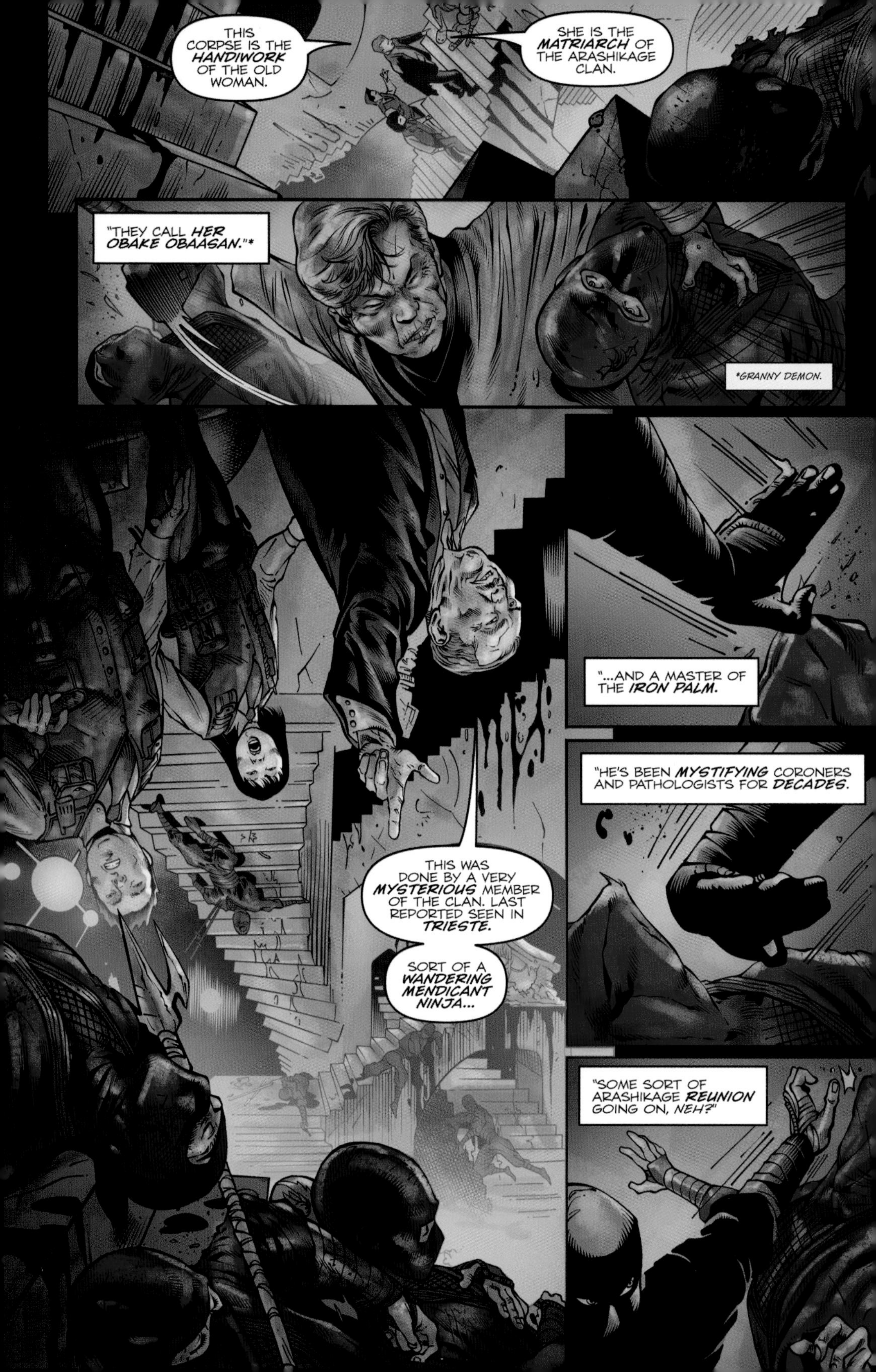

THIS CORPSE IS THE HANDIWORK OF THE OLD WOMAN.
SHE IS THE MATRIARCH OF THE ARASHIKAGE CLAN.
"THEY CALL HER OBAKE OBAASAN."*
*GRANNY DEMON.
"...AND A MASTER OF THE IRON PALM.
"HE'S BEEN MYSTIFYING CORONERS AND PATHOLOGISTS FOR DECADES.
THIS WAS DONE BY A VERY MYSTERIOUS MEMBER OF THE CLAN. LAST REPORTED SEEN IN TRIESTE.
SORT OF A WANDERING MENDICANT NINJA...
"SOME SORT OF ARASHIKAGE REUNION GOING ON, NEH?"

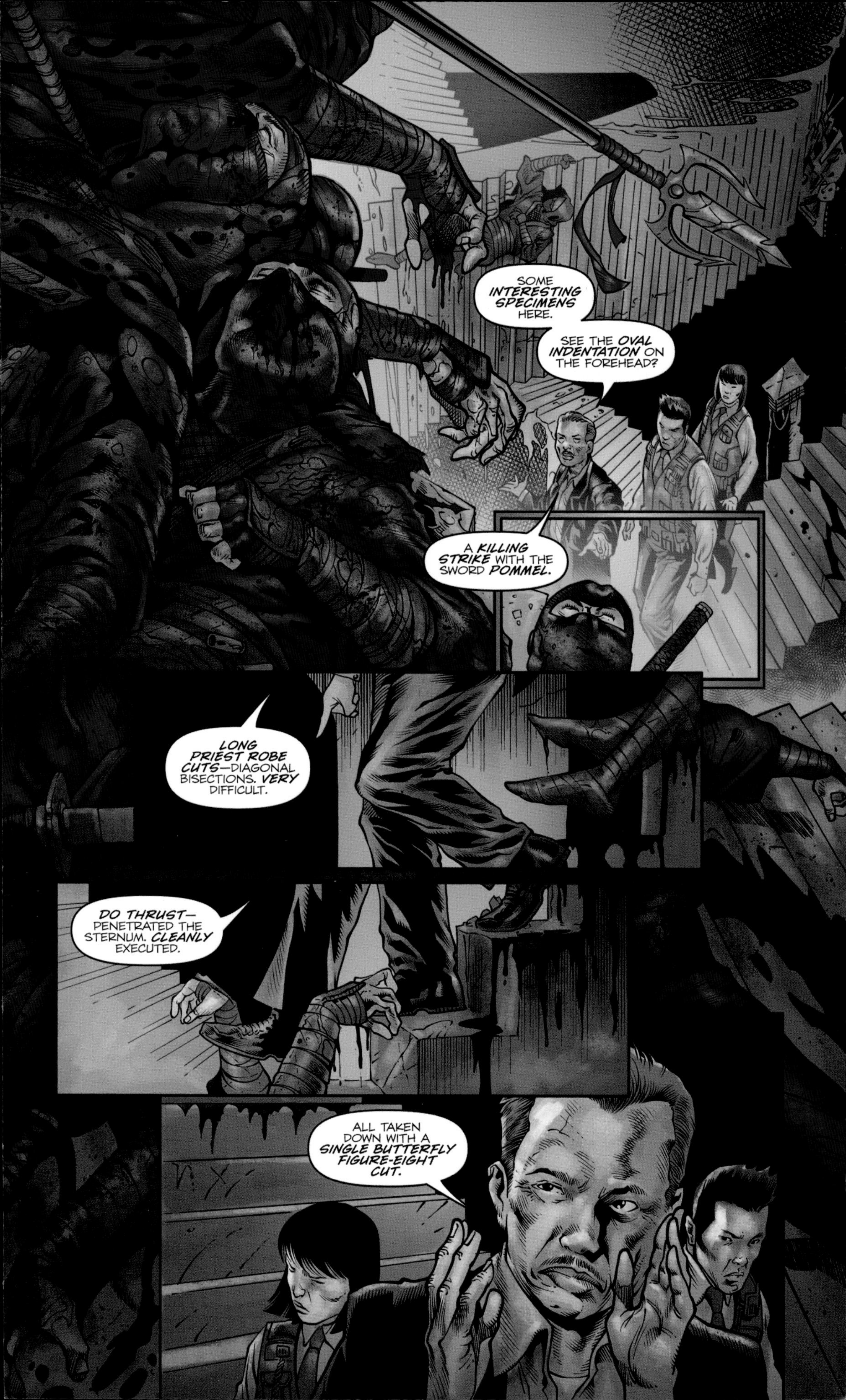
SOME INTERESTING SPECIMENS HERE.
SEE THE OVAL INDENTATION ON THE FOREHEAD?
A KILLING STRIKE WITH THE SWORD POMMEL.
LONG PRIEST ROBE CUTS—DIAGONAL BISECTIONS. VERY DIFFICULT.
DO THRUST—PENETRATED THE STERNUM. CLEANLY EXECUTED.
ALL TAKEN DOWN WITH A SINGLE BUTTERFLY FIGURE-EIGHT CUT.

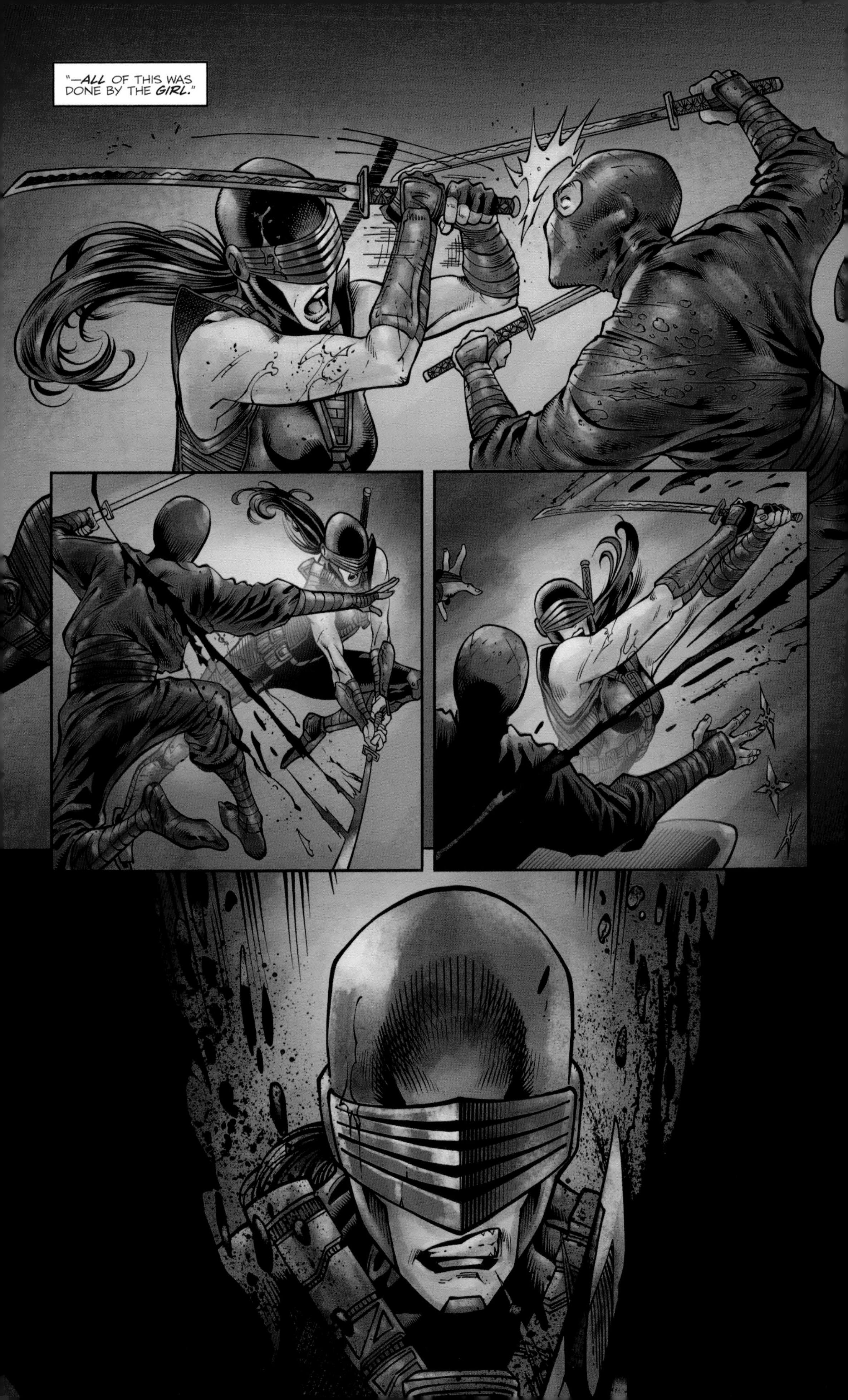
"—ALL OF THIS WAS DONE BY THE GIRL."

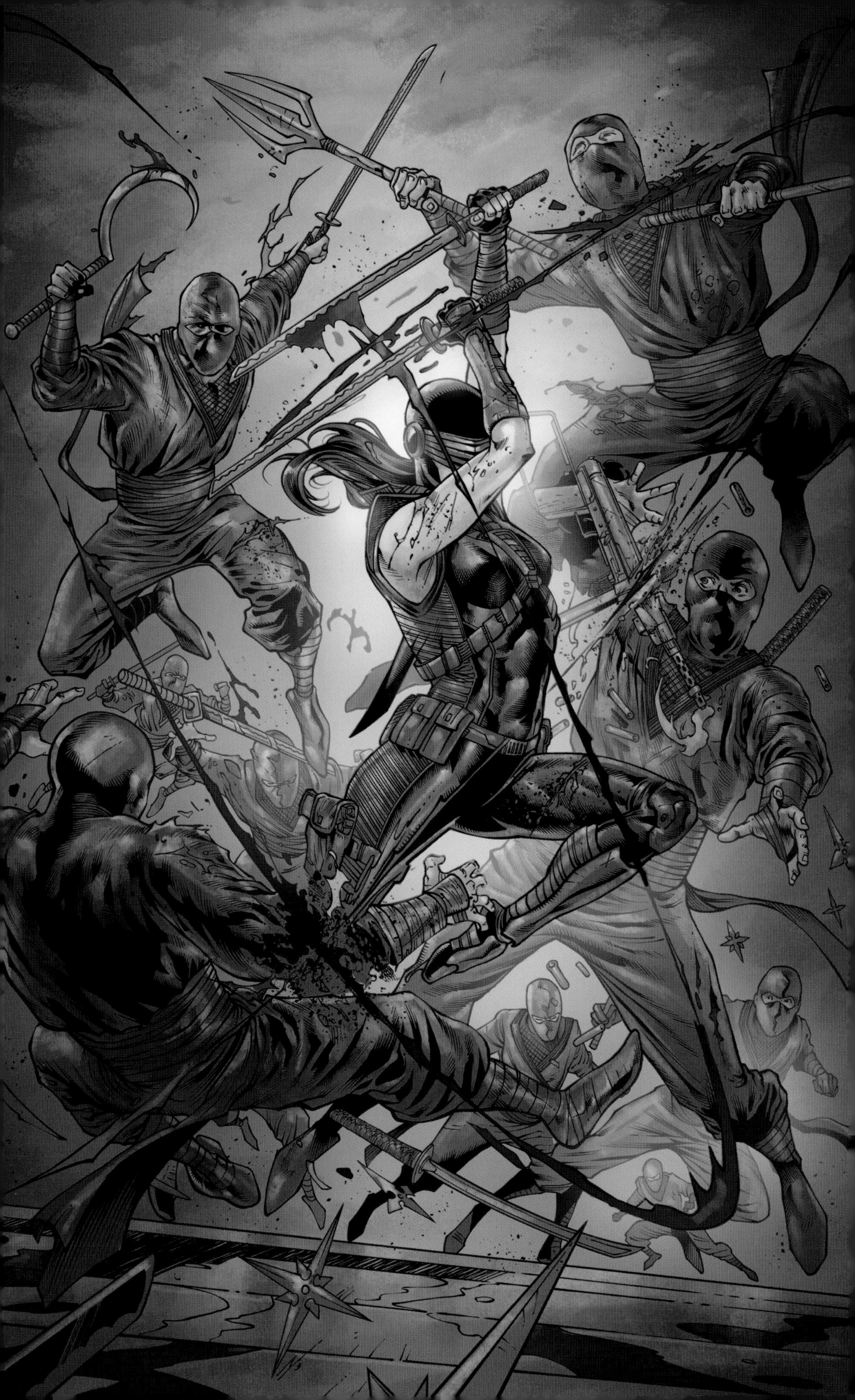

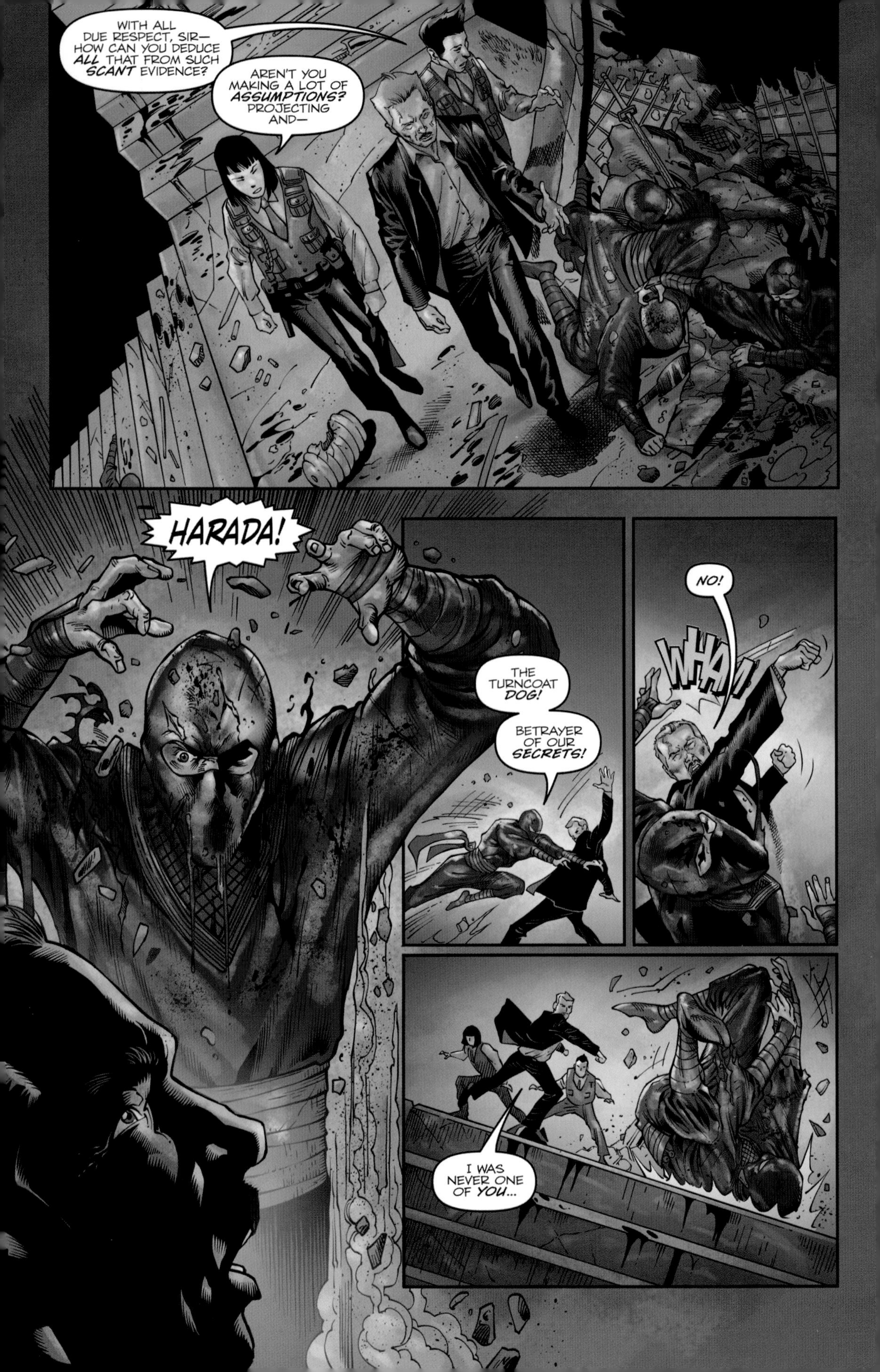

WITH ALL DUE RESPECT, SIR— HOW CAN YOU DEDUCE ALL THAT FROM SUCH SCANT EVIDENCE?
AREN'T YOU MAKING A LOT OF ASSUMPTIONS? PROJECTING AND—
HARADA!
THE TURNCOAT DOG!
BETRAYER OF OUR SECRETS!
NO!
WHAM
I WAS NEVER ONE OF YOU...

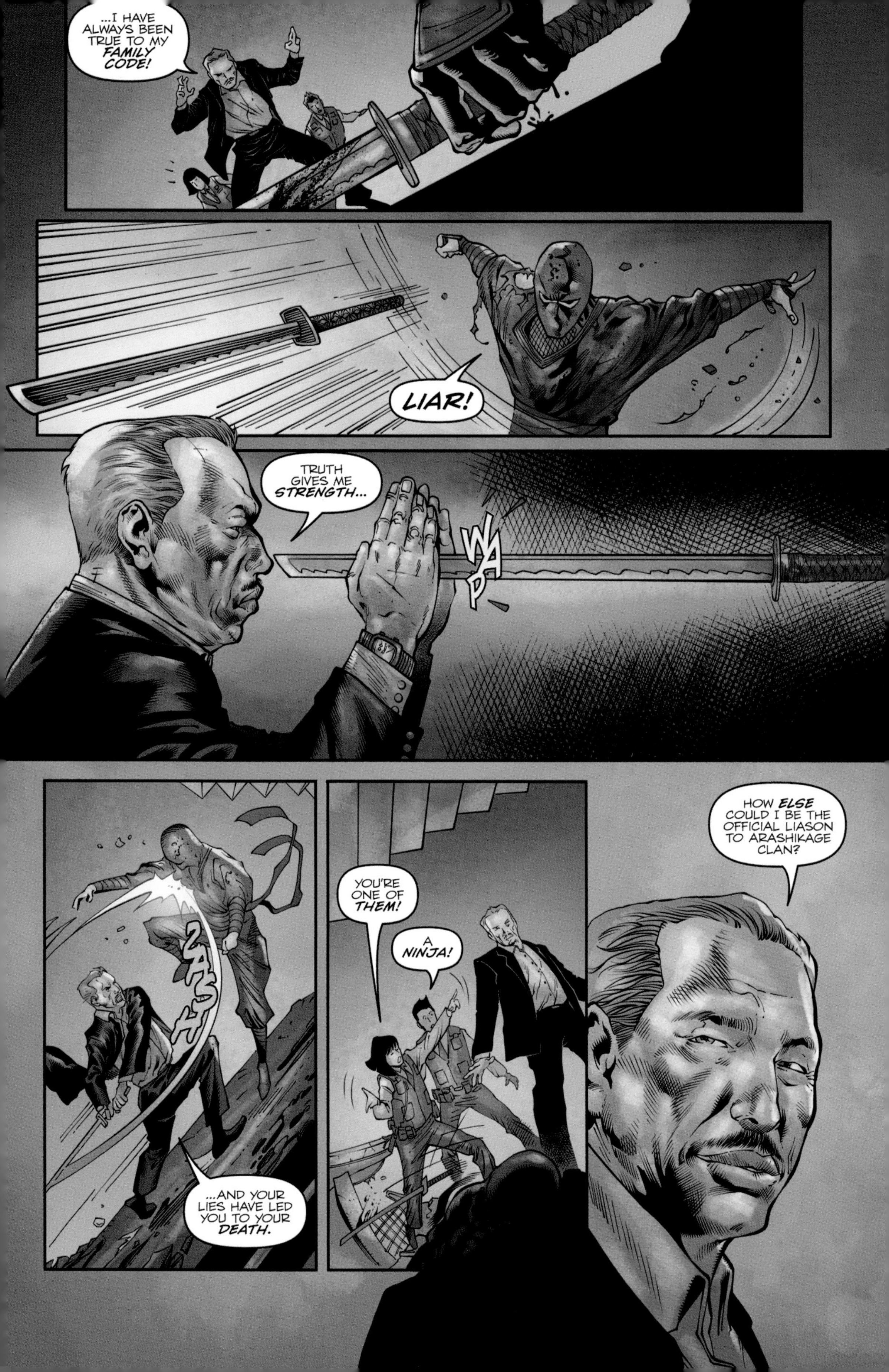
...I HAVE ALWAYS BEEN TRUE TO MY FAMILY CODE!
LIAR!
TRUTH GIVES ME STRENGTH...
WAP
ZASH
...AND YOUR LIES HAVE LED YOU TO YOUR DEATH.
YOU'RE ONE OF THEM!
A NINJA!
HOW ELSE COULD I BE THE OFFICIAL LIASON TO ARASHIKAGE CLAN?

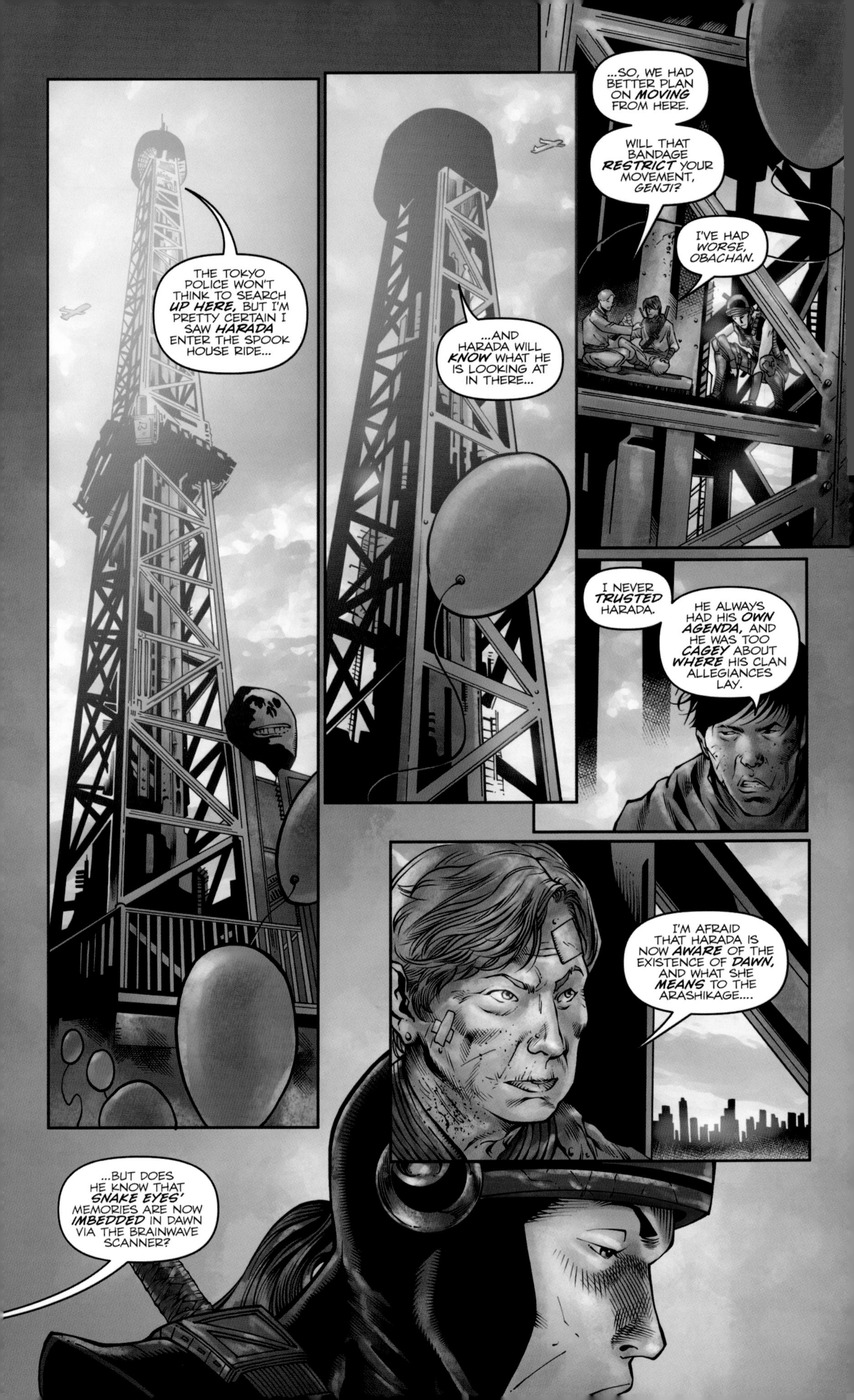
THE TOKYO POLICE WON'T THINK TO SEARCH UP HERE, BUT I'M PRETTY CERTAIN I SAW HARADA ENTER THE SPOOK HOUSE RIDE...
...AND HARADA WILL KNOW WHAT HE IS LOOKING AT IN THERE...
...SO, WE HAD BETTER PLAN ON MOVING FROM HERE.
WILL THAT BANDAGE RESTRICT YOUR MOVEMENT, GENJI?
I'VE HAD WORSE, OBACHAN.
I NEVER TRUSTED HARADA.
HE ALWAYS HAD HIS OWN AGENDA, AND HE WAS TOO CAGEY ABOUT WHERE HIS CLAN ALLEGIANCES LAY.
I'M AFRAID THAT HARADA IS NOW AWARE OF THE EXISTENCE OF DAWN, AND WHAT SHE MEANS TO THE ARASHIKAGE....
...BUT DOES HE KNOW THAT SNAKE EYES' MEMORIES ARE NOW IMBEDDED IN DAWN VIA THE BRAINWAVE SCANNER?

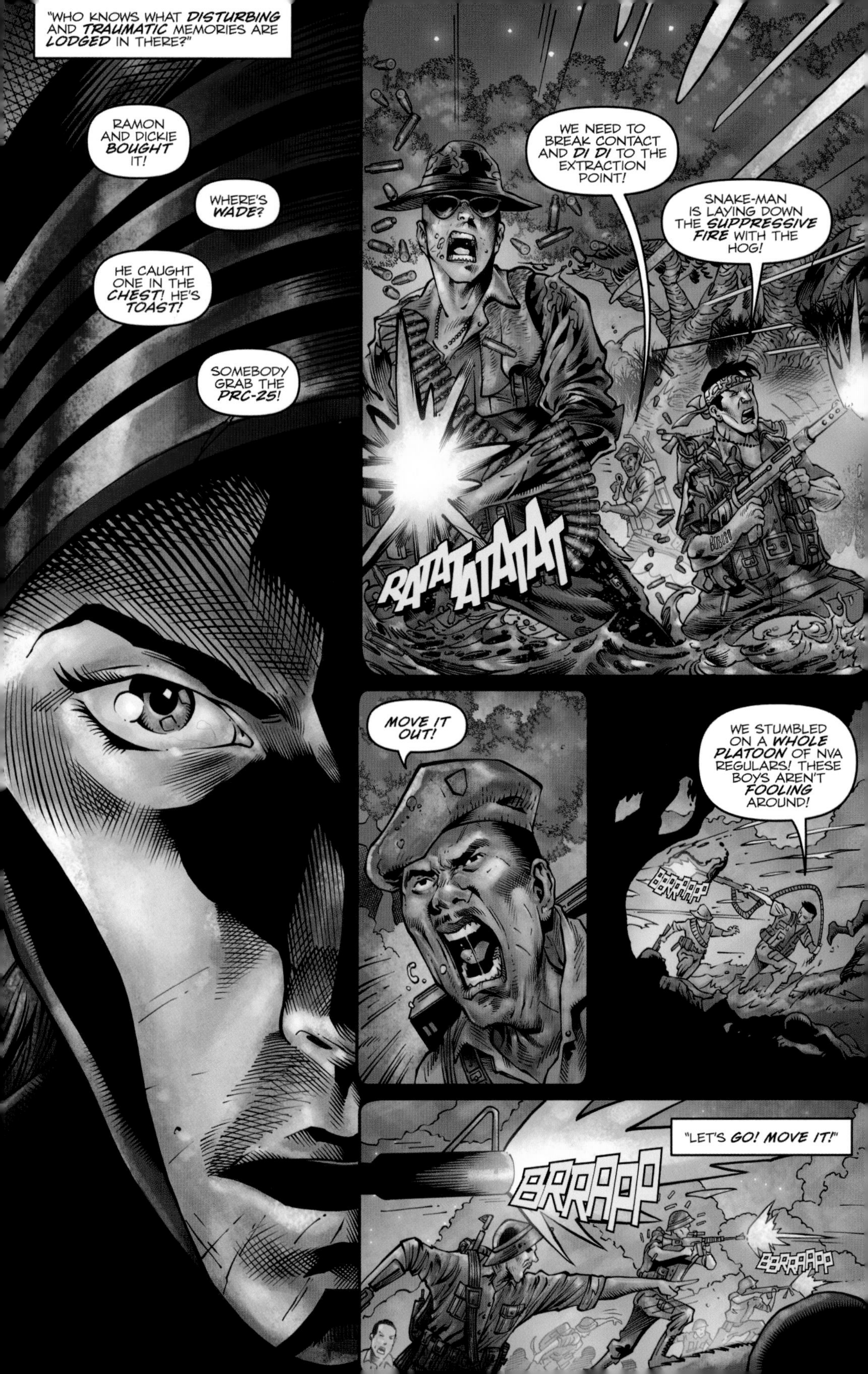
"WHO KNOWS WHAT DISTURBING AND TRAUMATIC MEMORIES ARE LODGED IN THERE?"
RAMON AND DICKIE BOUGHT IT!
WHERE'S WADE?
HE CAUGHT ONE IN THE CHEST! HE'S TOAST!
SOMEBODY GRAB THE PRC-25!
WE NEED TO BREAK CONTACT AND DI DI TO THE EXTRACTION POINT!
SNAKE-MAN IS LAYING DOWN THE SUPPRESSIVE FIRE WITH THE HOG!
RATATATATAT
MOVE IT OUT!
WE STUMBLED ON A WHOLE PLATOON OF NVA REGULARS! THESE BOYS AREN'T FOOLING AROUND!
BRRRAPP
"LET'S GO! MOVE IT!"
BRRAAPP
BRRRAAPP

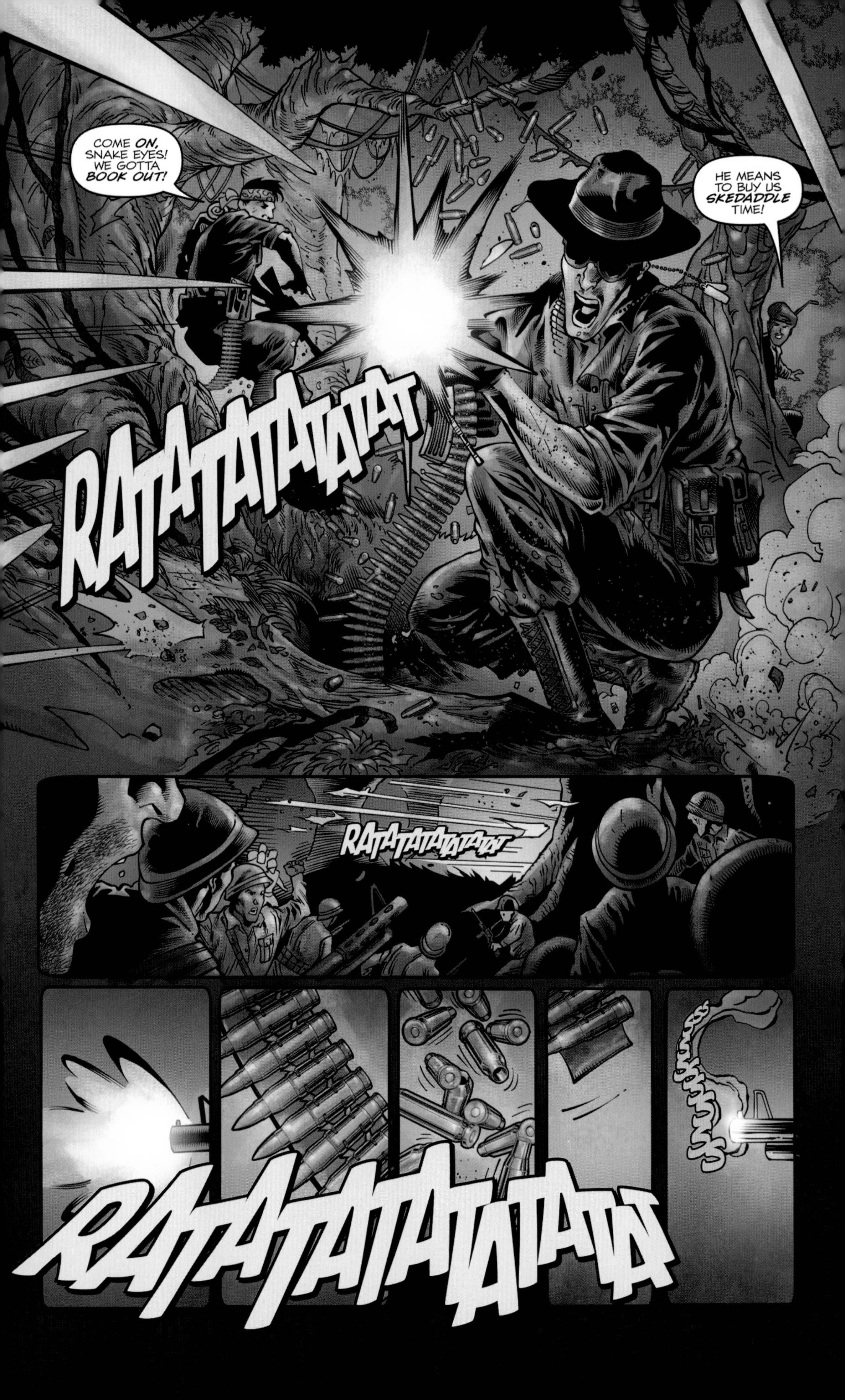
COME ON, SNAKE EYES! WE GOTTA BOOK OUT!
HE MEANS TO BUY US SKEDADDLE TIME!
RATATATATATAT
RATATATATATATAT
RATATATATATATAT

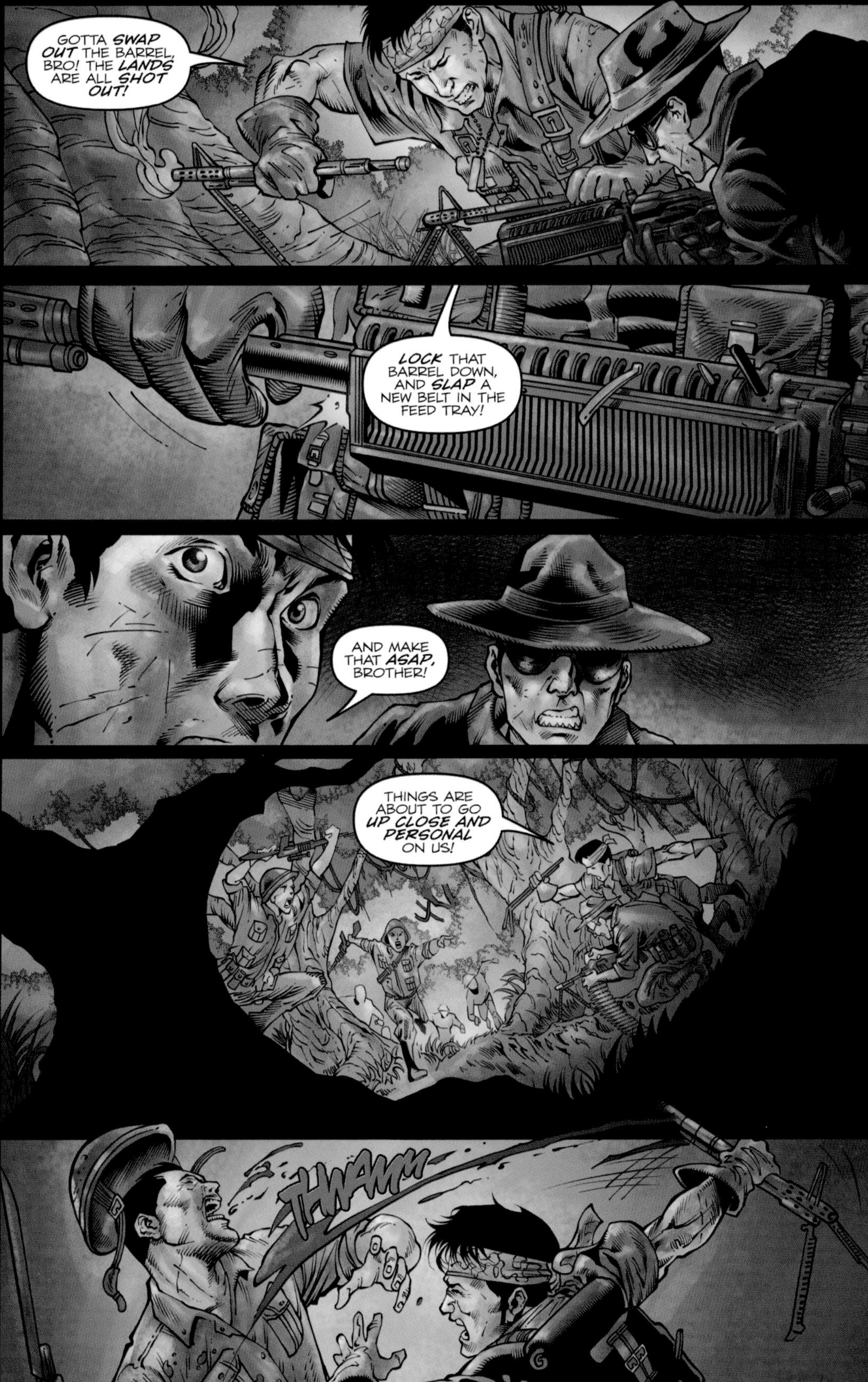
GOTTA SWAP OUT THE BARREL, BRO! THE LANDS ARE ALL SHOT OUT!
LOCK THAT BARREL DOWN, AND SLAP A NEW BELT IN THE FEED TRAY!
AND MAKE THAT ASAP, BROTHER!
THINGS ARE ABOUT TO GO UP CLOSE AND PERSONAL ON US!
THWAMM

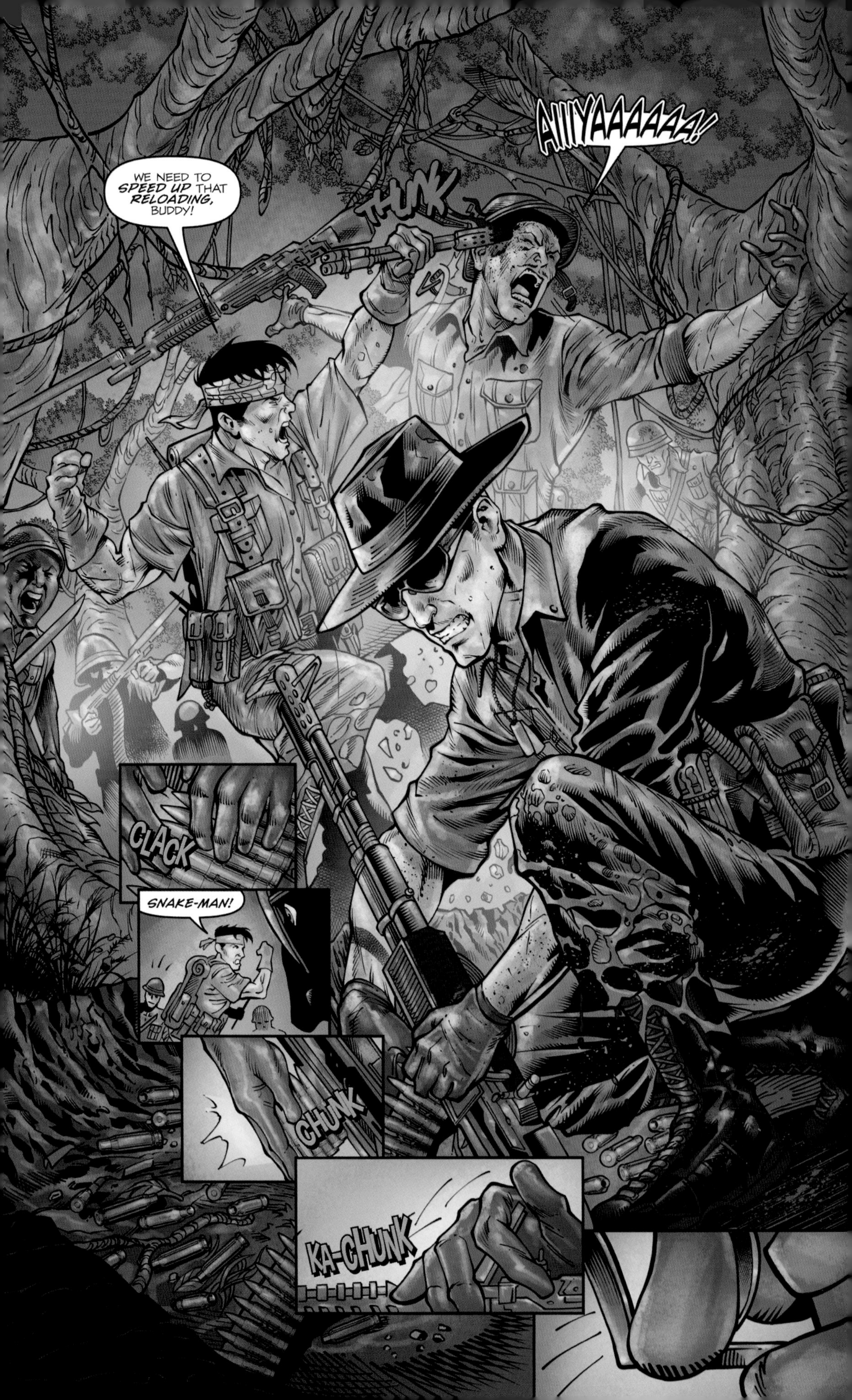
AIIIYAAAAAA!
WE NEED TO SPEED UP THAT RELOADING, BUDDY!
THUNK
CLACK
SNAKE-MAN!
CHUNK
KA-CHUNK

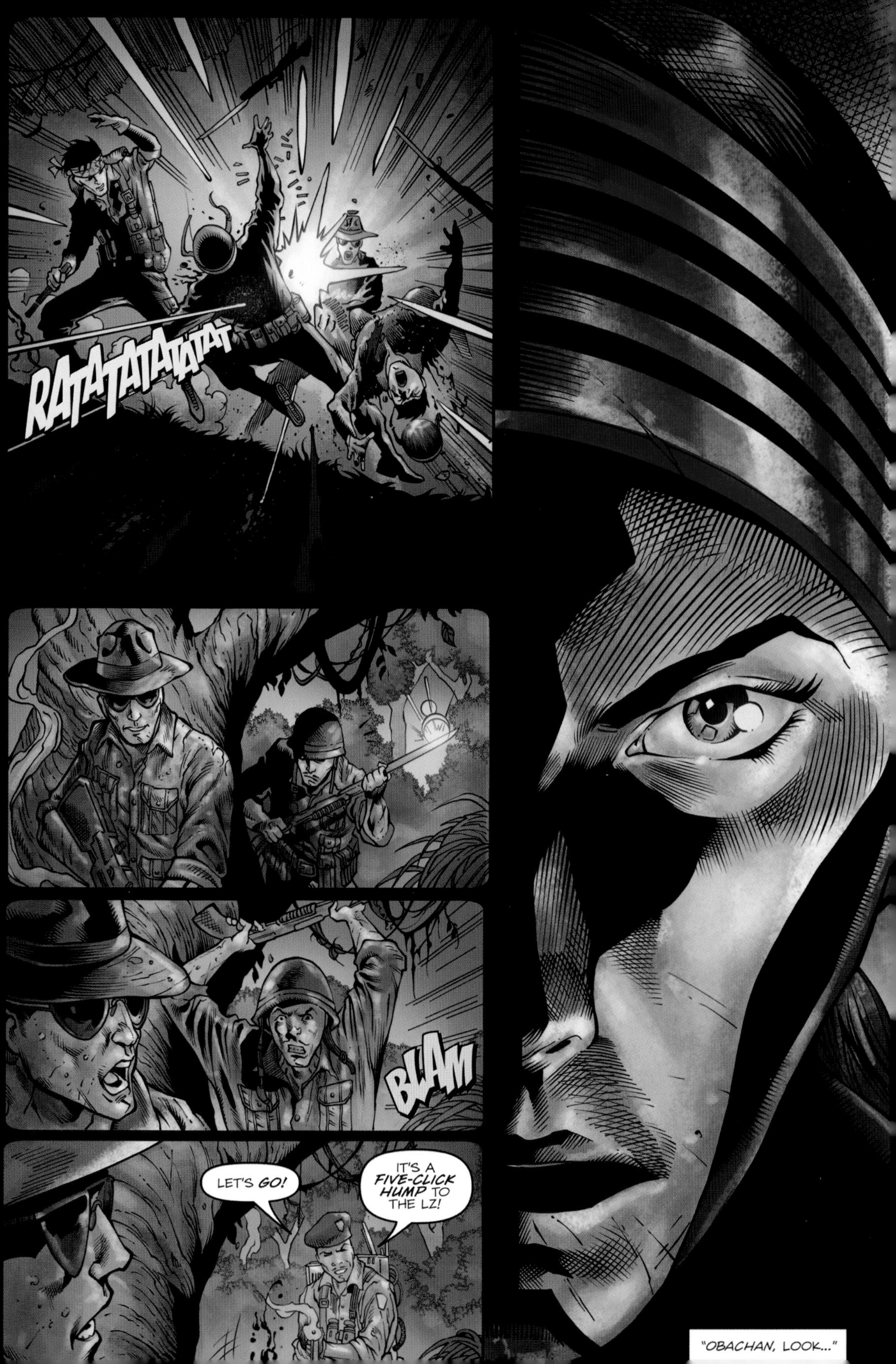
RATATATATATAT
BLAM
LET'S GO!
IT'S A FIVE-CLICK HUMP TO THE LZ!
"OBACHAN, LOOK..."

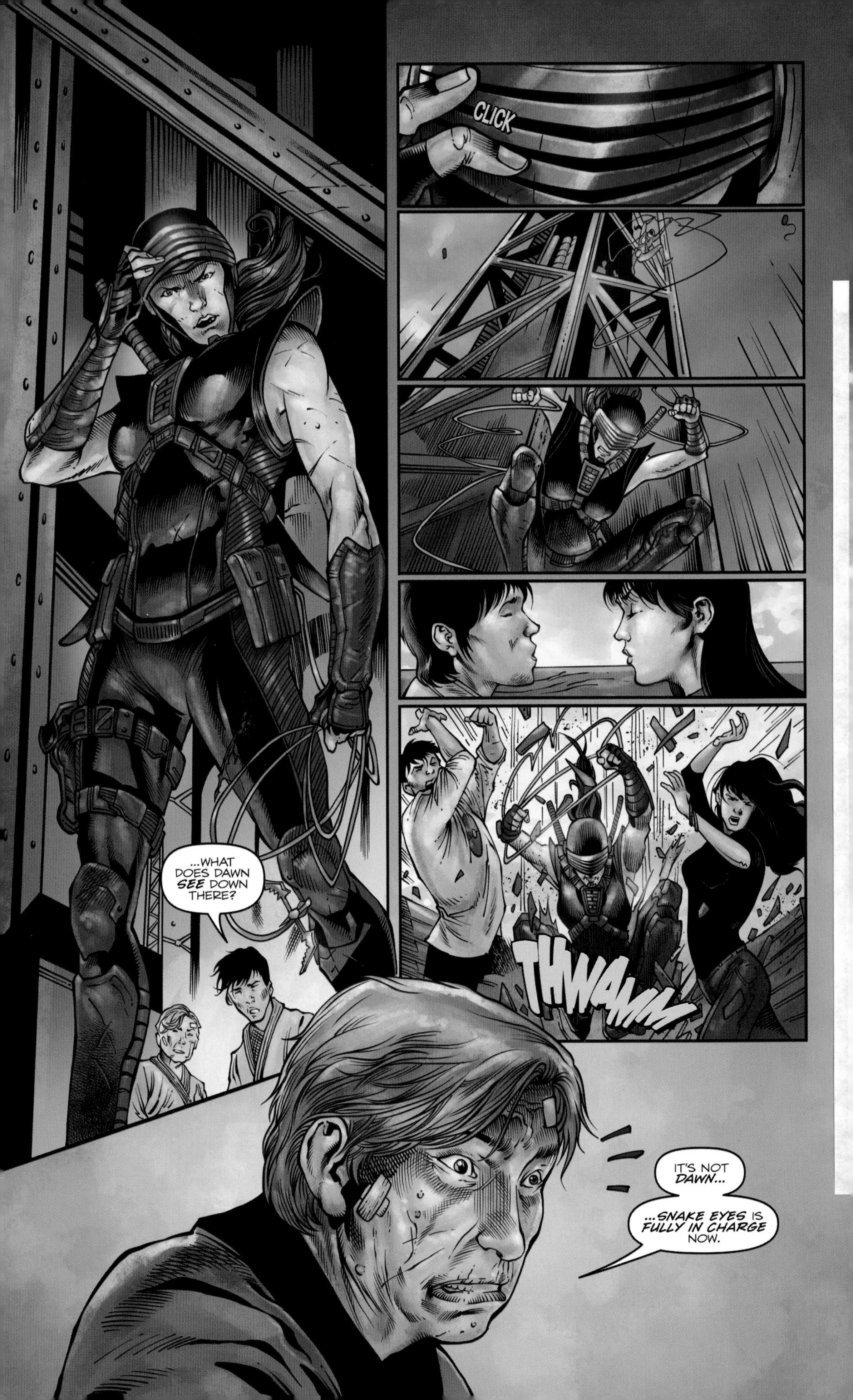
CLICK
...WHAT DOES DAWN SEE DOWN THERE?
THWAMM
IT'S NOT DAWN...
...SNAKE EYES IS FULLY IN CHARGE NOW.

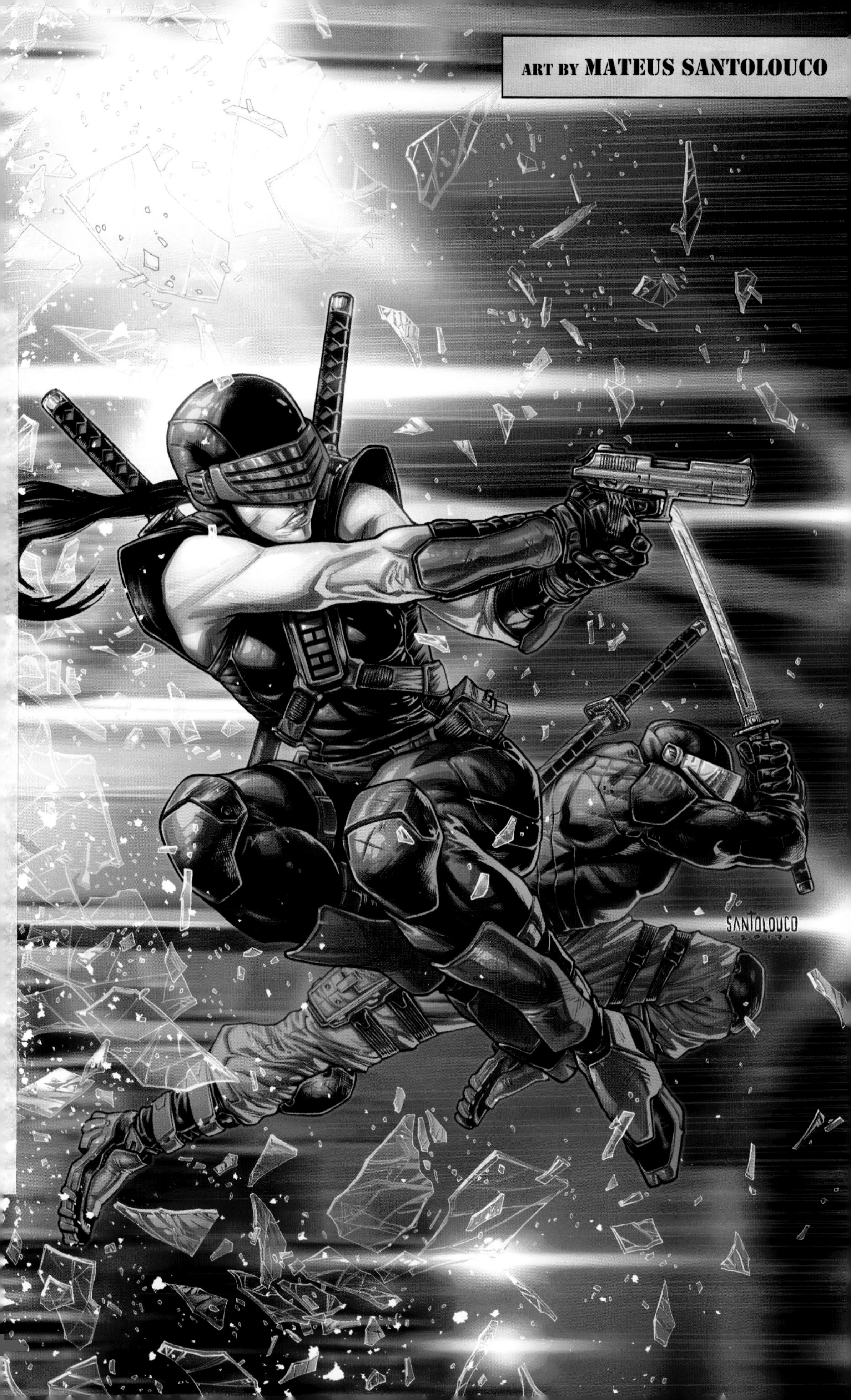
SANTOLOUCO
2017

ART BY **MATEUS SANTOLOUCO**

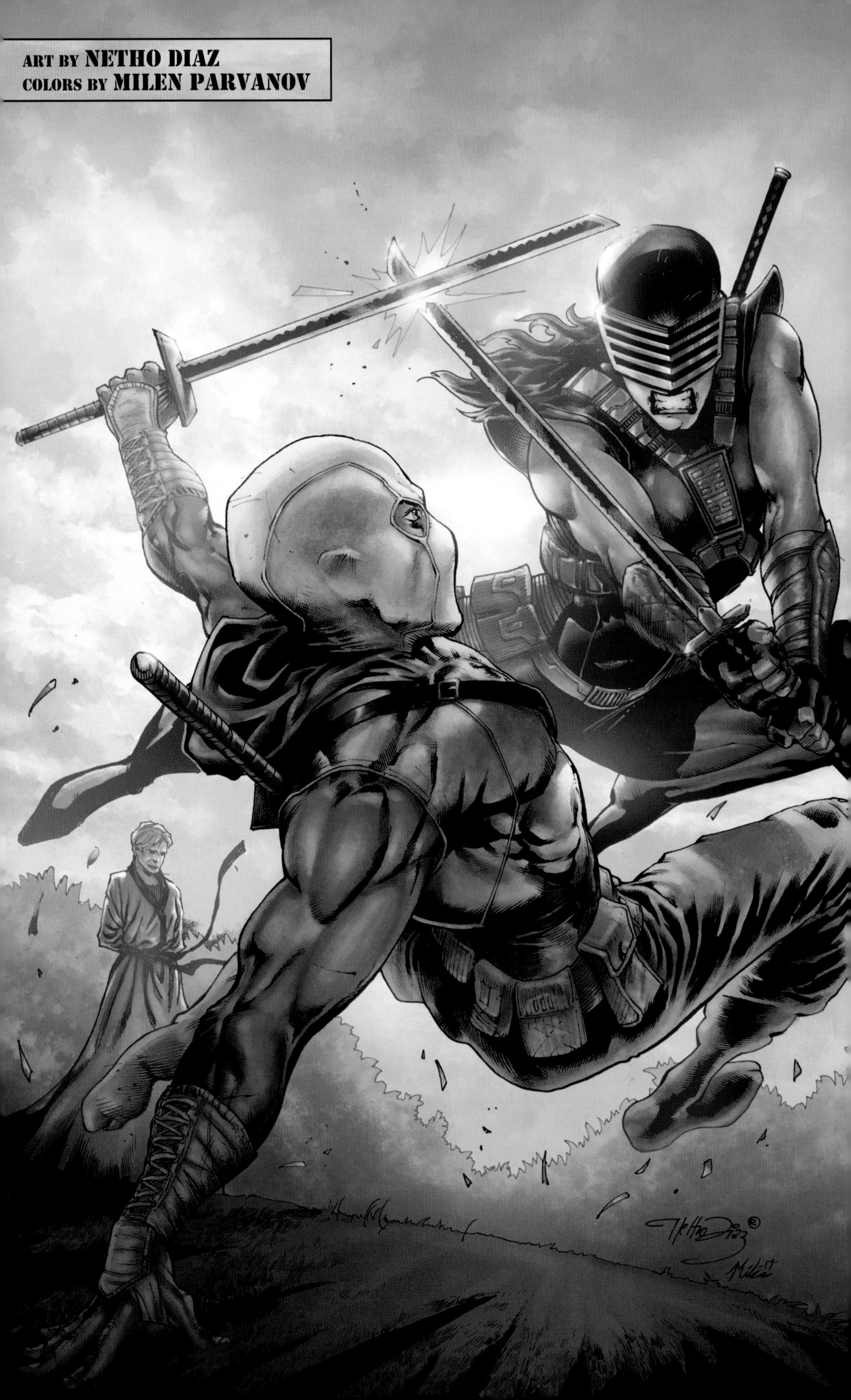

ART BY NETHO DIAZ
COLORS BY MILEN PARVANOV

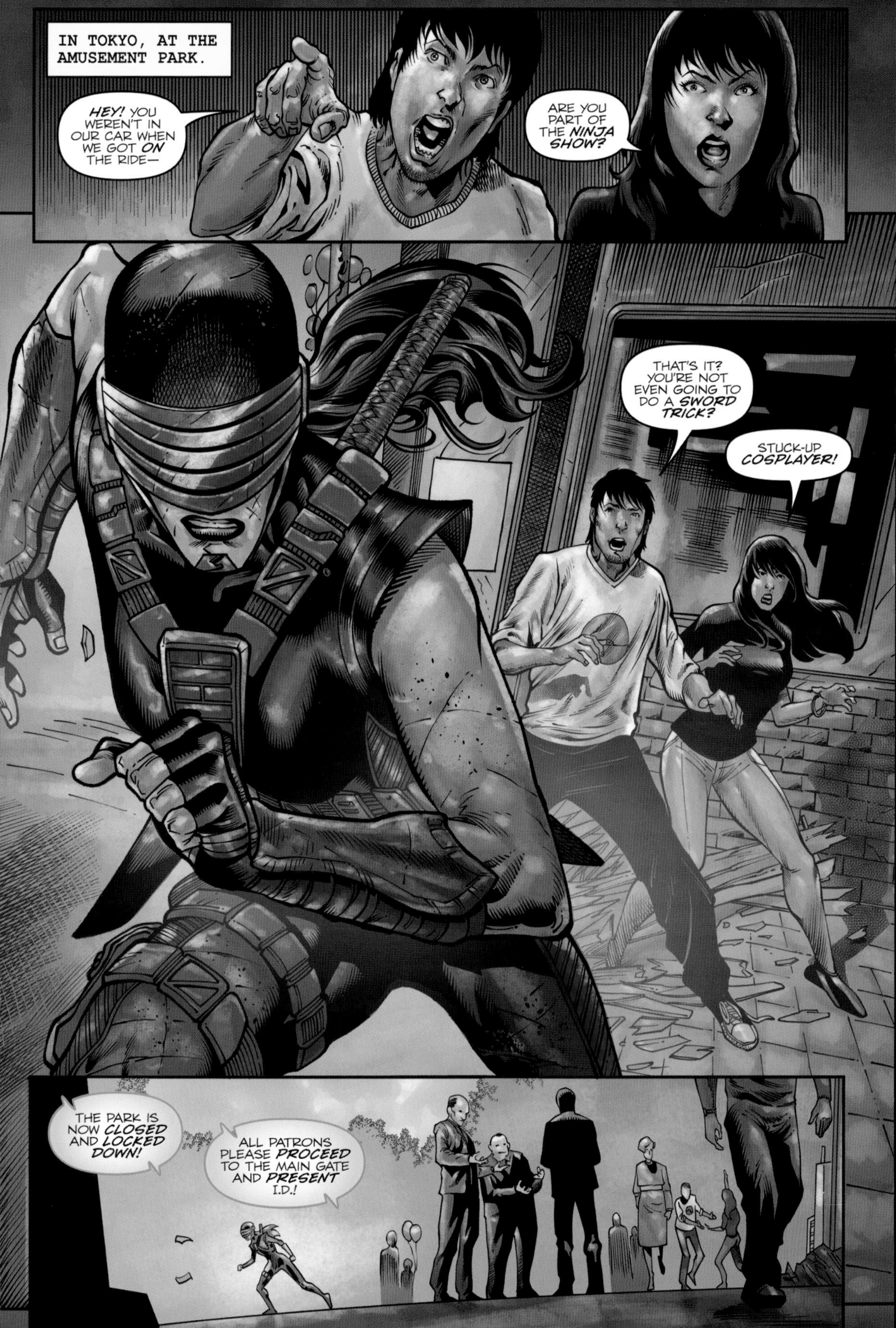
IN TOKYO, AT THE AMUSEMENT PARK.
HEY! YOU WEREN'T IN OUR CAR WHEN WE GOT ON THE RIDE—
ARE YOU PART OF THE NINJA SHOW?
THAT'S IT? YOU'RE NOT EVEN GOING TO DO A SWORD TRICK?
STUCK-UP COSPLAYER!
THE PARK IS NOW CLOSED AND LOCKED DOWN!
ALL PATRONS PLEASE PROCEED TO THE MAIN GATE AND PRESENT I.D.!

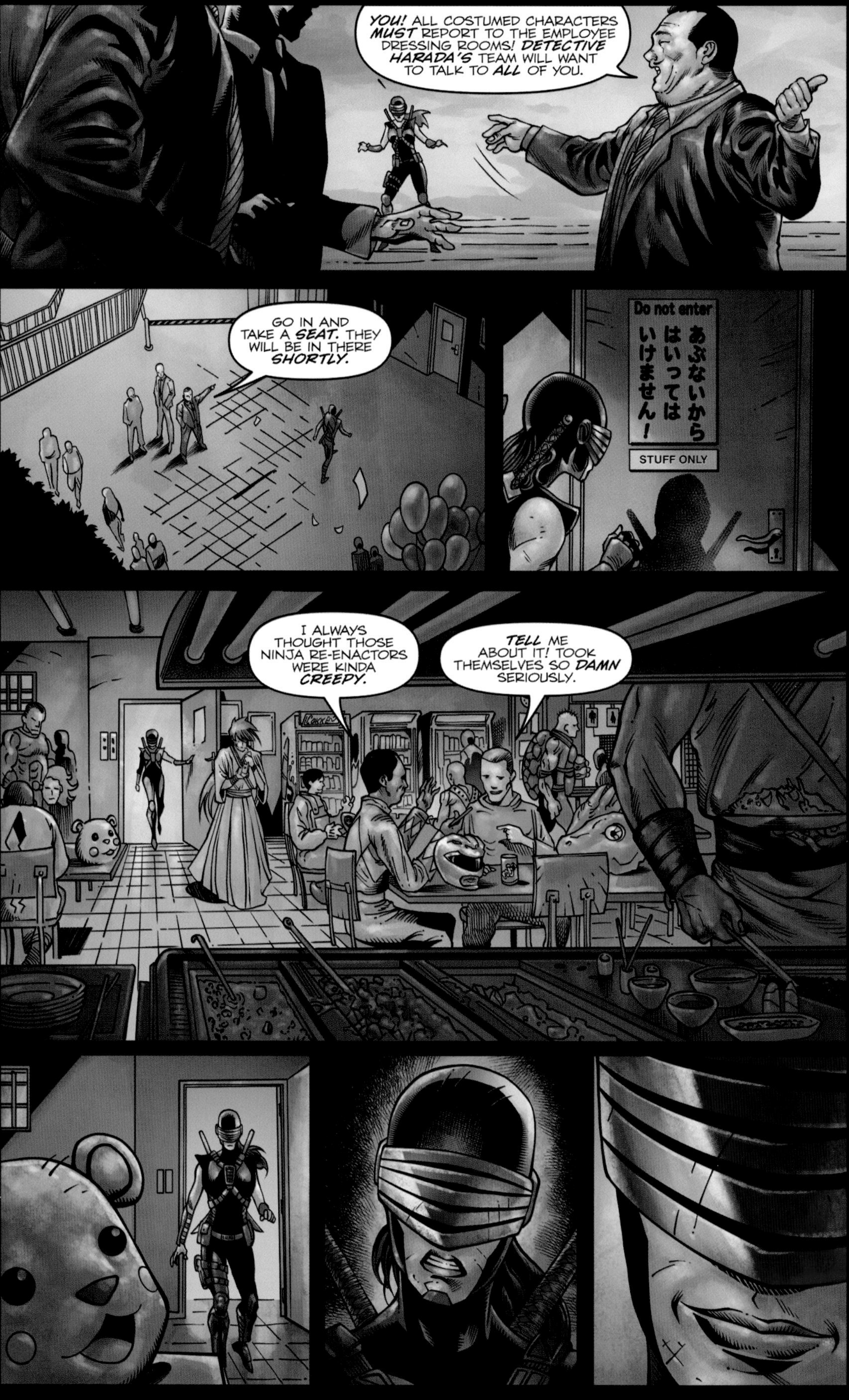

YOU! ALL COSTUMED CHARACTERS MUST REPORT TO THE EMPLOYEE DRESSING ROOMS! DETECTIVE HARADA'S TEAM WILL WANT TO TALK TO ALL OF YOU.
GO IN AND TAKE A SEAT. THEY WILL BE IN THERE SHORTLY.
Do not enter
あぶないから
はいっては
いけません!
STUFF ONLY
I ALWAYS THOUGHT THOSE NINJA RE-ENACTORS WERE KINDA CREEPY.
TELL ME ABOUT IT! TOOK THEMSELVES SO DAMN SERIOUSLY.

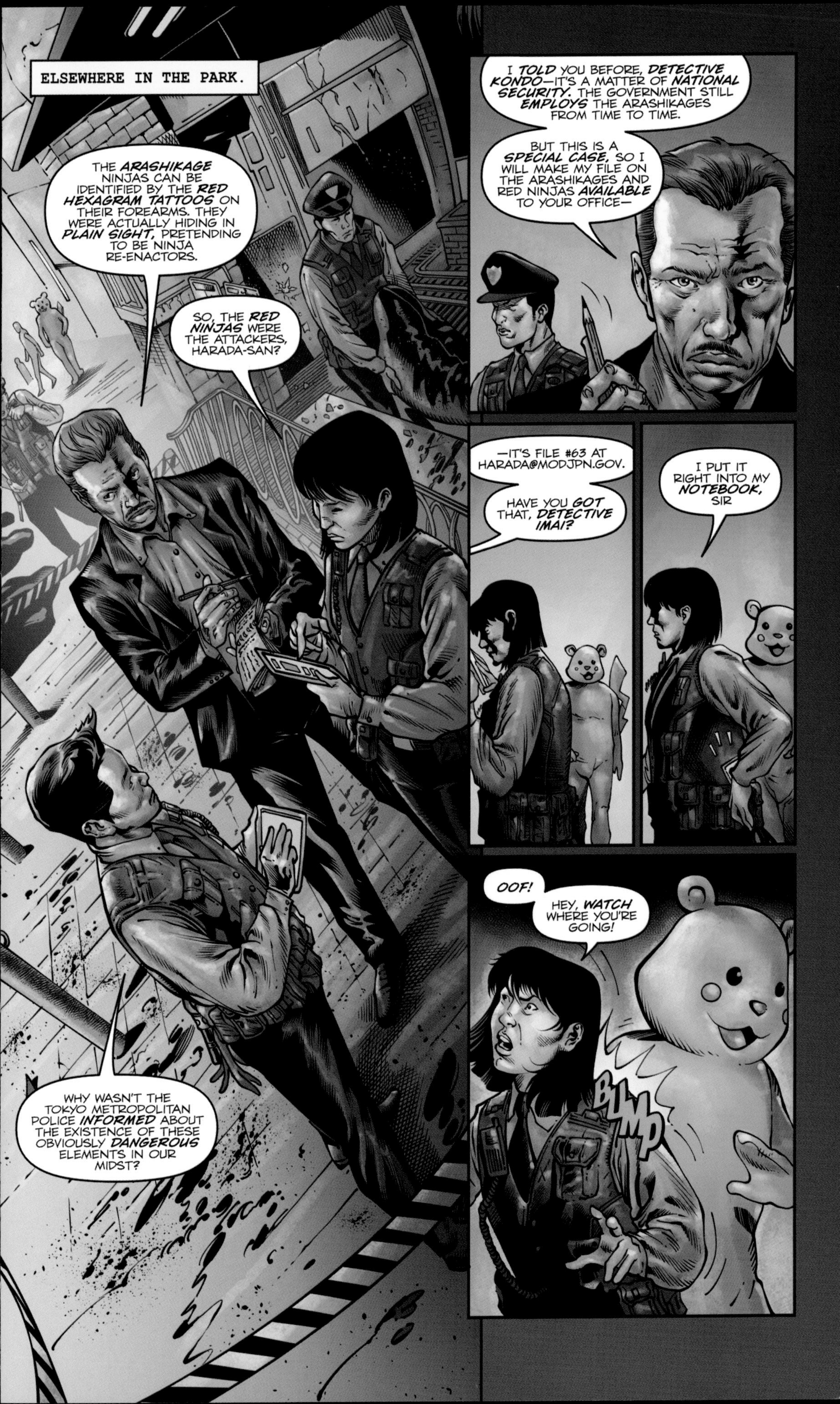
ELSEWHERE IN THE PARK.
THE ARASHIKAGE NINJAS CAN BE IDENTIFIED BY THE RED HEXAGRAM TATTOOS ON THEIR FOREARMS. THEY WERE ACTUALLY HIDING IN PLAIN SIGHT, PRETENDING TO BE NINJA RE-ENACTORS.
SO, THE RED NINJAS WERE THE ATTACKERS, HARADA-SAN?
WHY WASN'T THE TOKYO METROPOLITAN POLICE INFORMED ABOUT THE EXISTENCE OF THESE OBVIOUSLY DANGEROUS ELEMENTS IN OUR MIDST?
I TOLD YOU BEFORE, DETECTIVE KONDO—IT'S A MATTER OF NATIONAL SECURITY. THE GOVERNMENT STILL EMPLOYS THE ARASHIKAGES FROM TIME TO TIME.
BUT THIS IS A SPECIAL CASE, SO I WILL MAKE MY FILE ON THE ARASHIKAGES AND RED NINJAS AVAILABLE TO YOUR OFFICE—
—IT'S FILE #63 AT HARADA@MODJPN.GOV.
HAVE YOU GOT THAT, DETECTIVE IMAI?
I PUT IT RIGHT INTO MY NOTEBOOK, SIR
OOF!
HEY, WATCH WHERE YOU'RE GOING!
BUMP

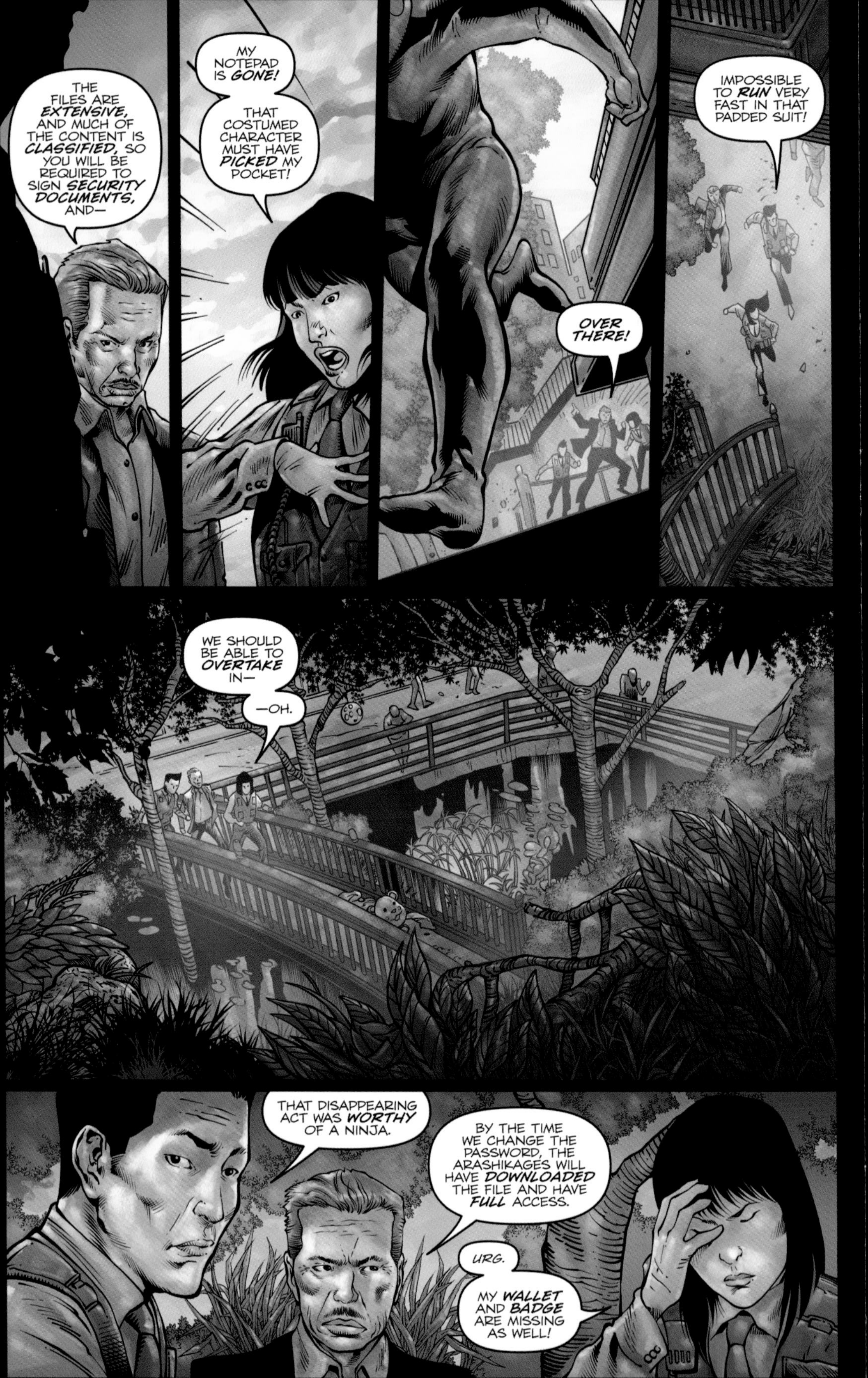
THE FILES ARE EXTENSIVE, AND MUCH OF THE CONTENT IS CLASSIFIED, SO YOU WILL BE REQUIRED TO SIGN SECURITY DOCUMENTS, AND—
MY NOTEPAD IS GONE!
THAT COSTUMED CHARACTER MUST HAVE PICKED MY POCKET!
OVER THERE!
IMPOSSIBLE TO RUN VERY FAST IN THAT PADDED SUIT!
WE SHOULD BE ABLE TO OVERTAKE IN—
—OH.
THAT DISAPPEARING ACT WAS WORTHY OF A NINJA.
BY THE TIME WE CHANGE THE PASSWORD, THE ARASHIKAGES WILL HAVE DOWNLOADED THE FILE AND HAVE FULL ACCESS.
URG.
MY WALLET AND BADGE ARE MISSING AS WELL!

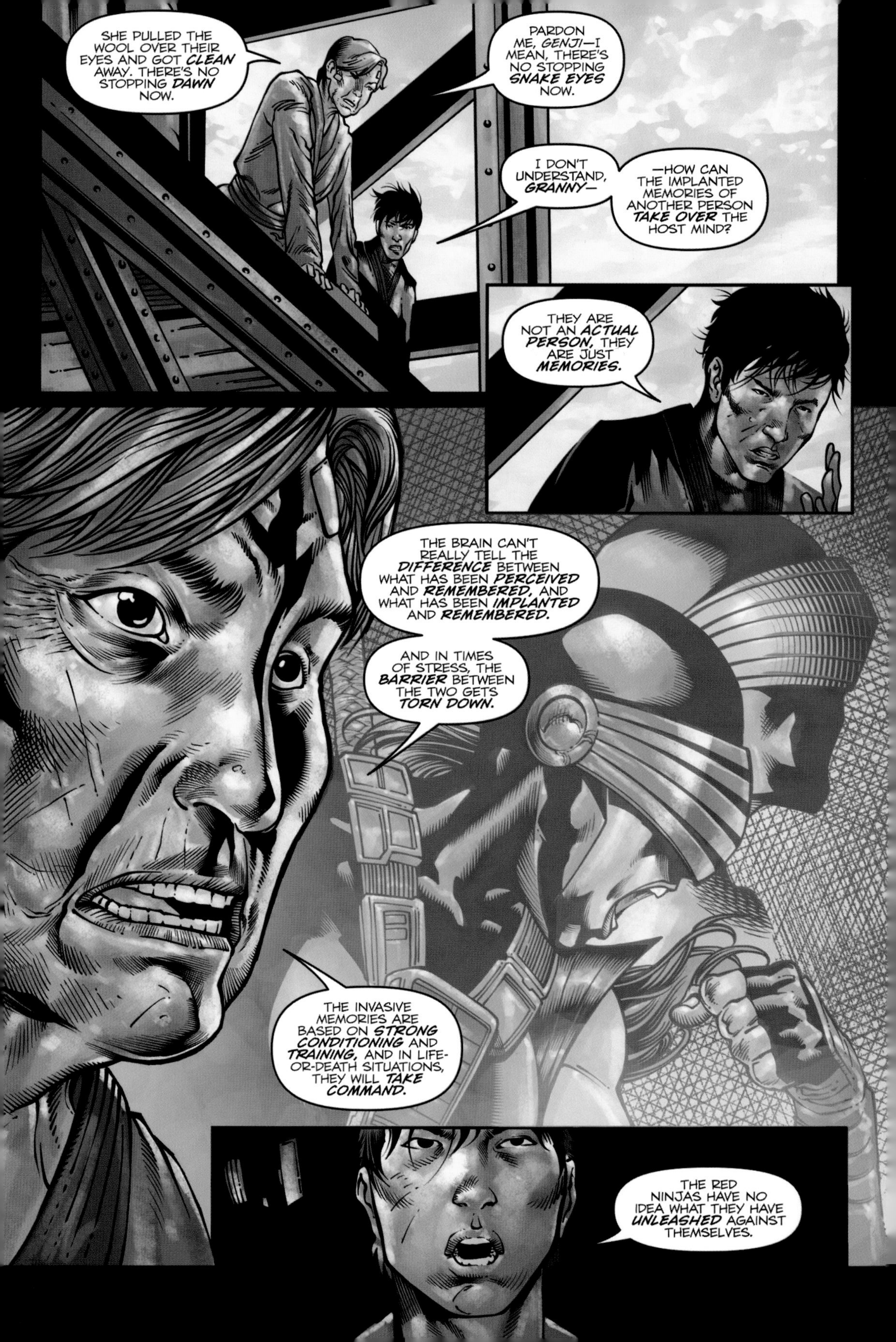
SHE PULLED THE WOOL OVER THEIR EYES AND GOT CLEAN AWAY. THERE'S NO STOPPING DAWN NOW.
PARDON ME, GENJI—I MEAN, THERE'S NO STOPPING SNAKE EYES NOW.
I DON'T UNDERSTAND, GRANNY—
—HOW CAN THE IMPLANTED MEMORIES OF ANOTHER PERSON TAKE OVER THE HOST MIND?
THEY ARE NOT AN ACTUAL PERSON, THEY ARE JUST MEMORIES.
THE BRAIN CAN'T REALLY TELL THE DIFFERENCE BETWEEN WHAT HAS BEEN PERCEIVED AND REMEMBERED, AND WHAT HAS BEEN IMPLANTED AND REMEMBERED.
AND IN TIMES OF STRESS, THE BARRIER BETWEEN THE TWO GETS TORN DOWN.
THE INVASIVE MEMORIES ARE BASED ON STRONG CONDITIONING AND TRAINING, AND IN LIFE-OR-DEATH SITUATIONS, THEY WILL TAKE COMMAND.
THE RED NINJAS HAVE NO IDEA WHAT THEY HAVE UNLEASHED AGAINST THEMSELVES.

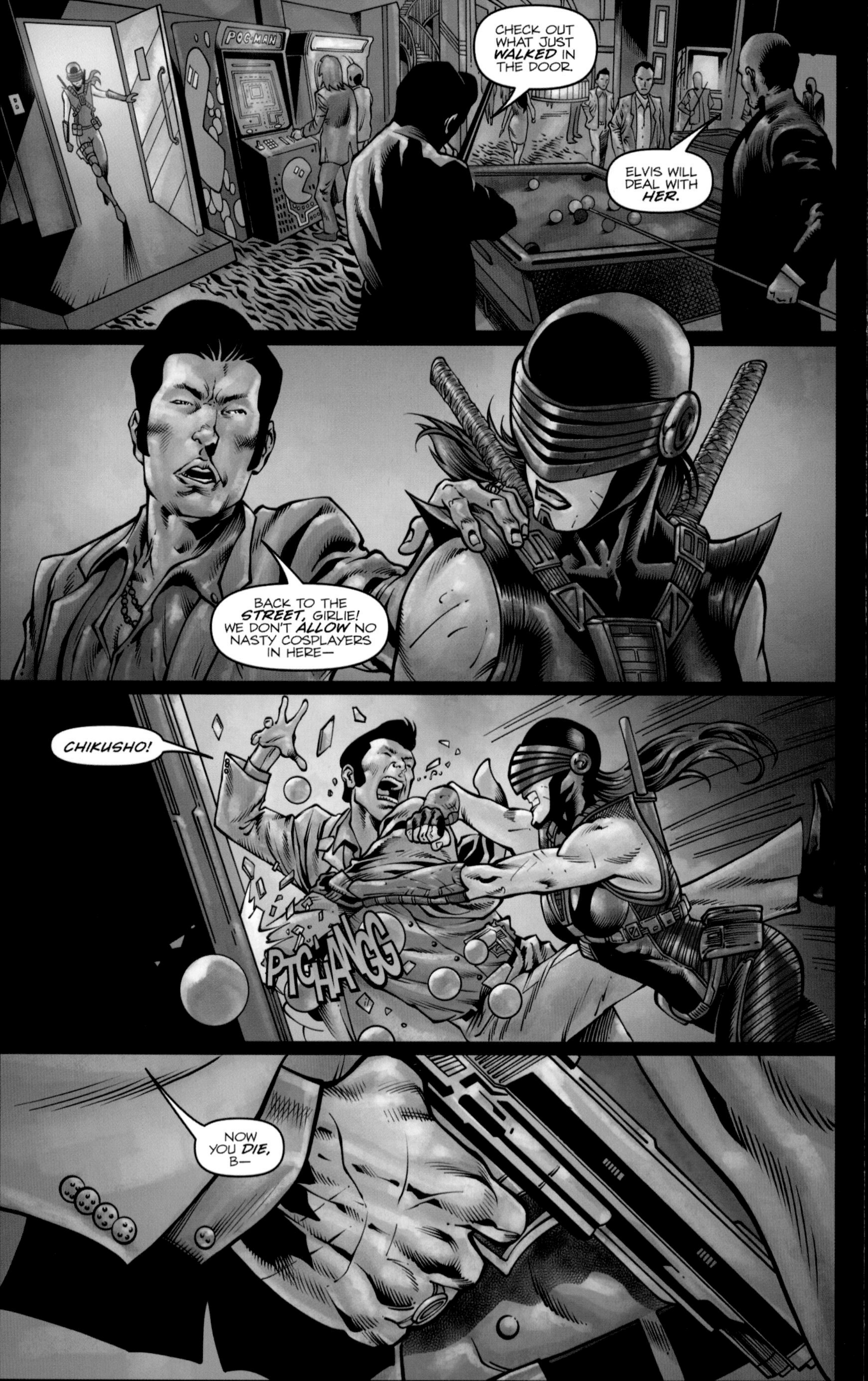
POC-MAN
CHECK OUT WHAT JUST WALKED IN THE DOOR.
ELVIS WILL DEAL WITH HER.
BACK TO THE STREET, GIRLIE! WE DON'T ALLOW NO NASTY COSPLAYERS IN HERE—
CHIKUSHO!
PTCHANGG
NOW YOU DIE, B—

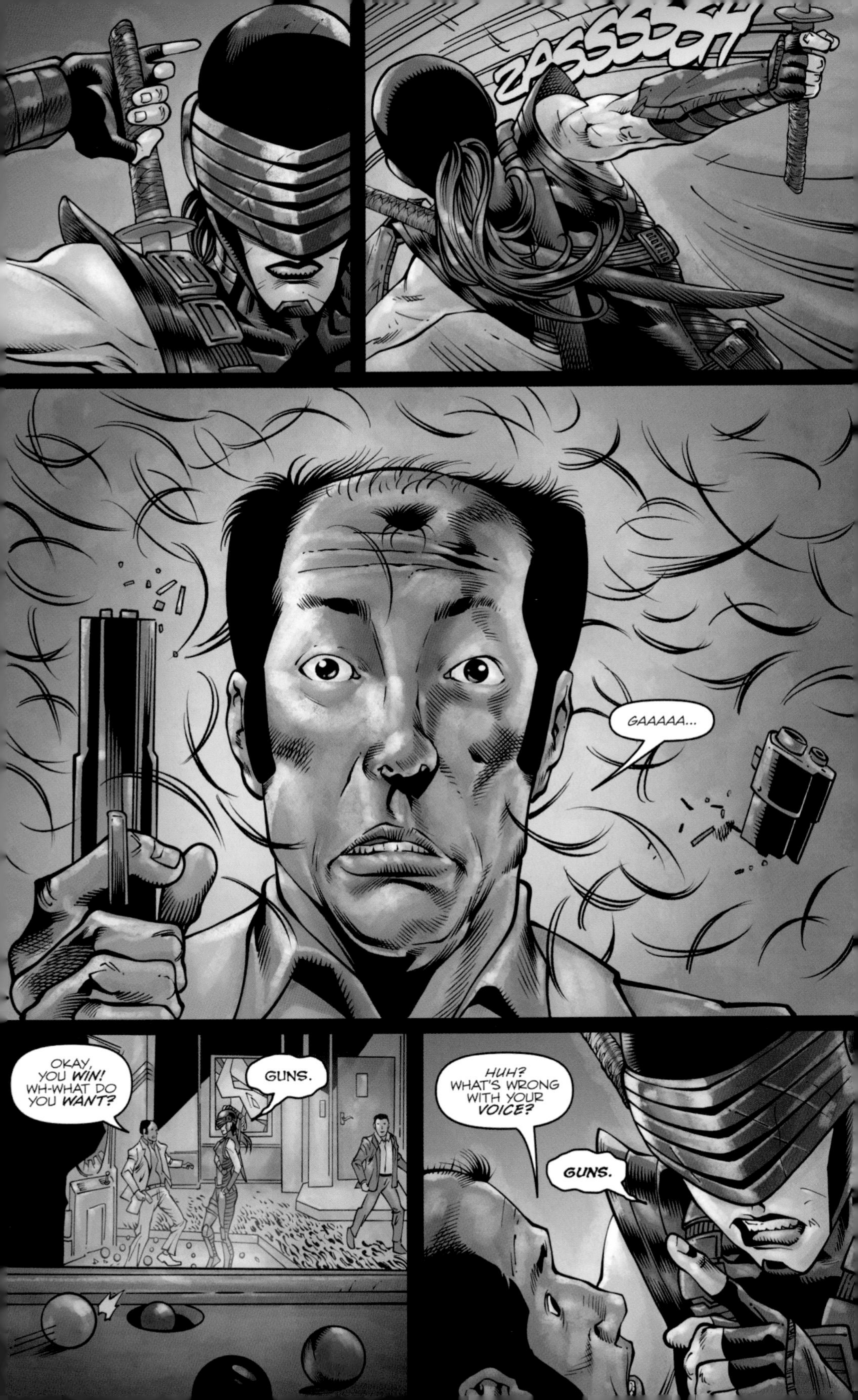
ZASSSSOOH
GAAAAA...
OKAY, YOU WIN! WH-WHAT DO YOU WANT?
GUNS.
HUH? WHAT'S WRONG WITH YOUR VOICE?
GUNS.

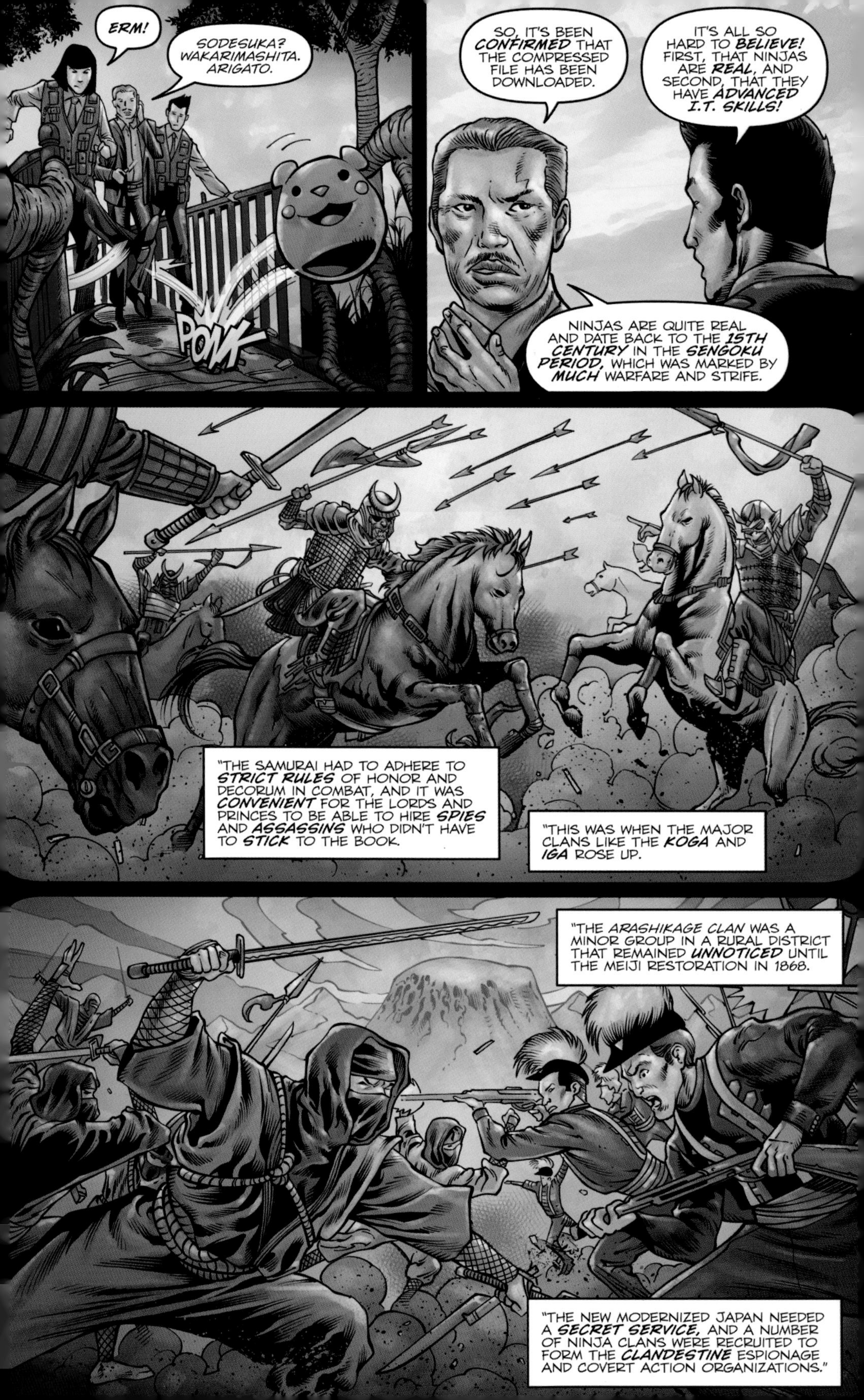

ERM!
SODESUKA? WAKARIMASHITA. ARIGATO.
POWK
SO, IT'S BEEN CONFIRMED THAT THE COMPRESSED FILE HAS BEEN DOWNLOADED.
IT'S ALL SO HARD TO BELIEVE! FIRST, THAT NINJAS ARE REAL, AND SECOND, THAT THEY HAVE ADVANCED I.T. SKILLS!
NINJAS ARE QUITE REAL AND DATE BACK TO THE 15TH CENTURY IN THE SENGOKU PERIOD, WHICH WAS MARKED BY MUCH WARFARE AND STRIFE.
"THE SAMURAI HAD TO ADHERE TO STRICT RULES OF HONOR AND DECORUM IN COMBAT, AND IT WAS CONVENIENT FOR THE LORDS AND PRINCES TO BE ABLE TO HIRE SPIES AND ASSASSINS WHO DIDN'T HAVE TO STICK TO THE BOOK.
"THIS WAS WHEN THE MAJOR CLANS LIKE THE KOGA AND IGA ROSE UP.
"THE ARASHIKAGE CLAN WAS A MINOR GROUP IN A RURAL DISTRICT THAT REMAINED UNNOTICED UNTIL THE MEIJI RESTORATION IN 1868.
"THE NEW MODERNIZED JAPAN NEEDED A SECRET SERVICE, AND A NUMBER OF NINJA CLANS WERE RECRUITED TO FORM THE CLANDESTINE ESPIONAGE AND COVERT ACTION ORGANIZATIONS."

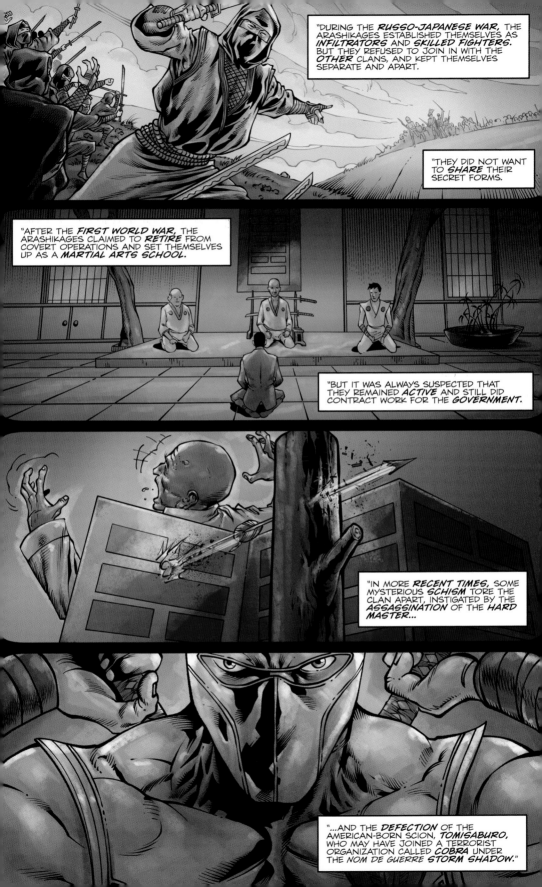

"DURING THE *RUSSO-JAPANESE WAR*, THE ARASHIKAGES ESTABLISHED THEMSELVES AS *INFILTRATORS* AND *SKILLED FIGHTERS*. BUT THEY REFUSED TO JOIN IN WITH THE *OTHER* CLANS, AND KEPT THEMSELVES SEPARATE AND APART.

"THEY DID NOT WANT TO *SHARE* THEIR SECRET FORMS.

"AFTER THE *FIRST WORLD WAR*, THE ARASHIKAGES CLAIMED TO *RETIRE* FROM COVERT OPERATIONS AND SET THEMSELVES UP AS A *MARTIAL ARTS SCHOOL*.

"BUT IT WAS ALWAYS SUSPECTED THAT THEY REMAINED *ACTIVE* AND STILL DID CONTRACT WORK FOR THE *GOVERNMENT*.

"IN MORE *RECENT TIMES*, SOME MYSTERIOUS *SCHISM* TORE THE CLAN APART, INSTIGATED BY THE *ASSASSINATION* OF THE *HARD MASTER*...

"...AND THE *DEFECTION* OF THE AMERICAN-BORN SCION, *TOMISABURO*, WHO MAY HAVE JOINED A TERRORIST ORGANIZATION CALLED *COBRA* UNDER THE *NOM DE GUERRE STORM SHADOW*."

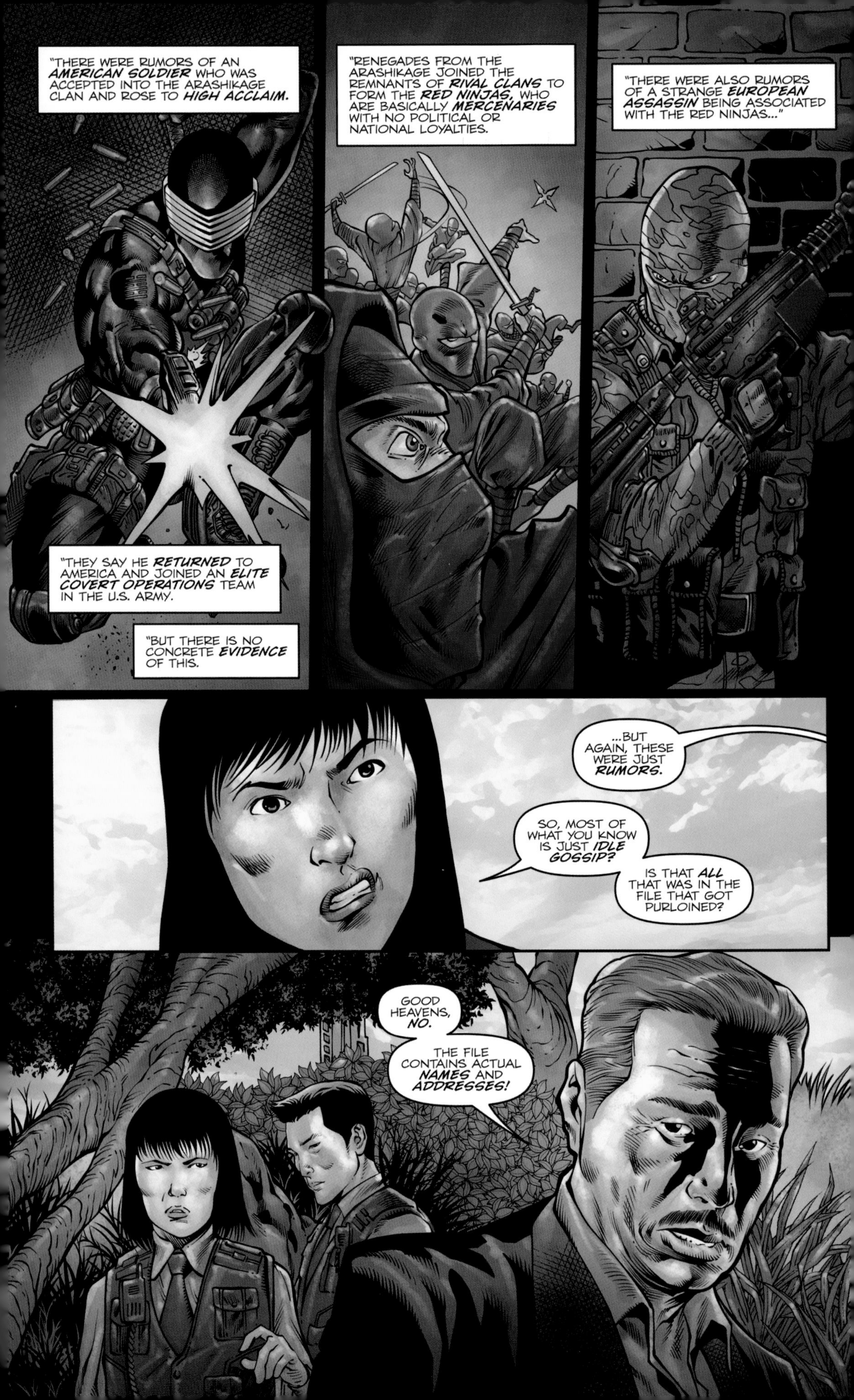
"THERE WERE RUMORS OF AN AMERICAN SOLDIER WHO WAS ACCEPTED INTO THE ARASHIKAGE CLAN AND ROSE TO HIGH ACCLAIM.
"THEY SAY HE RETURNED TO AMERICA AND JOINED AN ELITE COVERT OPERATIONS TEAM IN THE U.S. ARMY.
"BUT THERE IS NO CONCRETE EVIDENCE OF THIS.
"RENEGADES FROM THE ARASHIKAGE JOINED THE REMNANTS OF RIVAL CLANS TO FORM THE RED NINJAS, WHO ARE BASICALLY MERCENARIES WITH NO POLITICAL OR NATIONAL LOYALTIES.
"THERE WERE ALSO RUMORS OF A STRANGE EUROPEAN ASSASSIN BEING ASSOCIATED WITH THE RED NINJAS..."
...BUT AGAIN, THESE WERE JUST RUMORS.
SO, MOST OF WHAT YOU KNOW IS JUST IDLE GOSSIP?
IS THAT ALL THAT WAS IN THE FILE THAT GOT PURLOINED?
GOOD HEAVENS, NO.
THE FILE CONTAINS ACTUAL NAMES AND ADDRESSES!

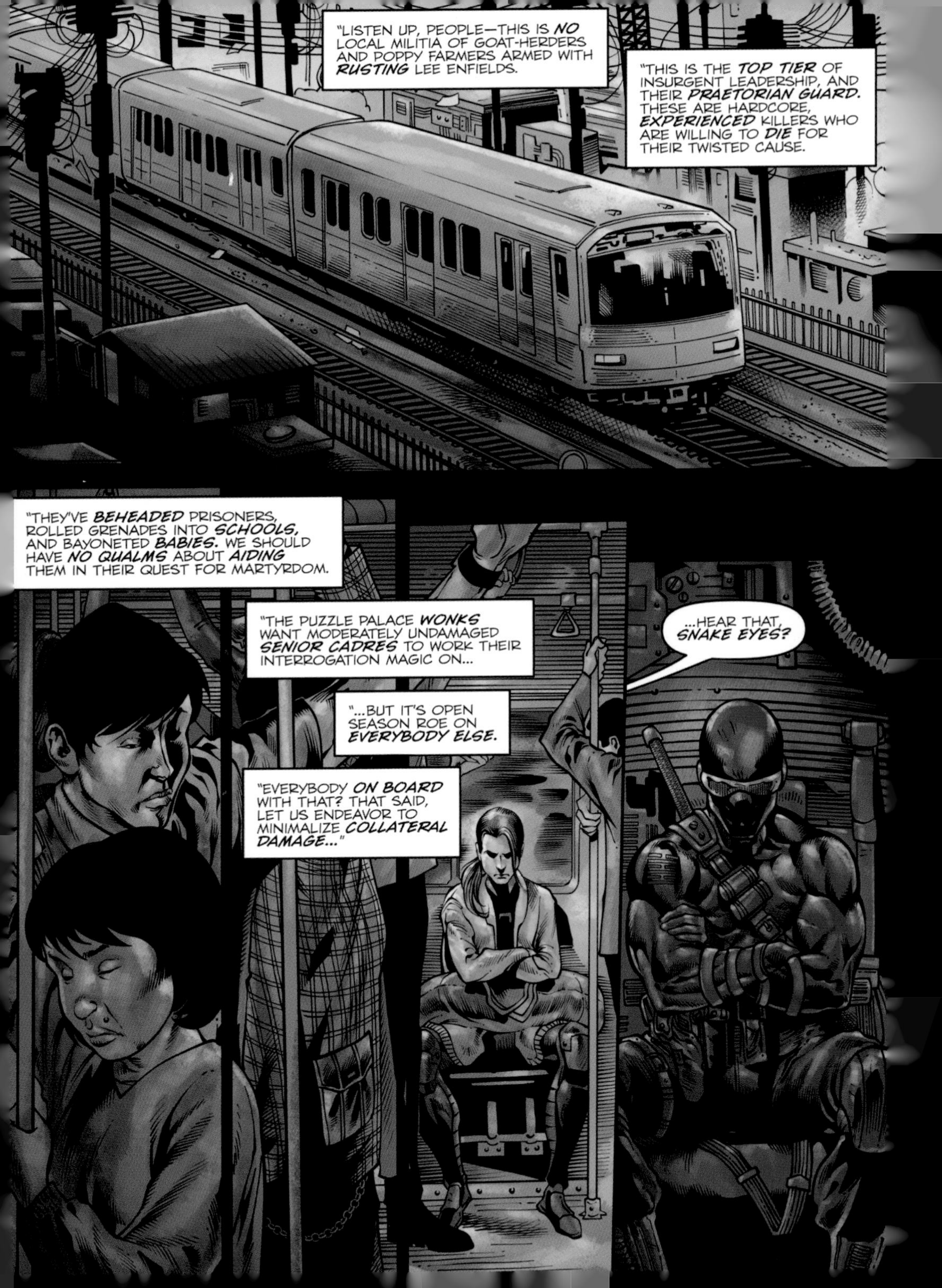
"LISTEN UP, PEOPLE—THIS IS NO LOCAL MILITIA OF GOAT-HERDERS AND POPPY FARMERS ARMED WITH RUSTING LEE ENFIELDS.
"THIS IS THE TOP TIER OF INSURGENT LEADERSHIP, AND THEIR PRAETORIAN GUARD. THESE ARE HARDCORE, EXPERIENCED KILLERS WHO ARE WILLING TO DIE FOR THEIR TWISTED CAUSE.
"THEY'VE BEHEADED PRISONERS, ROLLED GRENADES INTO SCHOOLS, AND BAYONETED BABIES. WE SHOULD HAVE NO QUALMS ABOUT AIDING THEM IN THEIR QUEST FOR MARTYRDOM.
"THE PUZZLE PALACE WONKS WANT MODERATELY UNDAMAGED SENIOR CADRES TO WORK THEIR INTERROGATION MAGIC ON...
"...BUT IT'S OPEN SEASON ROE ON EVERYBODY ELSE.
"EVERYBODY ON BOARD WITH THAT? THAT SAID, LET US ENDEAVOR TO MINIMALIZE COLLATERAL DAMAGE..."
...HEAR THAT, SNAKE EYES?

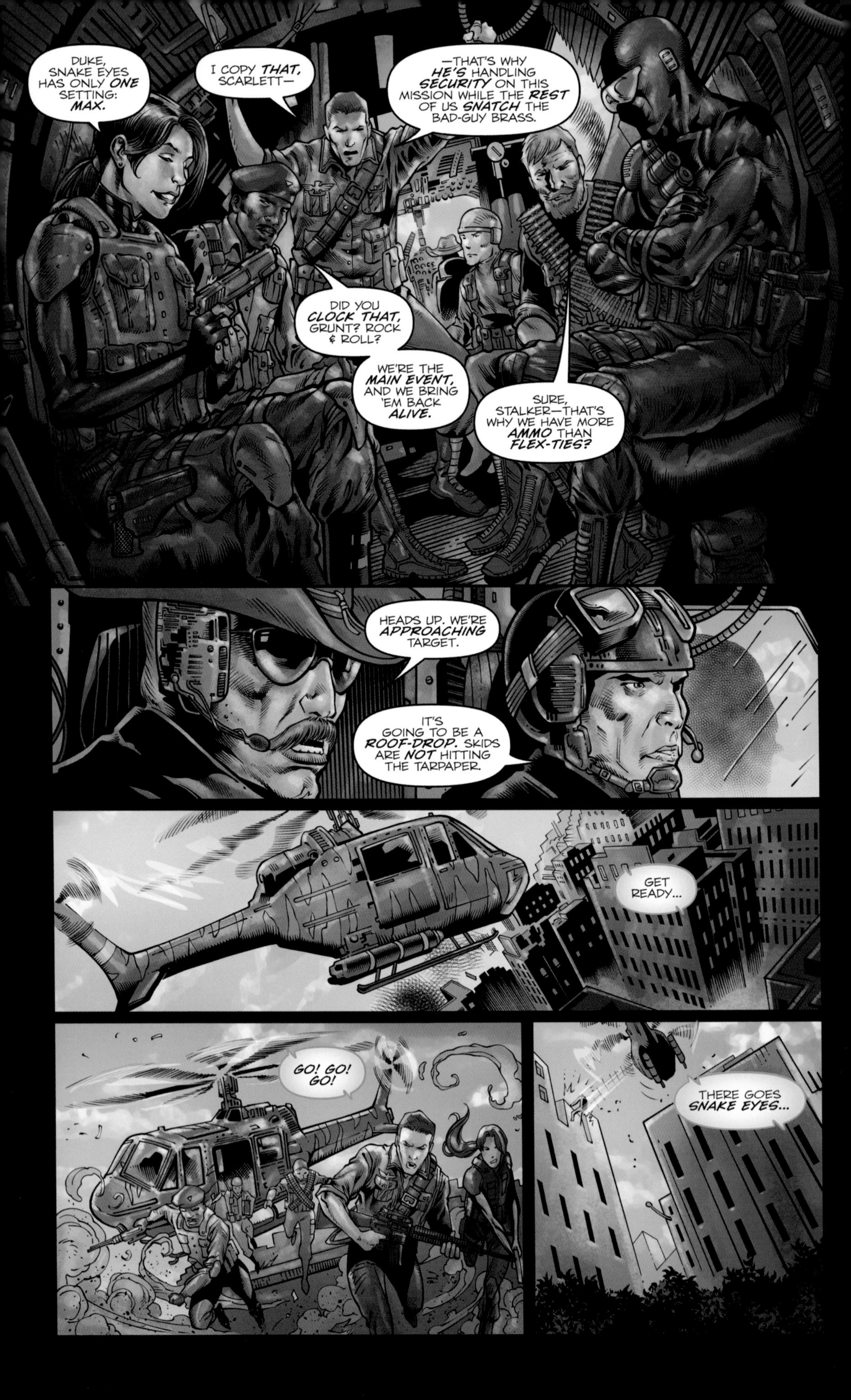
DUKE, SNAKE EYES HAS ONLY ONE SETTING: MAX.
I COPY THAT, SCARLETT—
—THAT'S WHY HE'S HANDLING SECURITY ON THIS MISSION WHILE THE REST OF US SNATCH THE BAD-GUY BRASS.
DID YOU CLOCK THAT, GRUNT? ROCK & ROLL?
WE'RE THE MAIN EVENT, AND WE BRING 'EM BACK ALIVE.
SURE, STALKER—THAT'S WHY WE HAVE MORE AMMO THAN FLEX-TIES?
HEADS UP. WE'RE APPROACHING TARGET.
IT'S GOING TO BE A ROOF-DROP. SKIDS ARE NOT HITTING THE TARPAPER.
GET READY...
GO! GO! GO!
THERE GOES SNAKE EYES...

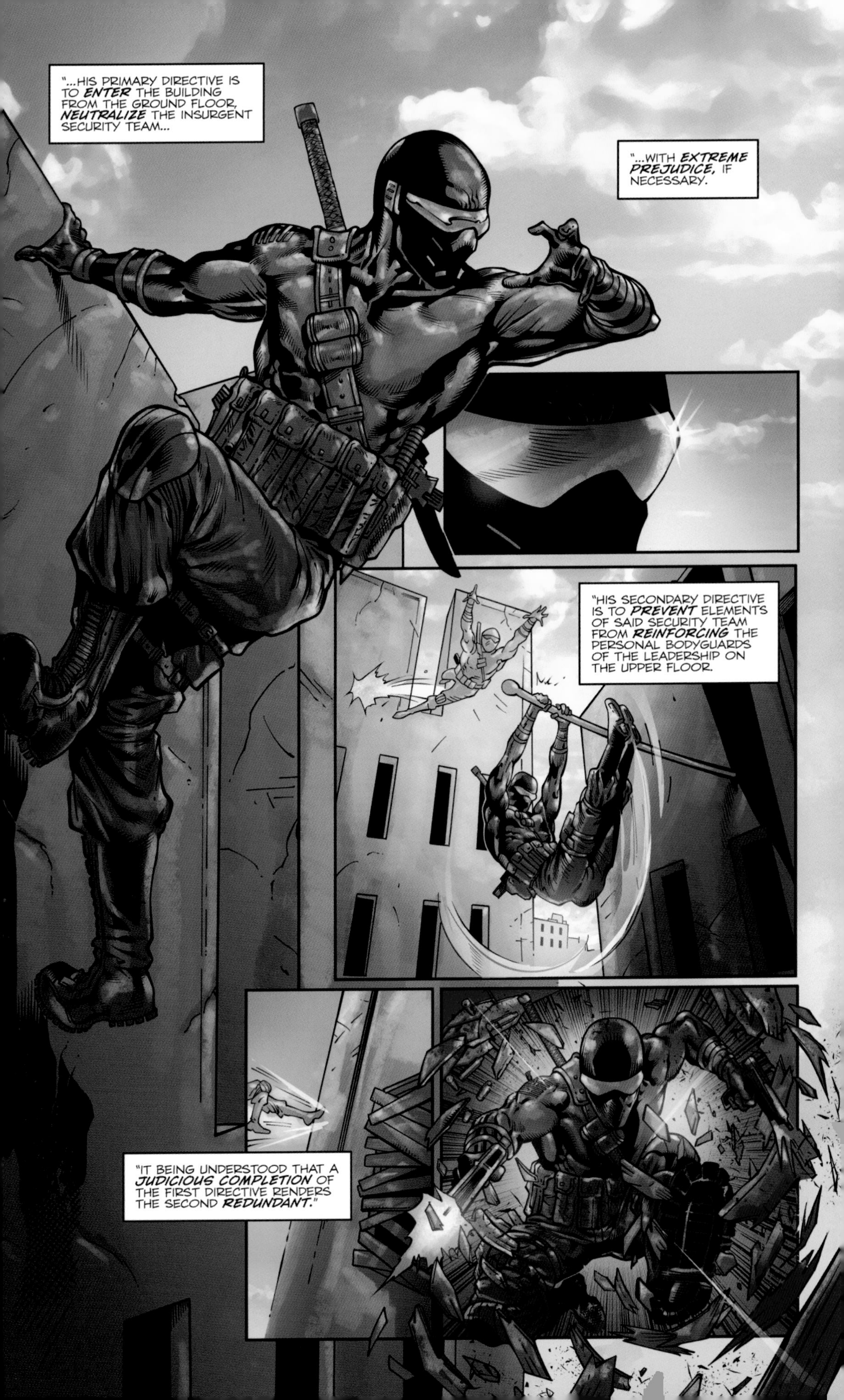
"...HIS PRIMARY DIRECTIVE IS TO ENTER THE BUILDING FROM THE GROUND FLOOR, NEUTRALIZE THE INSURGENT SECURITY TEAM...
"...WITH EXTREME PREJUDICE, IF NECESSARY.
"HIS SECONDARY DIRECTIVE IS TO PREVENT ELEMENTS OF SAID SECURITY TEAM FROM REINFORCING THE PERSONAL BODYGUARDS OF THE LEADERSHIP ON THE UPPER FLOOR.
"IT BEING UNDERSTOOD THAT A JUDICIOUS COMPLETION OF THE FIRST DIRECTIVE RENDERS THE SECOND REDUNDANT."

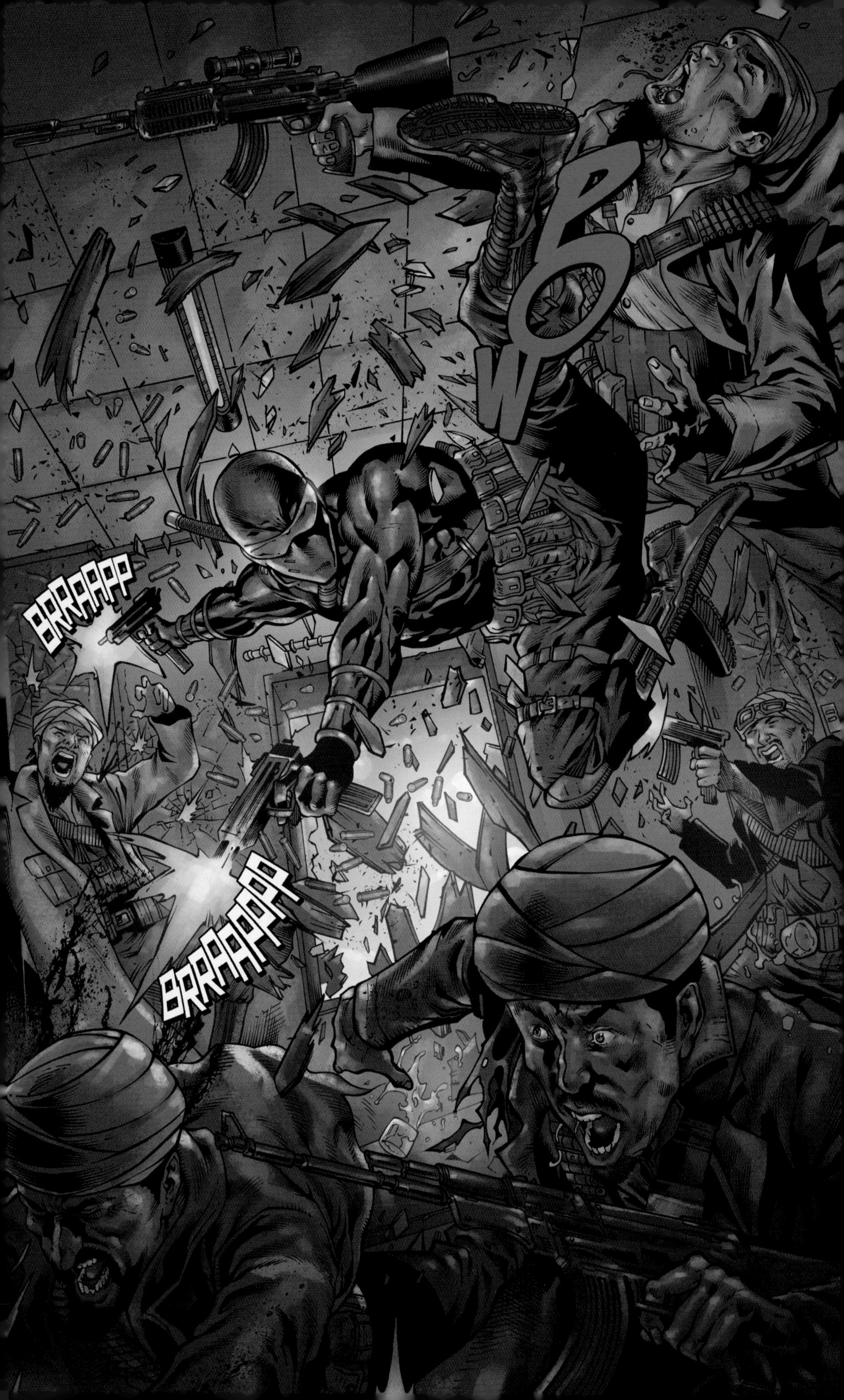
WBP
BRRAAPP
BRRAAPPP

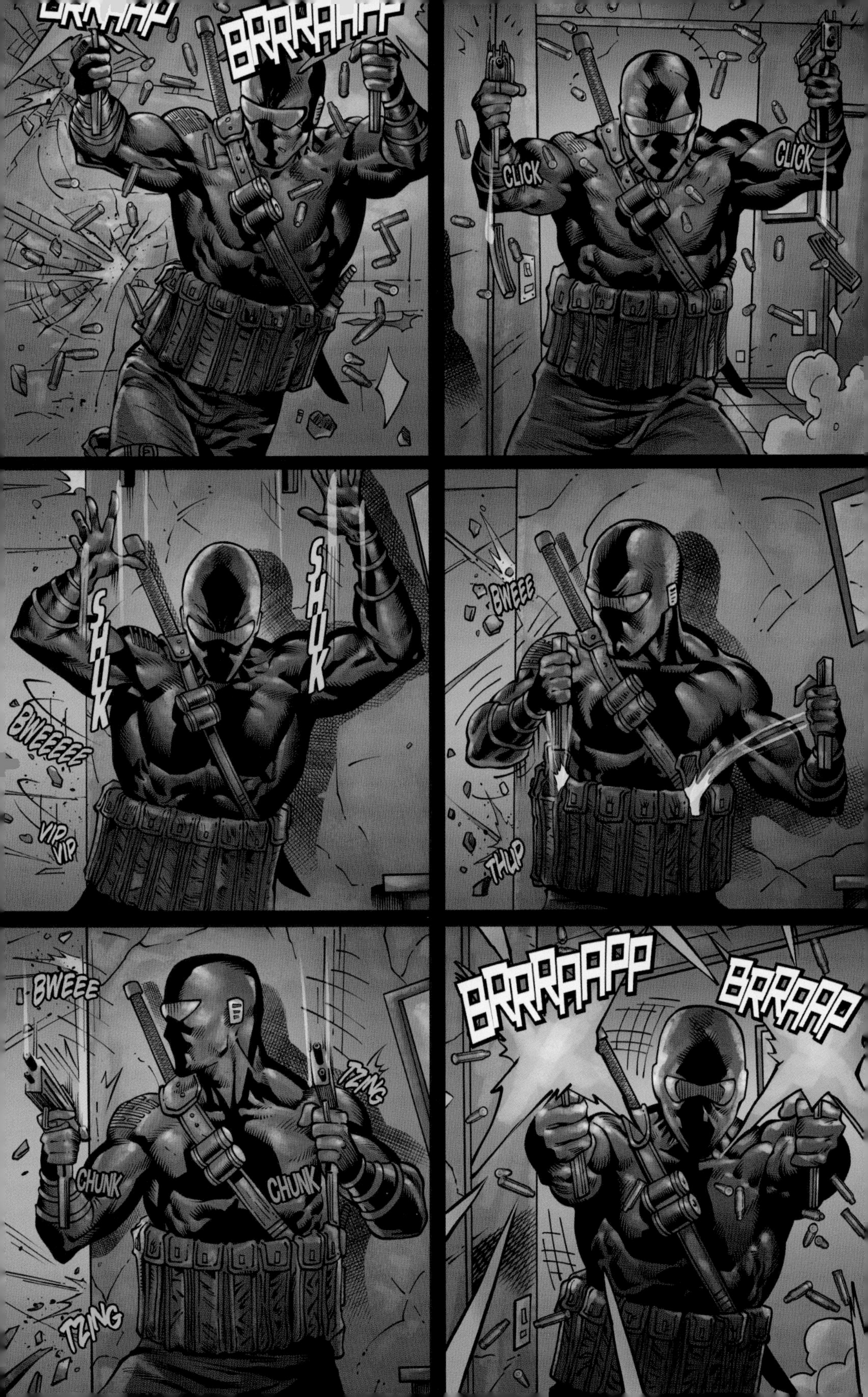
BRRRAHPP
CLICK
CLICK
SHUK
SHUK
BWEEEEE
VIP VIP
BWEEE
THUP
BWEEE
TZING
CHUNK
CHUNK
TZING
BRRRAAPP
BRRAAP

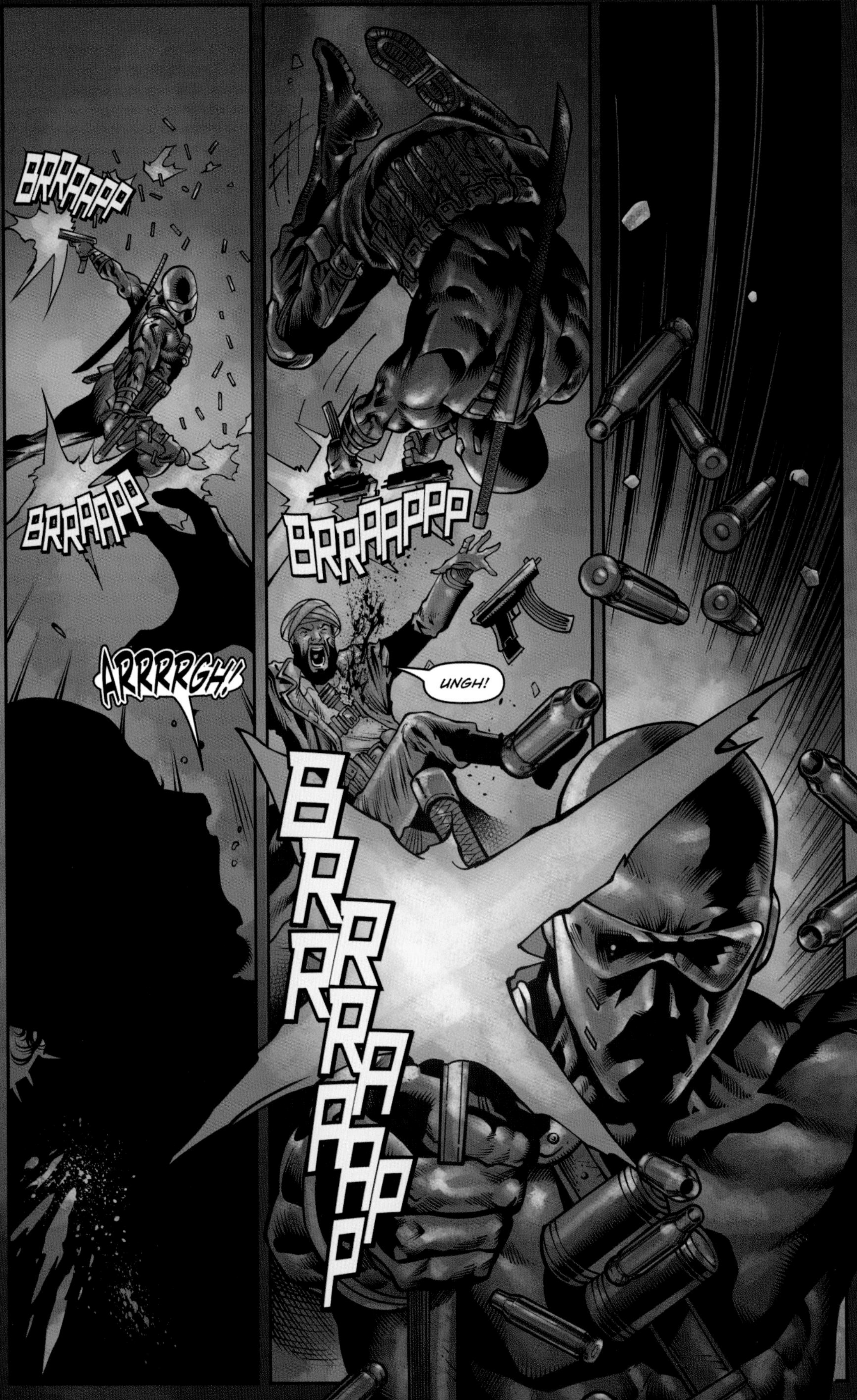
BRRAAPP
BRRAAPP
ARRRRGH!
BRRAAPPP
UNGH!
BRRRRRAAAAPP

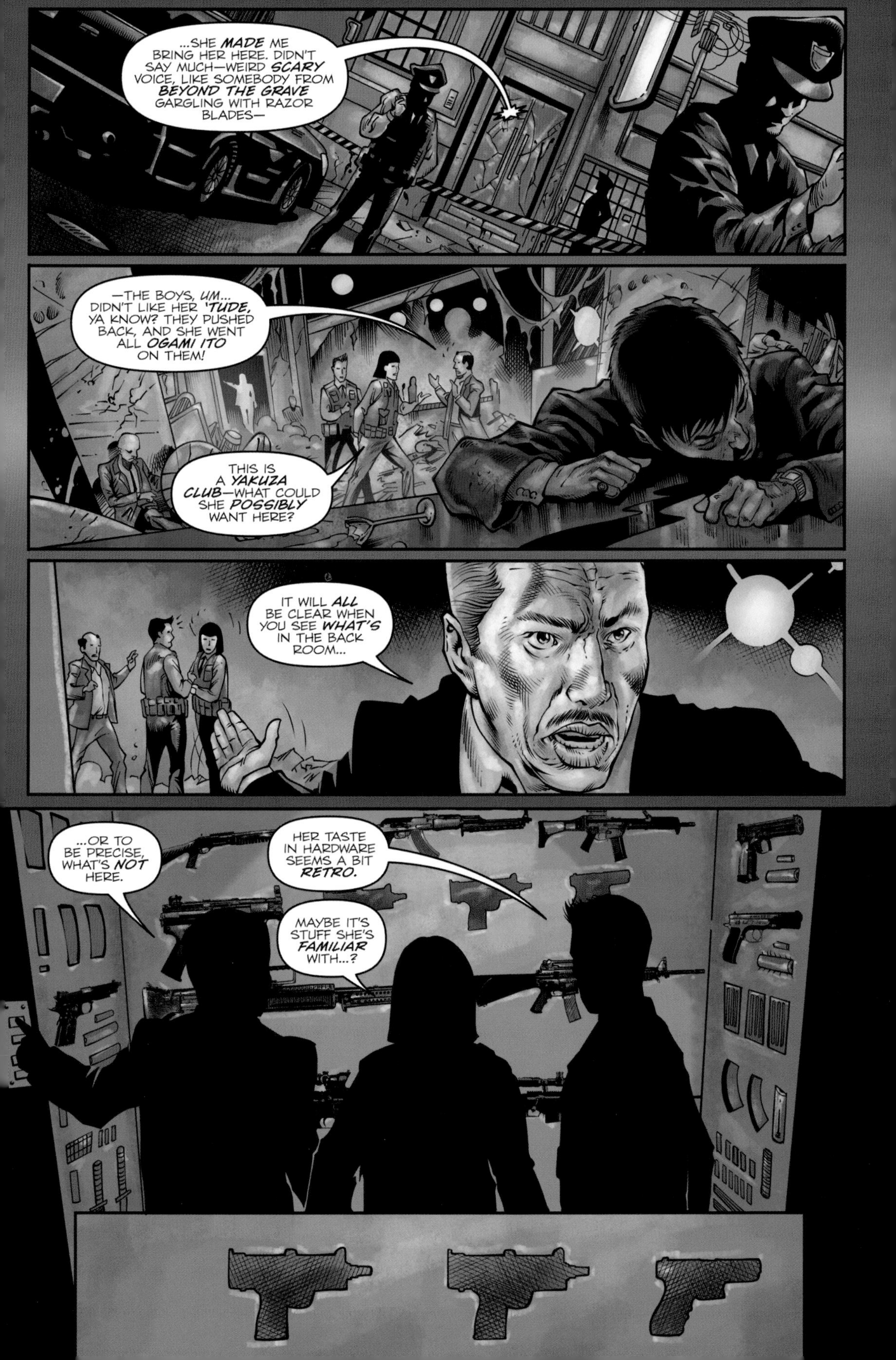
...SHE MADE ME BRING HER HERE. DIDN'T SAY MUCH—WEIRD SCARY VOICE, LIKE SOMEBODY FROM BEYOND THE GRAVE GARGLING WITH RAZOR BLADES—
—THE BOYS, UM... DIDN'T LIKE HER 'TUDE, YA KNOW? THEY PUSHED BACK, AND SHE WENT ALL OGAMI ITO ON THEM!
THIS IS A YAKUZA CLUB—WHAT COULD SHE POSSIBLY WANT HERE?
IT WILL ALL BE CLEAR WHEN YOU SEE WHAT'S IN THE BACK ROOM...
...OR TO BE PRECISE, WHAT'S NOT HERE.
HER TASTE IN HARDWARE SEEMS A BIT RETRO.
MAYBE IT'S STUFF SHE'S FAMILIAR WITH...?

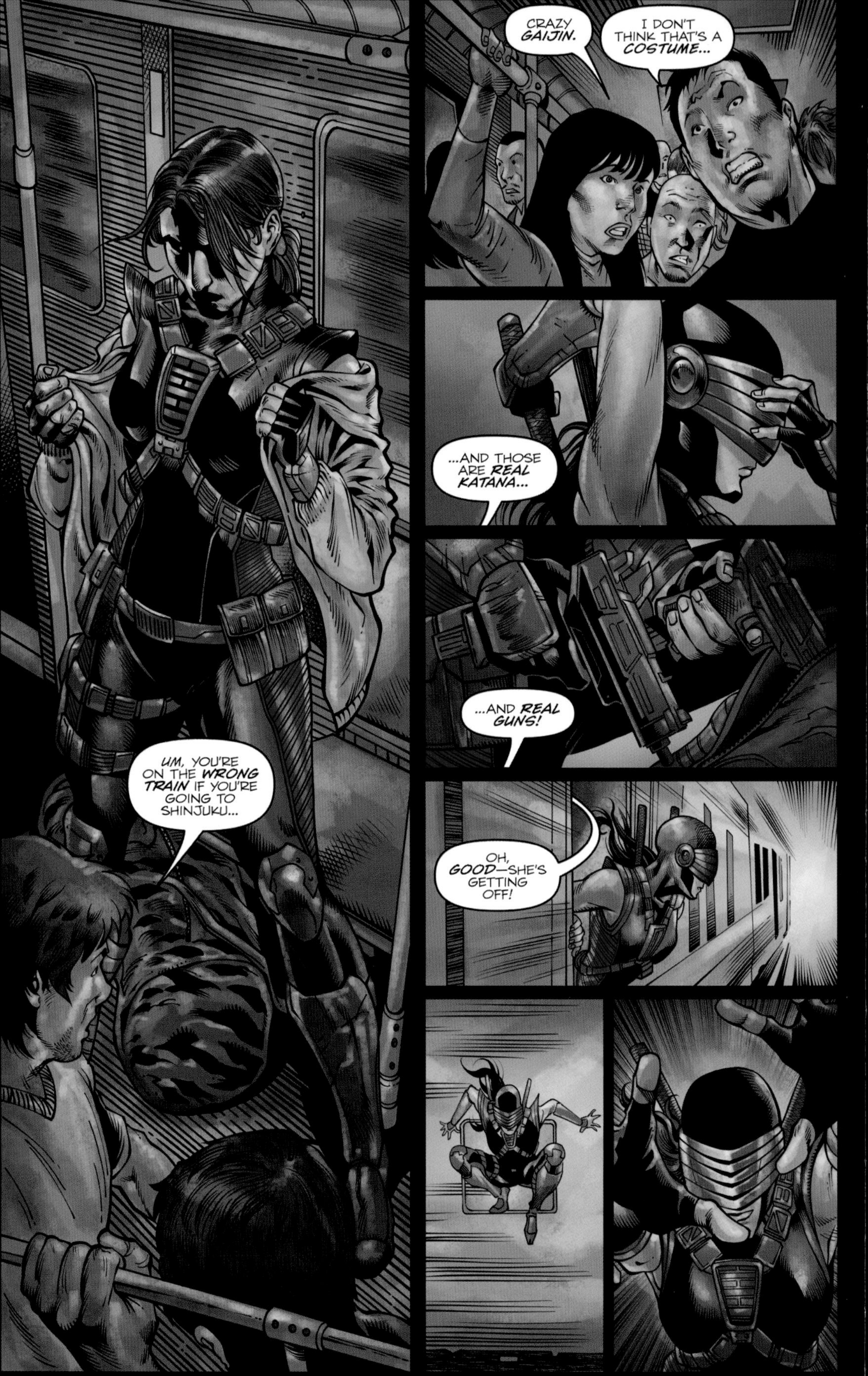
UM, YOU'RE ON THE WRONG TRAIN IF YOU'RE GOING TO SHINJUKU...
CRAZY GAIJIN.
I DON'T THINK THAT'S A COSTUME...
...AND THOSE ARE REAL KATANA...
...AND REAL GUNS!
OH, GOOD—SHE'S GETTING OFF!

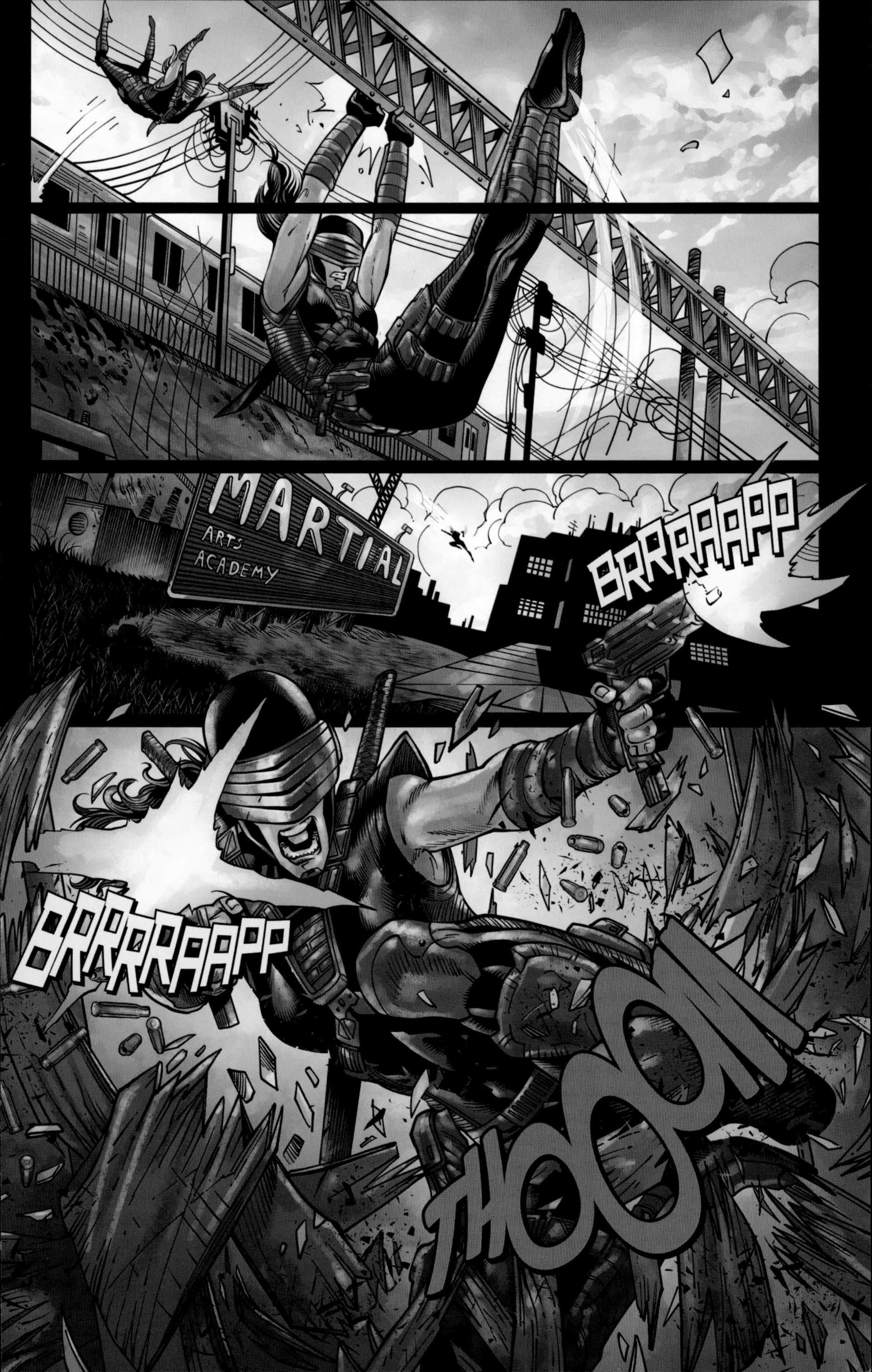
MARTIAL
ARTS
ACADEMY
BRRRAAPP
BRRRRAAPP
THOOM

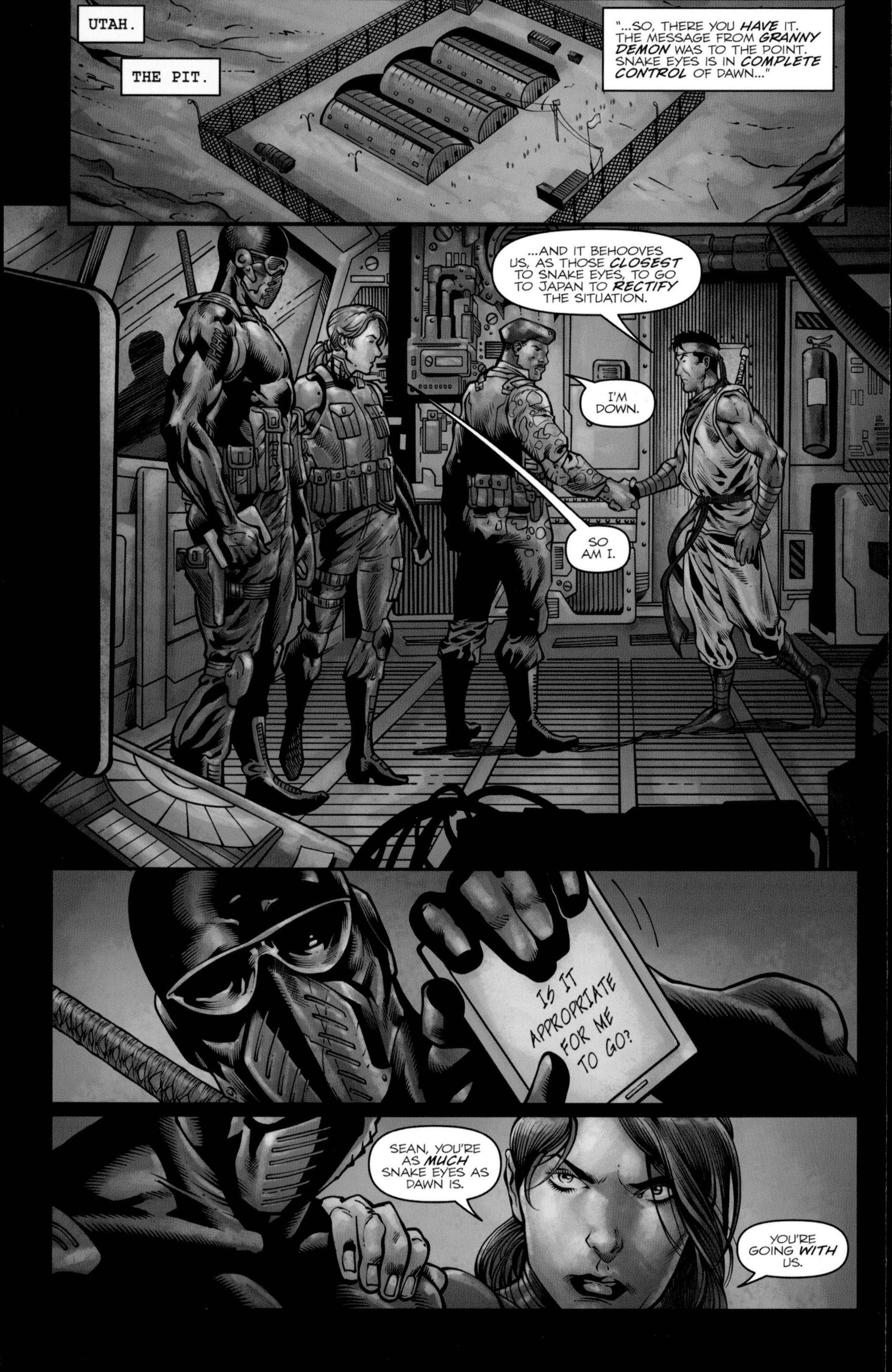
UTAH.
THE PIT.
"...SO, THERE YOU HAVE IT. THE MESSAGE FROM GRANNY DEMON WAS TO THE POINT. SNAKE EYES IS IN COMPLETE CONTROL OF DAWN..."
...AND IT BEHOOVES US, AS THOSE CLOSEST TO SNAKE EYES, TO GO TO JAPAN TO RECTIFY THE SITUATION.
I'M DOWN.
SO AM I.
IS IT APPROPRIATE FOR ME TO GO?
SEAN, YOU'RE AS MUCH SNAKE EYES AS DAWN IS.
YOU'RE GOING WITH US.

ART BY JOHN ROYLE & JAGDISH KUMAR
COLORS BY JAMES OFFREDI

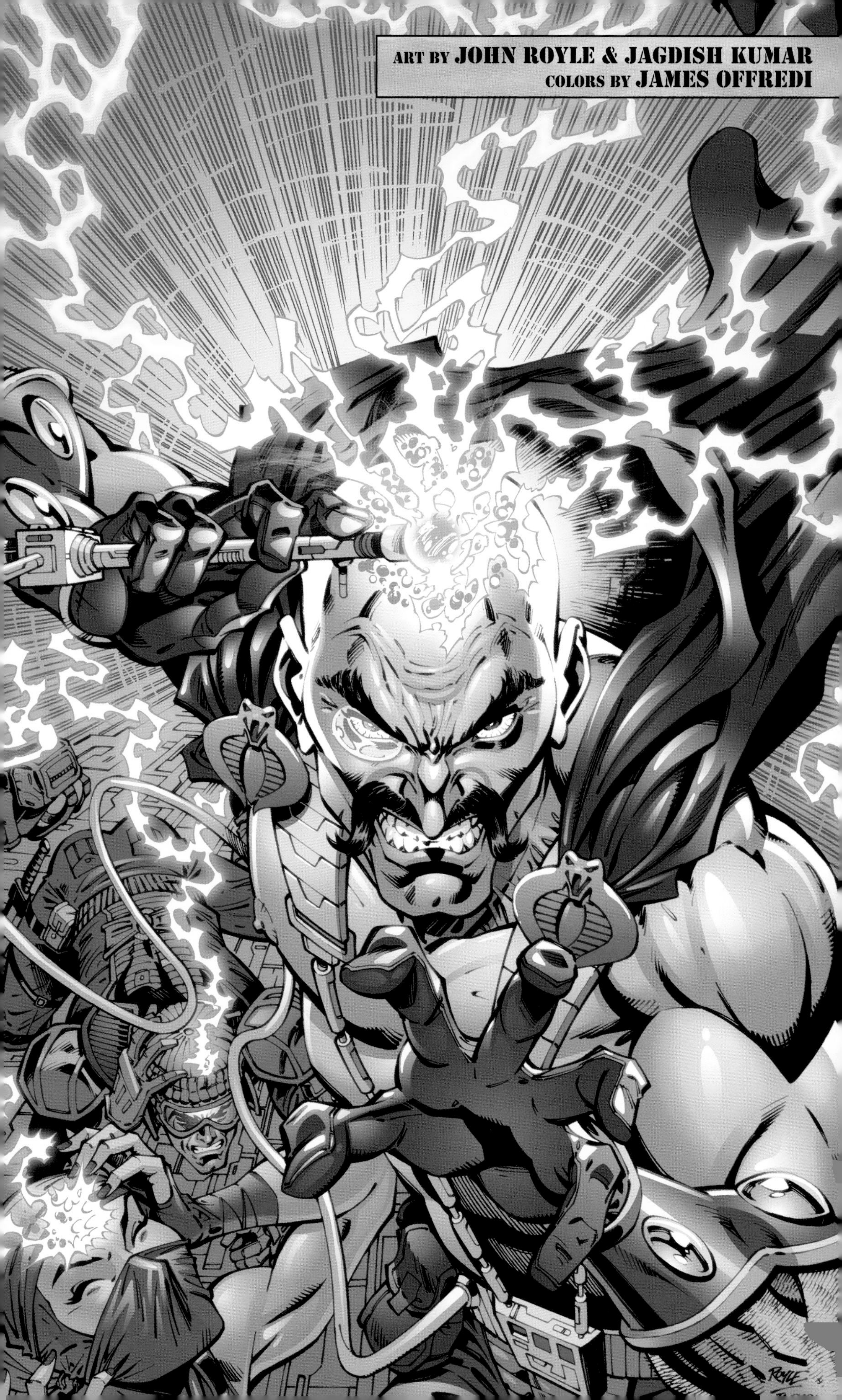

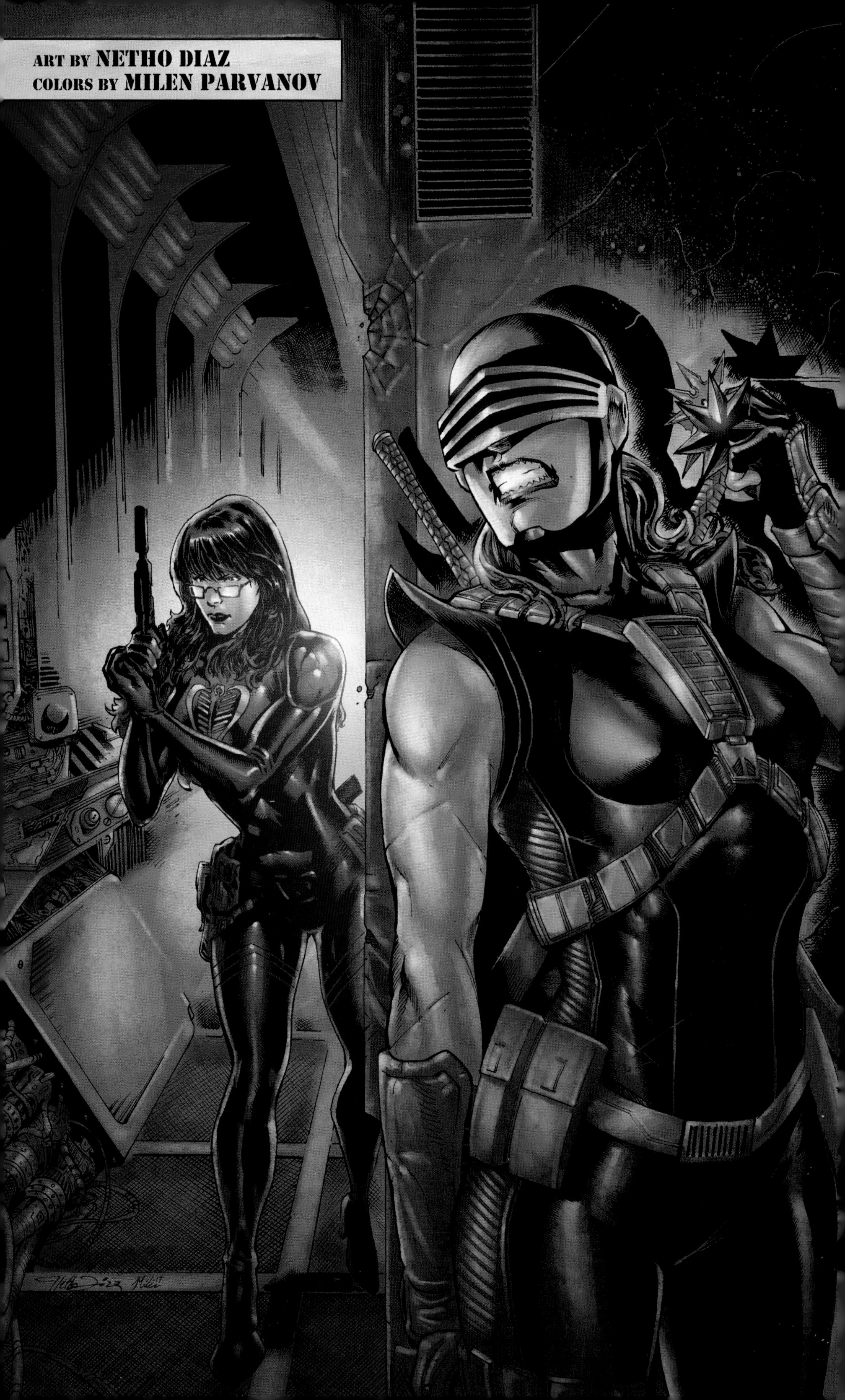
ART BY NETHO DIAZ
COLORS BY MILEN PARVANOV

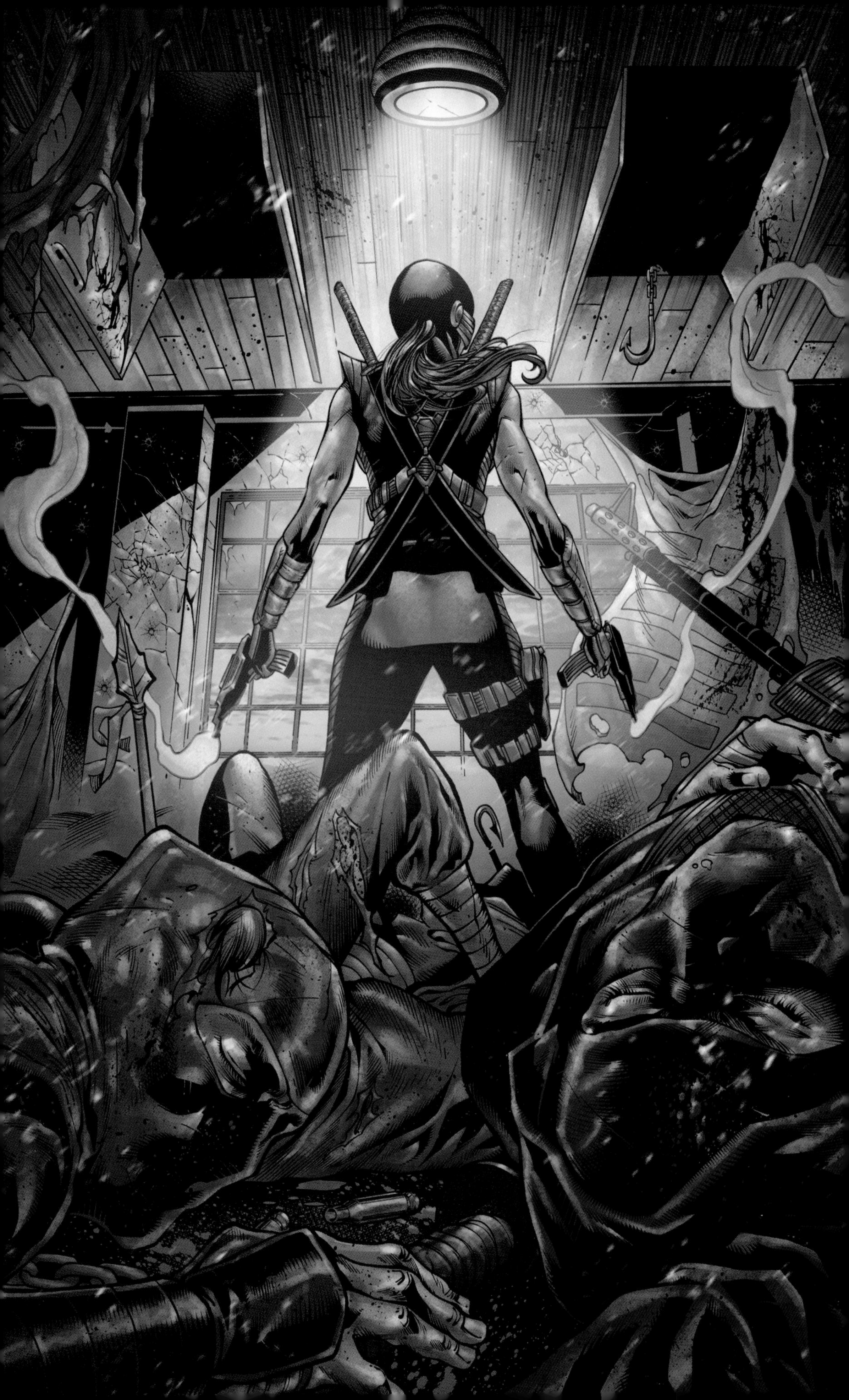

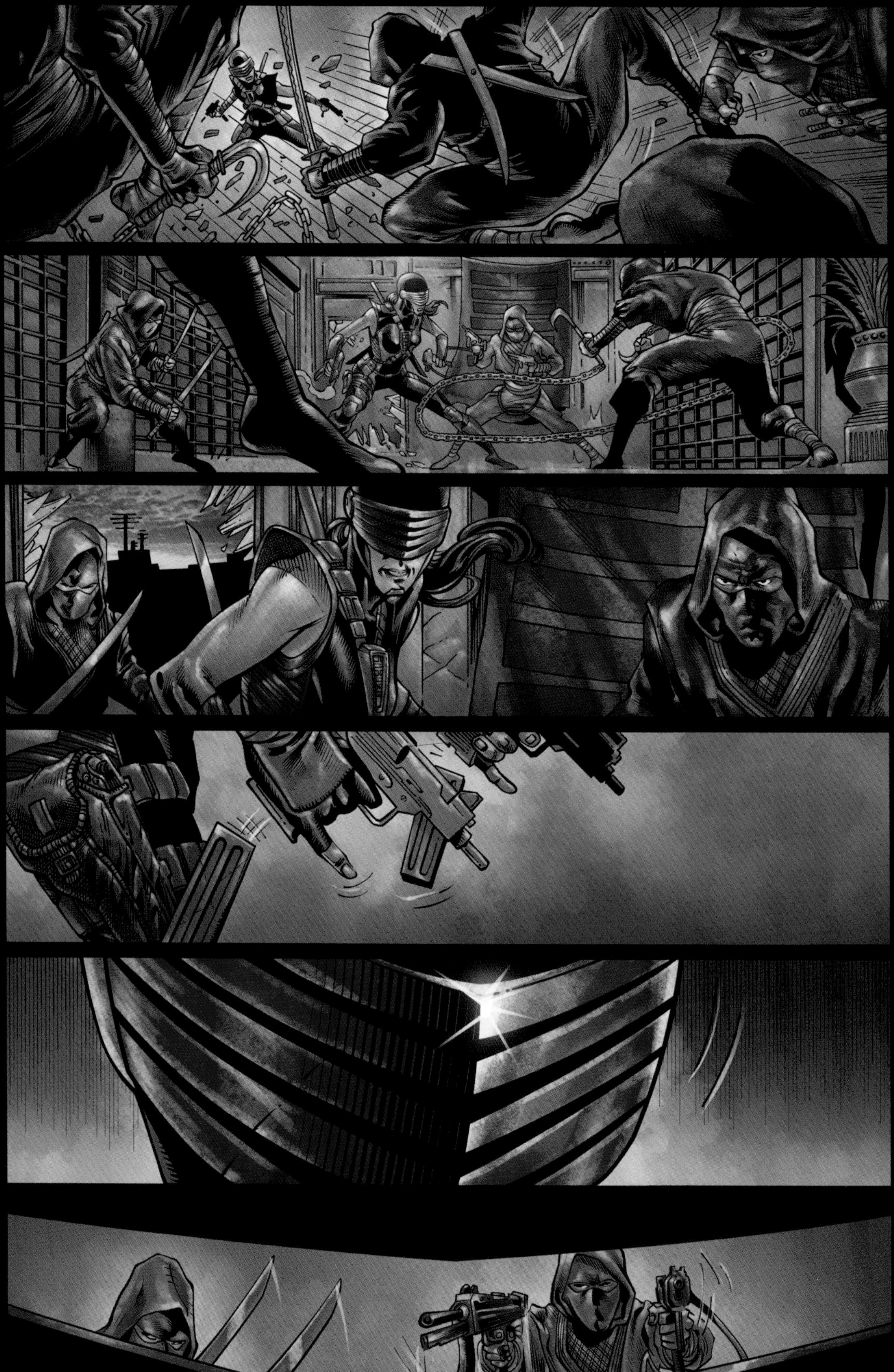

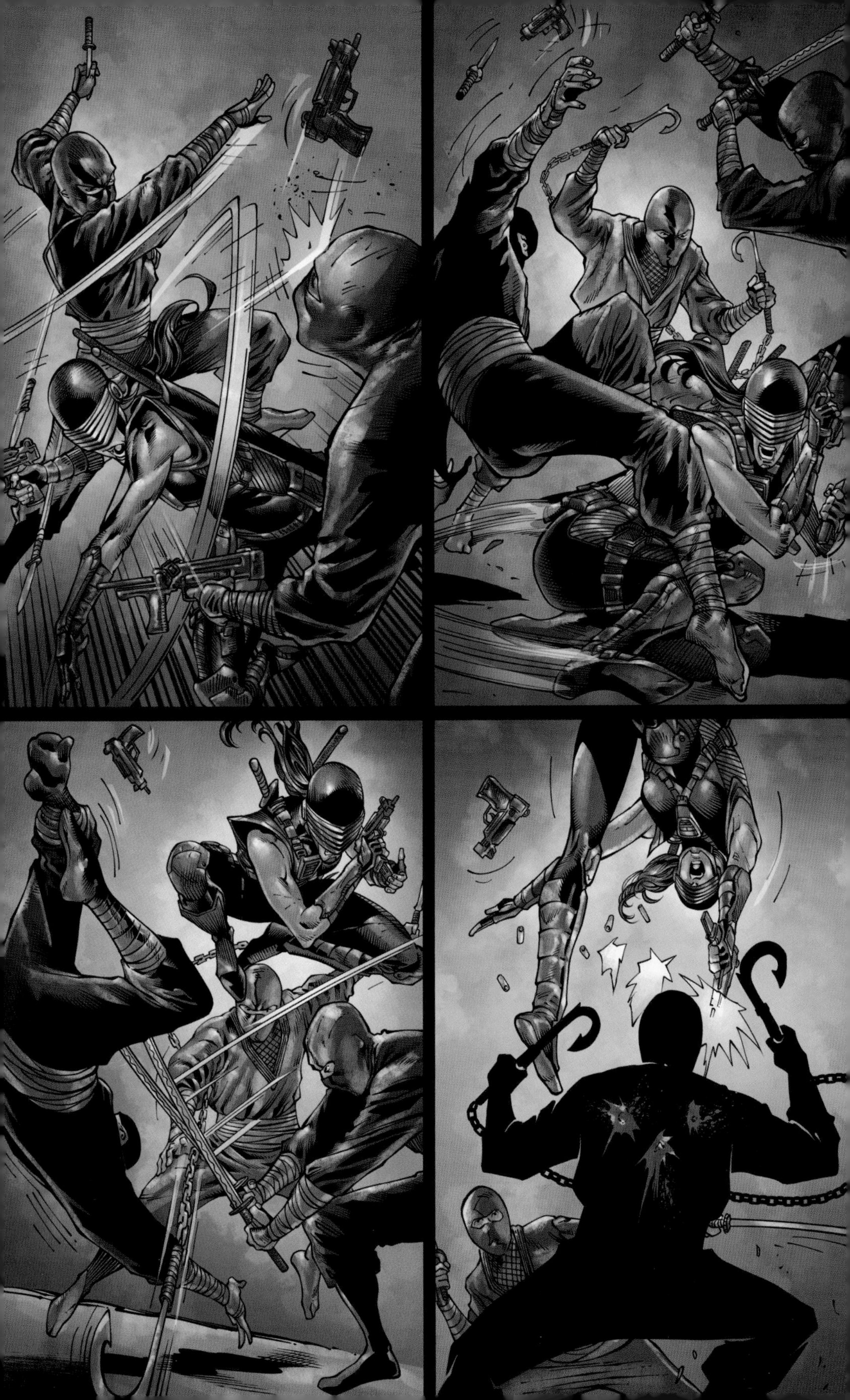

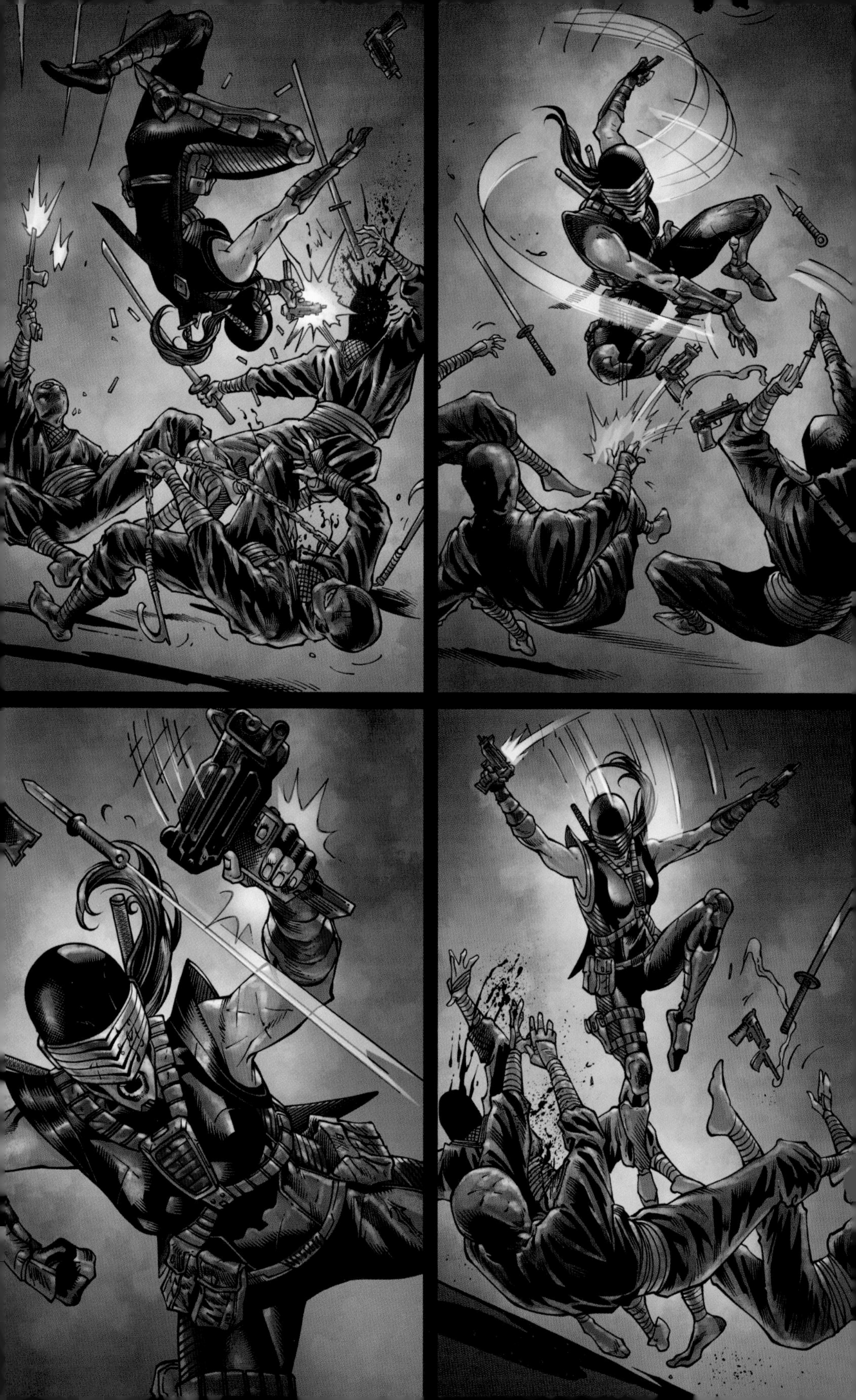

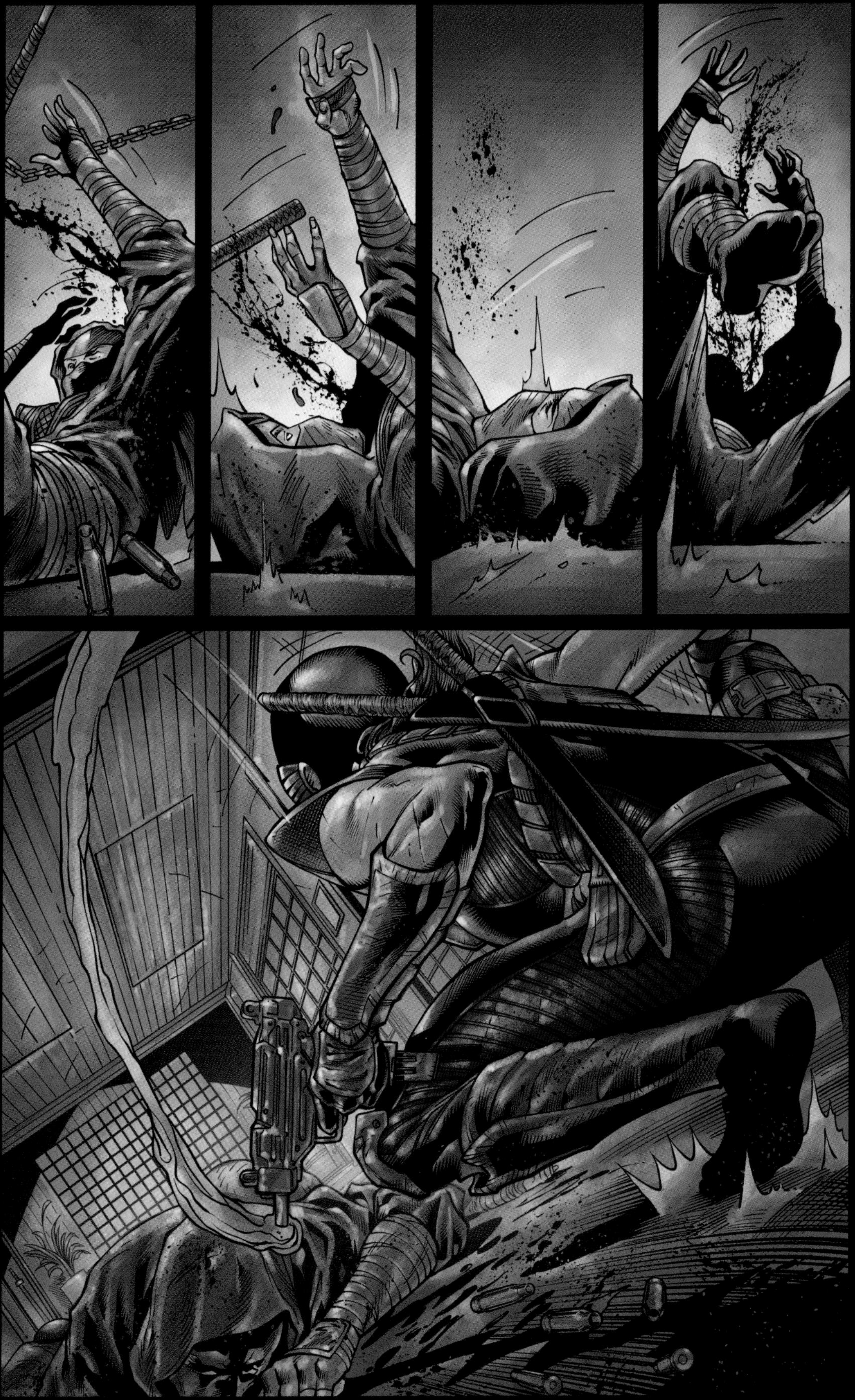

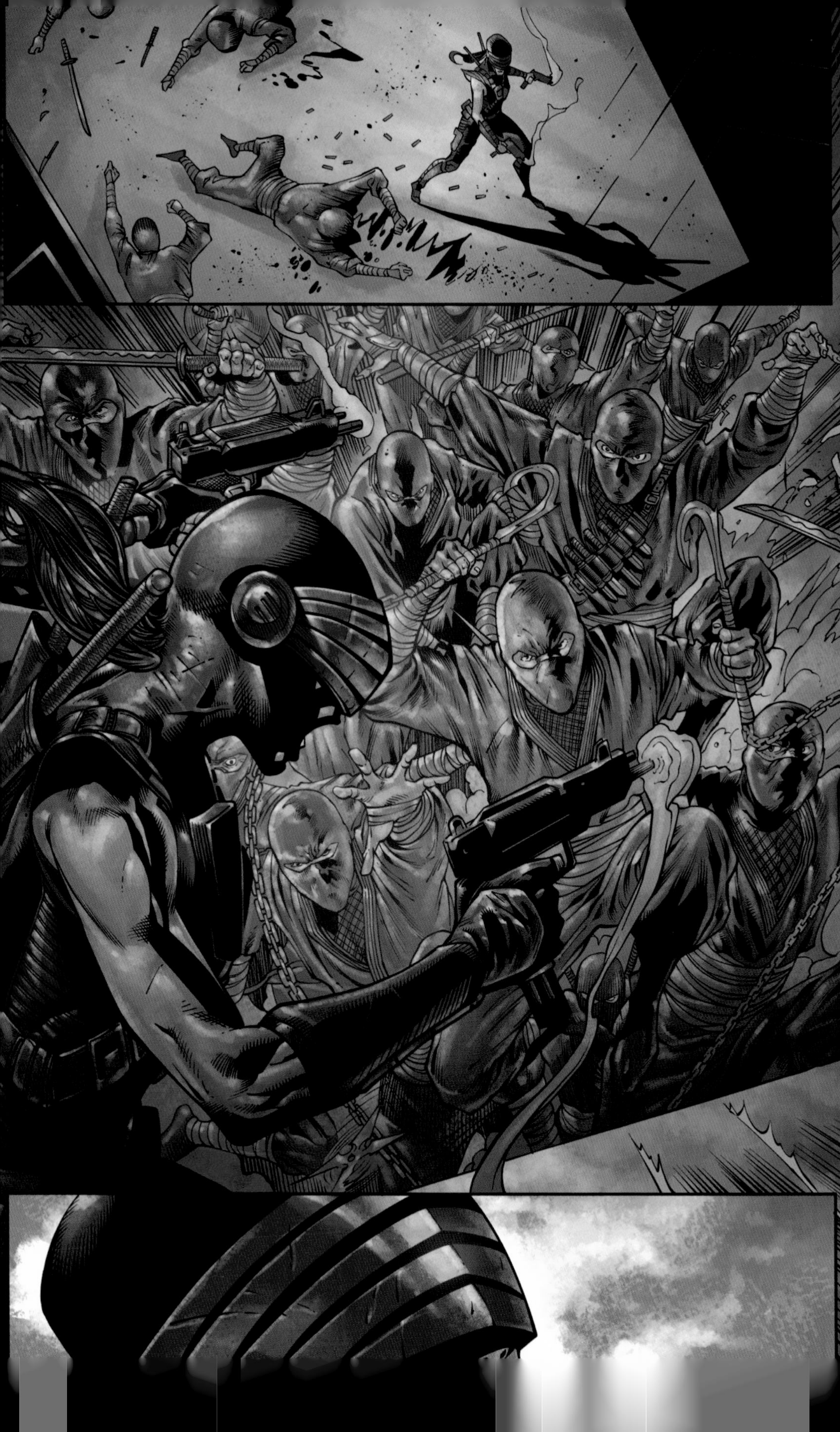

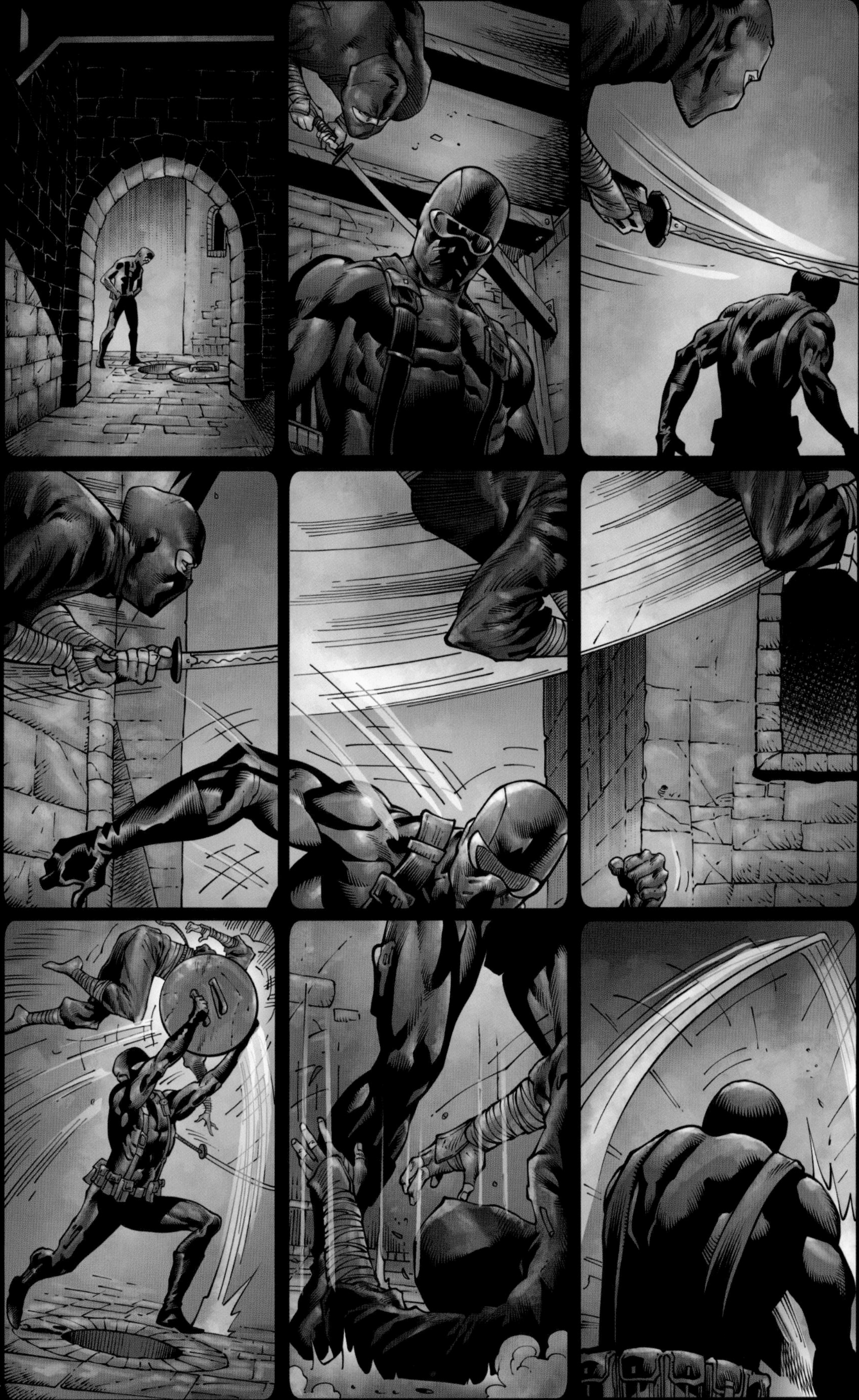

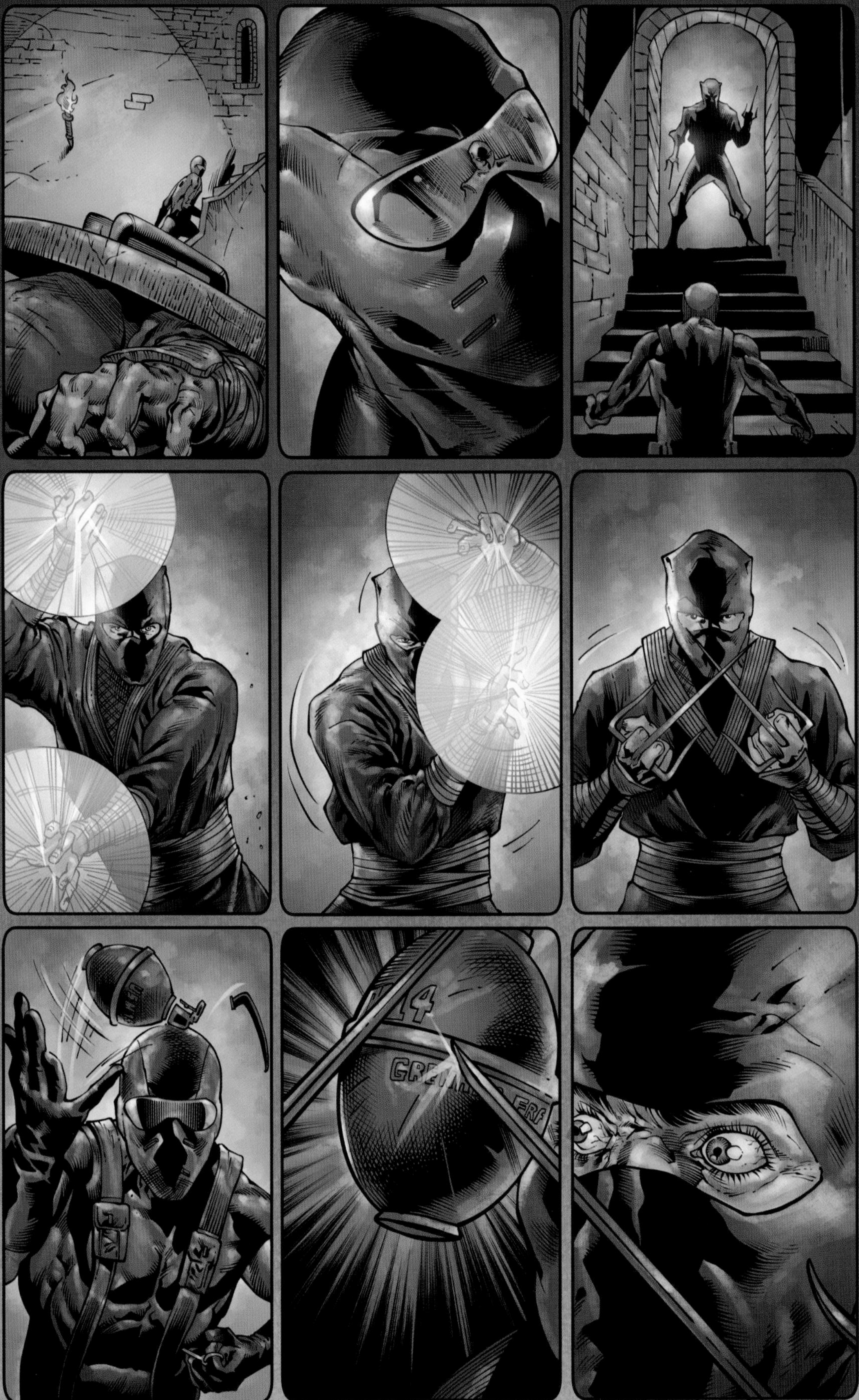

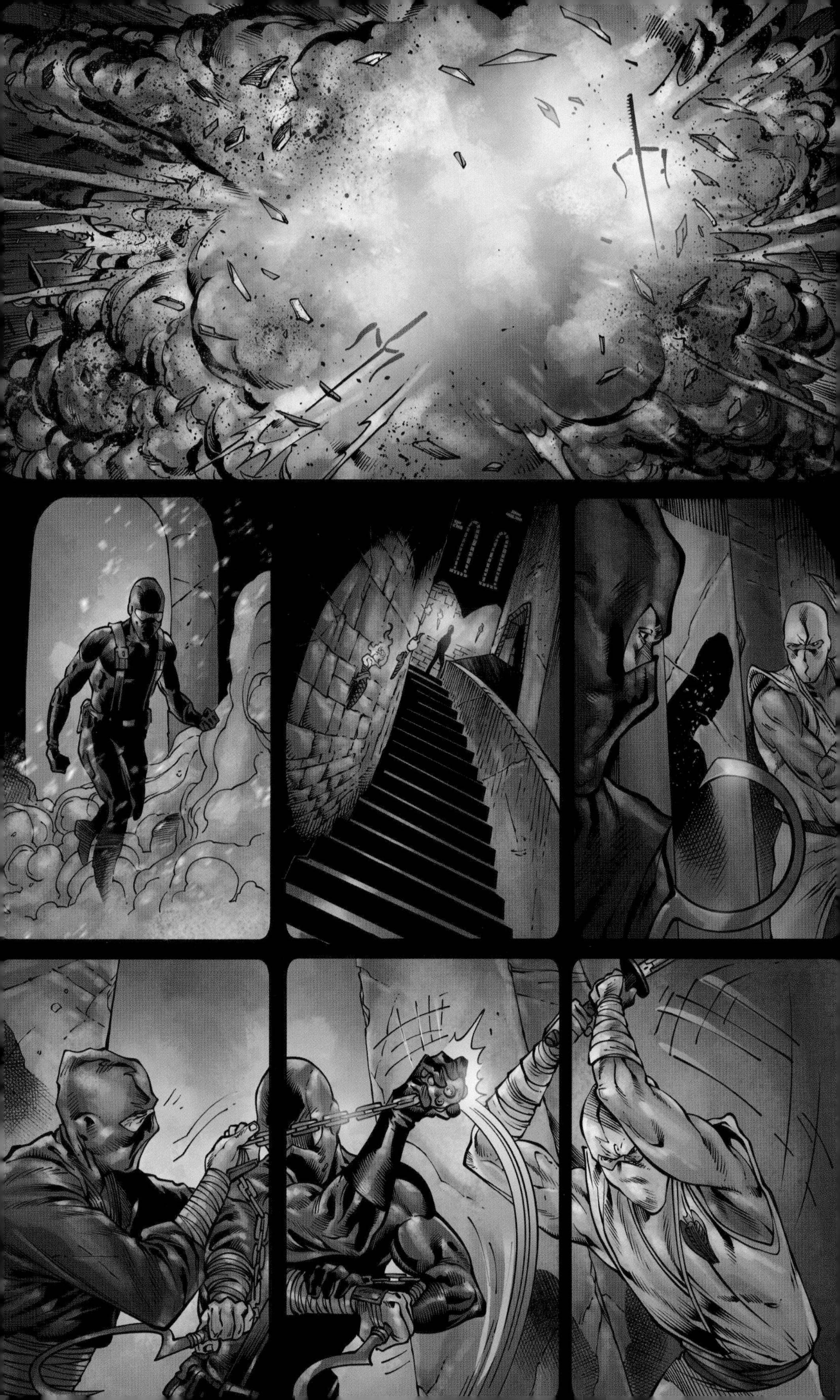

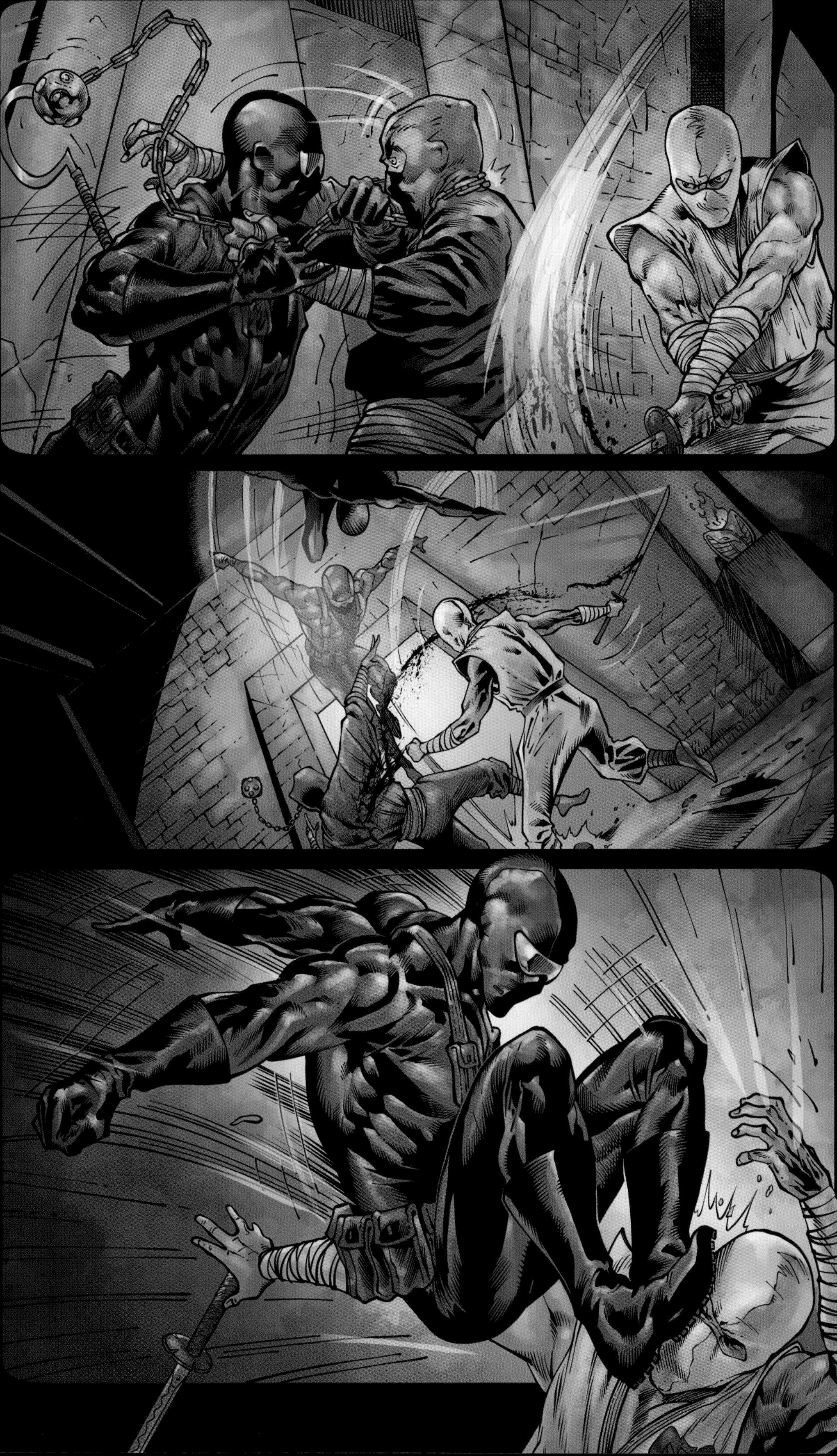

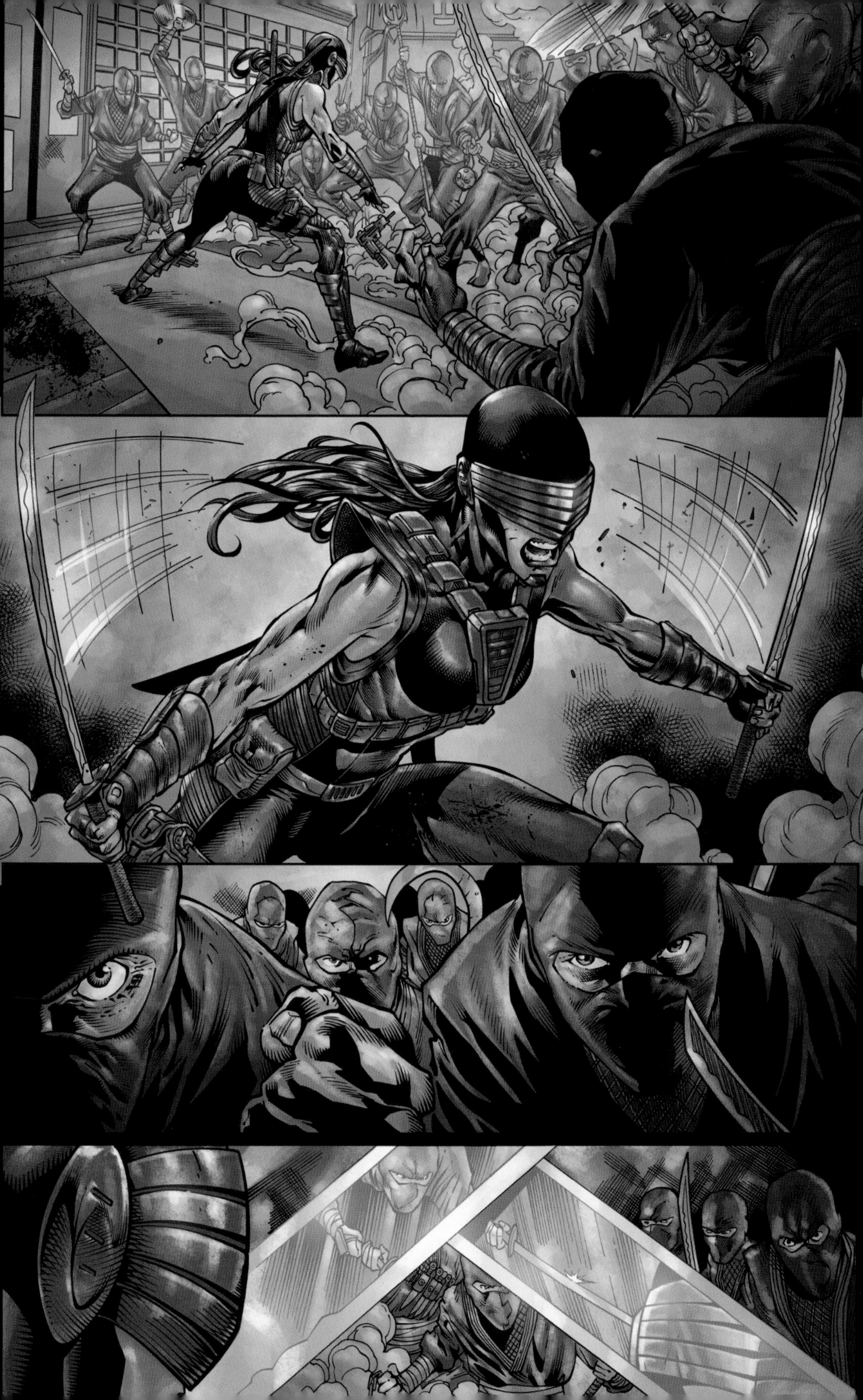

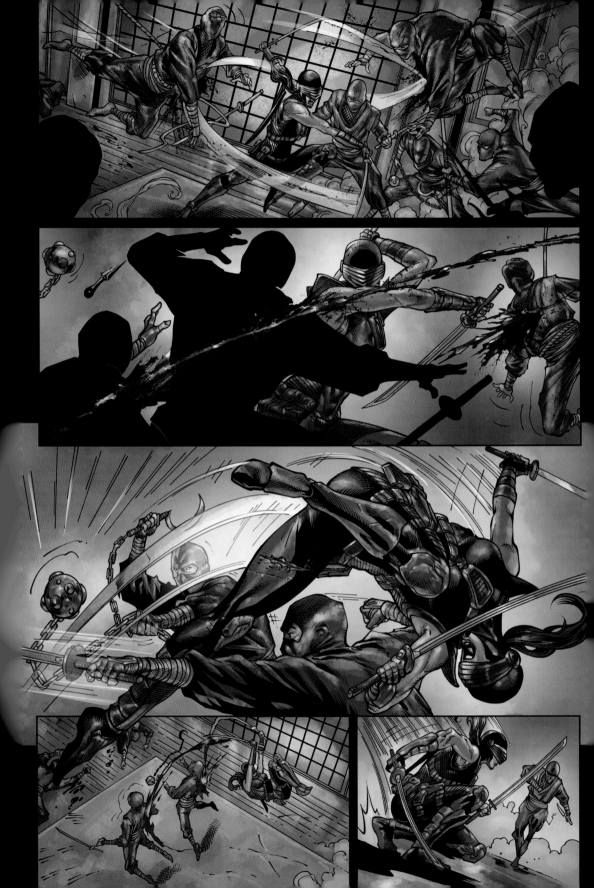

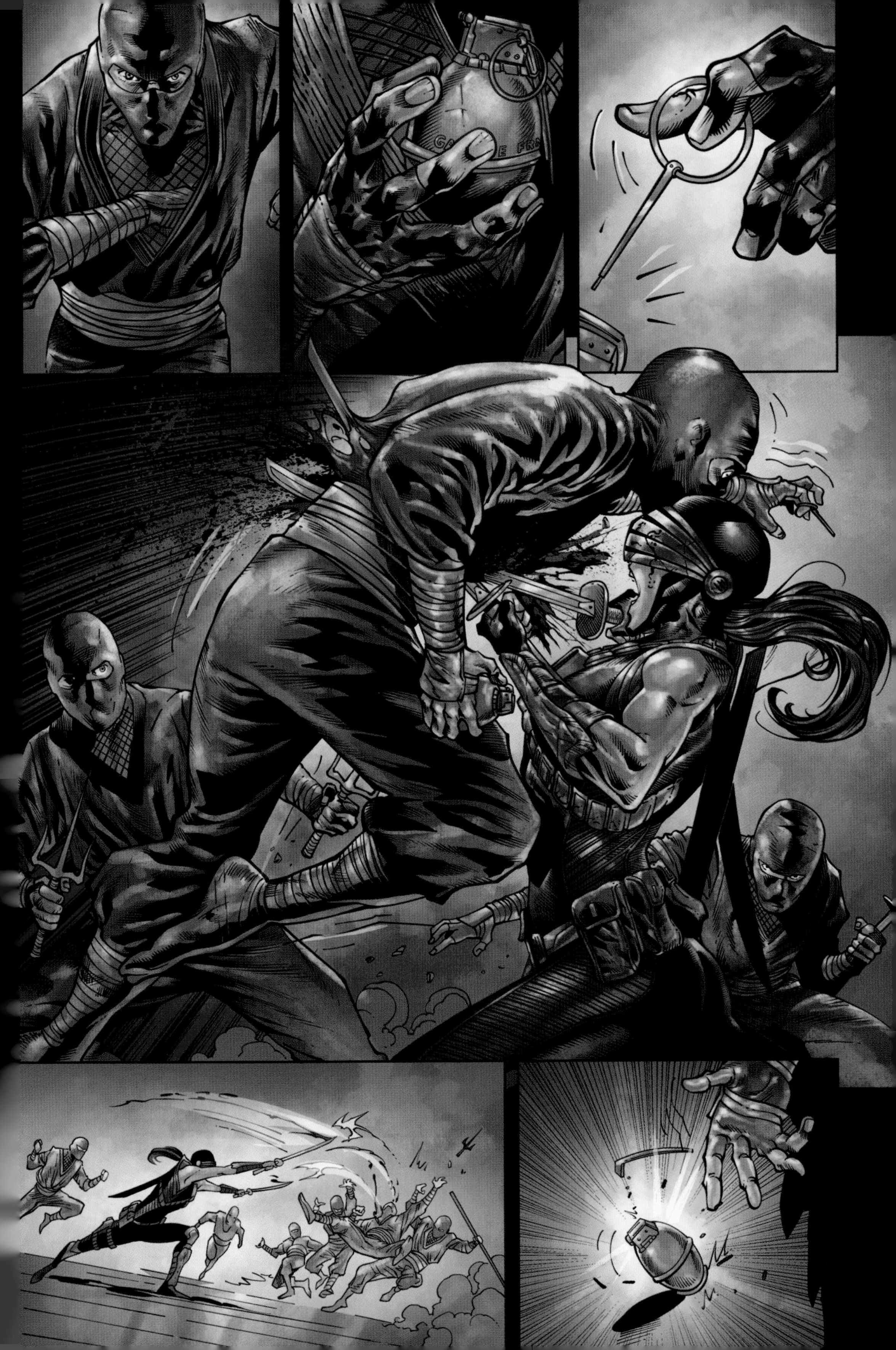

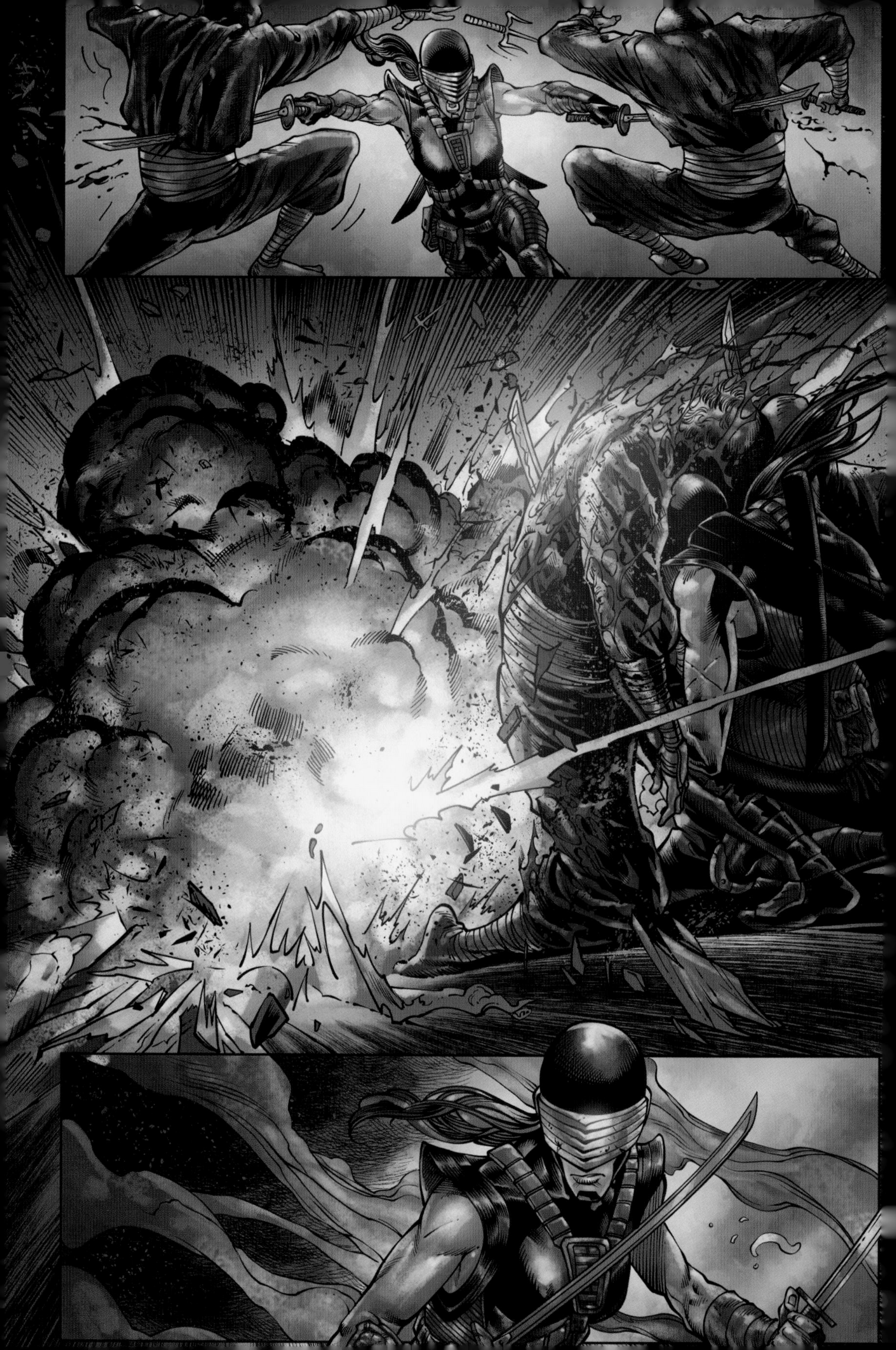

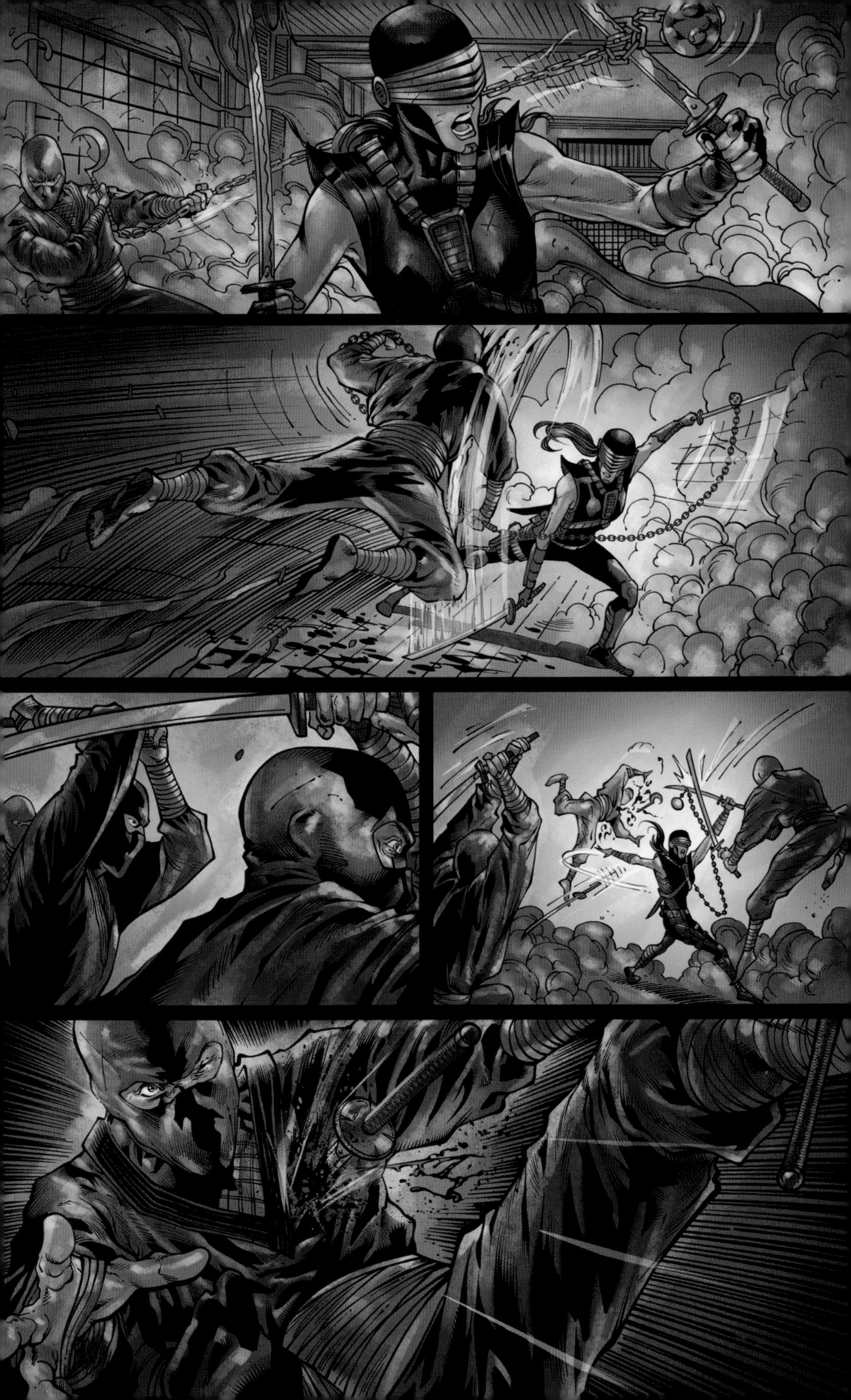

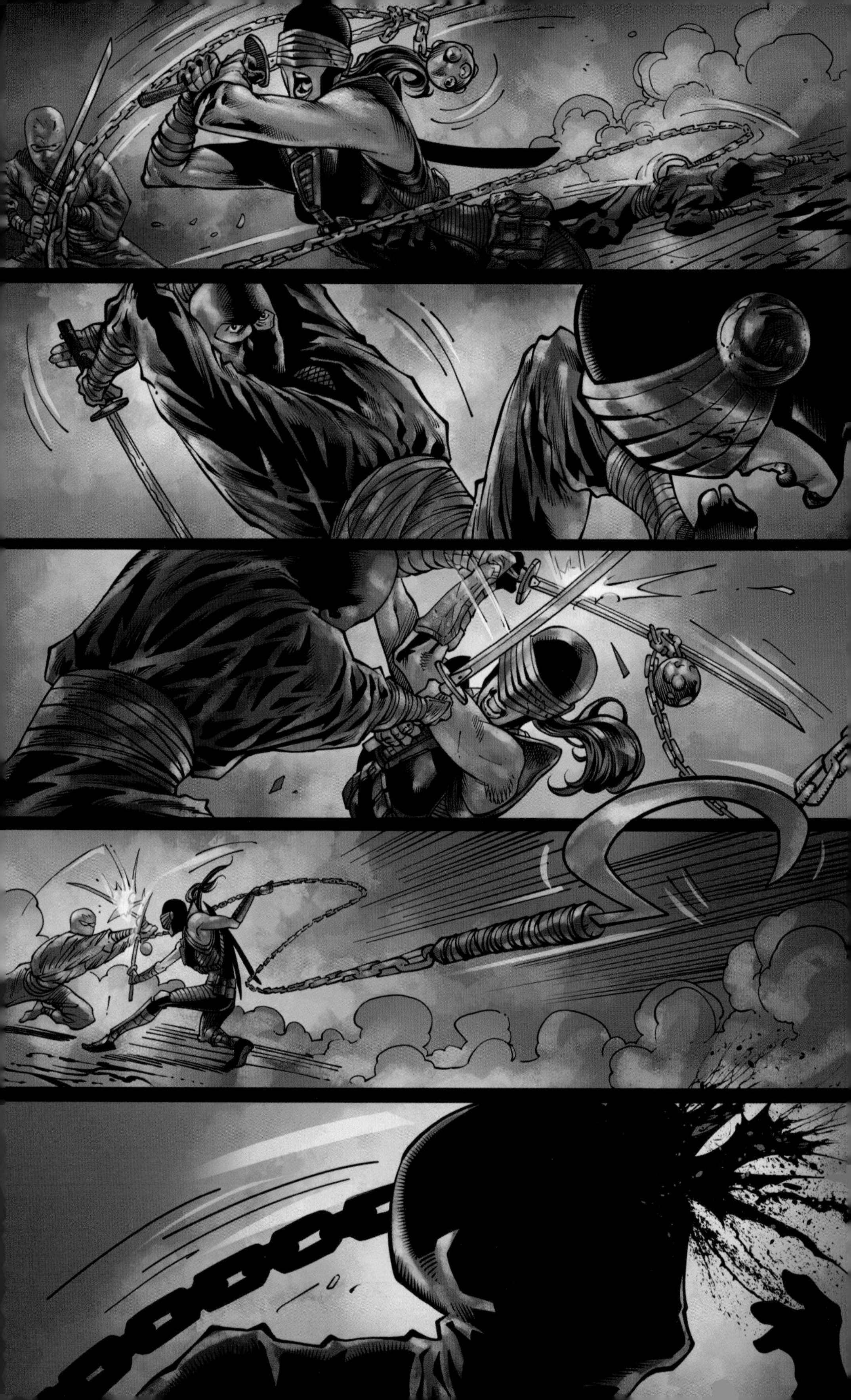

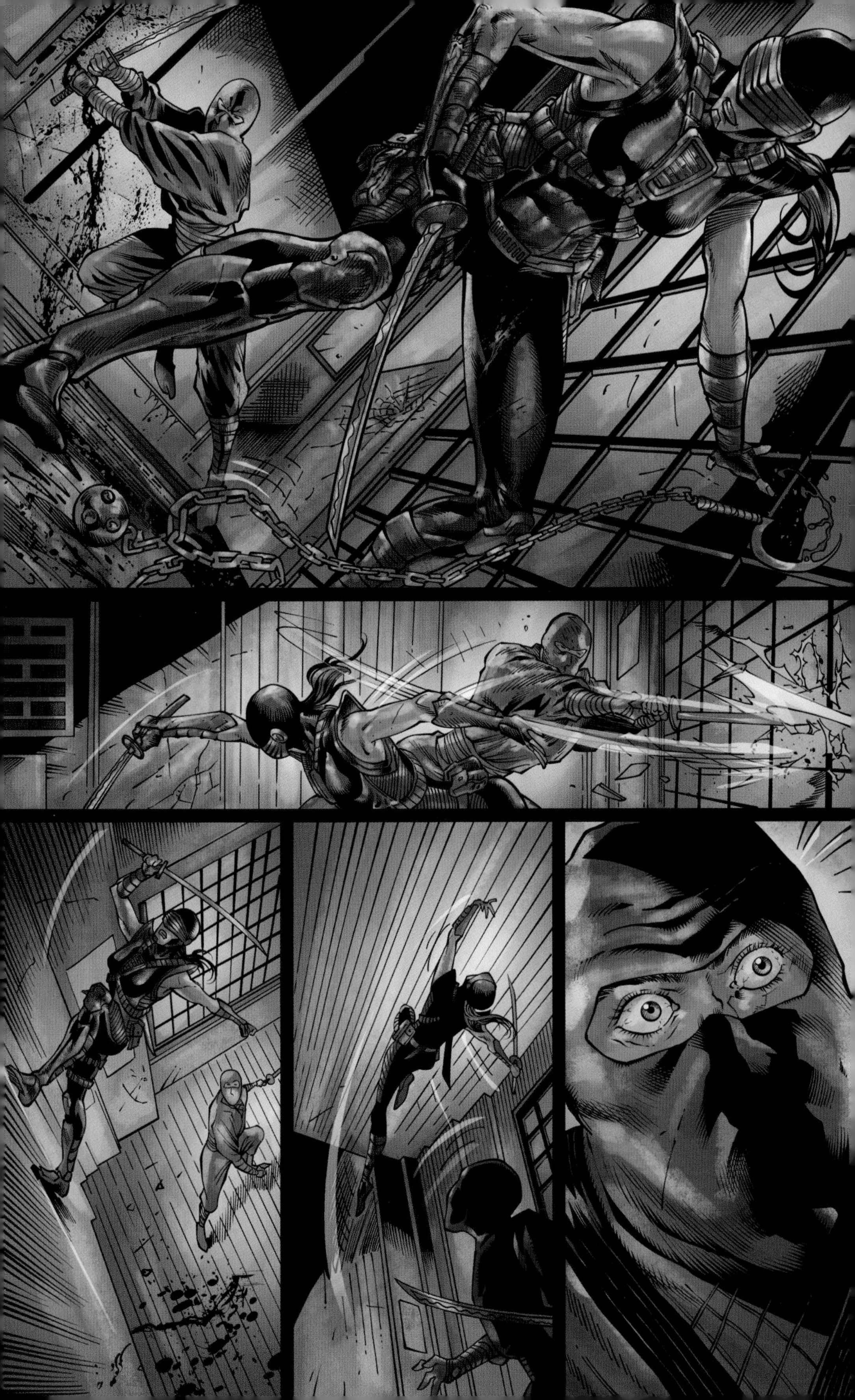

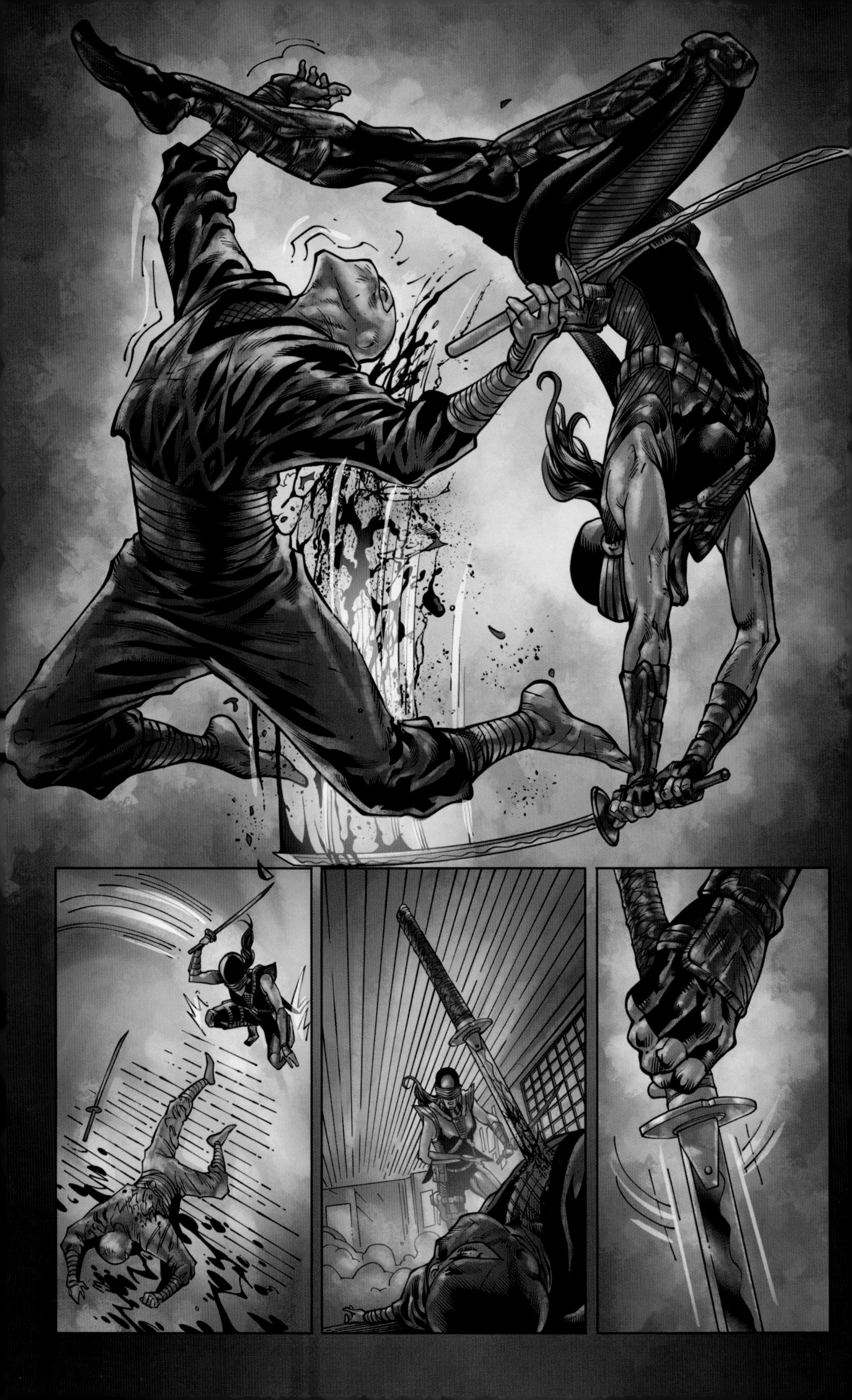

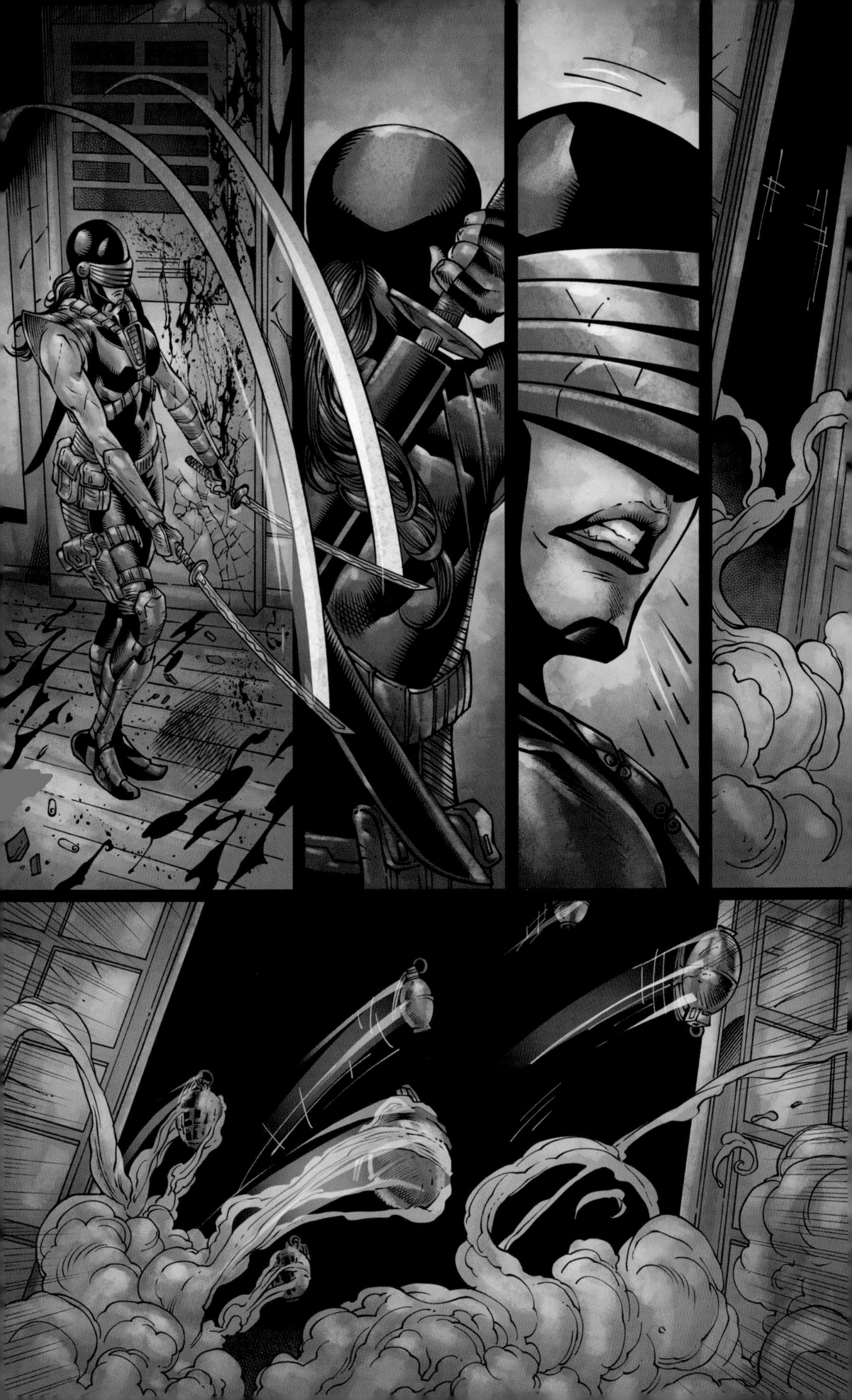

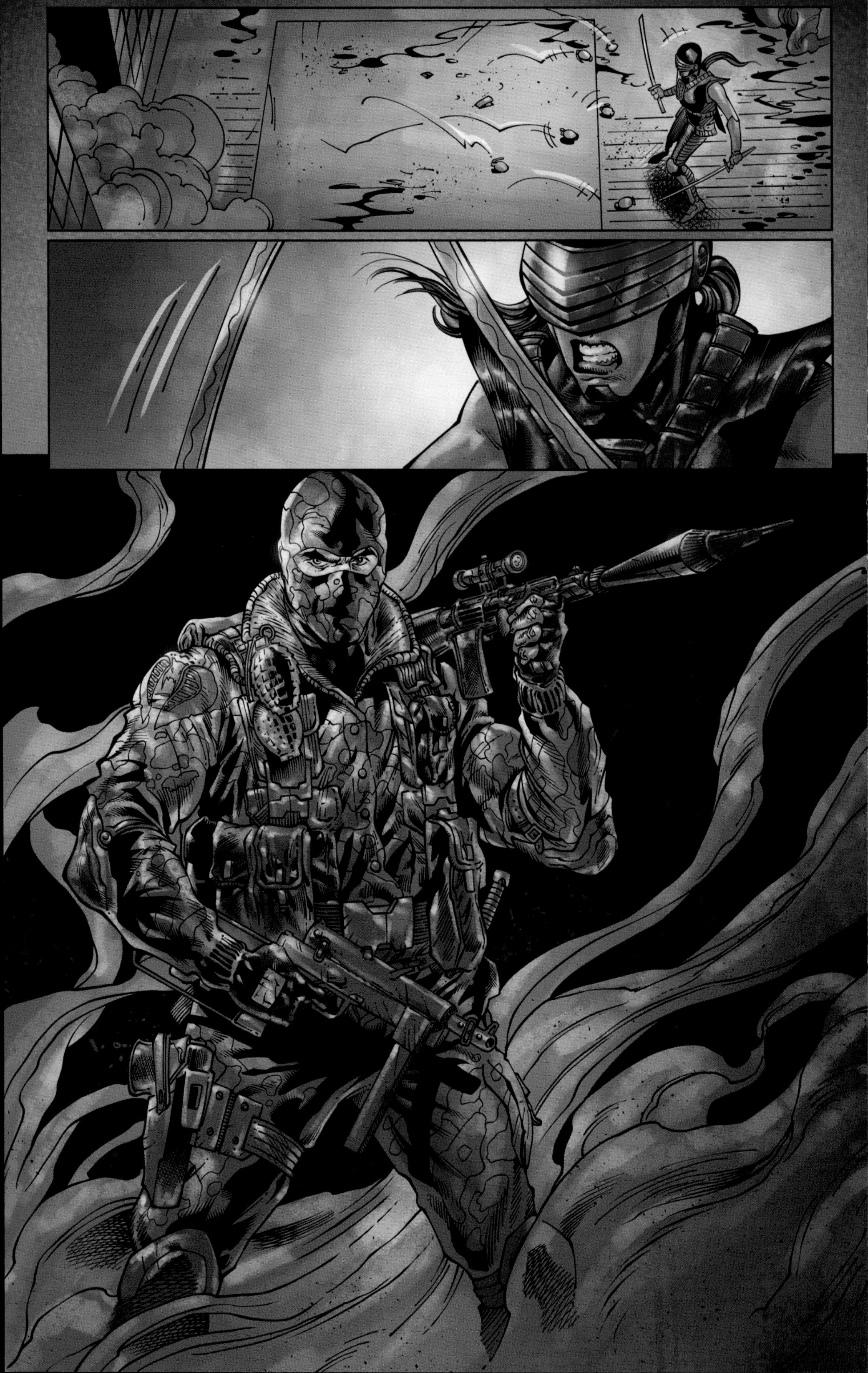

ART BY JAMIE SULLIVAN
COLORS BY JESSE HEAGY

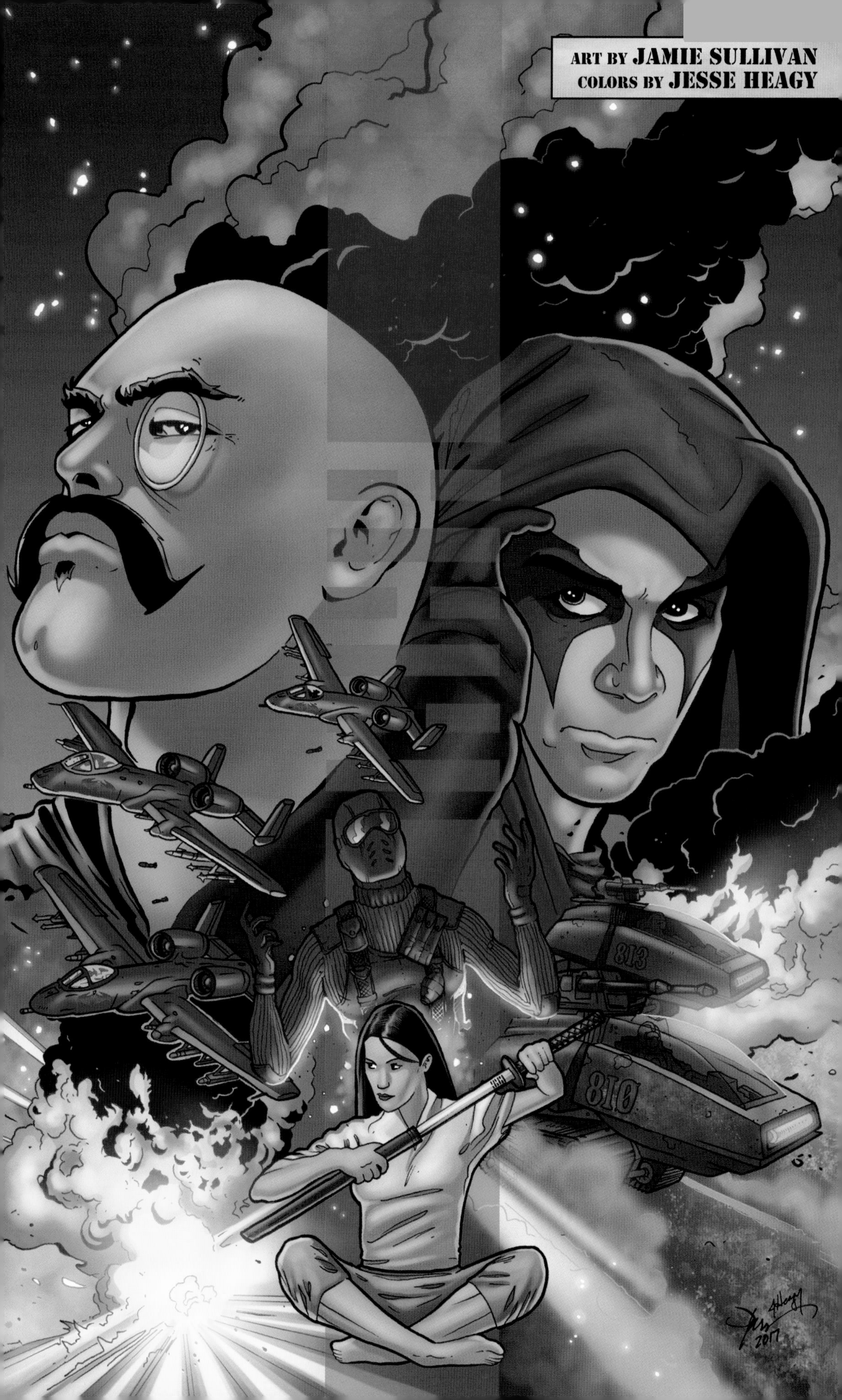
813
810

ART BY NETHO DIAZ
COLORS BY MILEN PARVANOV

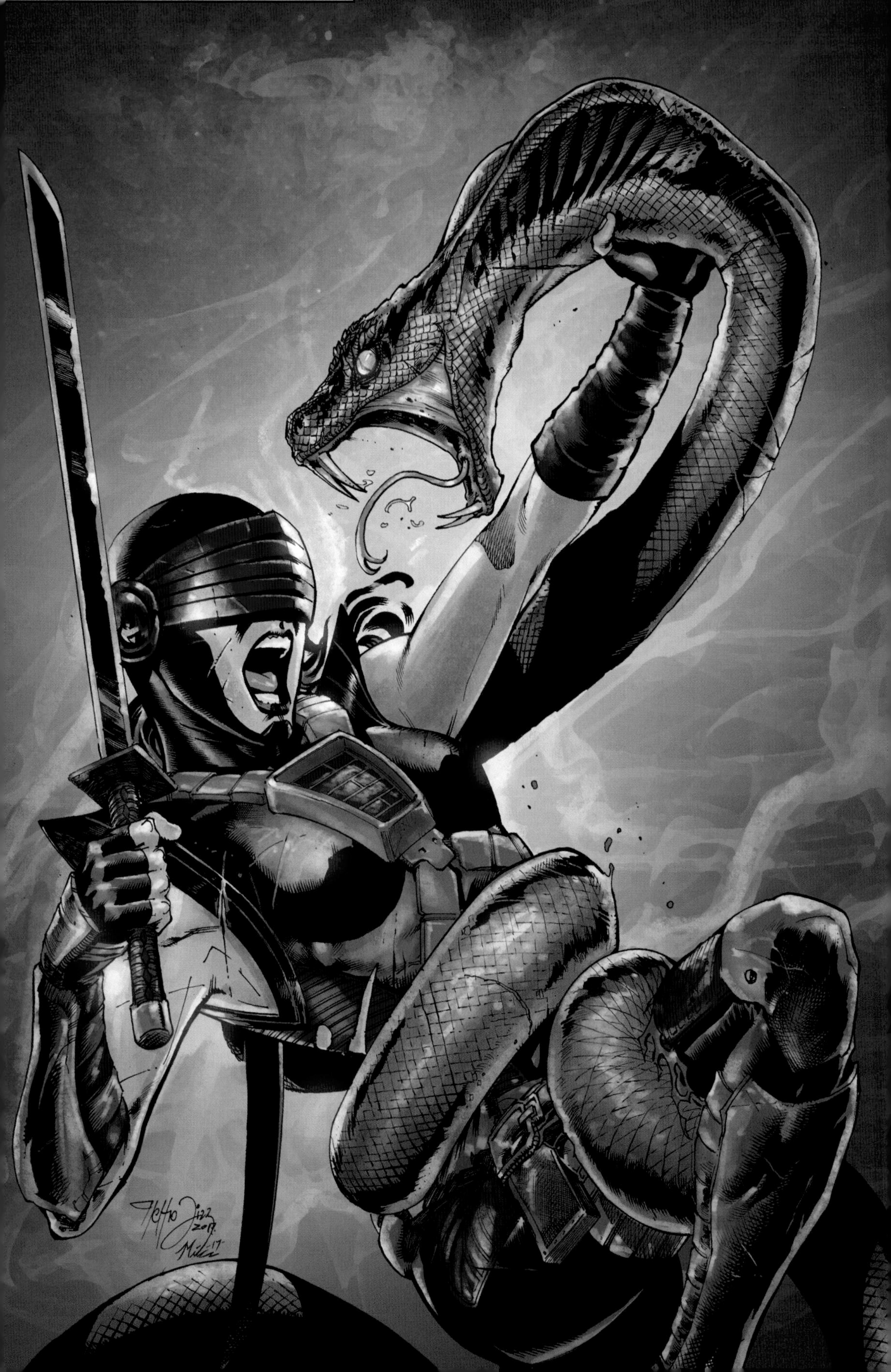

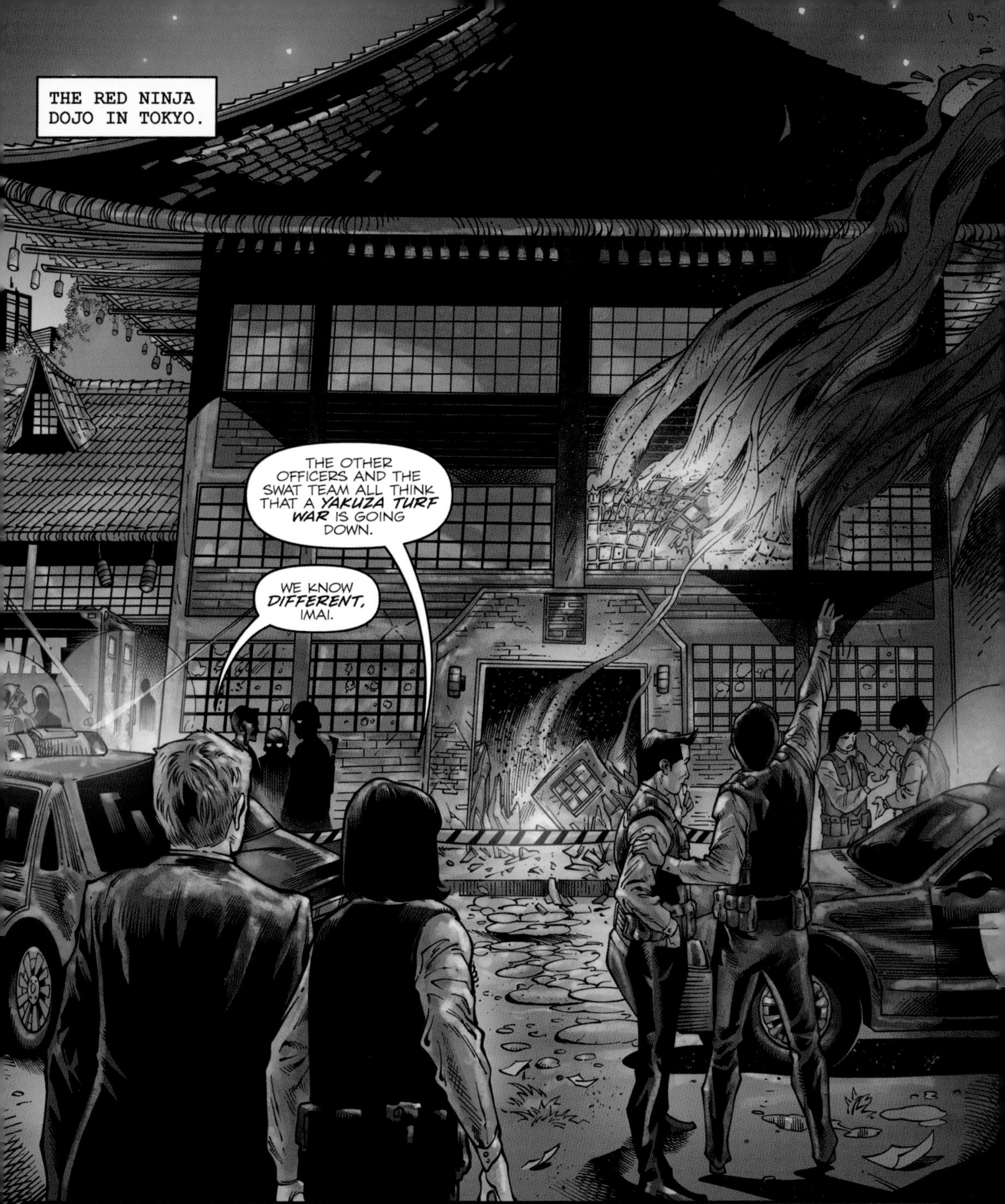
THE RED NINJA DOJO IN TOKYO.
THE OTHER OFFICERS AND THE SWAT TEAM ALL THINK THAT A YAKUZA TURF WAR IS GOING DOWN.
WE KNOW DIFFERENT, IMAI.

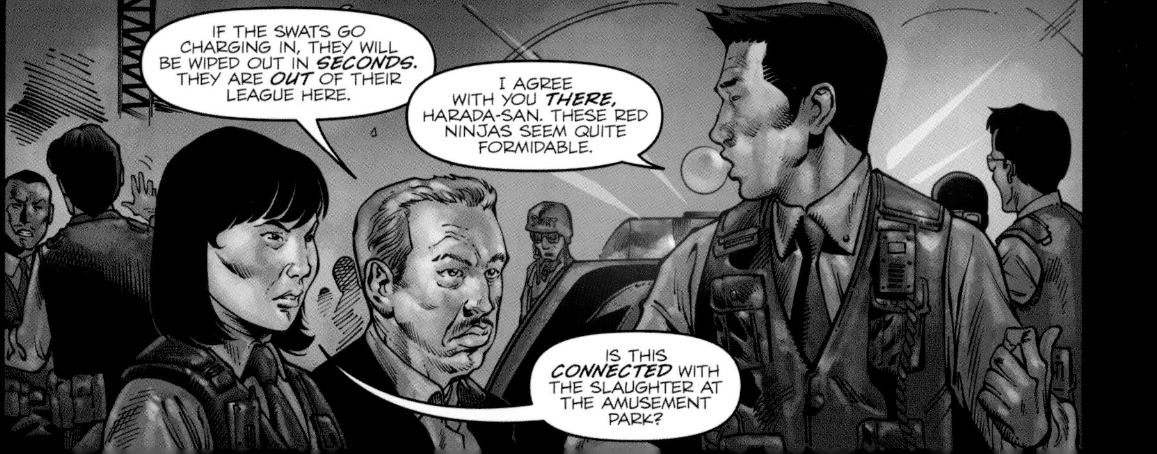
IF THE SWATS GO CHARGING IN, THEY WILL BE WIPED OUT IN SECONDS. THEY ARE OUT OF THEIR LEAGUE HERE.
I AGREE WITH YOU THERE, HARADA-SAN. THESE RED NINJAS SEEM QUITE FORMIDABLE.
IS THIS CONNECTED WITH THE SLAUGHTER AT THE AMUSEMENT PARK?

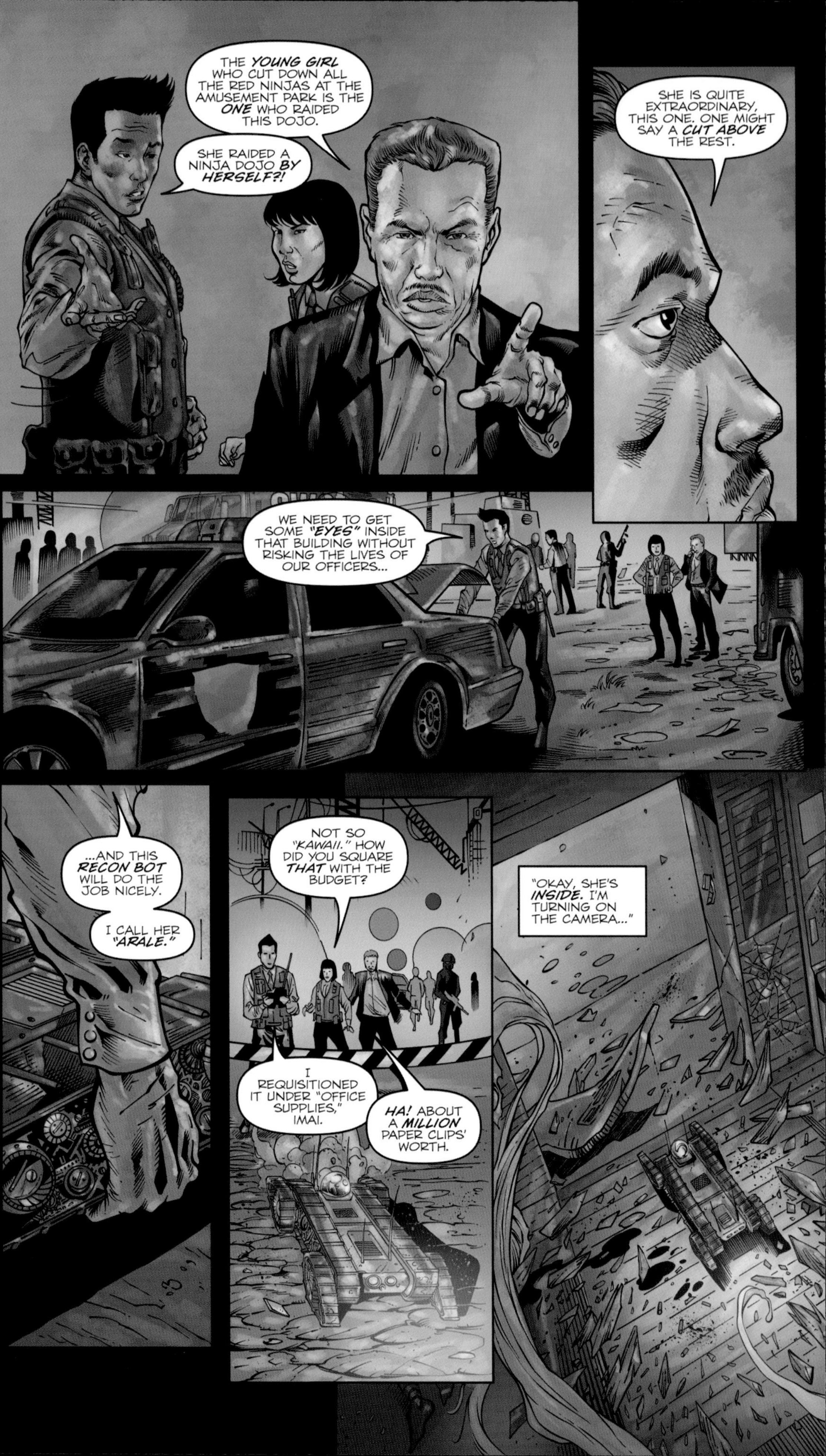

THE YOUNG GIRL WHO CUT DOWN ALL THE RED NINJAS AT THE AMUSEMENT PARK IS THE ONE WHO RAIDED THIS DOJO.
SHE RAIDED A NINJA DOJO BY HERSELF?!
SHE IS QUITE EXTRAORDINARY, THIS ONE. ONE MIGHT SAY A CUT ABOVE THE REST.
WE NEED TO GET SOME "EYES" INSIDE THAT BUILDING WITHOUT RISKING THE LIVES OF OUR OFFICERS...
...AND THIS RECON BOT WILL DO THE JOB NICELY.
I CALL HER "ARALE."
NOT SO "KAWAII." HOW DID YOU SQUARE THAT WITH THE BUDGET?
I REQUISITIONED IT UNDER "OFFICE SUPPLIES," IMAI.
HA! ABOUT A MILLION PAPER CLIPS' WORTH.
"OKAY, SHE'S INSIDE. I'M TURNING ON THE CAMERA..."

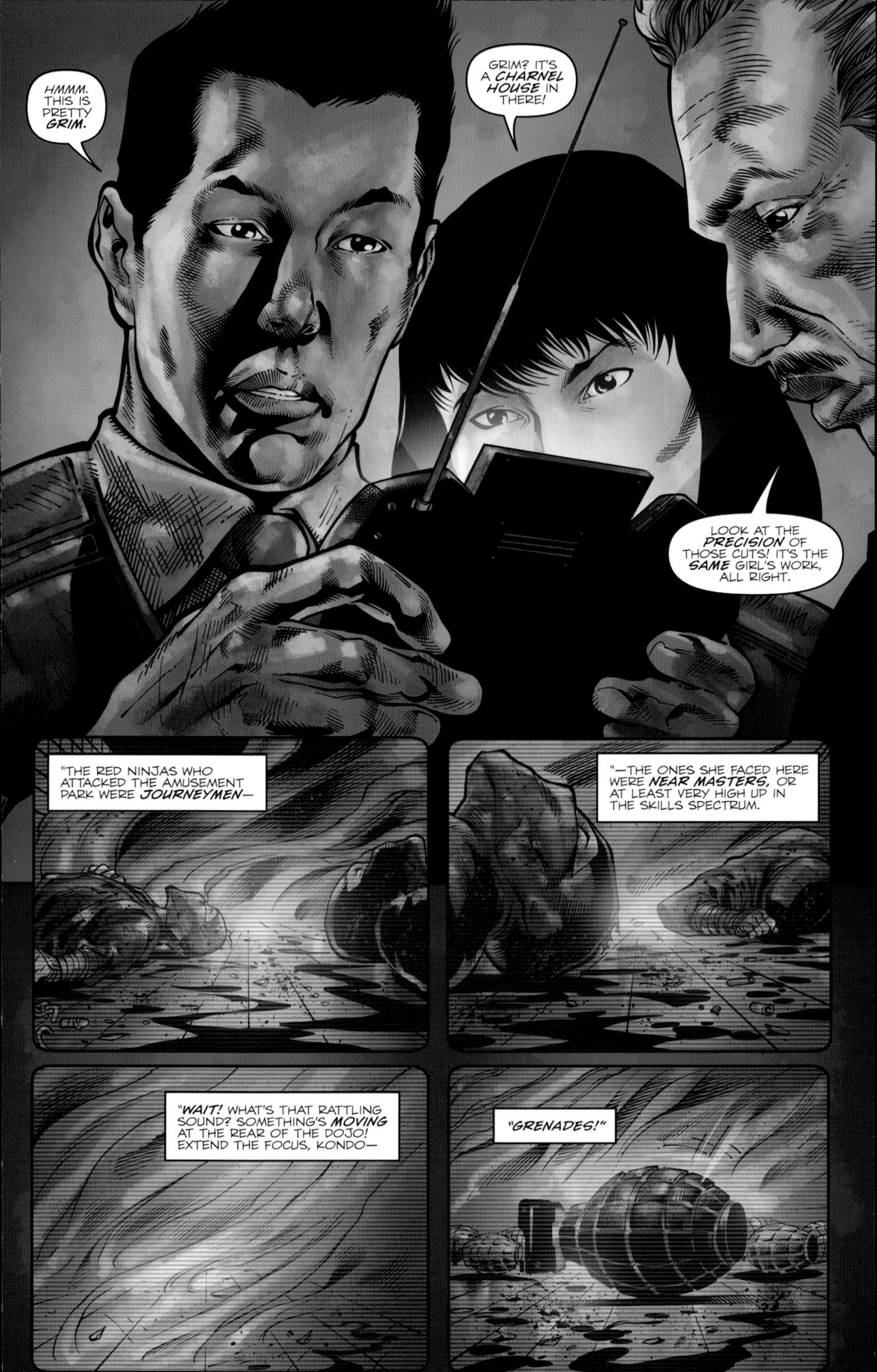
HMMM. THIS IS PRETTY GRIM.
GRIM? IT'S A CHARNEL HOUSE IN THERE!
LOOK AT THE PRECISION OF THOSE CUTS! IT'S THE SAME GIRL'S WORK, ALL RIGHT.
"THE RED NINJAS WHO ATTACKED THE AMUSEMENT PARK WERE JOURNEYMEN—
"—THE ONES SHE FACED HERE WERE NEAR MASTERS, OR AT LEAST VERY HIGH UP IN THE SKILLS SPECTRUM.
"WAIT! WHAT'S THAT RATTLING SOUND? SOMETHING'S MOVING AT THE REAR OF THE DOJO! EXTEND THE FOCUS, KONDO—
"GRENADES!"

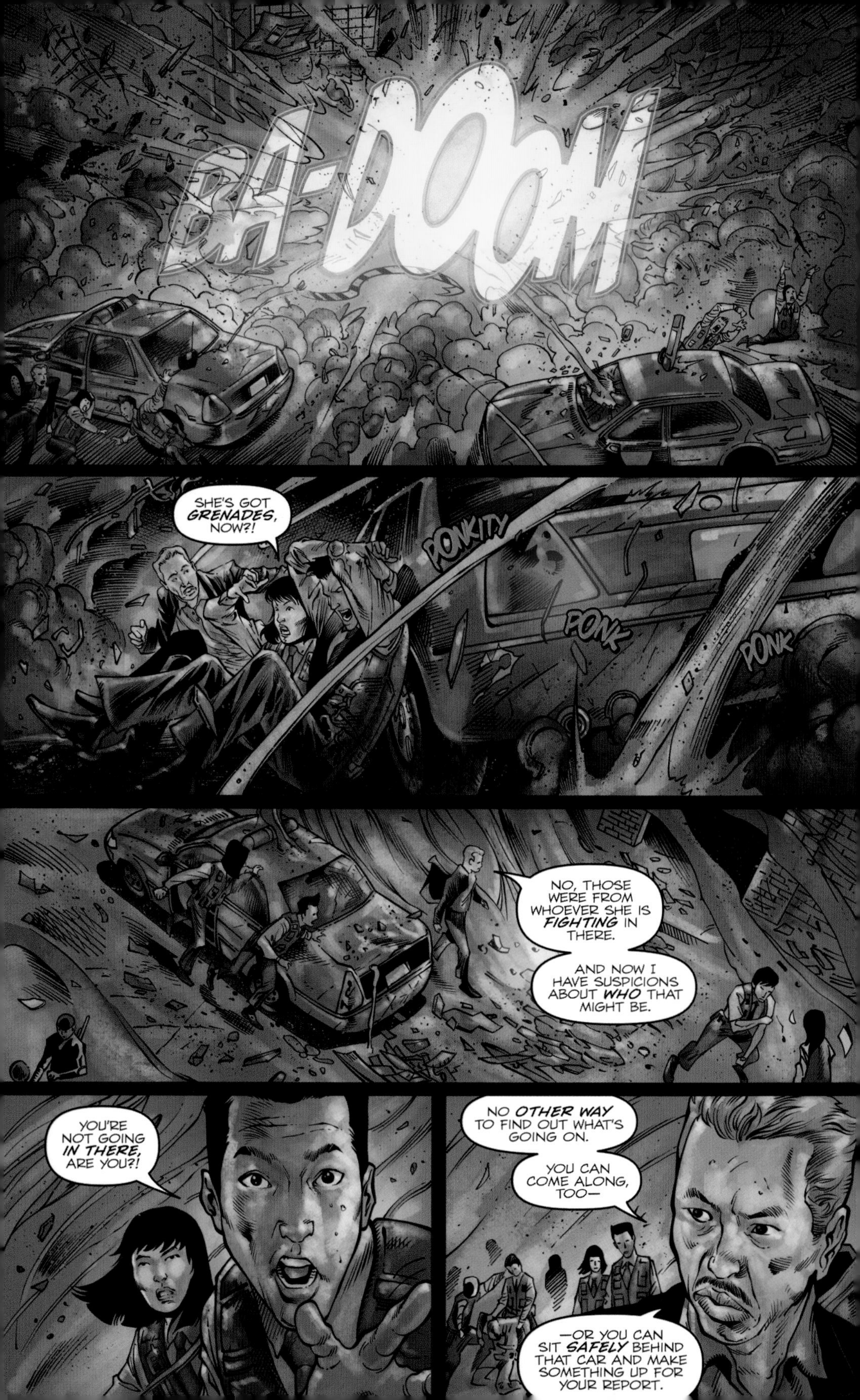
BA-DOOM
SHE'S GOT GRENADES, NOW?!
PONKITY
PONK
PONK
NO, THOSE WERE FROM WHOEVER SHE IS FIGHTING IN THERE.
AND NOW I HAVE SUSPICIONS ABOUT WHO THAT MIGHT BE.
YOU'RE NOT GOING IN THERE, ARE YOU?!
NO OTHER WAY TO FIND OUT WHAT'S GOING ON.
YOU CAN COME ALONG, TOO—
—OR YOU CAN SIT SAFELY BEHIND THAT CAR AND MAKE SOMETHING UP FOR YOUR REPORT.

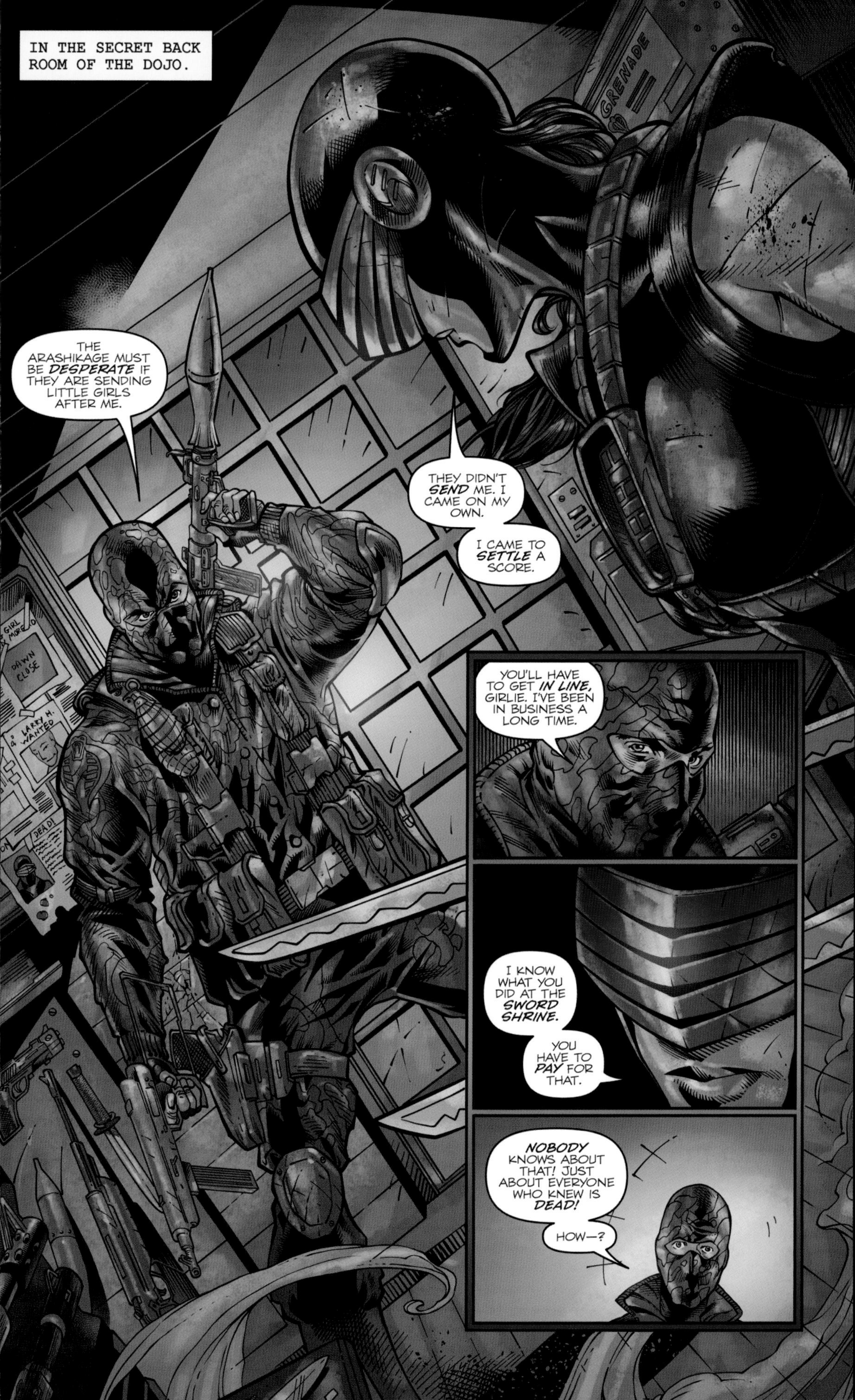
IN THE SECRET BACK ROOM OF THE DOJO.
THE ARASHIKAGE MUST BE DESPERATE IF THEY ARE SENDING LITTLE GIRLS AFTER ME.
THEY DIDN'T SEND ME. I CAME ON MY OWN.
I CAME TO SETTLE A SCORE.
GRENADE
YOU'LL HAVE TO GET IN LINE, GIRLIE. I'VE BEEN IN BUSINESS A LONG TIME.
I KNOW WHAT YOU DID AT THE SWORD SHRINE.
YOU HAVE TO PAY FOR THAT.
NOBODY KNOWS ABOUT THAT! JUST ABOUT EVERYONE WHO KNEW IS DEAD!
HOW—?

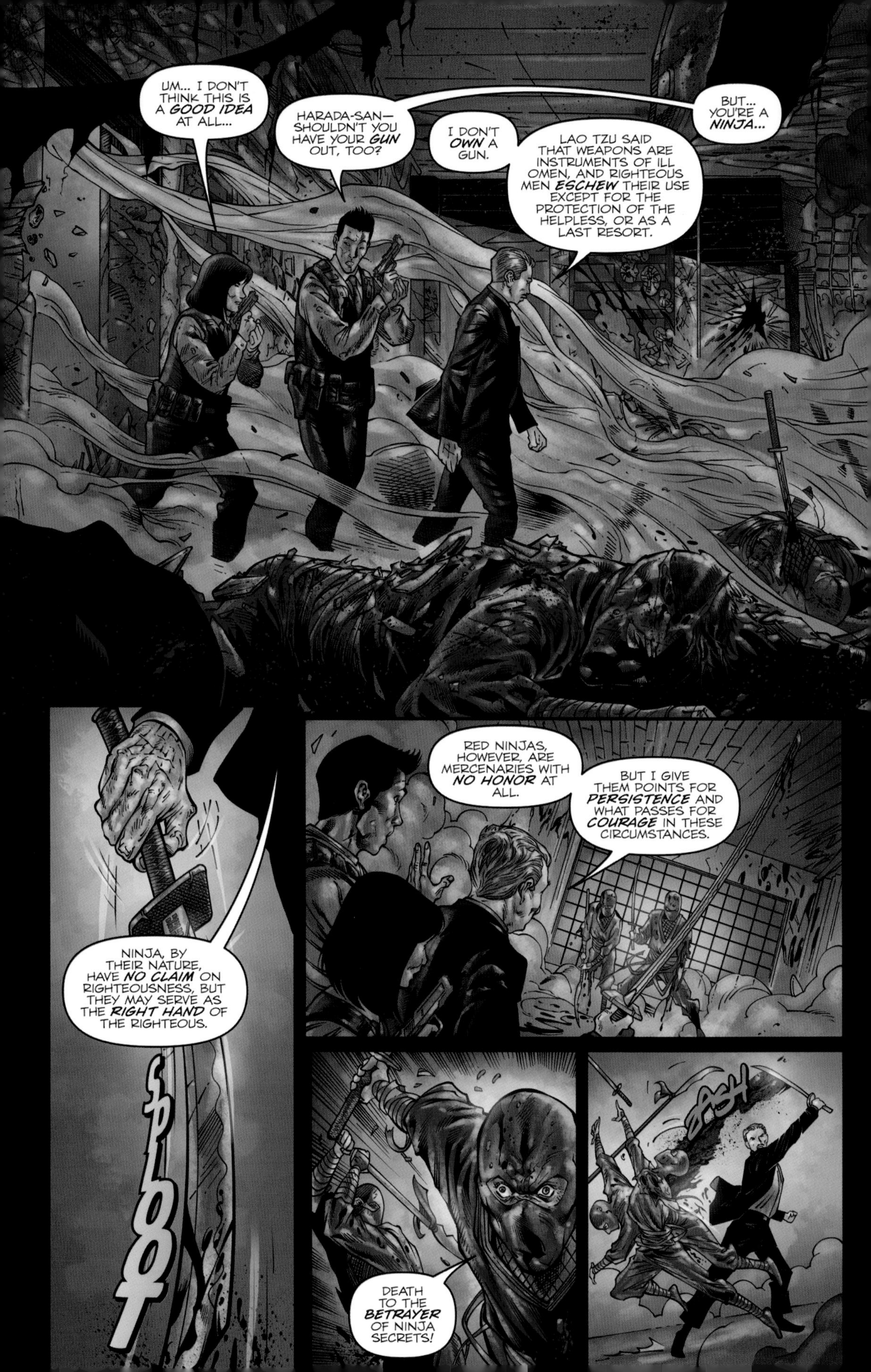
UM... I DON'T THINK THIS IS A GOOD IDEA AT ALL...
HARADA-SAN— SHOULDN'T YOU HAVE YOUR GUN OUT, TOO?
I DON'T OWN A GUN.
LAO TZU SAID THAT WEAPONS ARE INSTRUMENTS OF ILL OMEN, AND RIGHTEOUS MEN ESCHEW THEIR USE EXCEPT FOR THE PROTECTION OF THE HELPLESS, OR AS A LAST RESORT.
BUT... YOU'RE A NINJA...
NINJA, BY THEIR NATURE, HAVE NO CLAIM ON RIGHTEOUSNESS, BUT THEY MAY SERVE AS THE RIGHT HAND OF THE RIGHTEOUS.
SPLOOT
RED NINJAS, HOWEVER, ARE MERCENARIES WITH NO HONOR AT ALL.
BUT I GIVE THEM POINTS FOR PERSISTENCE AND WHAT PASSES FOR COURAGE IN THESE CIRCUMSTANCES.
DEATH TO THE BETRAYER OF NINJA SECRETS!

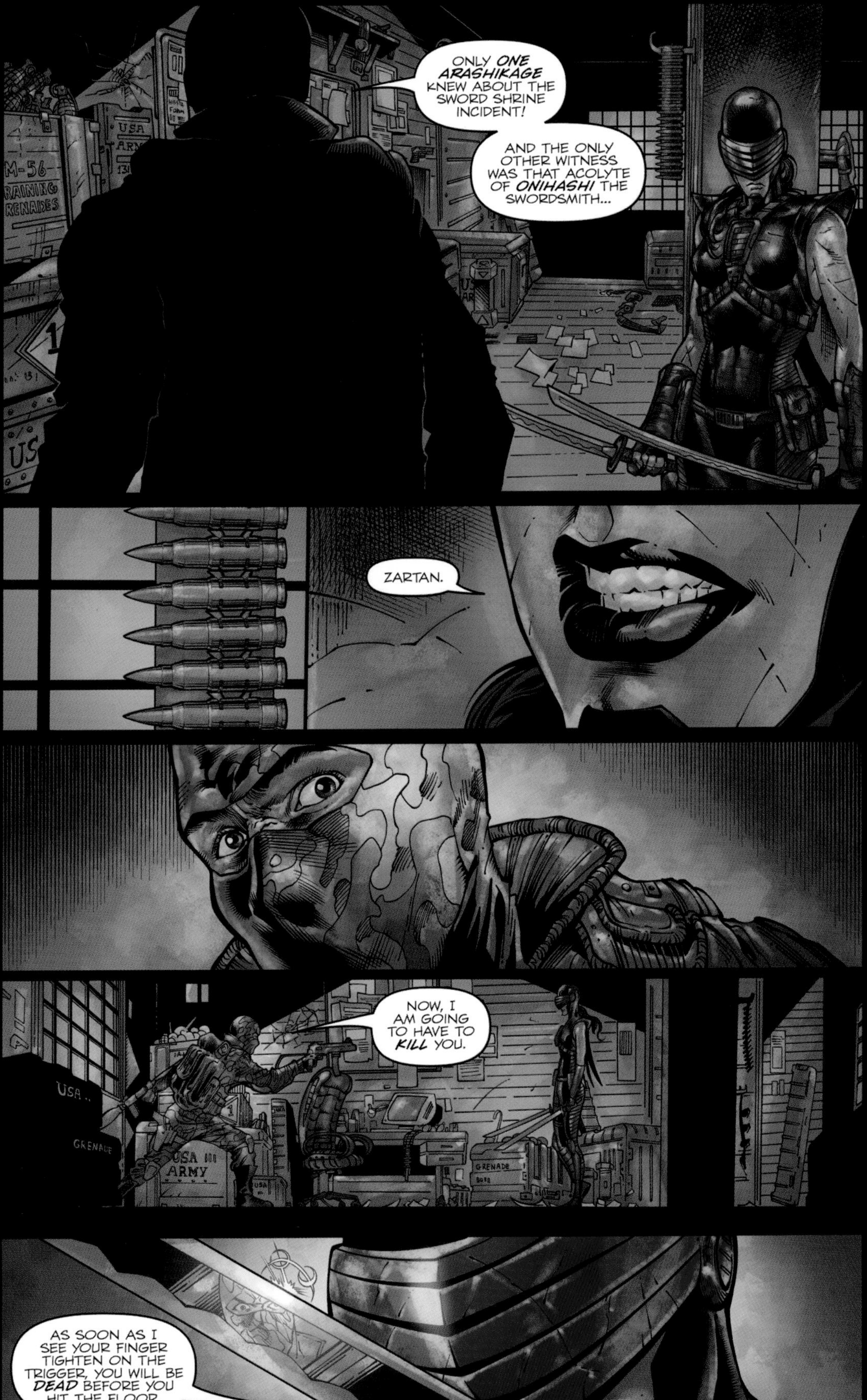
ONLY ONE ARASHIKAGE KNEW ABOUT THE SWORD SHRINE INCIDENT!
AND THE ONLY OTHER WITNESS WAS THAT ACOLYTE OF ONIHASHI THE SWORDSMITH...
ZARTAN.
NOW, I AM GOING TO HAVE TO KILL YOU.
AS SOON AS I SEE YOUR FINGER TIGHTEN ON THE TRIGGER, YOU WILL BE DEAD BEFORE YOU HIT THE FLOOR.

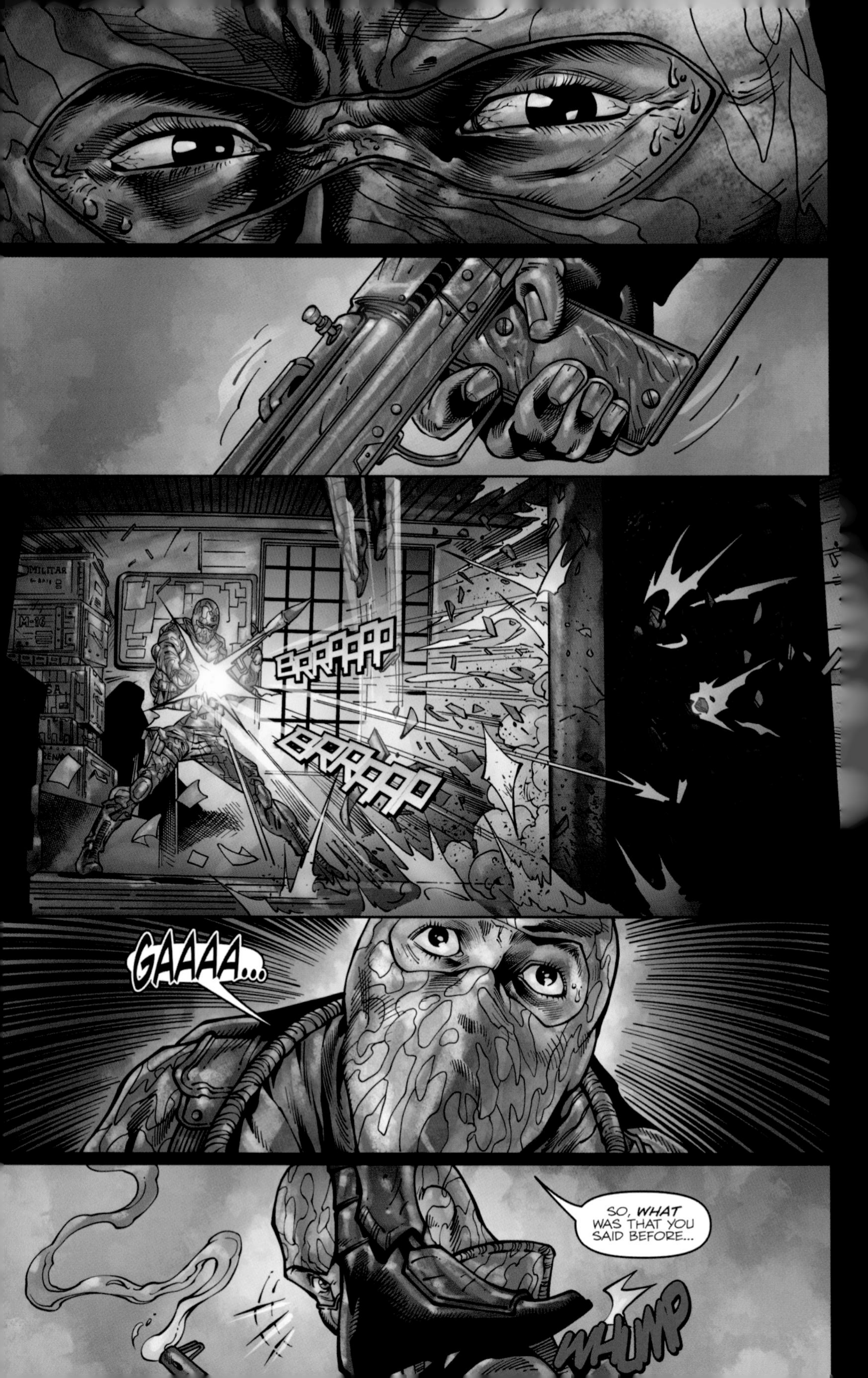
BRRAAAP
BRRAAAP
GAAAA...
SO, WHAT WAS THAT YOU SAID BEFORE...
WHUMP

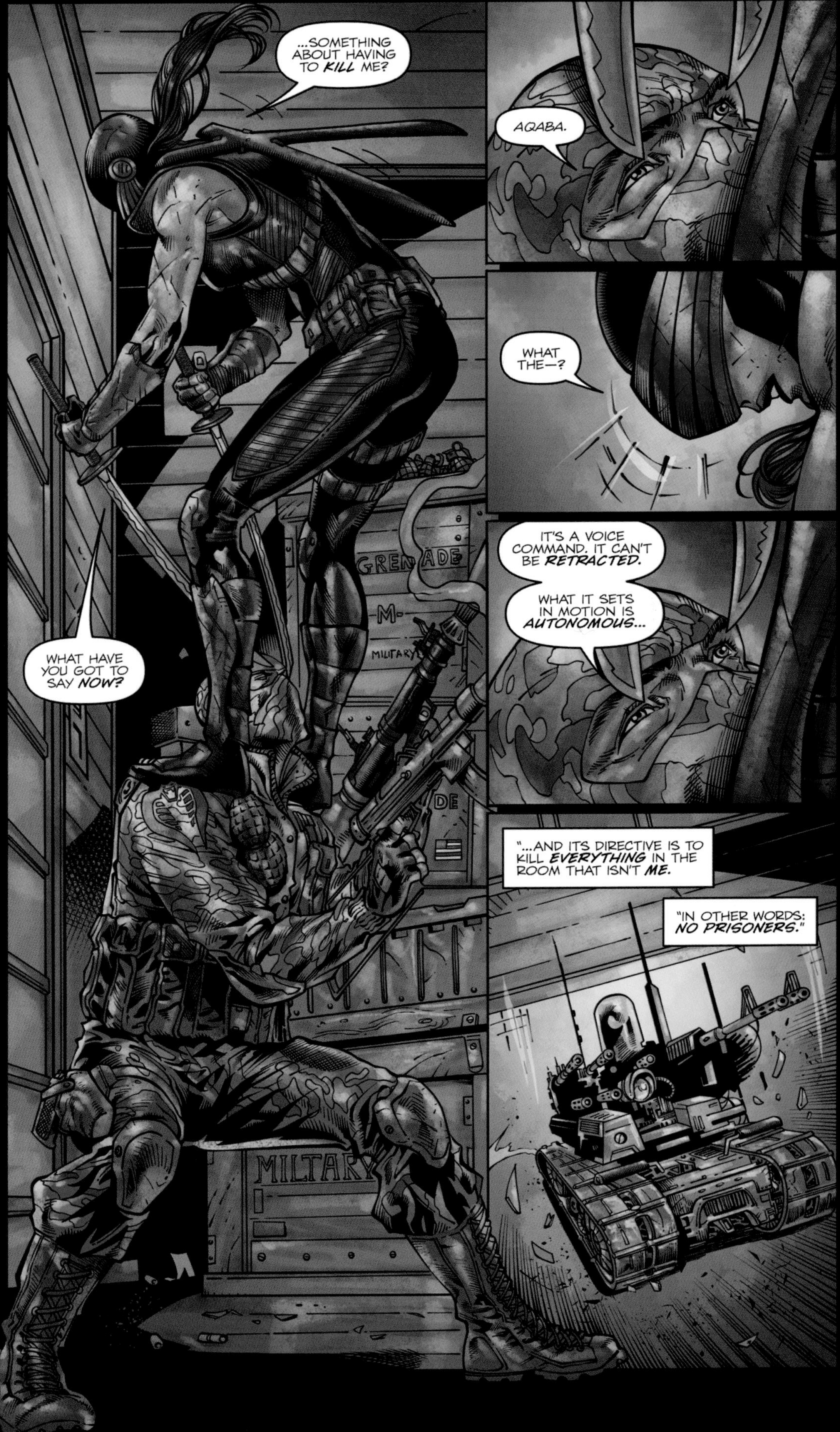

...SOMETHING ABOUT HAVING TO KILL ME?
WHAT HAVE YOU GOT TO SAY NOW?
AQABA.
WHAT THE—?
IT'S A VOICE COMMAND. IT CAN'T BE RETRACTED.
WHAT IT SETS IN MOTION IS AUTONOMOUS...
"...AND ITS DIRECTIVE IS TO KILL EVERYTHING IN THE ROOM THAT ISN'T ME.
"IN OTHER WORDS: NO PRISONERS."
GRENADE
M
MILITARY
DE
MILTARY

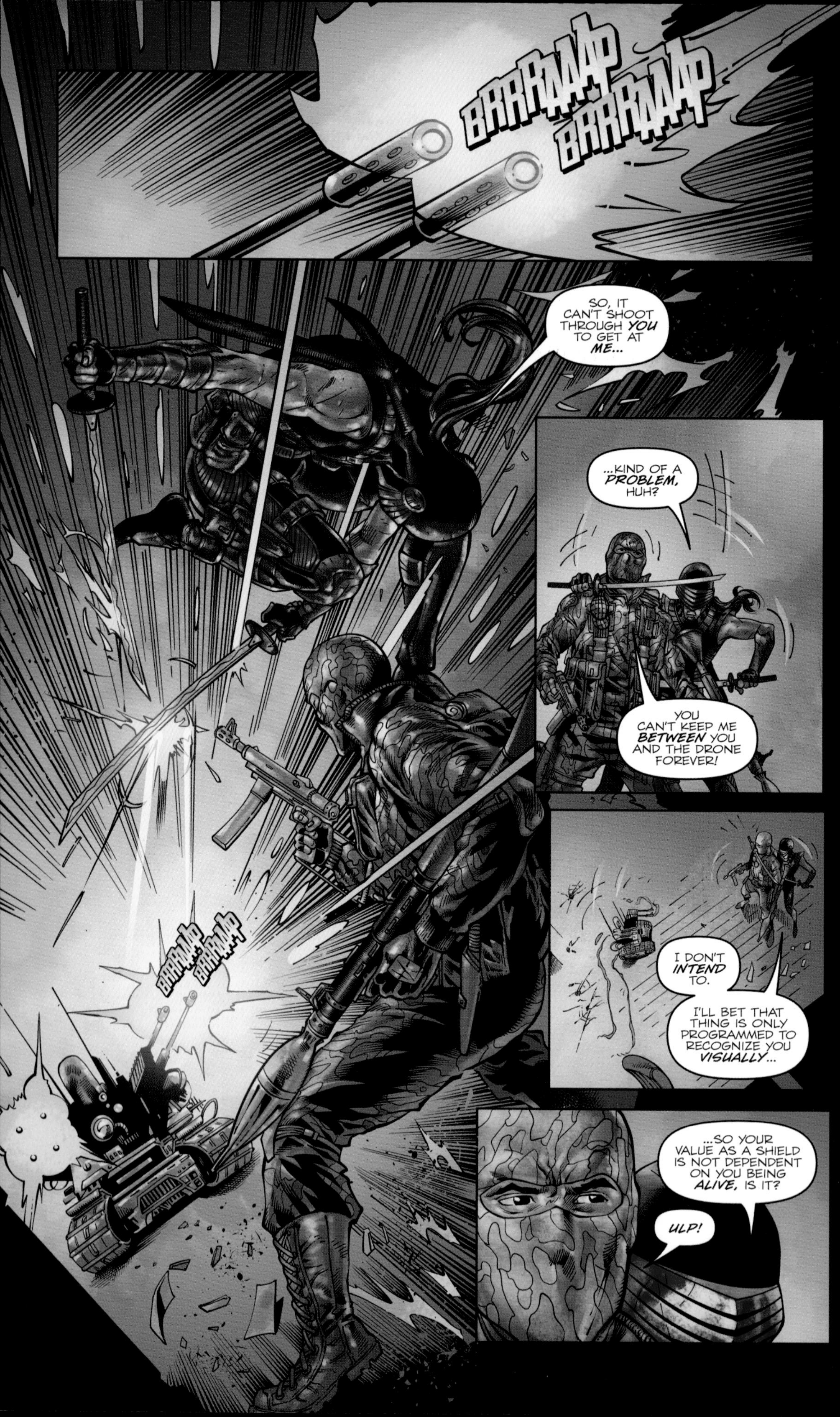
BRRRAAAP BRRRAAAP
SO, IT CAN'T SHOOT THROUGH *YOU* TO GET AT *ME*...
...KIND OF A *PROBLEM,* HUH?
YOU CAN'T KEEP ME *BETWEEN* YOU AND THE DRONE FOREVER!
BRRRAAAP BRRRAAAP
I DON'T *INTEND* TO.
I'LL BET THAT THING IS ONLY PROGRAMMED TO RECOGNIZE YOU *VISUALLY*...
...SO YOUR VALUE AS A SHIELD IS NOT DEPENDENT ON YOU BEING *ALIVE,* IS IT?
ULP!

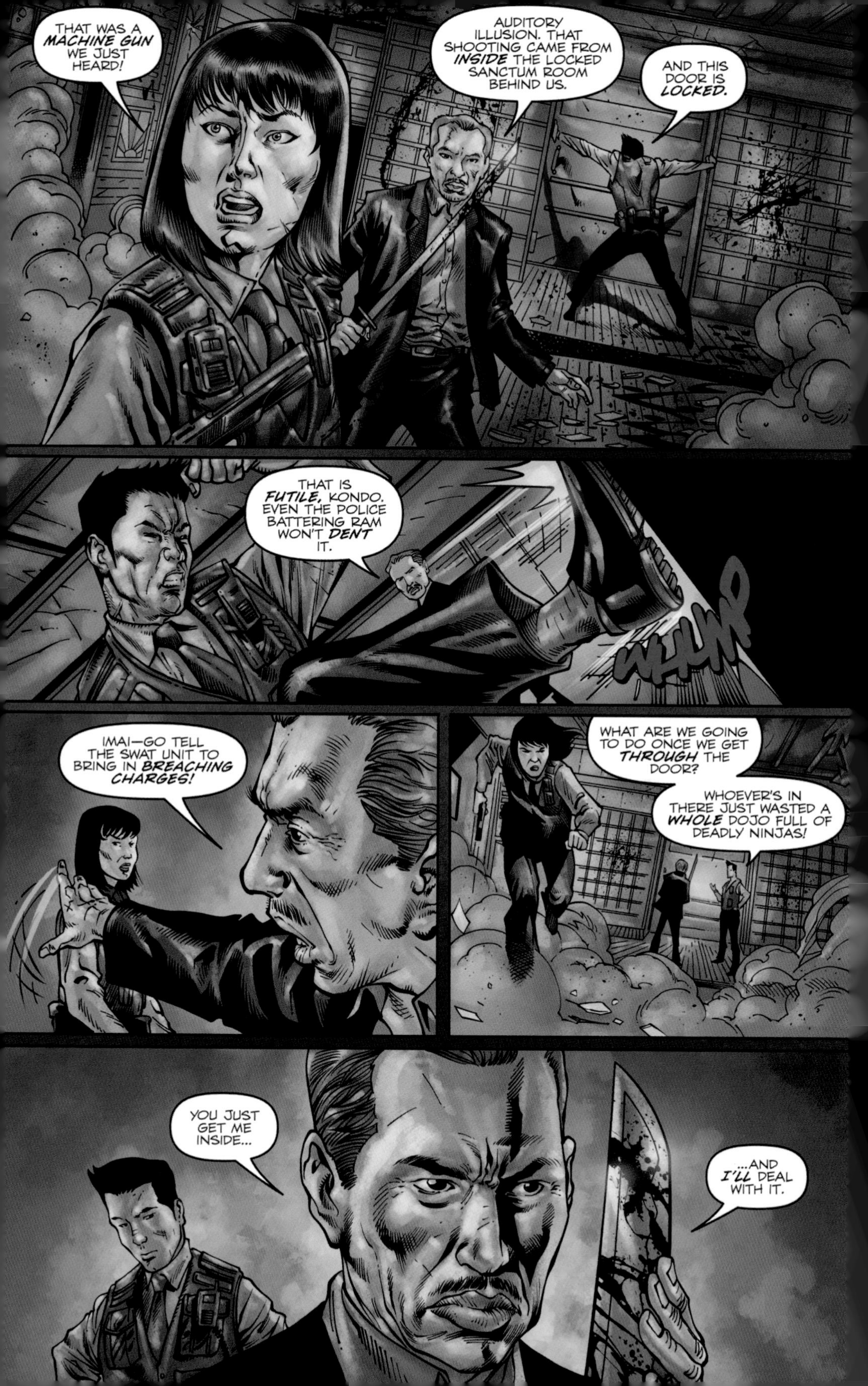
THAT WAS A MACHINE GUN WE JUST HEARD!
AUDITORY ILLUSION. THAT SHOOTING CAME FROM INSIDE THE LOCKED SANCTUM ROOM BEHIND US.
AND THIS DOOR IS LOCKED.
THAT IS FUTILE, KONDO. EVEN THE POLICE BATTERING RAM WON'T DENT IT.
WHUMP
IMAI—GO TELL THE SWAT UNIT TO BRING IN BREACHING CHARGES!
WHAT ARE WE GOING TO DO ONCE WE GET THROUGH THE DOOR?
WHOEVER'S IN THERE JUST WASTED A WHOLE DOJO FULL OF DEADLY NINJAS!
YOU JUST GET ME INSIDE...
...AND I'LL DEAL WITH IT.

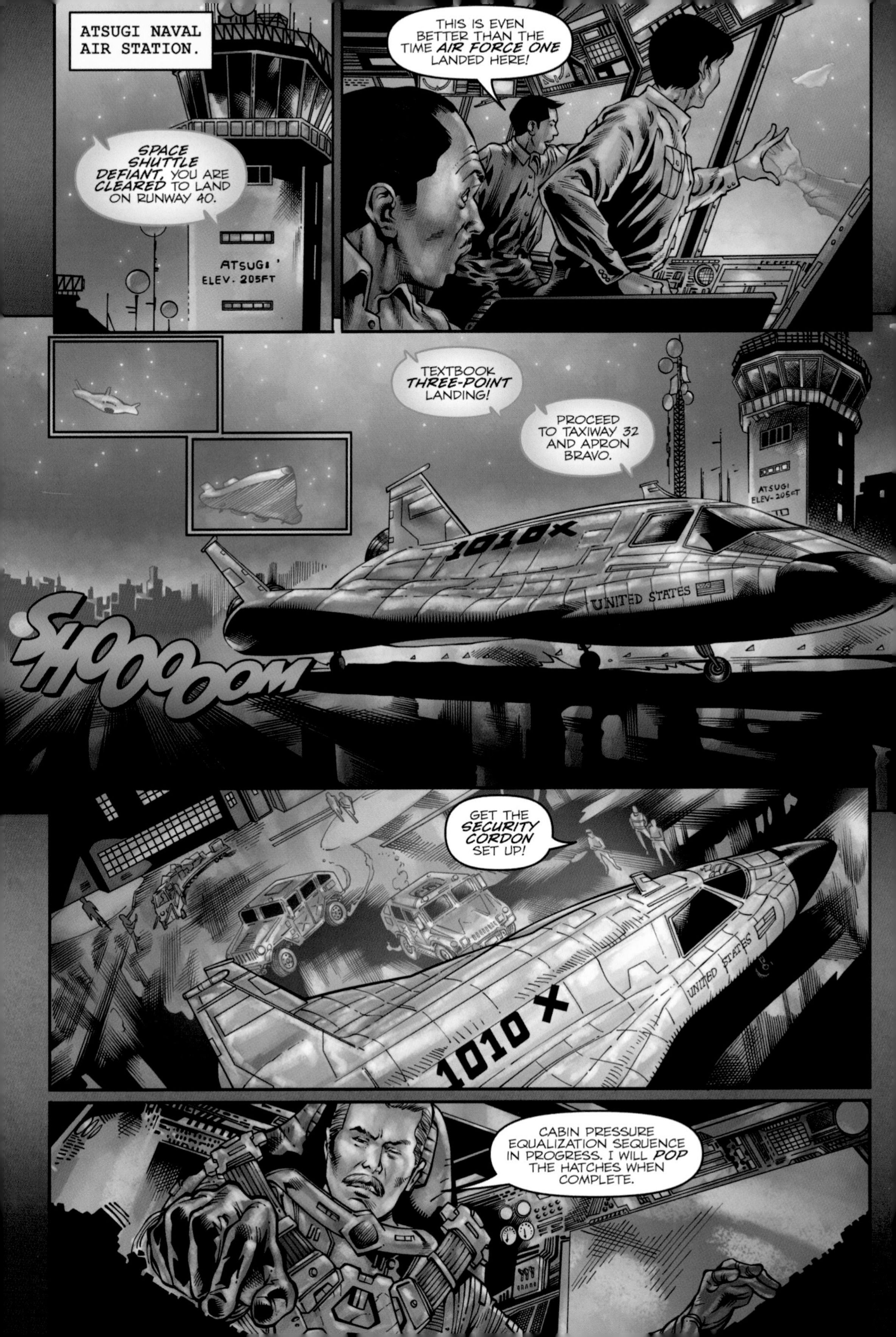
ATSUGI NAVAL AIR STATION.
SPACE SHUTTLE DEFIANT, YOU ARE CLEARED TO LAND ON RUNWAY 40.
ATSUGI ELEV. 205FT
THIS IS EVEN BETTER THAN THE TIME AIR FORCE ONE LANDED HERE!
TEXTBOOK THREE-POINT LANDING!
PROCEED TO TAXIWAY 32 AND APRON BRAVO.
SHOOOOOM
1010X
UNITED STATES
ATSUGI ELEV-205FT
GET THE SECURITY CORDON SET UP!
1010 X
UNITED STATES
CABIN PRESSURE EQUALIZATION SEQUENCE IN PROGRESS. I WILL POP THE HATCHES WHEN COMPLETE.

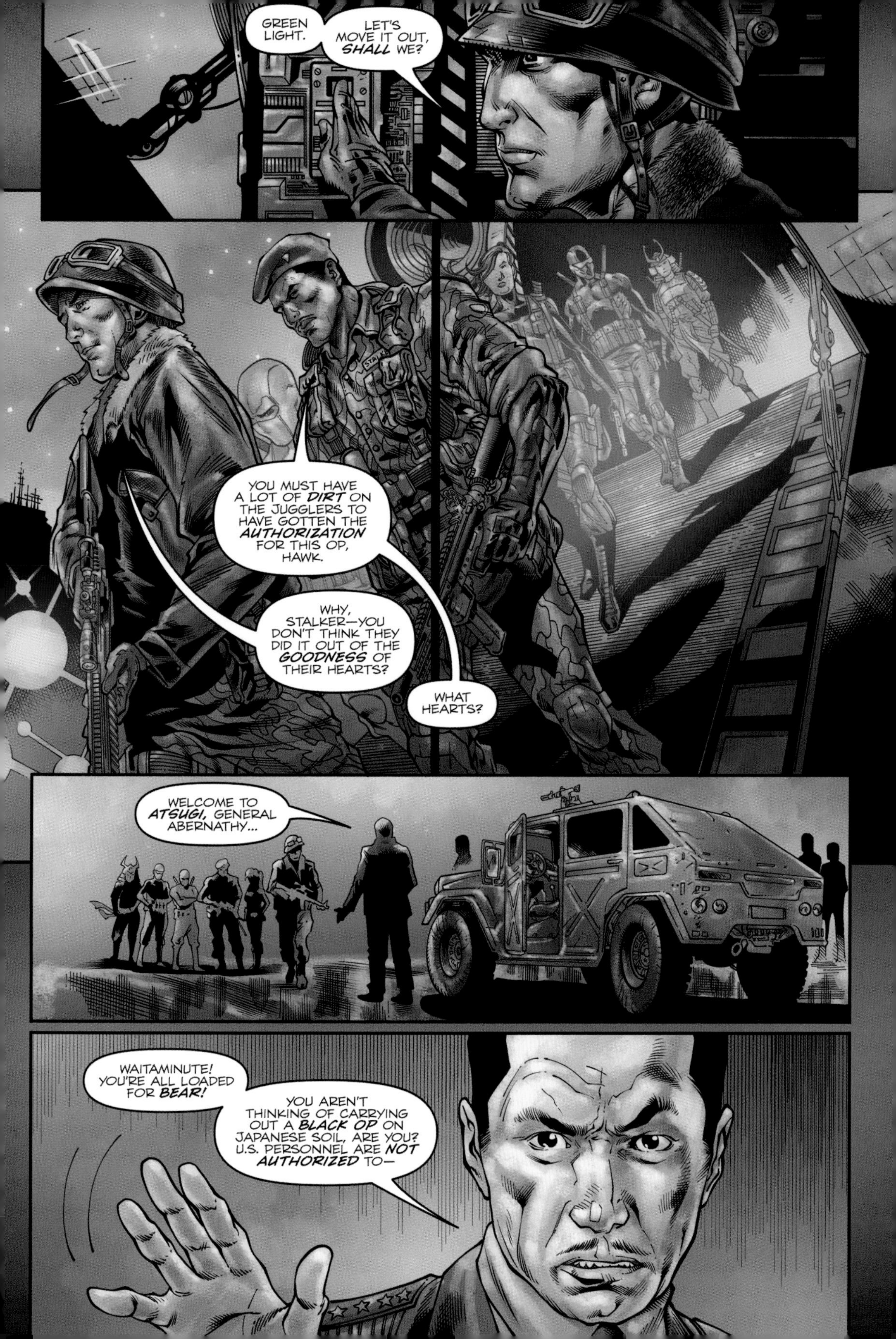
GREEN LIGHT.
LET'S MOVE IT OUT, SHALL WE?
YOU MUST HAVE A LOT OF DIRT ON THE JUGGLERS TO HAVE GOTTEN THE AUTHORIZATION FOR THIS OP, HAWK.
WHY, STALKER—YOU DON'T THINK THEY DID IT OUT OF THE GOODNESS OF THEIR HEARTS?
WHAT HEARTS?
WELCOME TO ATSUGI, GENERAL ABERNATHY...
WAITAMINUTE! YOU'RE ALL LOADED FOR BEAR!
YOU AREN'T THINKING OF CARRYING OUT A BLACK OP ON JAPANESE SOIL, ARE YOU? U.S. PERSONNEL ARE NOT AUTHORIZED TO—

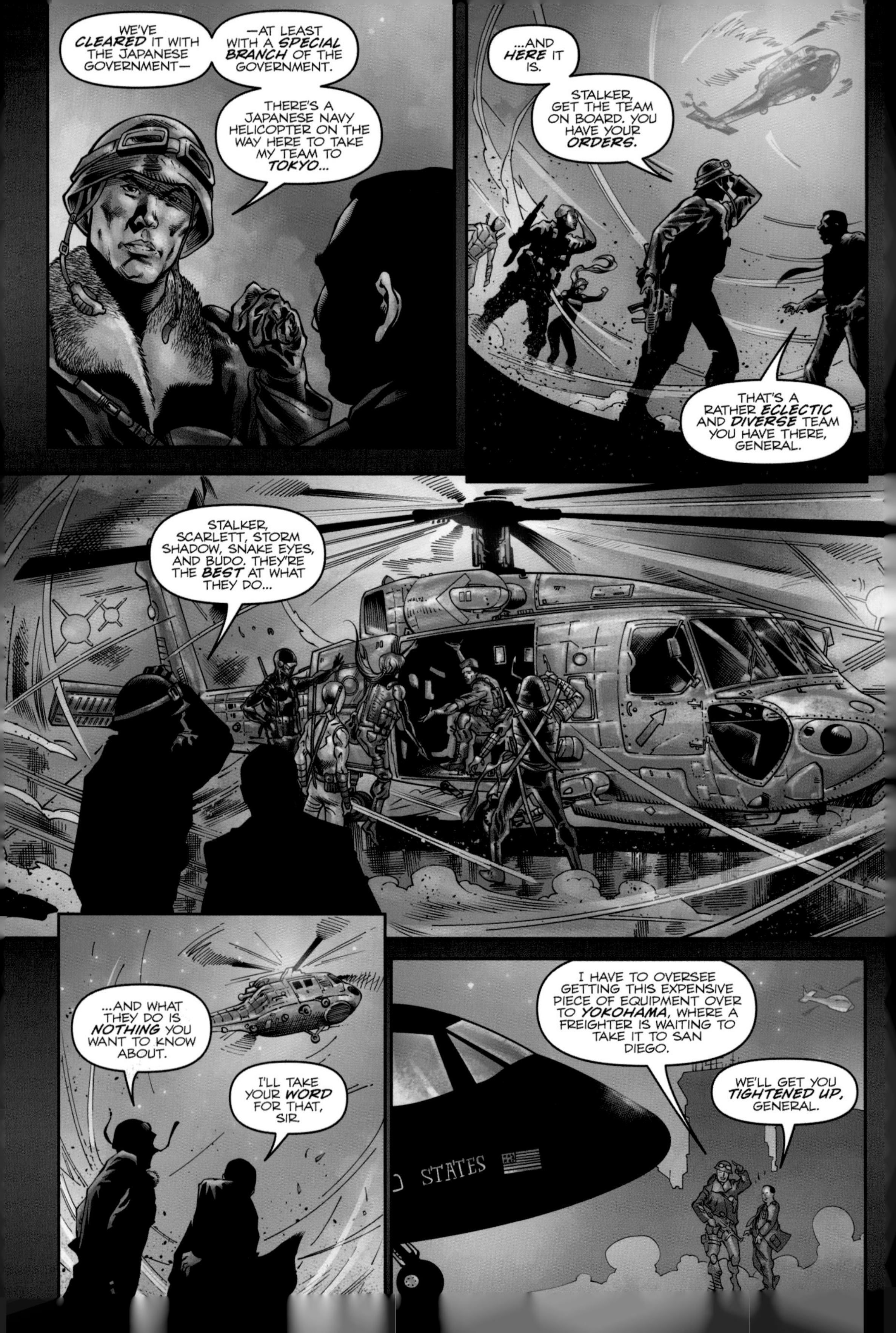
WE'VE CLEARED IT WITH THE JAPANESE GOVERNMENT—
—AT LEAST WITH A SPECIAL BRANCH OF THE GOVERNMENT.
THERE'S A JAPANESE NAVY HELICOPTER ON THE WAY HERE TO TAKE MY TEAM TO TOKYO...
...AND HERE IT IS.
STALKER, GET THE TEAM ON BOARD. YOU HAVE YOUR ORDERS.
THAT'S A RATHER ECLECTIC AND DIVERSE TEAM YOU HAVE THERE, GENERAL.
STALKER, SCARLETT, STORM SHADOW, SNAKE EYES, AND BUDO. THEY'RE THE BEST AT WHAT THEY DO...
...AND WHAT THEY DO IS NOTHING YOU WANT TO KNOW ABOUT.
I'LL TAKE YOUR WORD FOR THAT, SIR.
I HAVE TO OVERSEE GETTING THIS EXPENSIVE PIECE OF EQUIPMENT OVER TO YOKOHAMA, WHERE A FREIGHTER IS WAITING TO TAKE IT TO SAN DIEGO.
WE'LL GET YOU TIGHTENED UP, GENERAL.
STATES

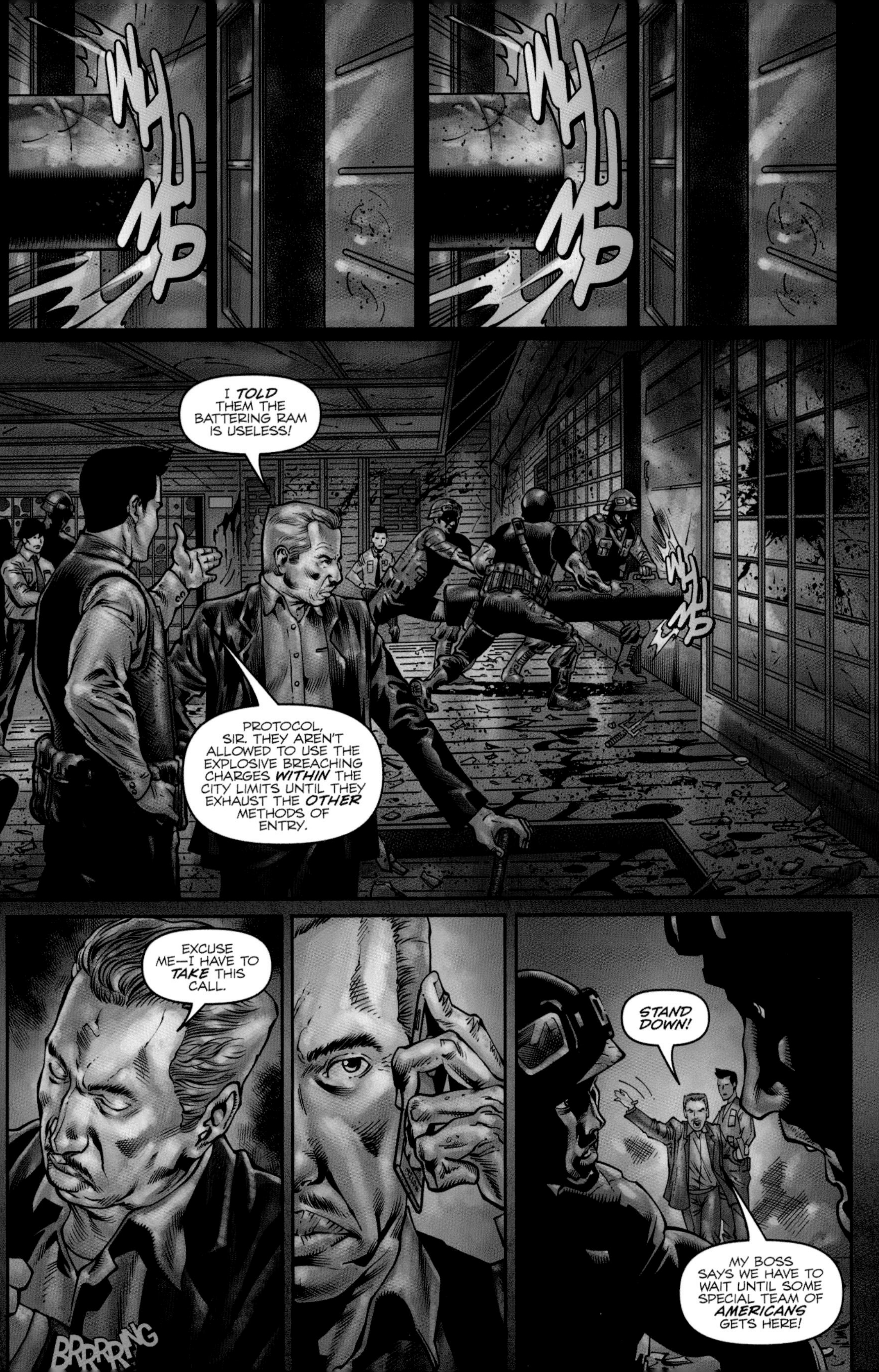
WHUMP
WHUMP
I TOLD THEM THE BATTERING RAM IS USELESS!
WHUMP
PROTOCOL, SIR. THEY AREN'T ALLOWED TO USE THE EXPLOSIVE BREACHING CHARGES WITHIN THE CITY LIMITS UNTIL THEY EXHAUST THE OTHER METHODS OF ENTRY.
EXCUSE ME—I HAVE TO TAKE THIS CALL.
BRRRRING
STAND DOWN!
MY BOSS SAYS WE HAVE TO WAIT UNTIL SOME SPECIAL TEAM OF AMERICANS GETS HERE!

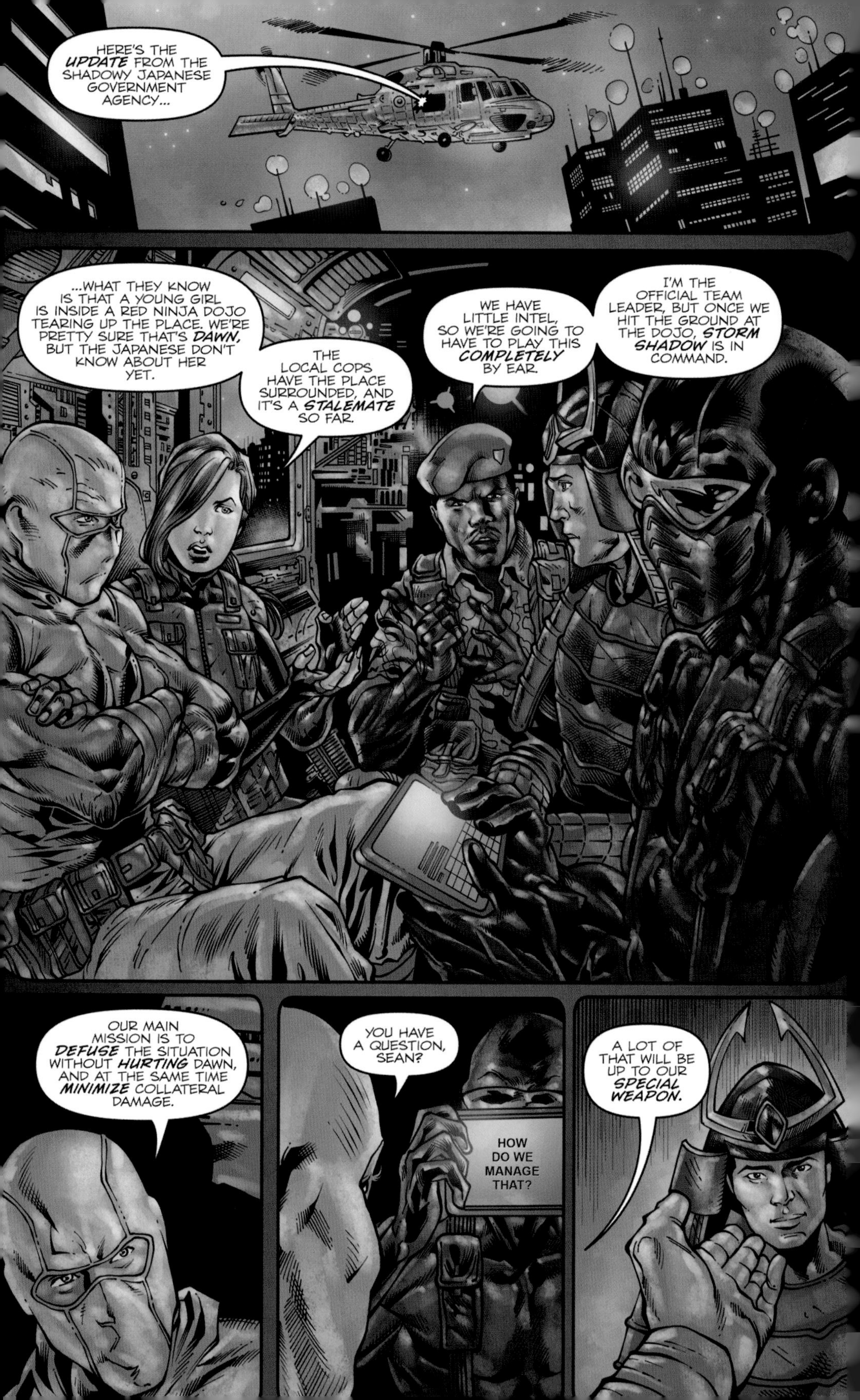
HERE'S THE UPDATE FROM THE SHADOWY JAPANESE GOVERNMENT AGENCY...
...WHAT THEY KNOW IS THAT A YOUNG GIRL IS INSIDE A RED NINJA DOJO TEARING UP THE PLACE. WE'RE PRETTY SURE THAT'S DAWN, BUT THE JAPANESE DON'T KNOW ABOUT HER YET.
THE LOCAL COPS HAVE THE PLACE SURROUNDED, AND IT'S A STALEMATE SO FAR.
WE HAVE LITTLE INTEL, SO WE'RE GOING TO HAVE TO PLAY THIS COMPLETELY BY EAR.
I'M THE OFFICIAL TEAM LEADER, BUT ONCE WE HIT THE GROUND AT THE DOJO, STORM SHADOW IS IN COMMAND.
OUR MAIN MISSION IS TO DEFUSE THE SITUATION WITHOUT HURTING DAWN, AND AT THE SAME TIME MINIMIZE COLLATERAL DAMAGE.
YOU HAVE A QUESTION, SEAN?
HOW DO WE MANAGE THAT?
A LOT OF THAT WILL BE UP TO OUR SPECIAL WEAPON.

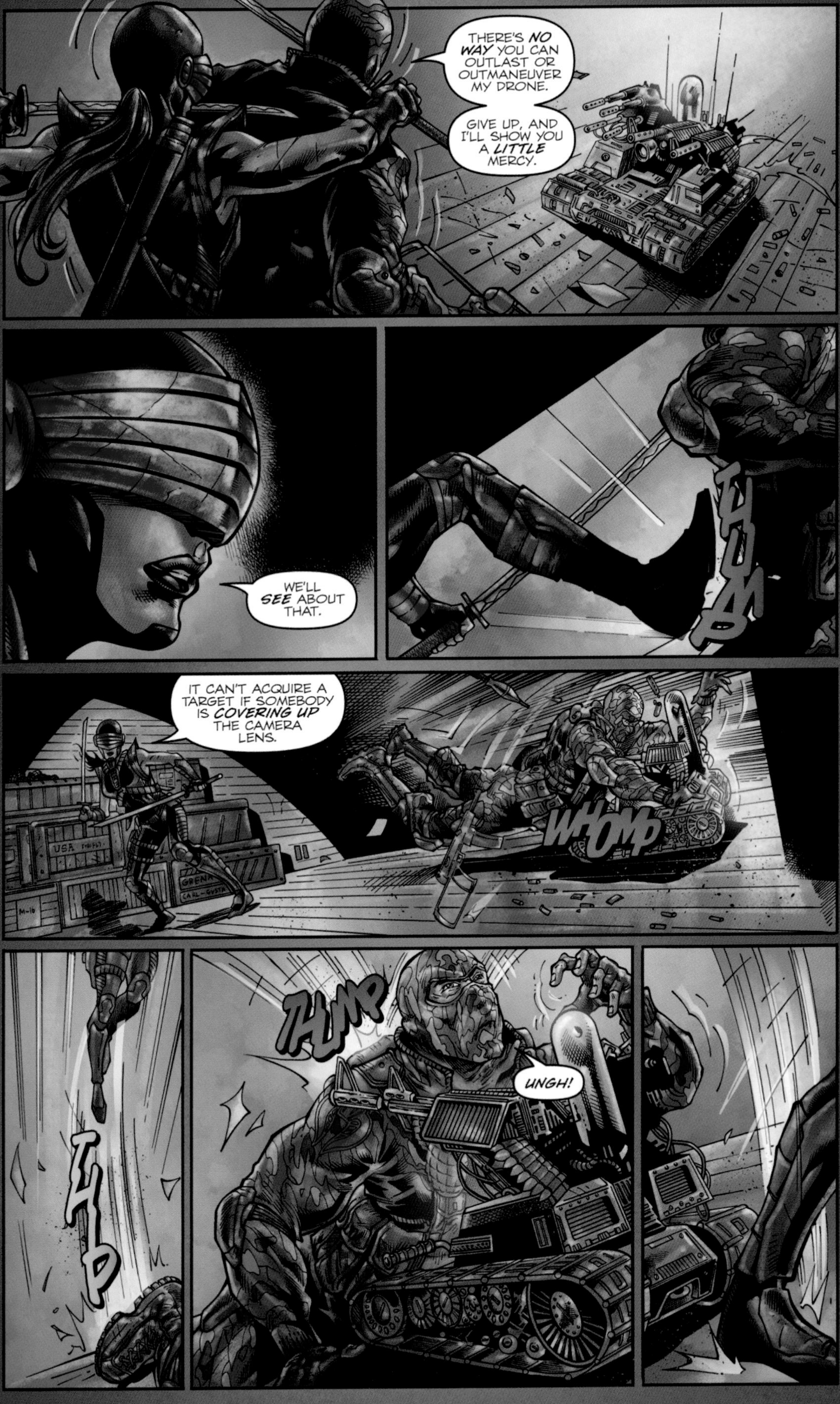
THERE'S NO WAY YOU CAN OUTLAST OR OUTMANEUVER MY DRONE.
GIVE UP, AND I'LL SHOW YOU A LITTLE MERCY.
WE'LL SEE ABOUT THAT.
THUMP
IT CAN'T ACQUIRE A TARGET IF SOMEBODY IS COVERING UP THE CAMERA LENS.
WHOMP
THUMP
UNGH!
THP

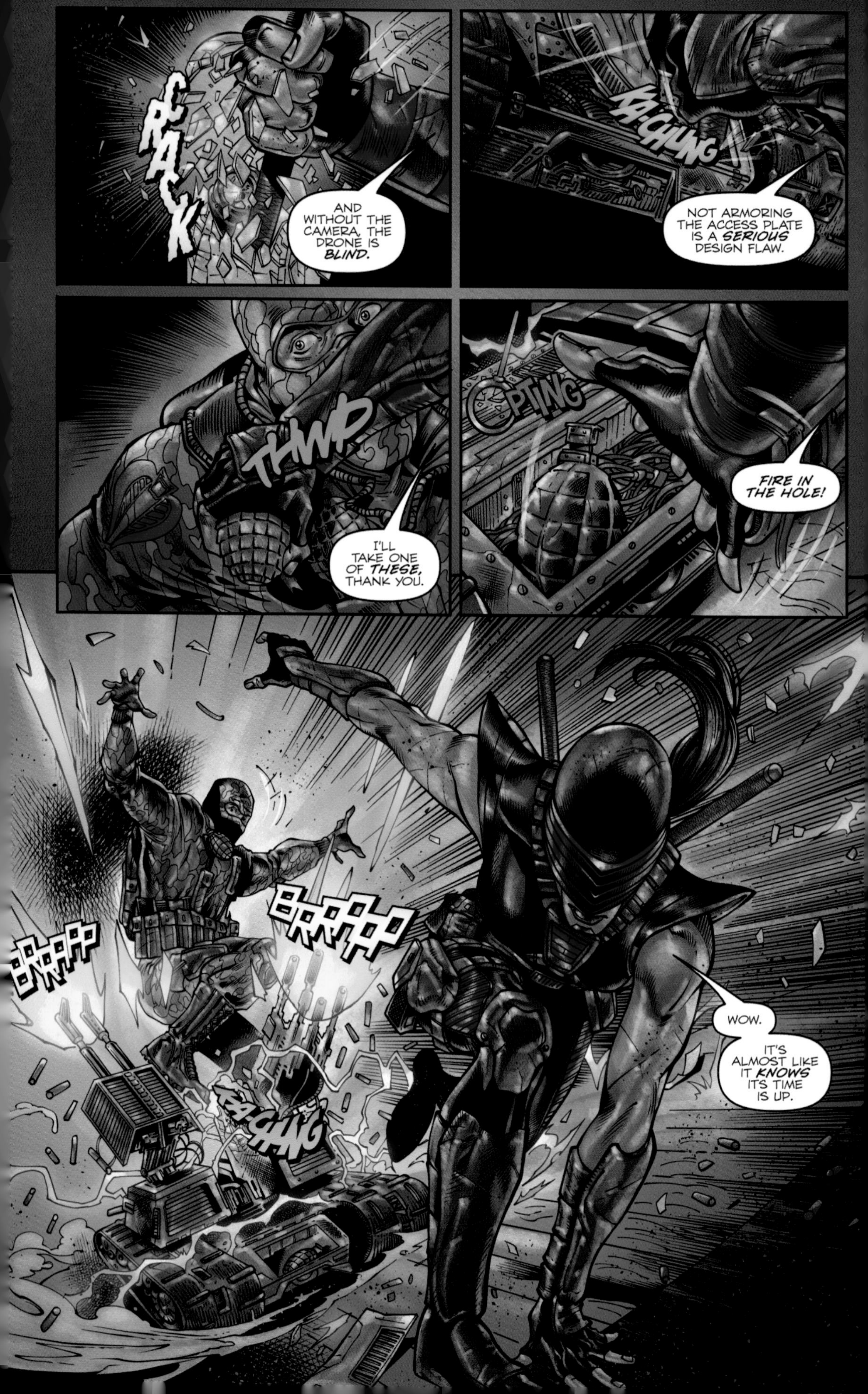
CRACK
AND WITHOUT THE CAMERA, THE DRONE IS *BLIND.*
KA-CHUNG
NOT ARMORING THE ACCESS PLATE IS A *SERIOUS* DESIGN FLAW.
THWP
I'LL TAKE ONE OF *THESE,* THANK YOU.
PTING
FIRE IN THE HOLE!
BRRAPP
BRRAPP
KA-CHANG
WOW.
IT'S ALMOST LIKE IT *KNOWS* ITS TIME IS UP.

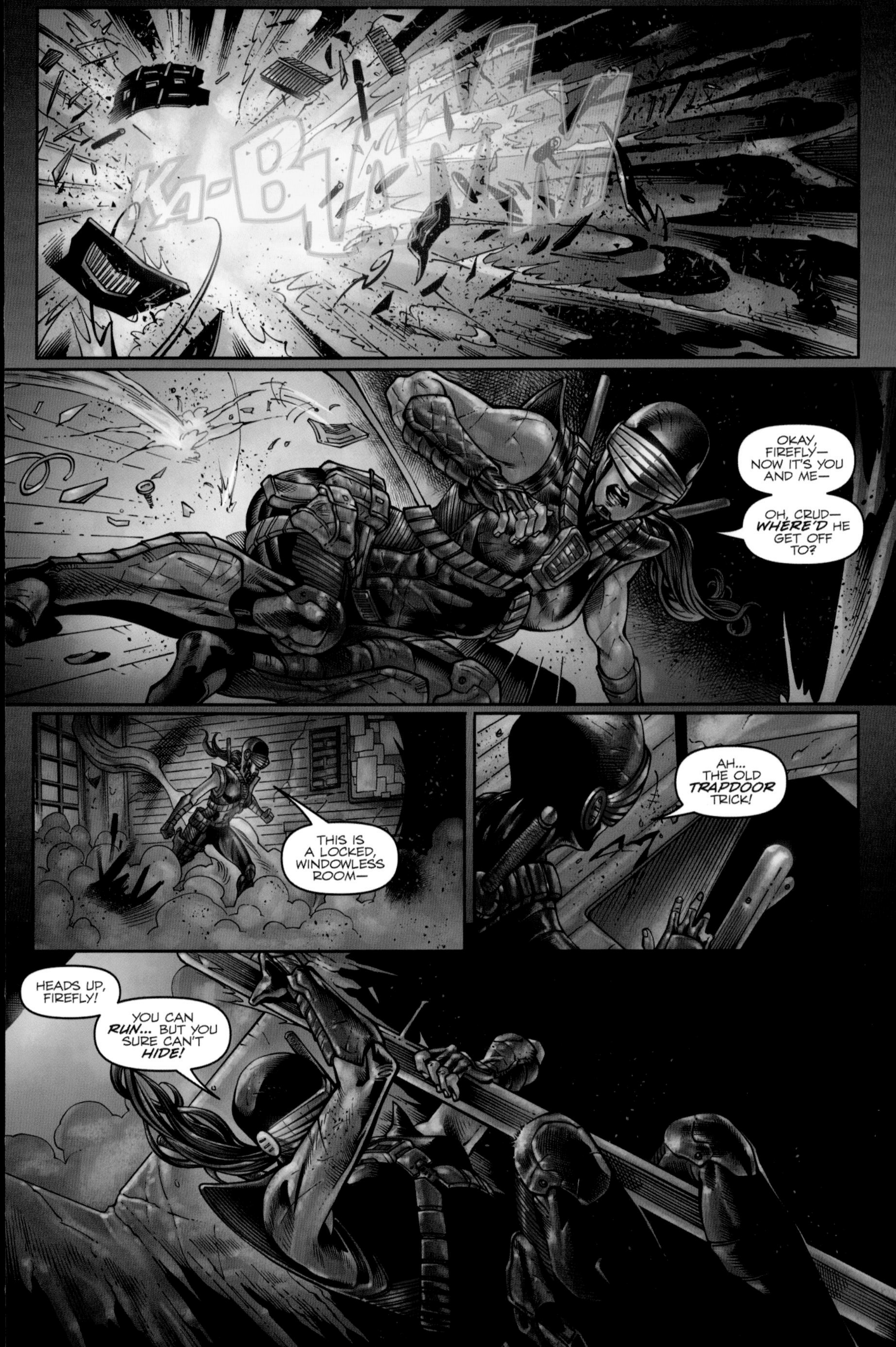
KA-BLAMM
OKAY, FIREFLY— NOW IT'S YOU AND ME—
OH, CRUD— WHERE'D HE GET OFF TO?
THIS IS A LOCKED, WINDOWLESS ROOM—
AH... THE OLD TRAPDOOR TRICK!
HEADS UP, FIREFLY!
YOU CAN RUN... BUT YOU SURE CAN'T HIDE!

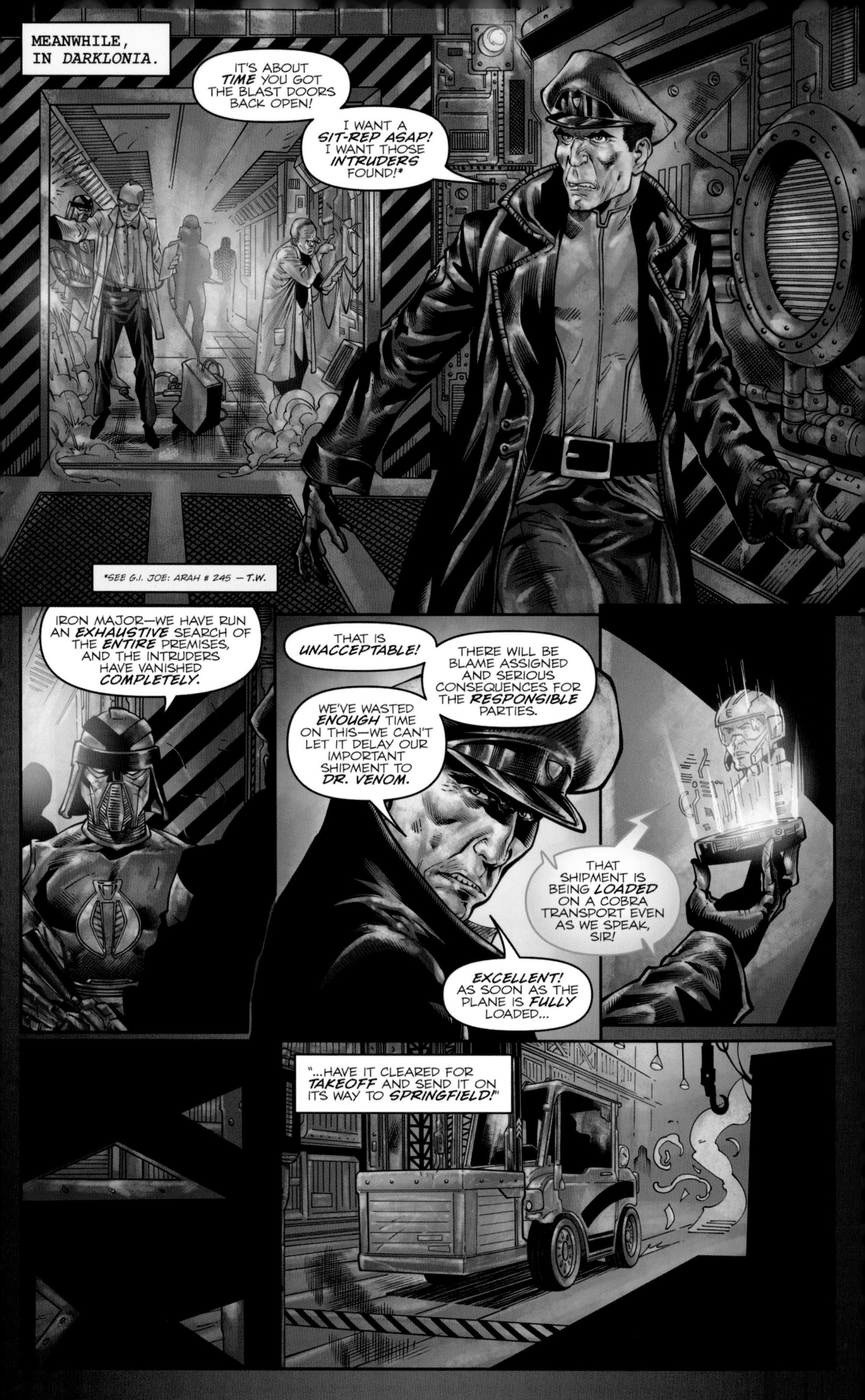
MEANWHILE, IN DARKLONIA.
IT'S ABOUT TIME YOU GOT THE BLAST DOORS BACK OPEN!
I WANT A SIT-REP ASAP! I WANT THOSE INTRUDERS FOUND!*
*SEE G.I. JOE: ARAH # 245 —T.W.
IRON MAJOR—WE HAVE RUN AN EXHAUSTIVE SEARCH OF THE ENTIRE PREMISES, AND THE INTRUDERS HAVE VANISHED COMPLETELY.
THAT IS UNACCEPTABLE!
THERE WILL BE BLAME ASSIGNED AND SERIOUS CONSEQUENCES FOR THE RESPONSIBLE PARTIES.
WE'VE WASTED ENOUGH TIME ON THIS—WE CAN'T LET IT DELAY OUR IMPORTANT SHIPMENT TO DR. VENOM.
THAT SHIPMENT IS BEING LOADED ON A COBRA TRANSPORT EVEN AS WE SPEAK, SIR!
EXCELLENT! AS SOON AS THE PLANE IS FULLY LOADED...
"...HAVE IT CLEARED FOR TAKEOFF AND SEND IT ON ITS WAY TO SPRINGFIELD!"

SKETCH BY HARVEY TOLIBAO
COLORS BY HMT STUDIOS' GAB SANTOS & KEVIN ANTHONY DECASTRO

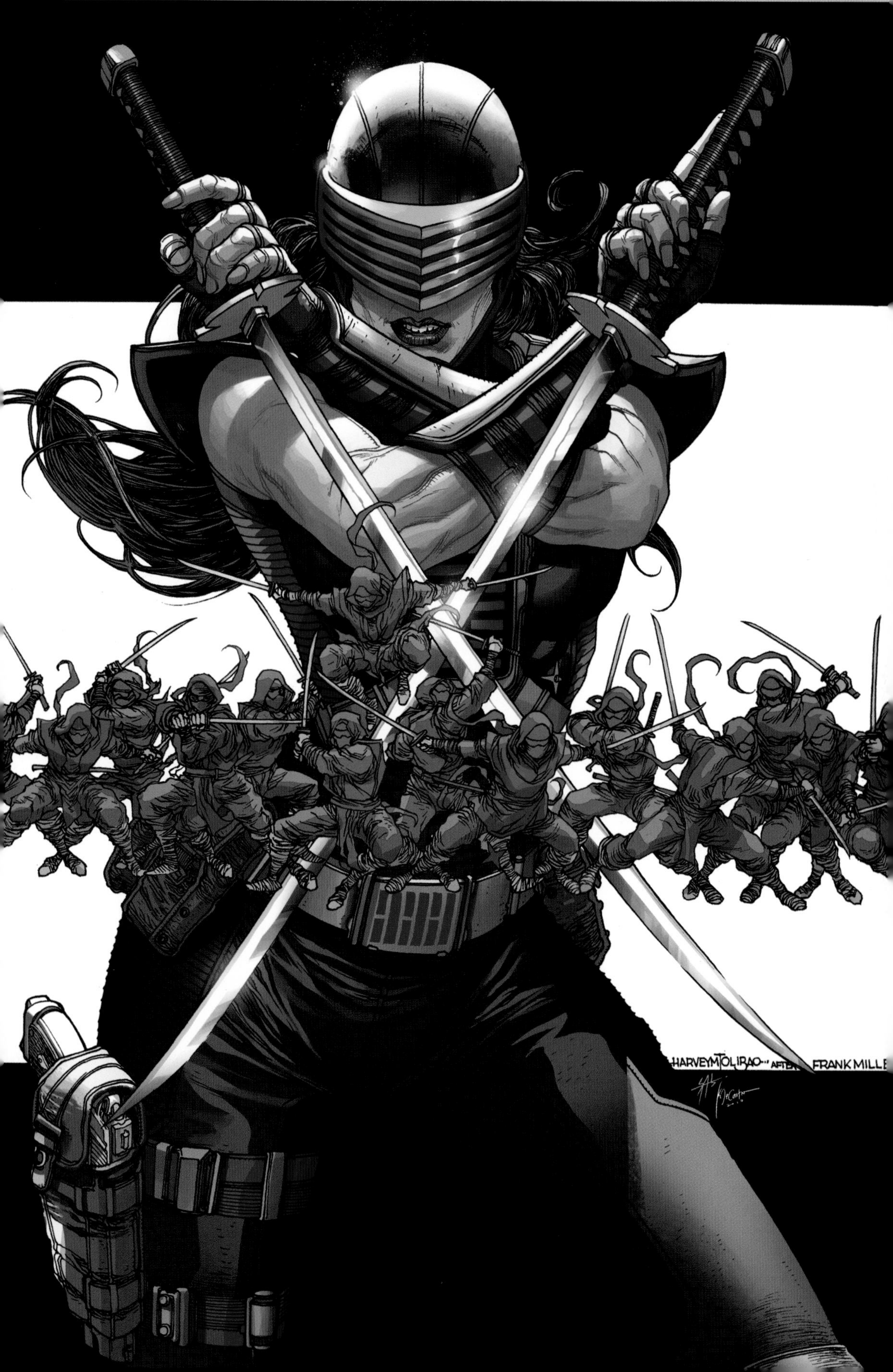
HARVEYMTOLIBAO AFTE FRANK MILLE

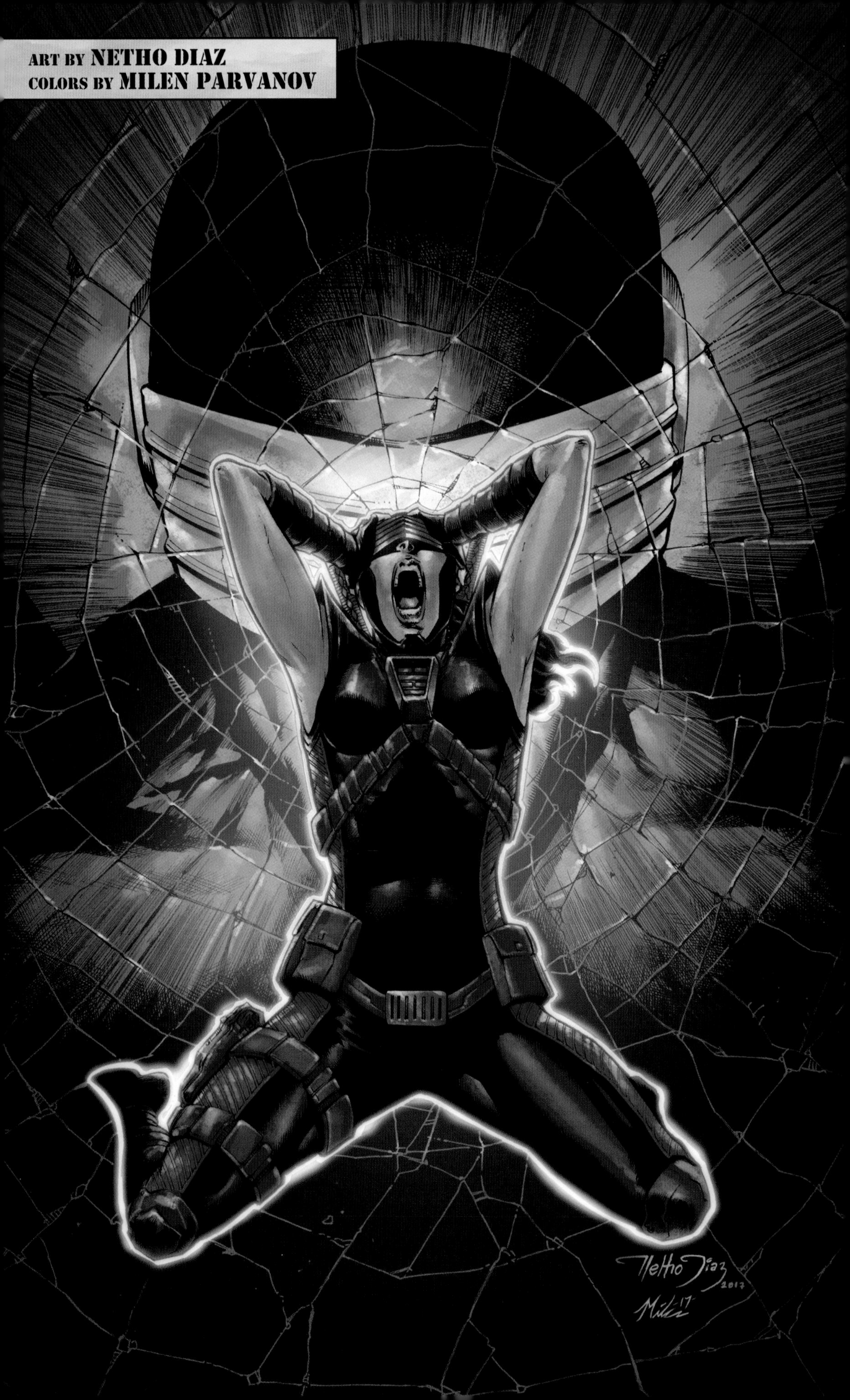

ART BY NETHO DIAZ
COLORS BY MILEN PARVANOV

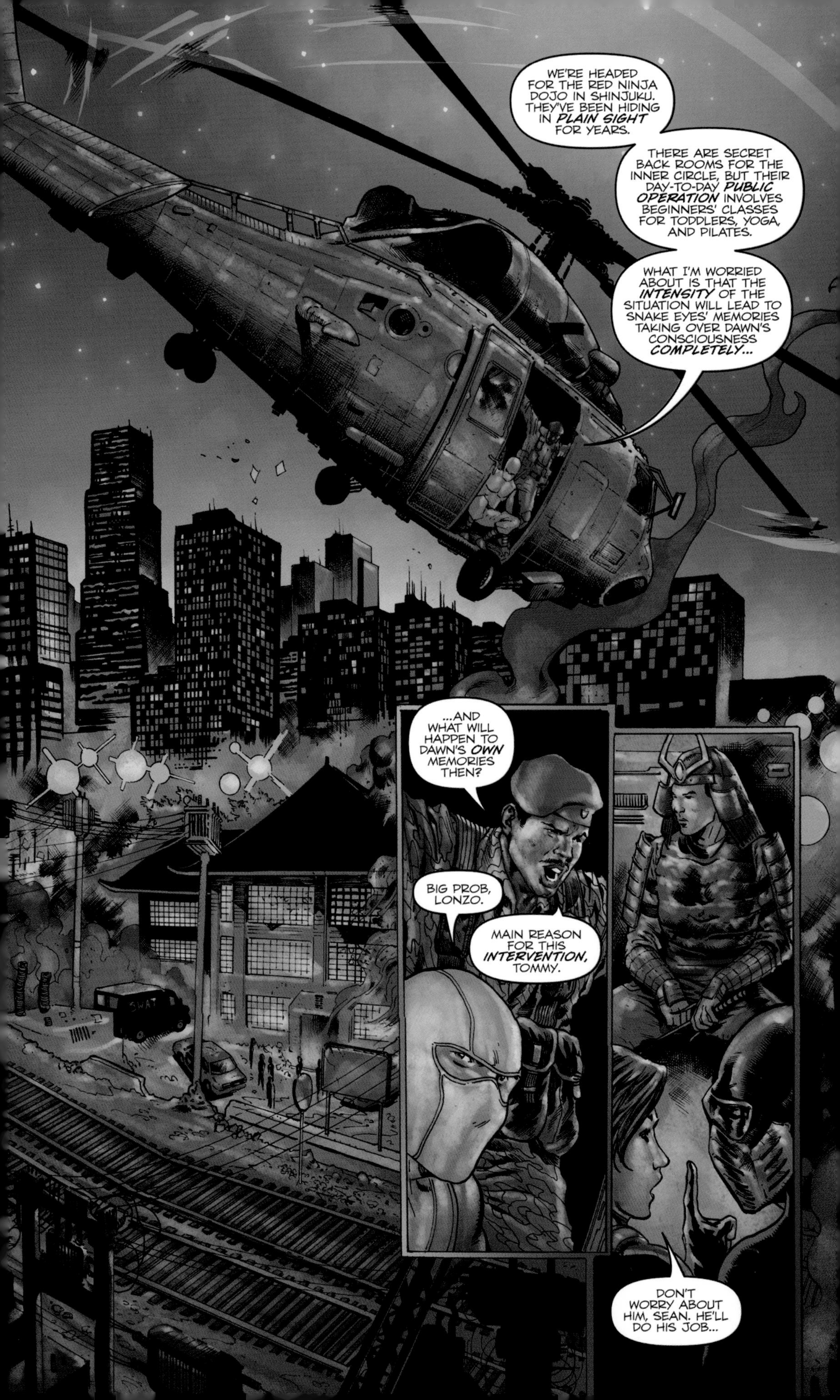
WE'RE HEADED FOR THE RED NINJA DOJO IN SHINJUKU. THEY'VE BEEN HIDING IN *PLAIN SIGHT* FOR YEARS.
THERE ARE SECRET BACK ROOMS FOR THE INNER CIRCLE, BUT THEIR DAY-TO-DAY *PUBLIC OPERATION* INVOLVES BEGINNERS' CLASSES FOR TODDLERS, YOGA, AND PILATES.
WHAT I'M WORRIED ABOUT IS THAT THE *INTENSITY* OF THE SITUATION WILL LEAD TO SNAKE EYES' MEMORIES TAKING OVER DAWN'S CONSCIOUSNESS *COMPLETELY*...
...AND WHAT WILL HAPPEN TO DAWN'S *OWN* MEMORIES THEN?
BIG PROB, LONZO.
MAIN REASON FOR THIS *INTERVENTION,* TOMMY.
DON'T WORRY ABOUT HIM, SEAN. HE'LL DO HIS JOB...

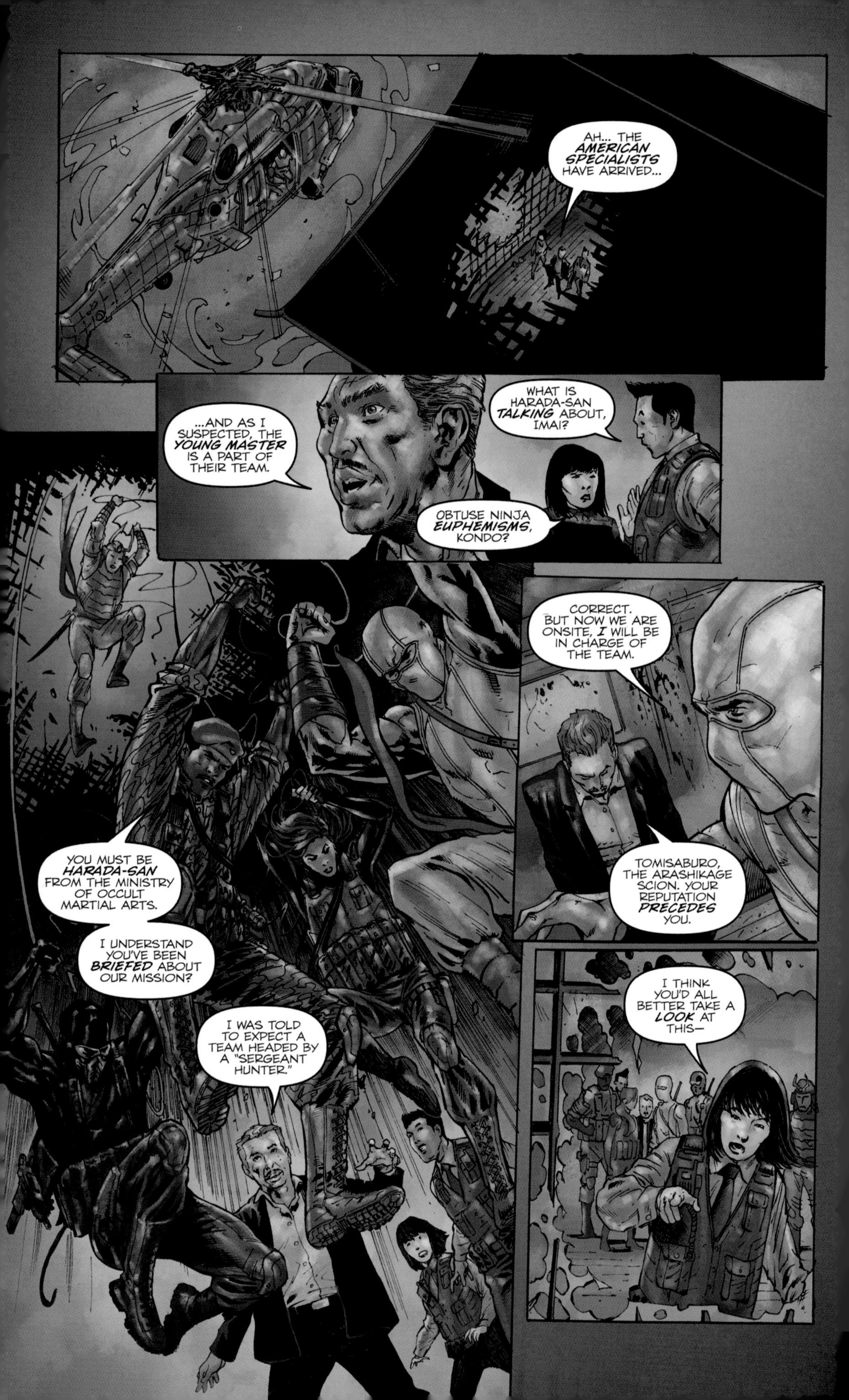
AH... THE AMERICAN SPECIALISTS HAVE ARRIVED...
...AND AS I SUSPECTED, THE YOUNG MASTER IS A PART OF THEIR TEAM.
WHAT IS HARADA-SAN TALKING ABOUT, IMAI?
OBTUSE NINJA EUPHEMISMS, KONDO?
YOU MUST BE HARADA-SAN FROM THE MINISTRY OF OCCULT MARTIAL ARTS.
I UNDERSTAND YOU'VE BEEN BRIEFED ABOUT OUR MISSION?
I WAS TOLD TO EXPECT A TEAM HEADED BY A "SERGEANT HUNTER."
CORRECT. BUT NOW WE ARE ONSITE, I WILL BE IN CHARGE OF THE TEAM.
TOMISABURO, THE ARASHIKAGE SCION. YOUR REPUTATION PRECEDES YOU.
I THINK YOU'D ALL BETTER TAKE A LOOK AT THIS—

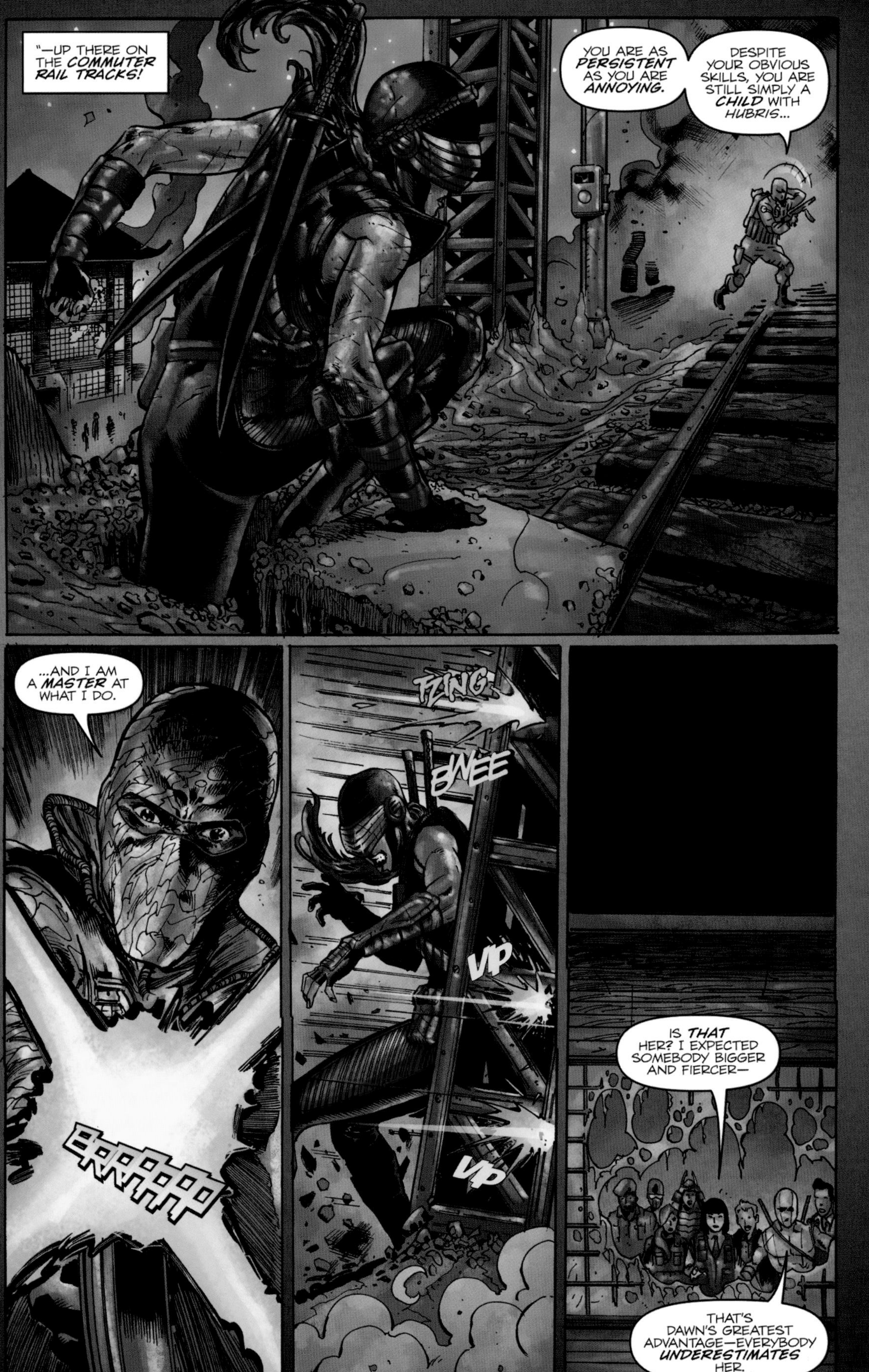

"—UP THERE ON THE COMMUTER RAIL TRACKS!
YOU ARE AS PERSISTENT AS YOU ARE ANNOYING.
DESPITE YOUR OBVIOUS SKILLS, YOU ARE STILL SIMPLY A CHILD WITH HUBRIS...
...AND I AM A MASTER AT WHAT I DO.
TZING
BWEE
VIP
VIP
IS THAT HER? I EXPECTED SOMEBODY BIGGER AND FIERCER—
THAT'S DAWN'S GREATEST ADVANTAGE—EVERYBODY UNDERESTIMATES HER.

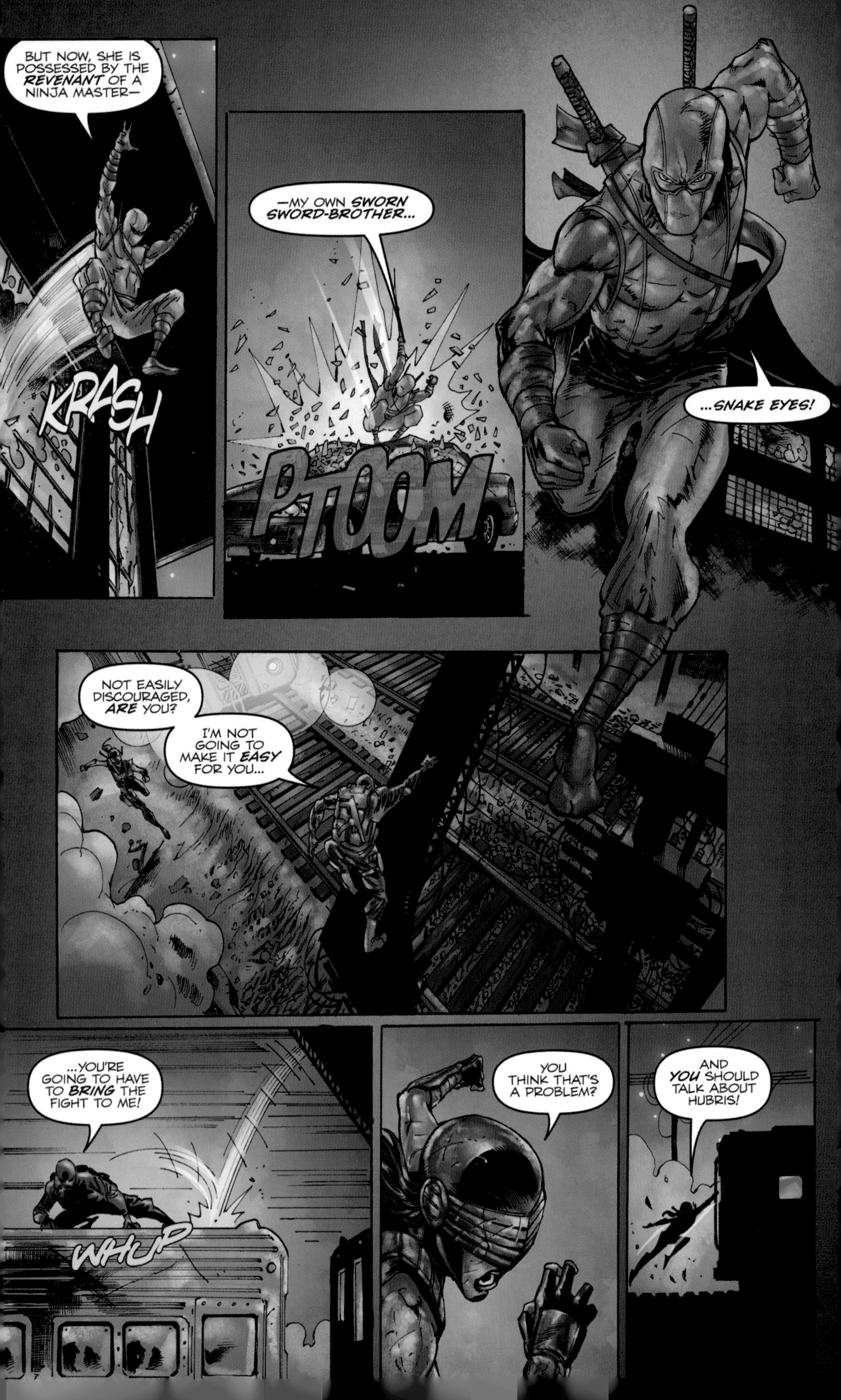
BUT NOW, SHE IS POSSESSED BY THE REVENANT OF A NINJA MASTER—
KRASH
—MY OWN SWORN SWORD-BROTHER...
PTOOM
...SNAKE EYES!
NOT EASILY DISCOURAGED, ARE YOU?
I'M NOT GOING TO MAKE IT EASY FOR YOU...
...YOU'RE GOING TO HAVE TO BRING THE FIGHT TO ME!
WHUP
YOU THINK THAT'S A PROBLEM?
AND YOU SHOULD TALK ABOUT HUBRIS!

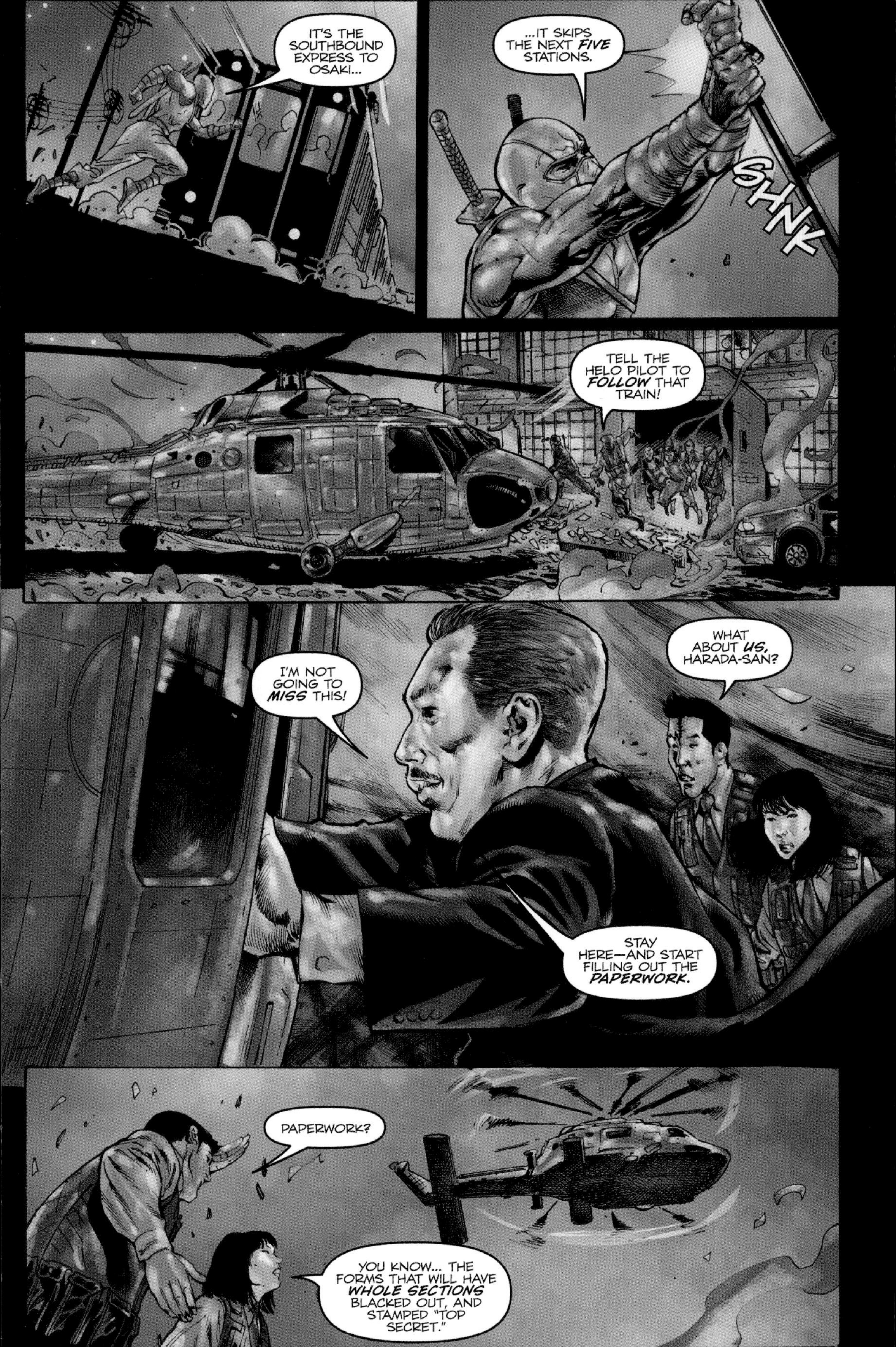
IT'S THE SOUTHBOUND EXPRESS TO OSAKI...
...IT SKIPS THE NEXT FIVE STATIONS.
SHNK
TELL THE HELO PILOT TO FOLLOW THAT TRAIN!
I'M NOT GOING TO MISS THIS!
WHAT ABOUT US, HARADA-SAN?
STAY HERE—AND START FILLING OUT THE PAPERWORK.
PAPERWORK?
YOU KNOW... THE FORMS THAT WILL HAVE WHOLE SECTIONS BLACKED OUT, AND STAMPED "TOP SECRET."

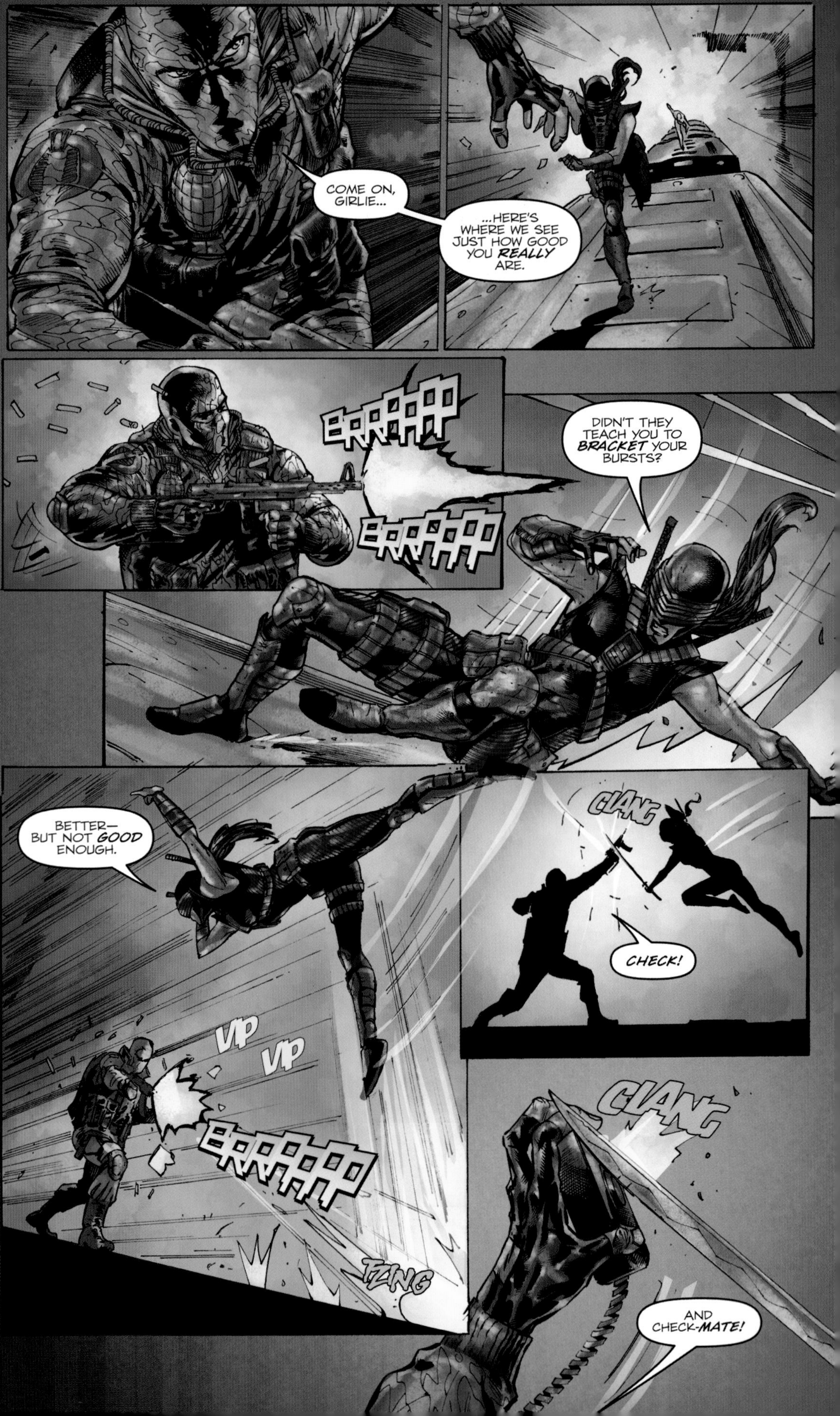
COME ON, GIRLIE...
...HERE'S WHERE WE SEE JUST HOW GOOD YOU REALLY ARE.
BRRRRRR
BRRRRRR
DIDN'T THEY TEACH YOU TO BRACKET YOUR BURSTS?
BETTER— BUT NOT GOOD ENOUGH.
VIP
VIP
BRRRRRRR
TZING
CLANG
CHECK!
CLANG
AND CHECK-MATE!

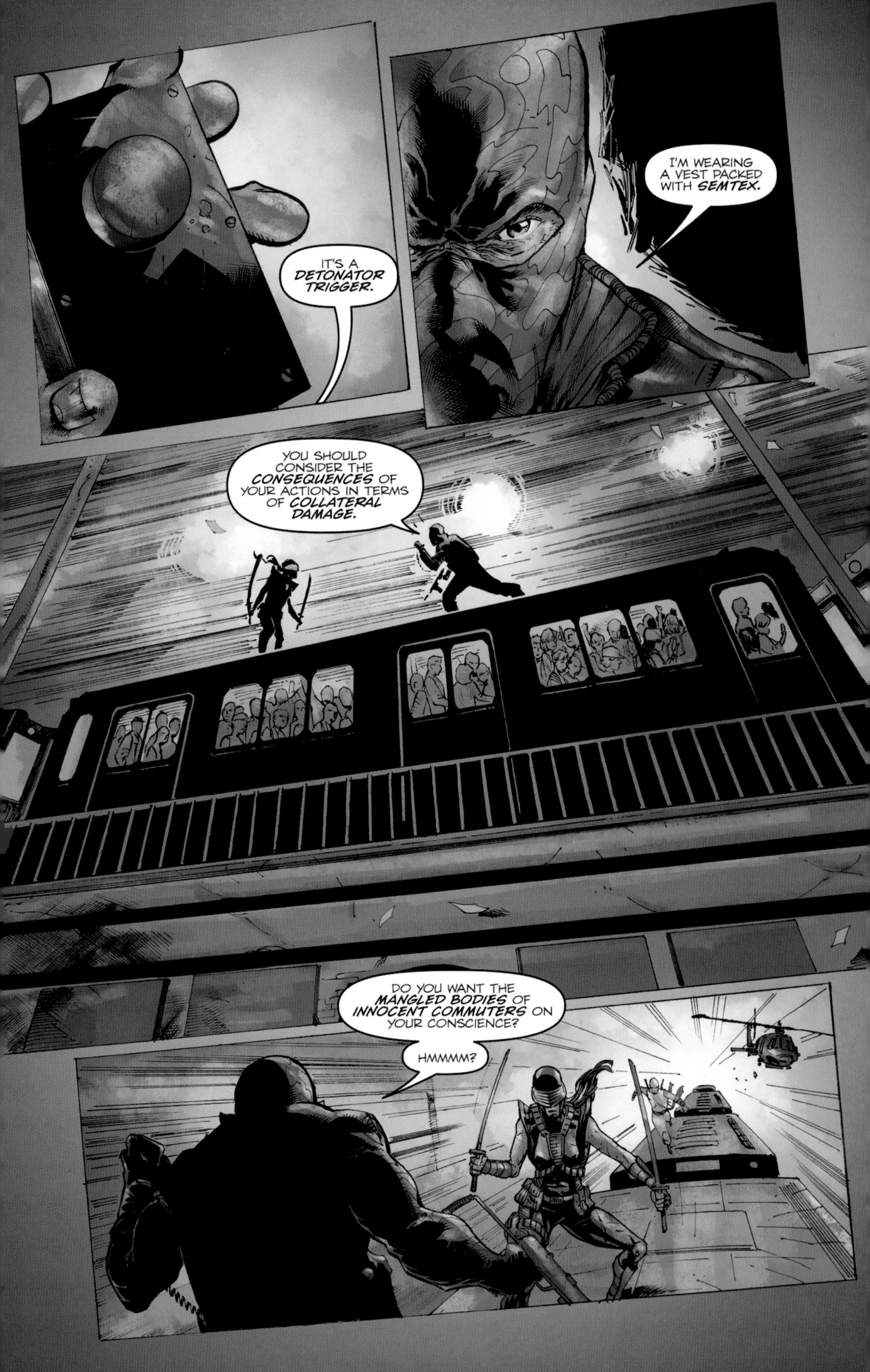

IT'S A DETONATOR TRIGGER.
I'M WEARING A VEST PACKED WITH SEMTEX.
YOU SHOULD CONSIDER THE CONSEQUENCES OF YOUR ACTIONS IN TERMS OF COLLATERAL DAMAGE.
DO YOU WANT THE MANGLED BODIES OF INNOCENT COMMUTERS ON YOUR CONSCIENCE?
HMMMM?

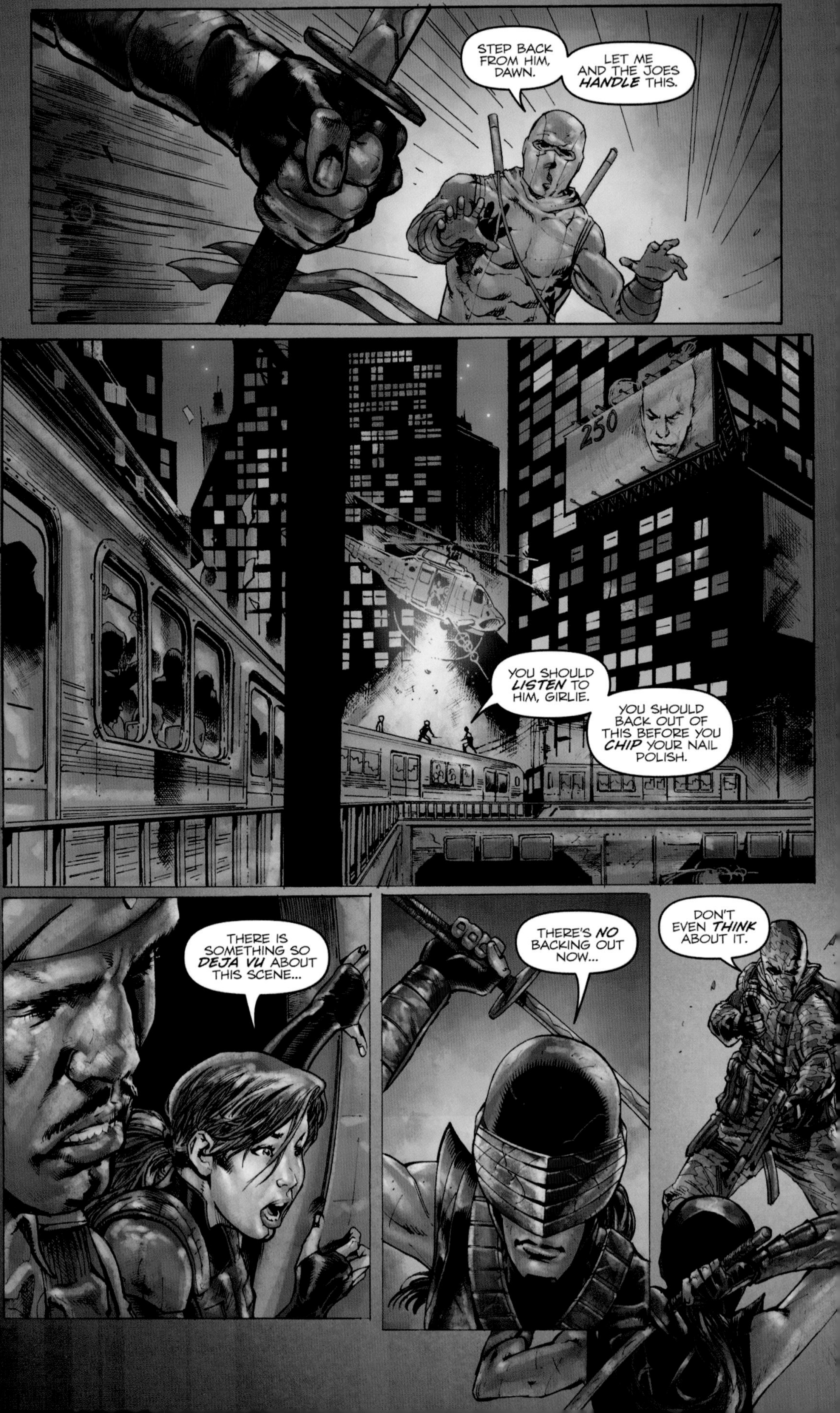
STEP BACK FROM HIM, DAWN.
LET ME AND THE JOES HANDLE THIS.
250
YOU SHOULD LISTEN TO HIM, GIRLIE.
YOU SHOULD BACK OUT OF THIS BEFORE YOU CHIP YOUR NAIL POLISH.
THERE IS SOMETHING SO DEJA VU ABOUT THIS SCENE...
THERE'S NO BACKING OUT NOW...
DON'T EVEN THINK ABOUT IT.

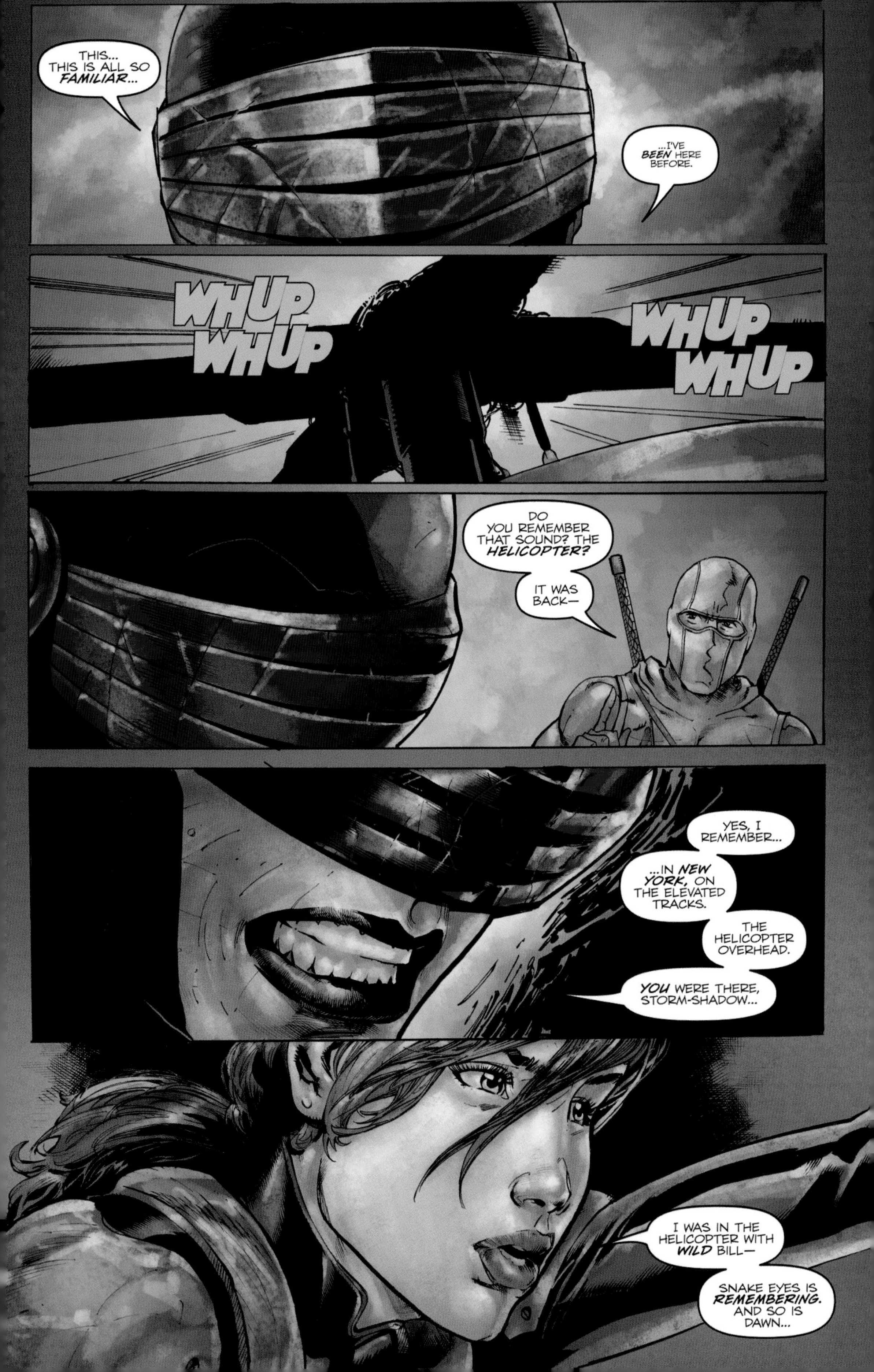
THIS... THIS IS ALL SO FAMILIAR...
...I'VE BEEN HERE BEFORE.
WHUP WHUP
WHUP WHUP
DO YOU REMEMBER THAT SOUND? THE HELICOPTER?
IT WAS BACK—
YES, I REMEMBER...
...IN NEW YORK, ON THE ELEVATED TRACKS.
THE HELICOPTER OVERHEAD.
YOU WERE THERE, STORM-SHADOW...
I WAS IN THE HELICOPTER WITH WILD BILL—
SNAKE EYES IS REMEMBERING. AND SO IS DAWN...

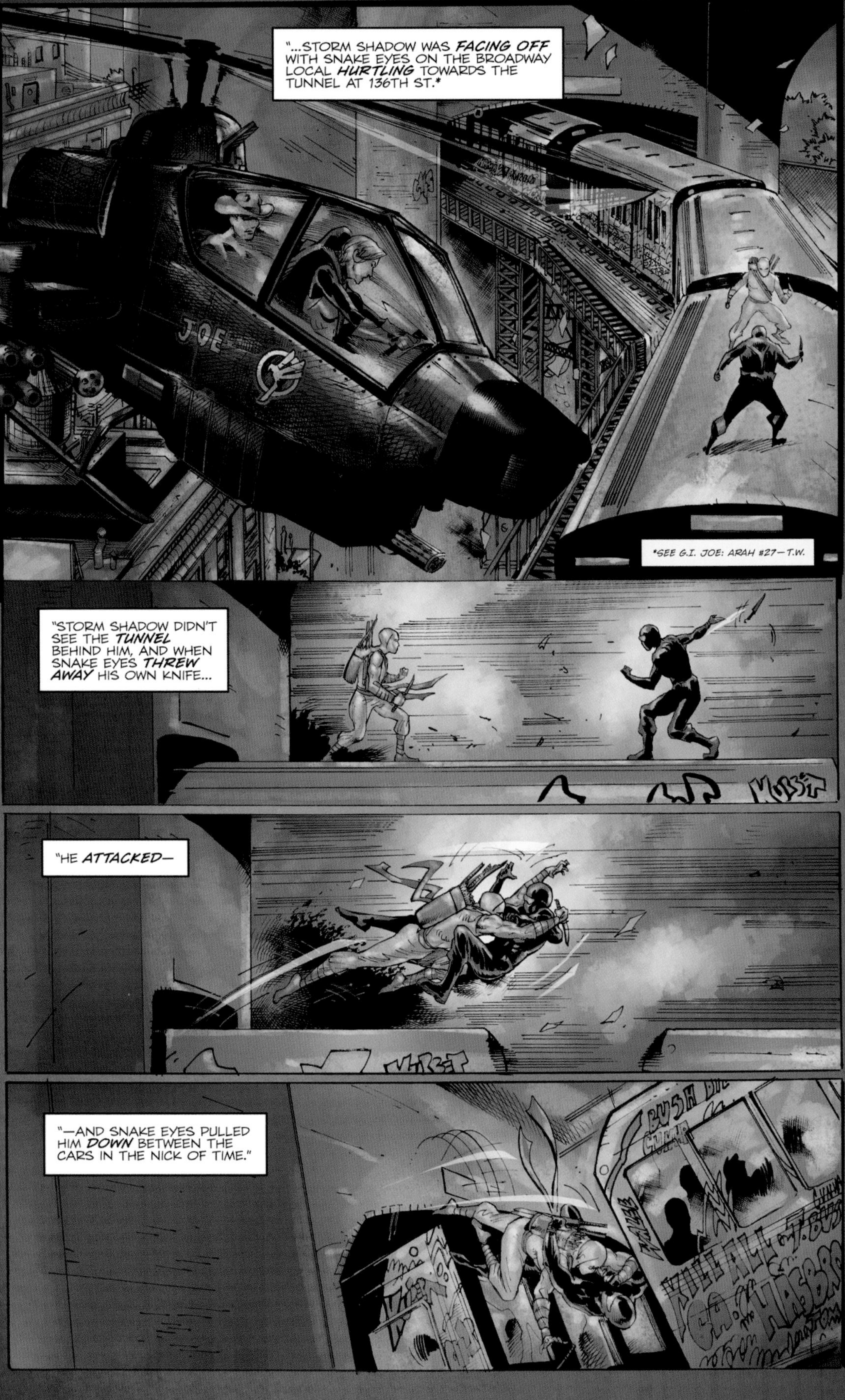
"...STORM SHADOW WAS FACING OFF WITH SNAKE EYES ON THE BROADWAY LOCAL HURTLING TOWARDS THE TUNNEL AT 136TH ST.*
JOE
*SEE G.I. JOE: ARAH #27—T.W.
"STORM SHADOW DIDN'T SEE THE TUNNEL BEHIND HIM, AND WHEN SNAKE EYES THREW AWAY HIS OWN KNIFE...
"HE ATTACKED—
"—AND SNAKE EYES PULLED HIM DOWN BETWEEN THE CARS IN THE NICK OF TIME."

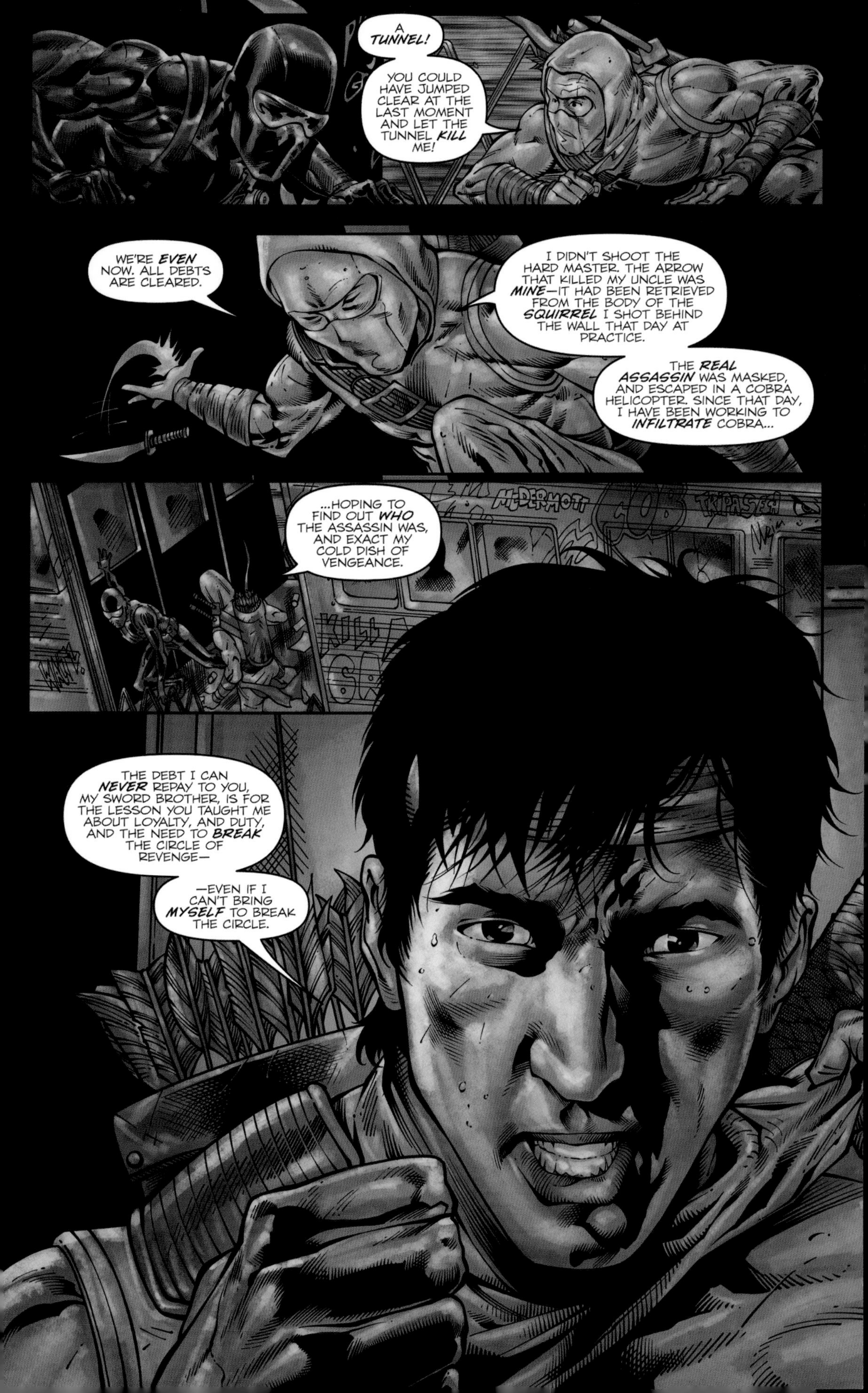

A TUNNEL!
YOU COULD HAVE JUMPED CLEAR AT THE LAST MOMENT AND LET THE TUNNEL KILL ME!
WE'RE EVEN NOW. ALL DEBTS ARE CLEARED.
I DIDN'T SHOOT THE HARD MASTER. THE ARROW THAT KILLED MY UNCLE WAS MINE—IT HAD BEEN RETRIEVED FROM THE BODY OF THE SQUIRREL I SHOT BEHIND THE WALL THAT DAY AT PRACTICE.
THE REAL ASSASSIN WAS MASKED, AND ESCAPED IN A COBRA HELICOPTER. SINCE THAT DAY, I HAVE BEEN WORKING TO INFILTRATE COBRA...
...HOPING TO FIND OUT WHO THE ASSASSIN WAS, AND EXACT MY COLD DISH OF VENGEANCE.
THE DEBT I CAN NEVER REPAY TO YOU, MY SWORD BROTHER, IS FOR THE LESSON YOU TAUGHT ME ABOUT LOYALTY, AND DUTY, AND THE NEED TO BREAK THE CIRCLE OF REVENGE—
—EVEN IF I CAN'T BRING MYSELF TO BREAK THE CIRCLE.

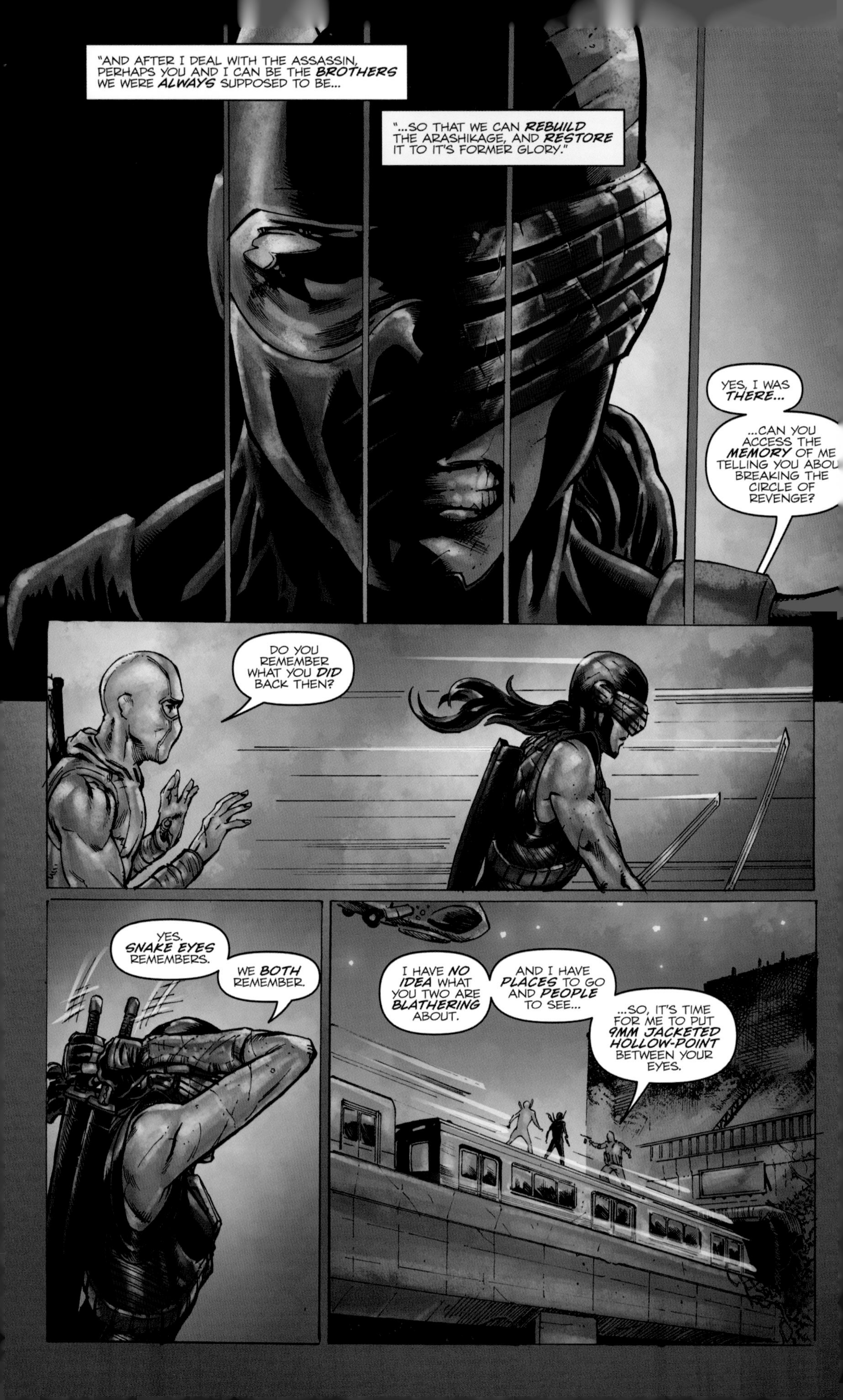
"AND AFTER I DEAL WITH THE ASSASSIN, PERHAPS YOU AND I CAN BE THE BROTHERS WE WERE ALWAYS SUPPOSED TO BE...
"...SO THAT WE CAN REBUILD THE ARASHIKAGE, AND RESTORE IT TO IT'S FORMER GLORY."
YES, I WAS THERE...
...CAN YOU ACCESS THE MEMORY OF ME TELLING YOU ABOU BREAKING THE CIRCLE OF REVENGE?
DO YOU REMEMBER WHAT YOU DID BACK THEN?
YES. SNAKE EYES REMEMBERS.
WE BOTH REMEMBER.
I HAVE NO IDEA WHAT YOU TWO ARE BLATHERING ABOUT.
AND I HAVE PLACES TO GO AND PEOPLE TO SEE...
...SO, IT'S TIME FOR ME TO PUT 9MM JACKETED HOLLOW-POINT BETWEEN YOUR EYES.

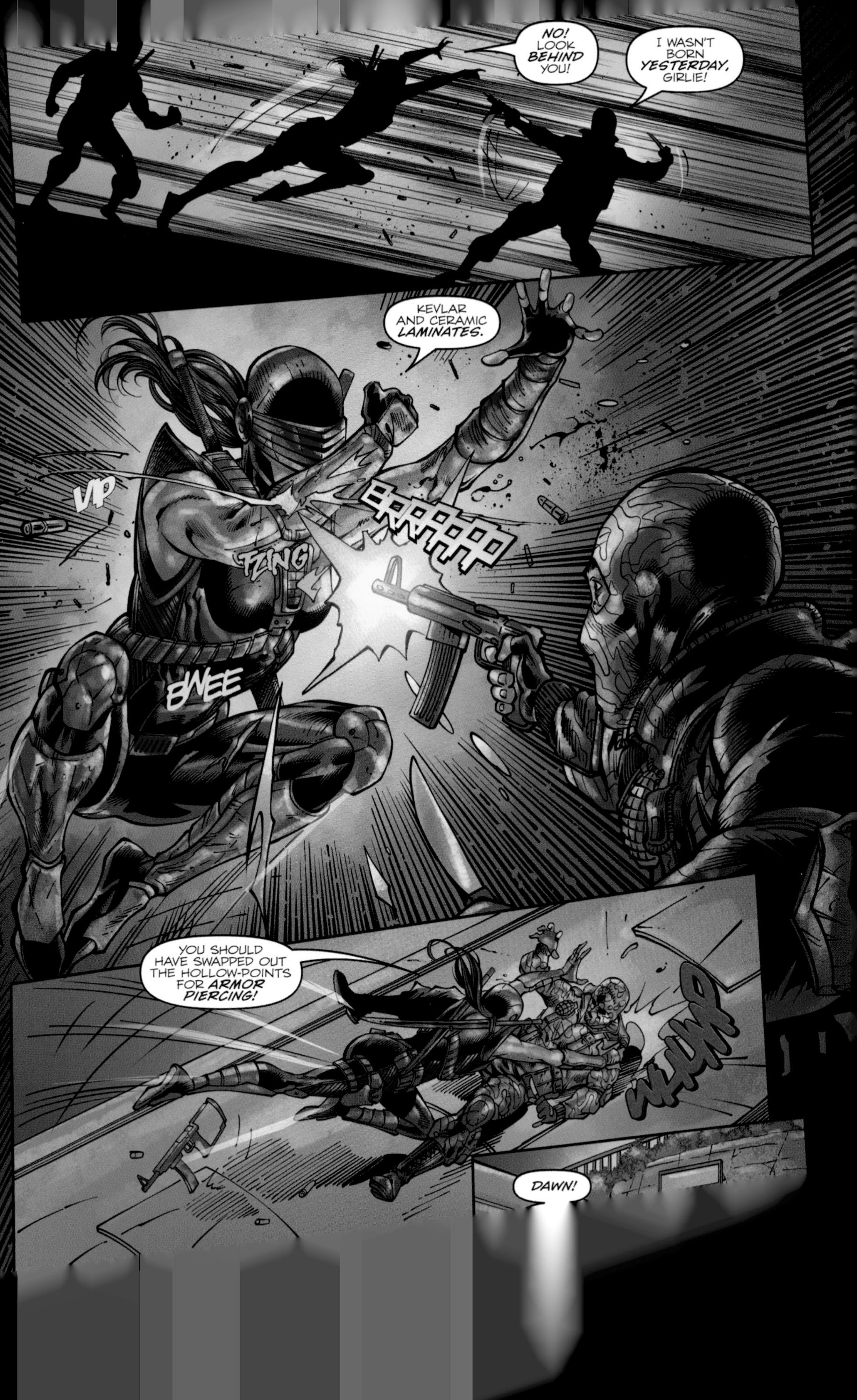
NO! LOOK BEHIND YOU!
I WASN'T BORN YESTERDAY, GIRLIE!
KEVLAR AND CERAMIC LAMINATES.
VIP
BRRRRRP
FZING
BWEE
YOU SHOULD HAVE SWAPPED OUT THE HOLLOW-POINTS FOR ARMOR PIERCING!
WHUMP
DAWN!

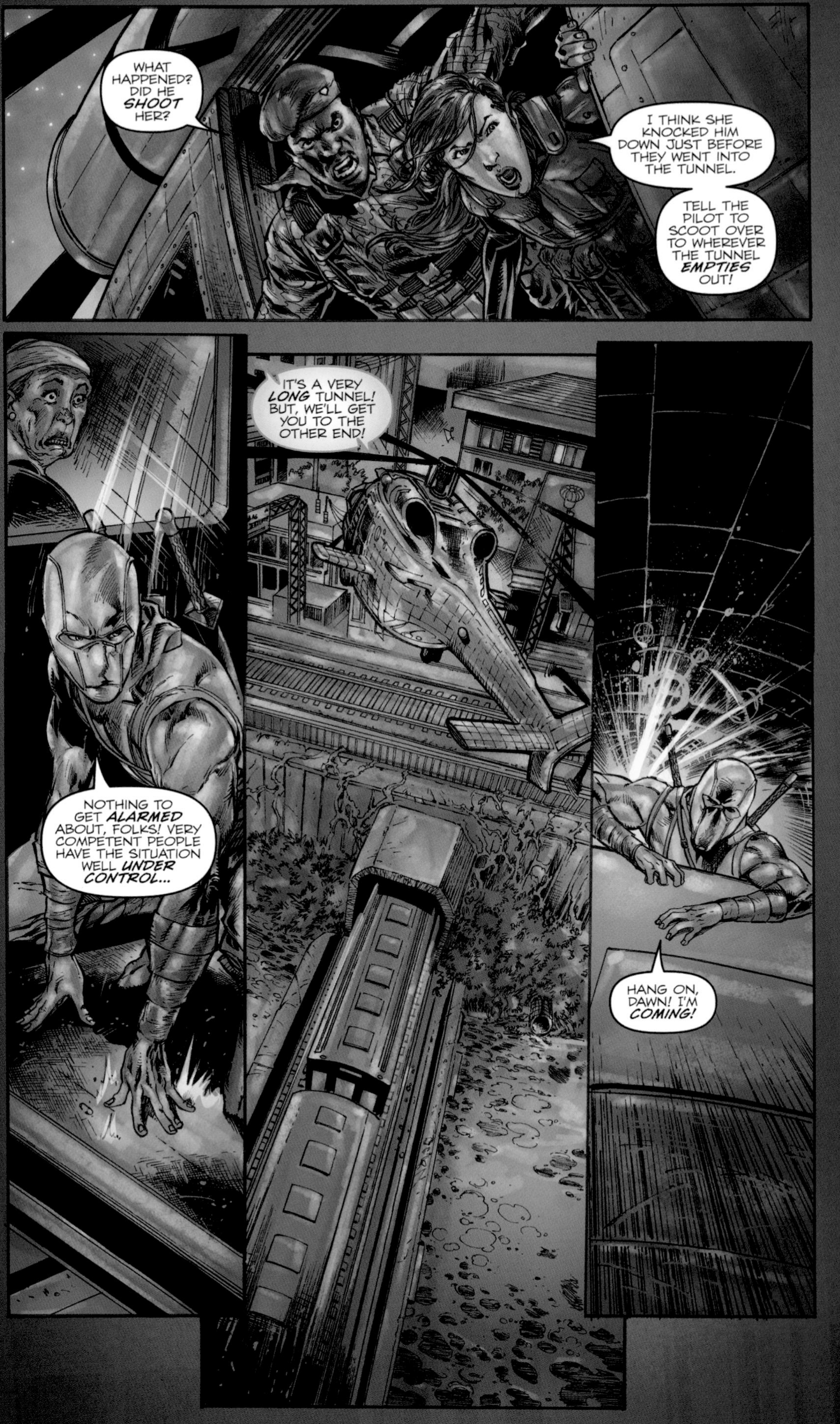
WHAT HAPPENED? DID HE SHOOT HER?
I THINK SHE KNOCKED HIM DOWN JUST BEFORE THEY WENT INTO THE TUNNEL.
TELL THE PILOT TO SCOOT OVER TO WHEREVER THE TUNNEL EMPTIES OUT!
NOTHING TO GET ALARMED ABOUT, FOLKS! VERY COMPETENT PEOPLE HAVE THE SITUATION WELL UNDER CONTROL...
IT'S A VERY LONG TUNNEL! BUT, WE'LL GET YOU TO THE OTHER END!
HANG ON, DAWN! I'M COMING!

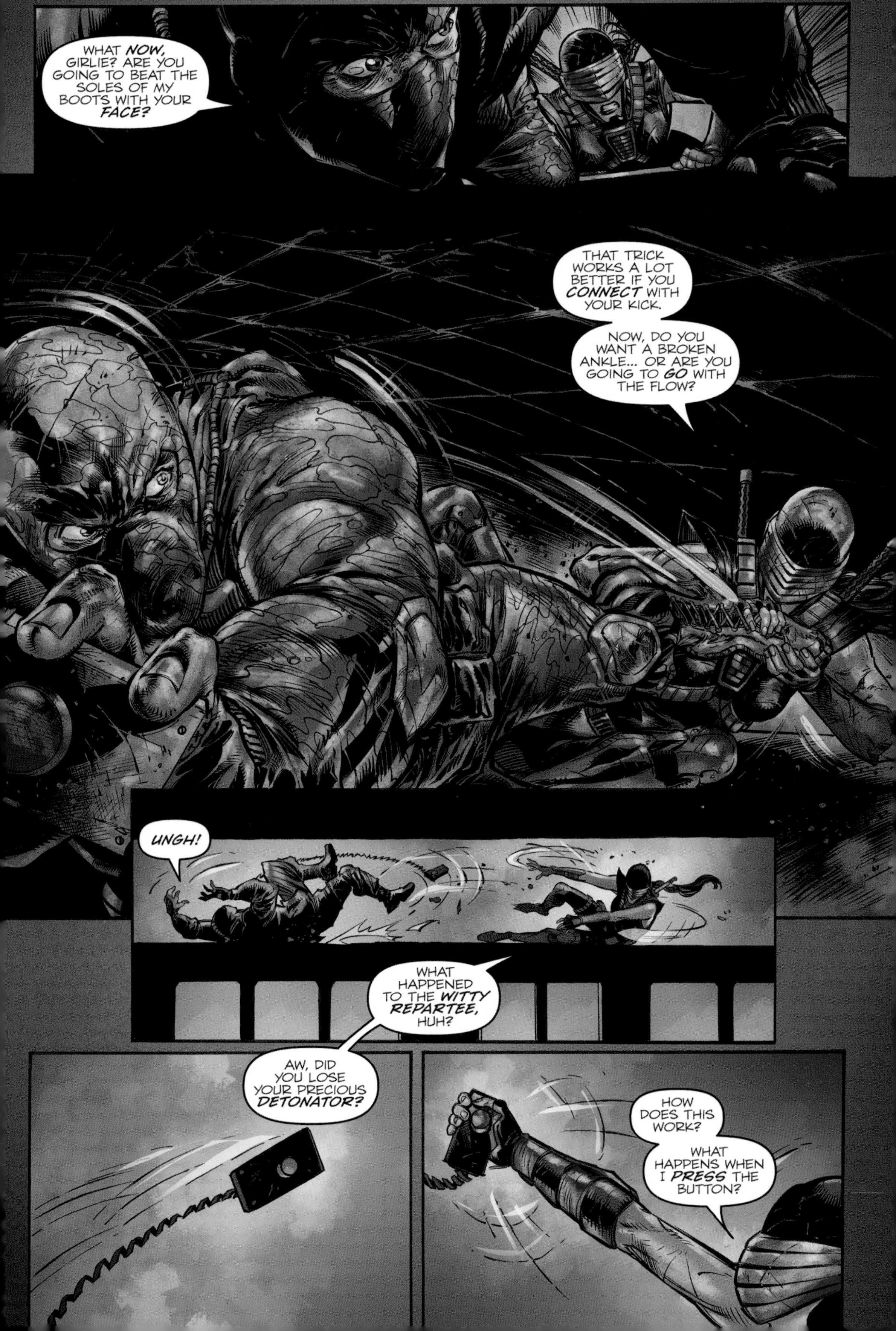
WHAT NOW, GIRLIE? ARE YOU GOING TO BEAT THE SOLES OF MY BOOTS WITH YOUR FACE?
THAT TRICK WORKS A LOT BETTER IF YOU CONNECT WITH YOUR KICK.
NOW, DO YOU WANT A BROKEN ANKLE... OR ARE YOU GOING TO GO WITH THE FLOW?
UNGH!
WHAT HAPPENED TO THE WITTY REPARTEE, HUH?
AW, DID YOU LOSE YOUR PRECIOUS DETONATOR?
HOW DOES THIS WORK?
WHAT HAPPENS WHEN I PRESS THE BUTTON?

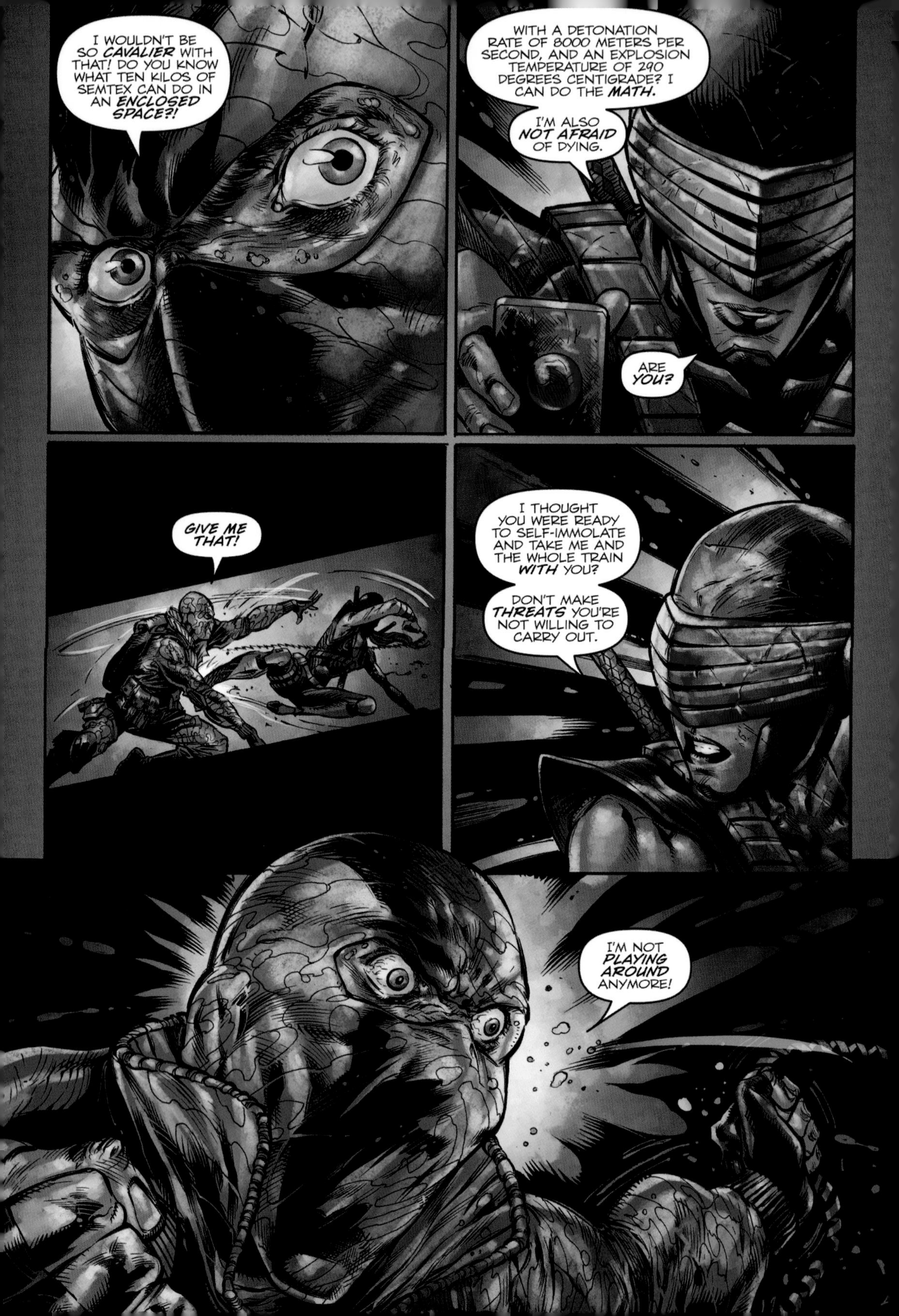
I WOULDN'T BE SO CAVALIER WITH THAT! DO YOU KNOW WHAT TEN KILOS OF SEMTEX CAN DO IN AN ENCLOSED SPACE?!
WITH A DETONATION RATE OF 8000 METERS PER SECOND, AND AN EXPLOSION TEMPERATURE OF 290 DEGREES CENTIGRADE? I CAN DO THE MATH.
I'M ALSO NOT AFRAID OF DYING.
ARE YOU?
GIVE ME THAT!
I THOUGHT YOU WERE READY TO SELF-IMMOLATE AND TAKE ME AND THE WHOLE TRAIN WITH YOU?
DON'T MAKE THREATS YOU'RE NOT WILLING TO CARRY OUT.
I'M NOT PLAYING AROUND ANYMORE!

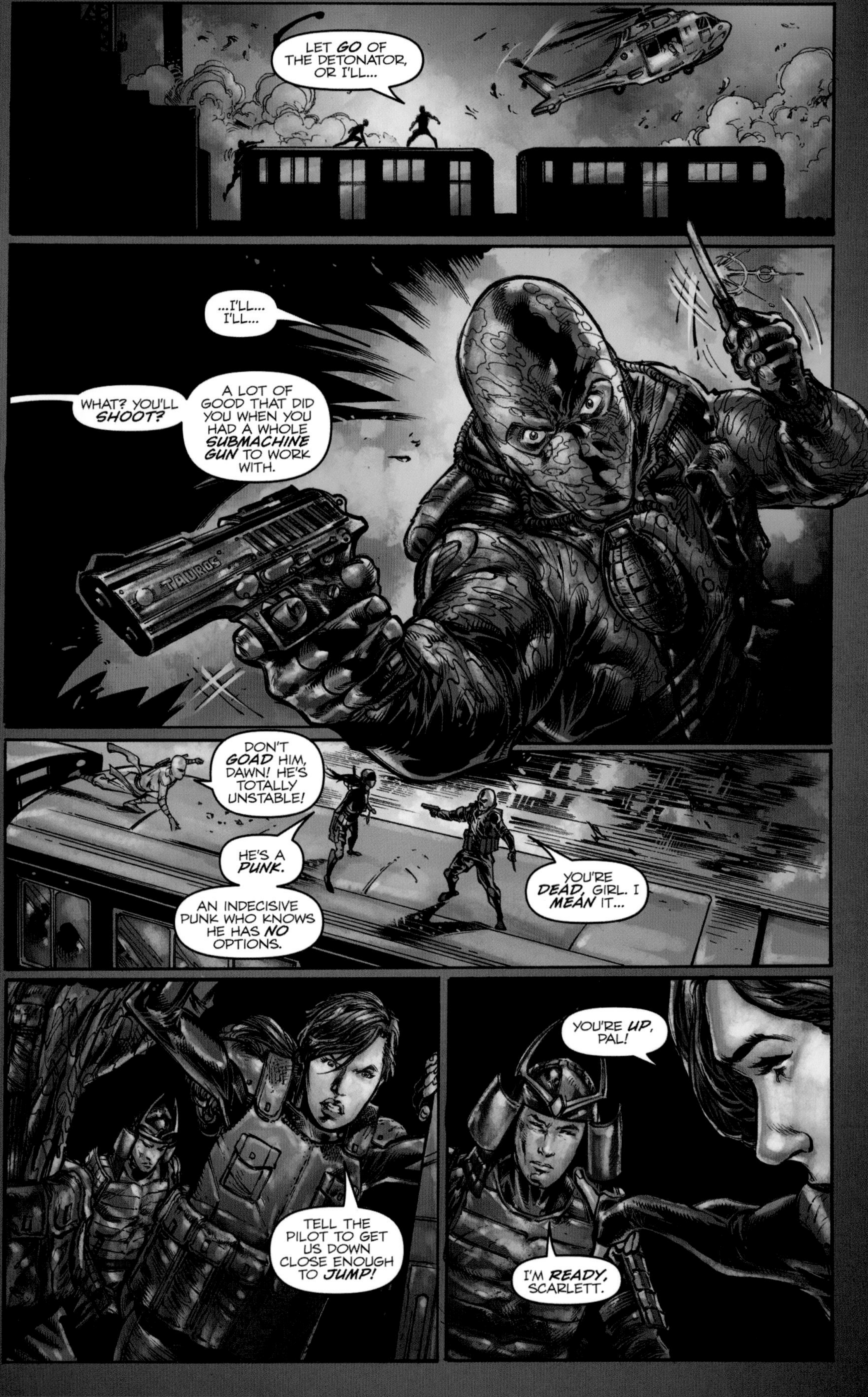
LET GO OF THE DETONATOR, OR I'LL...
...I'LL... I'LL...
WHAT? YOU'LL SHOOT?
A LOT OF GOOD THAT DID YOU WHEN YOU HAD A WHOLE SUBMACHINE GUN TO WORK WITH.
TAUROS
DON'T GOAD HIM, DAWN! HE'S TOTALLY UNSTABLE!
HE'S A PUNK.
AN INDECISIVE PUNK WHO KNOWS HE HAS NO OPTIONS.
YOU'RE DEAD, GIRL. I MEAN IT...
TELL THE PILOT TO GET US DOWN CLOSE ENOUGH TO JUMP!
YOU'RE UP, PAL!
I'M READY, SCARLETT.

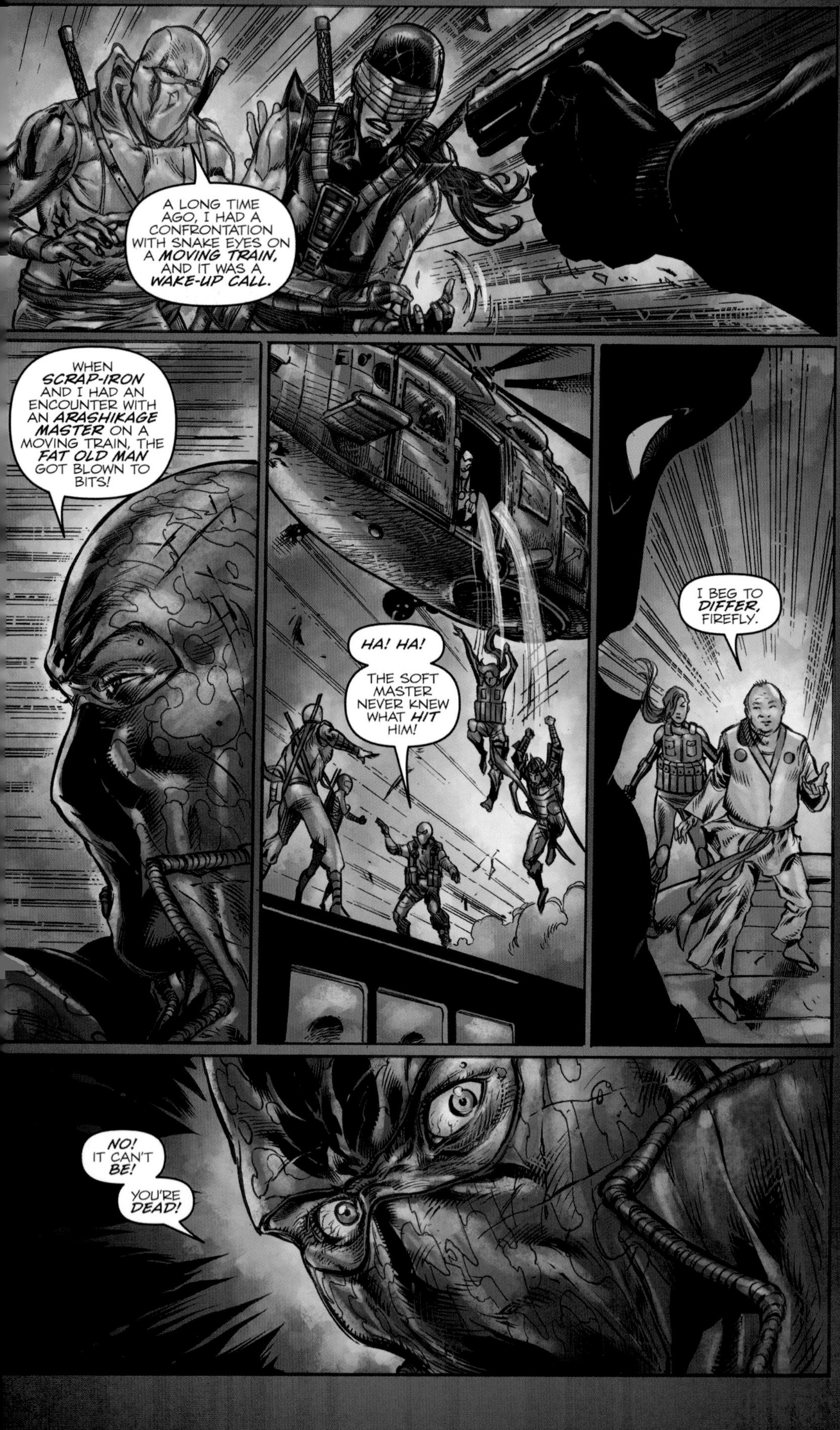
A LONG TIME AGO, I HAD A CONFRONTATION WITH SNAKE EYES ON A MOVING TRAIN, AND IT WAS A WAKE-UP CALL.
WHEN SCRAP-IRON AND I HAD AN ENCOUNTER WITH AN ARASHIKAGE MASTER ON A MOVING TRAIN, THE FAT OLD MAN GOT BLOWN TO BITS!
HA! HA!
THE SOFT MASTER NEVER KNEW WHAT HIT HIM!
I BEG TO DIFFER, FIREFLY.
NO! IT CAN'T BE!
YOU'RE DEAD!

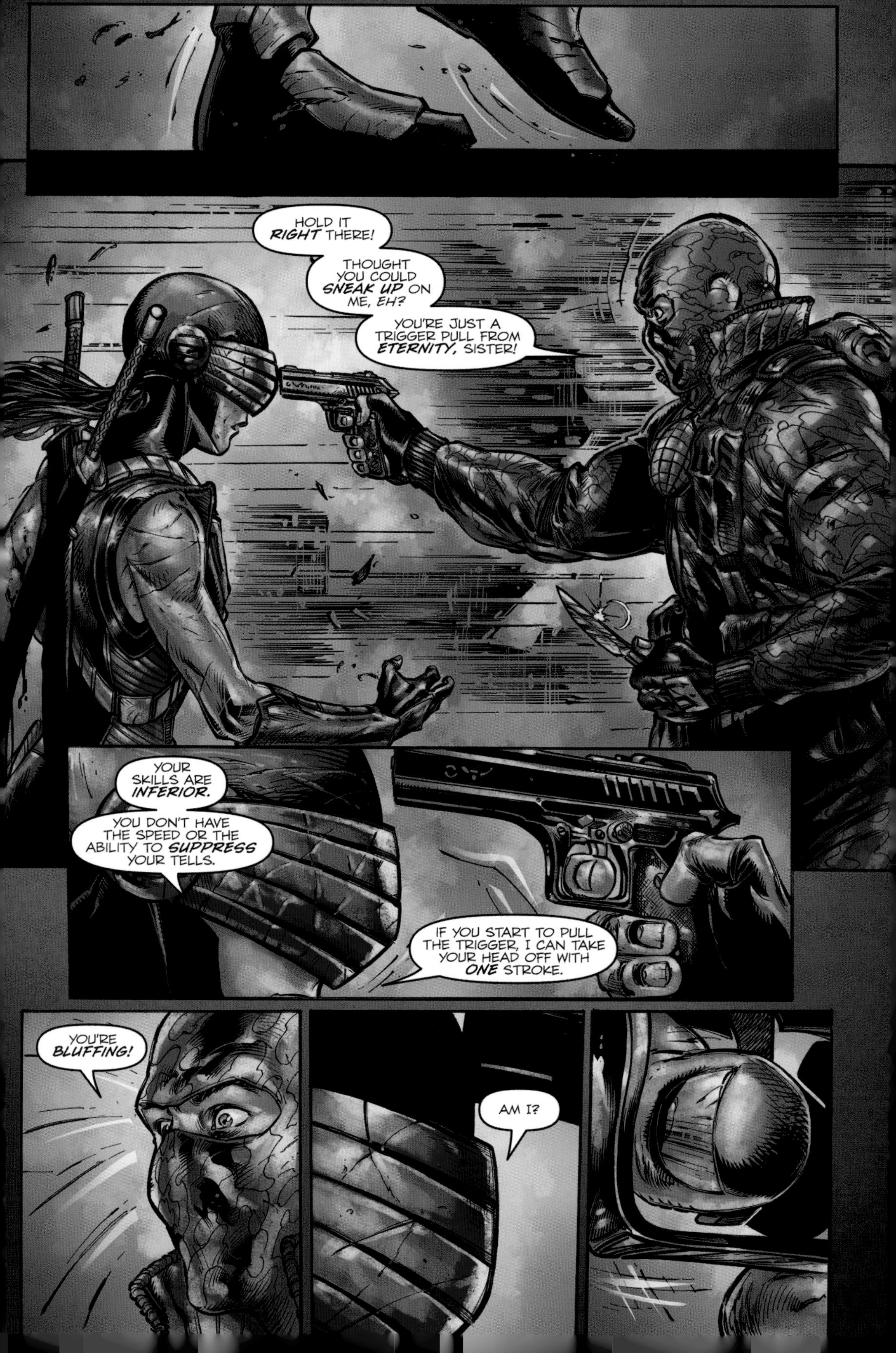
HOLD IT RIGHT THERE!
THOUGHT YOU COULD SNEAK UP ON ME, EH?
YOU'RE JUST A TRIGGER PULL FROM ETERNITY, SISTER!
YOUR SKILLS ARE INFERIOR.
YOU DON'T HAVE THE SPEED OR THE ABILITY TO SUPPRESS YOUR TELLS.
IF YOU START TO PULL THE TRIGGER, I CAN TAKE YOUR HEAD OFF WITH ONE STROKE.
YOU'RE BLUFFING!
AM I?

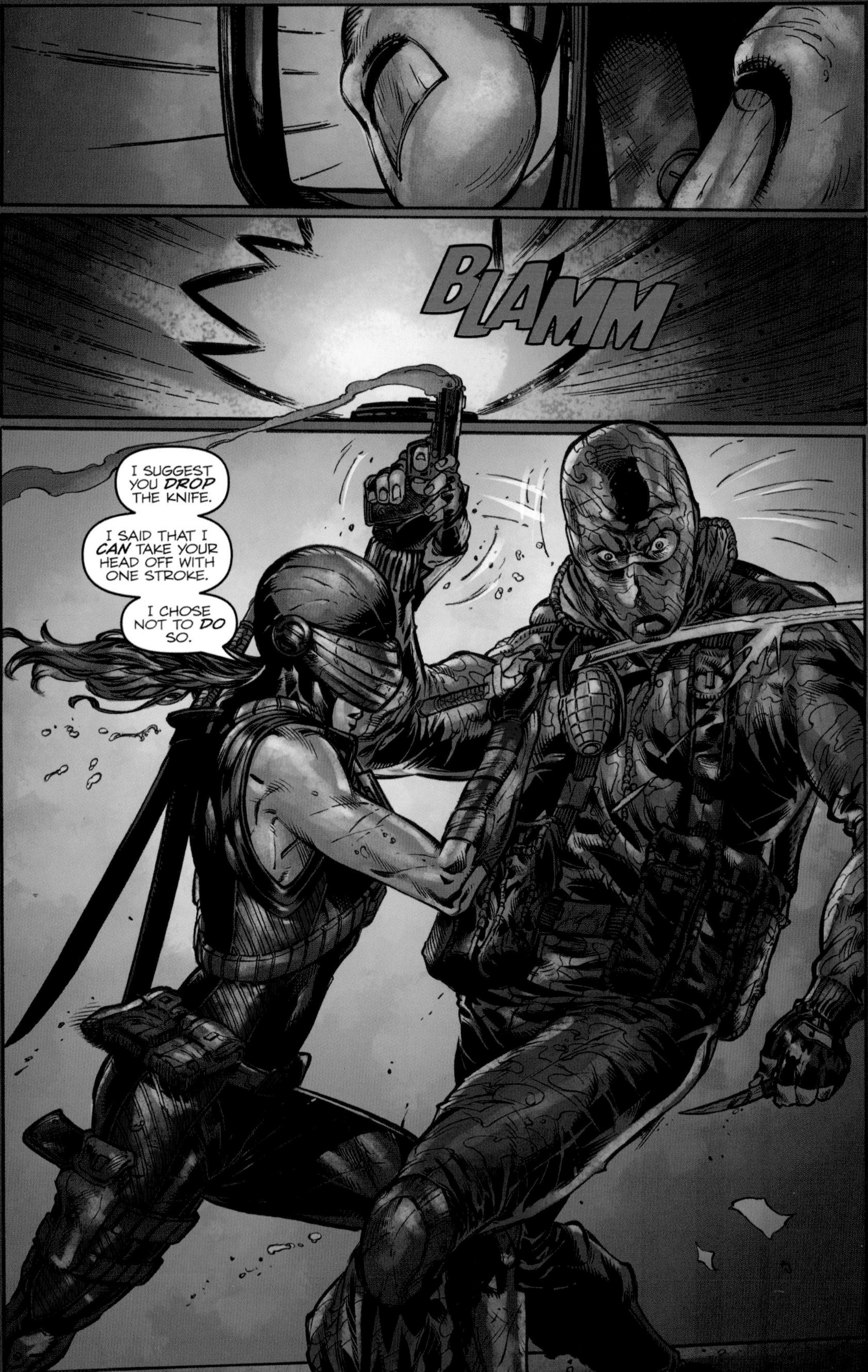
BLAMM
I SUGGEST YOU DROP THE KNIFE.
I SAID THAT I CAN TAKE YOUR HEAD OFF WITH ONE STROKE.
I CHOSE NOT TO DO SO.

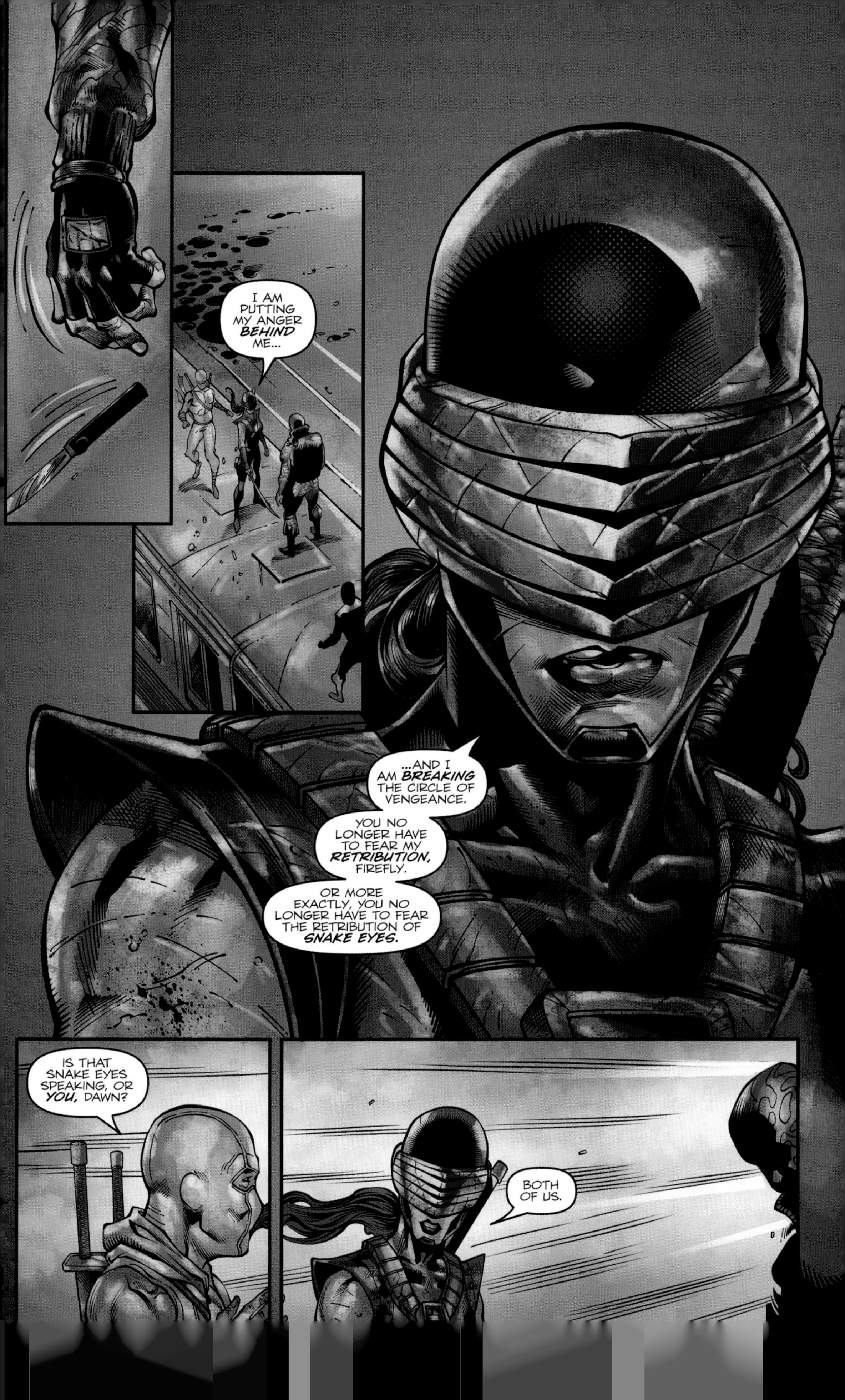

I AM PUTTING MY ANGER BEHIND ME...
...AND I AM BREAKING THE CIRCLE OF VENGEANCE.
YOU NO LONGER HAVE TO FEAR MY RETRIBUTION, FIREFLY.
OR MORE EXACTLY, YOU NO LONGER HAVE TO FEAR THE RETRIBUTION OF SNAKE EYES.
IS THAT SNAKE EYES SPEAKING, OR YOU, DAWN?
BOTH OF US.

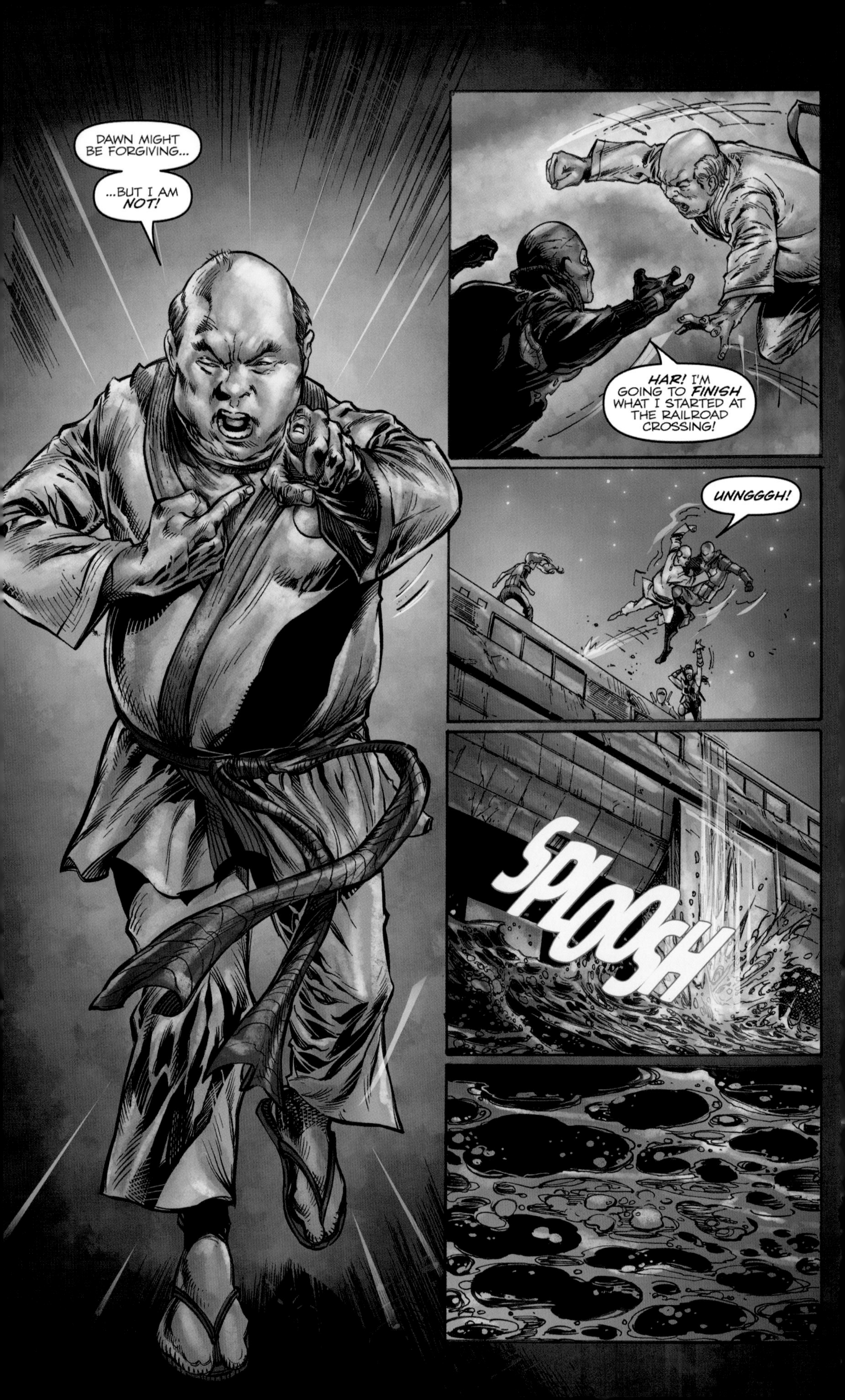
DAWN MIGHT BE FORGIVING...
...BUT I AM NOT!
HAR! I'M GOING TO FINISH WHAT I STARTED AT THE RAILROAD CROSSING!
UNNGGGH!
SPLOOSH

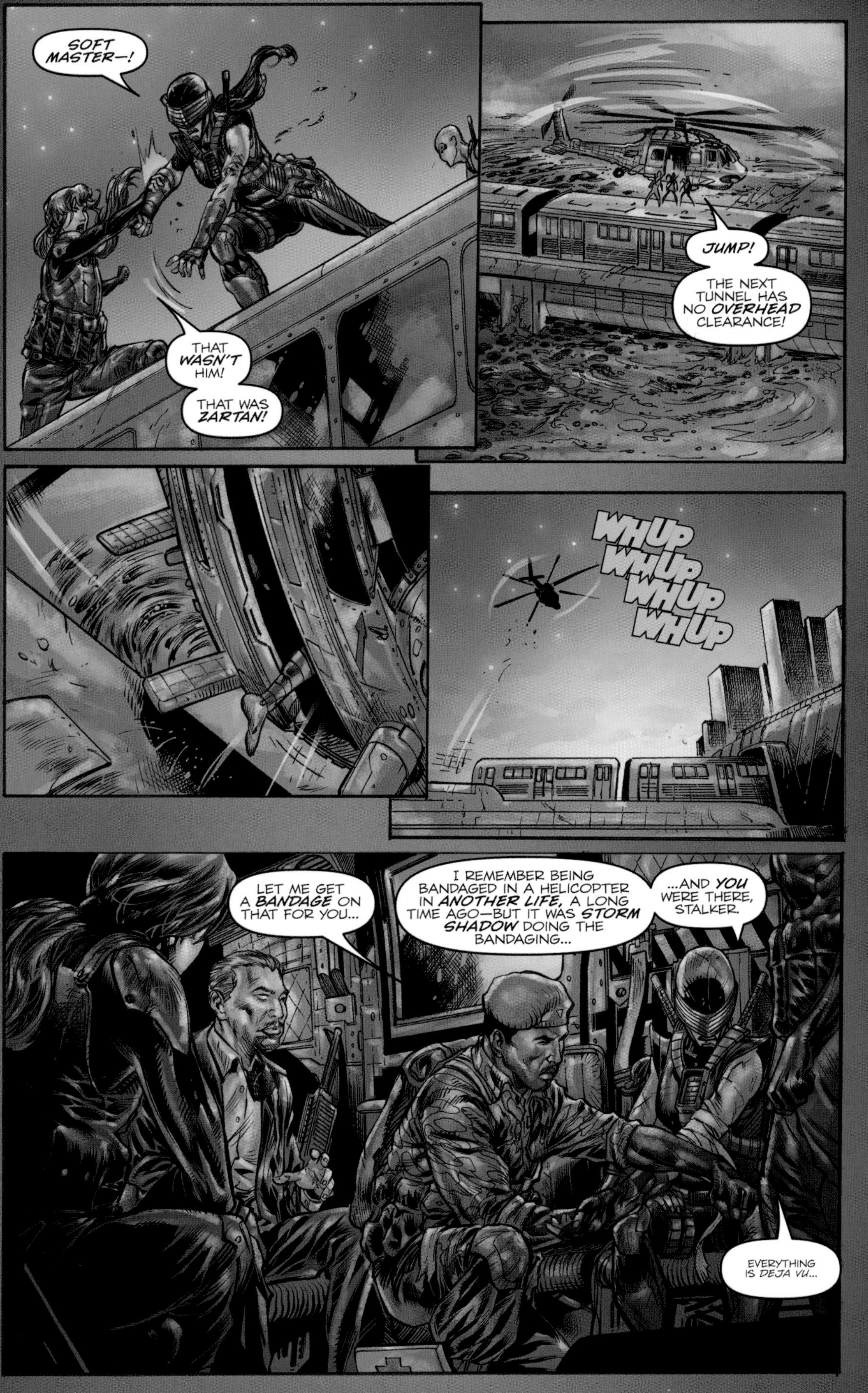
SOFT MASTER—!
THAT WASN'T HIM!
THAT WAS ZARTAN!
JUMP!
THE NEXT TUNNEL HAS NO OVERHEAD CLEARANCE!
WHUP WHUP WHUP WHUP
LET ME GET A BANDAGE ON THAT FOR YOU...
I REMEMBER BEING BANDAGED IN A HELICOPTER IN ANOTHER LIFE, A LONG TIME AGO—BUT IT WAS STORM SHADOW DOING THE BANDAGING...
...AND YOU WERE THERE, STALKER.
EVERYTHING IS DEJA VU...

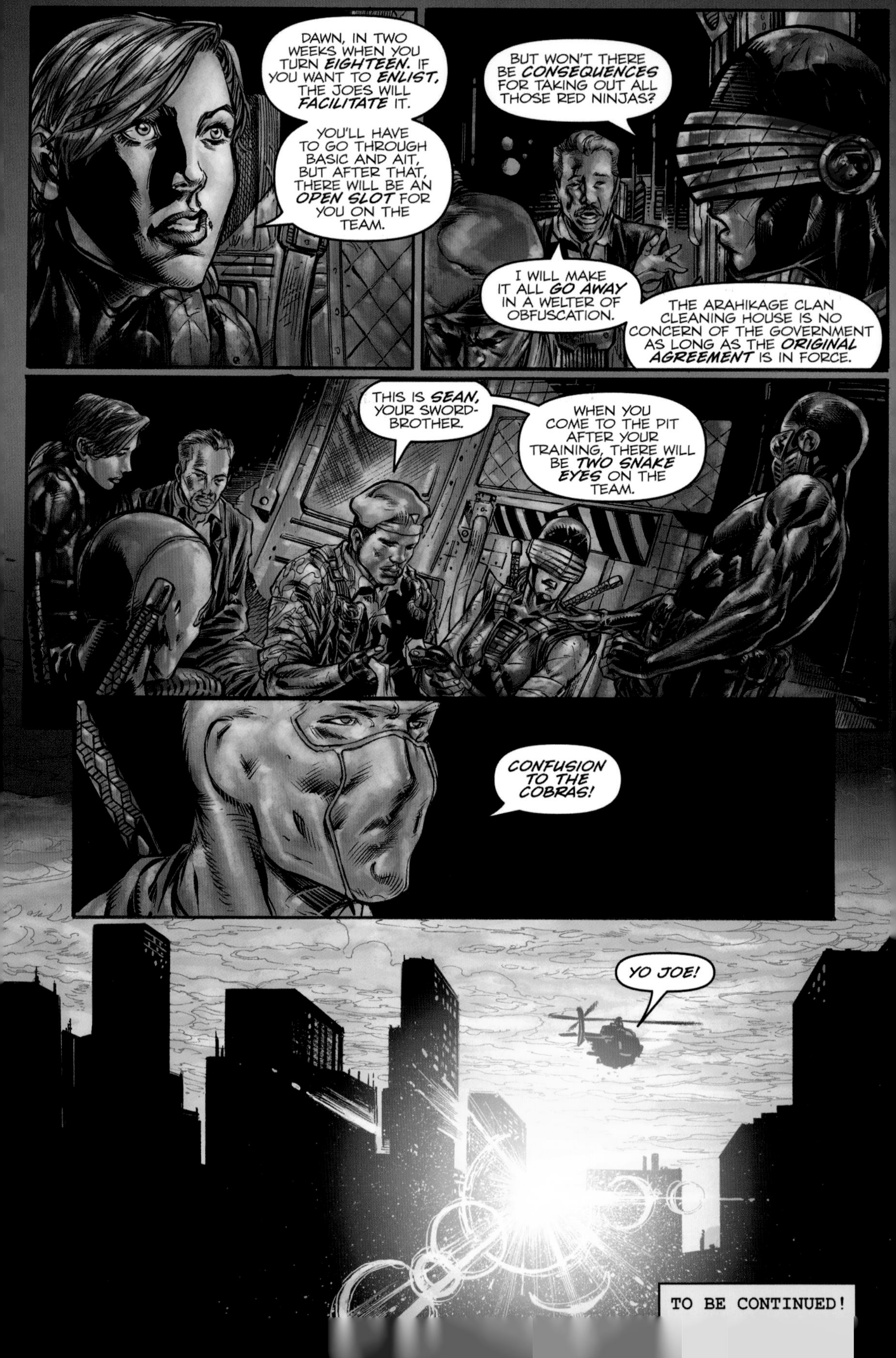

DAWN, IN TWO WEEKS WHEN YOU TURN EIGHTEEN. IF YOU WANT TO ENLIST, THE JOES WILL FACILITATE IT.
YOU'LL HAVE TO GO THROUGH BASIC AND AIT, BUT AFTER THAT, THERE WILL BE AN OPEN SLOT FOR YOU ON THE TEAM.
BUT WON'T THERE BE CONSEQUENCES FOR TAKING OUT ALL THOSE RED NINJAS?
I WILL MAKE IT ALL GO AWAY IN A WELTER OF OBFUSCATION.
THE ARAHIKAGE CLAN CLEANING HOUSE IS NO CONCERN OF THE GOVERNMENT AS LONG AS THE ORIGINAL AGREEMENT IS IN FORCE.
THIS IS SEAN, YOUR SWORD-BROTHER.
WHEN YOU COME TO THE PIT AFTER YOUR TRAINING, THERE WILL BE TWO SNAKE EYES ON THE TEAM.
CONFUSION TO THE COBRAS!
YO JOE!
TO BE CONTINUED!

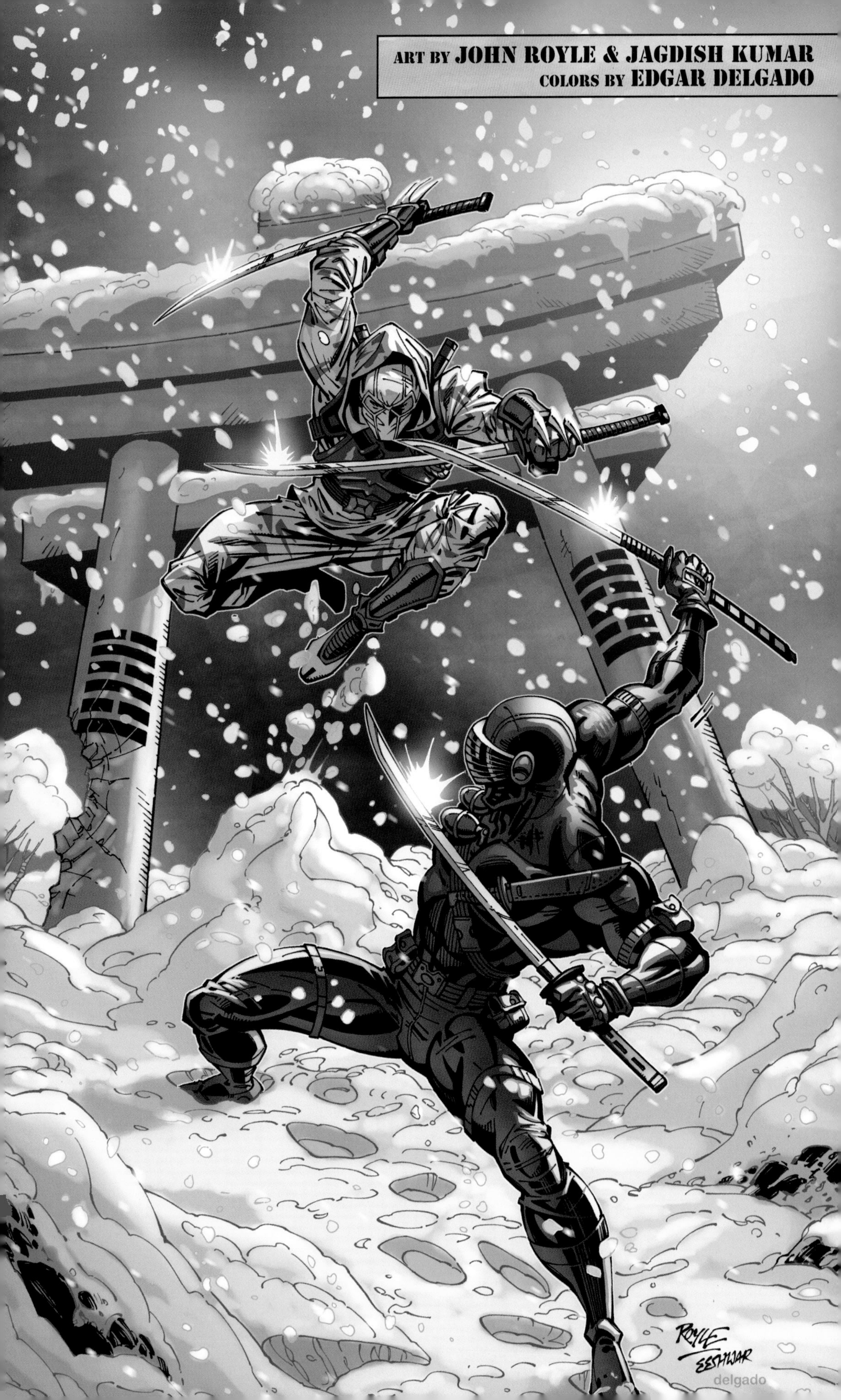
ART BY JOHN ROYLE & JAGDISH KUMAR
COLORS BY EDGAR DELGADO
ROYLE
EESHWAR
delgado

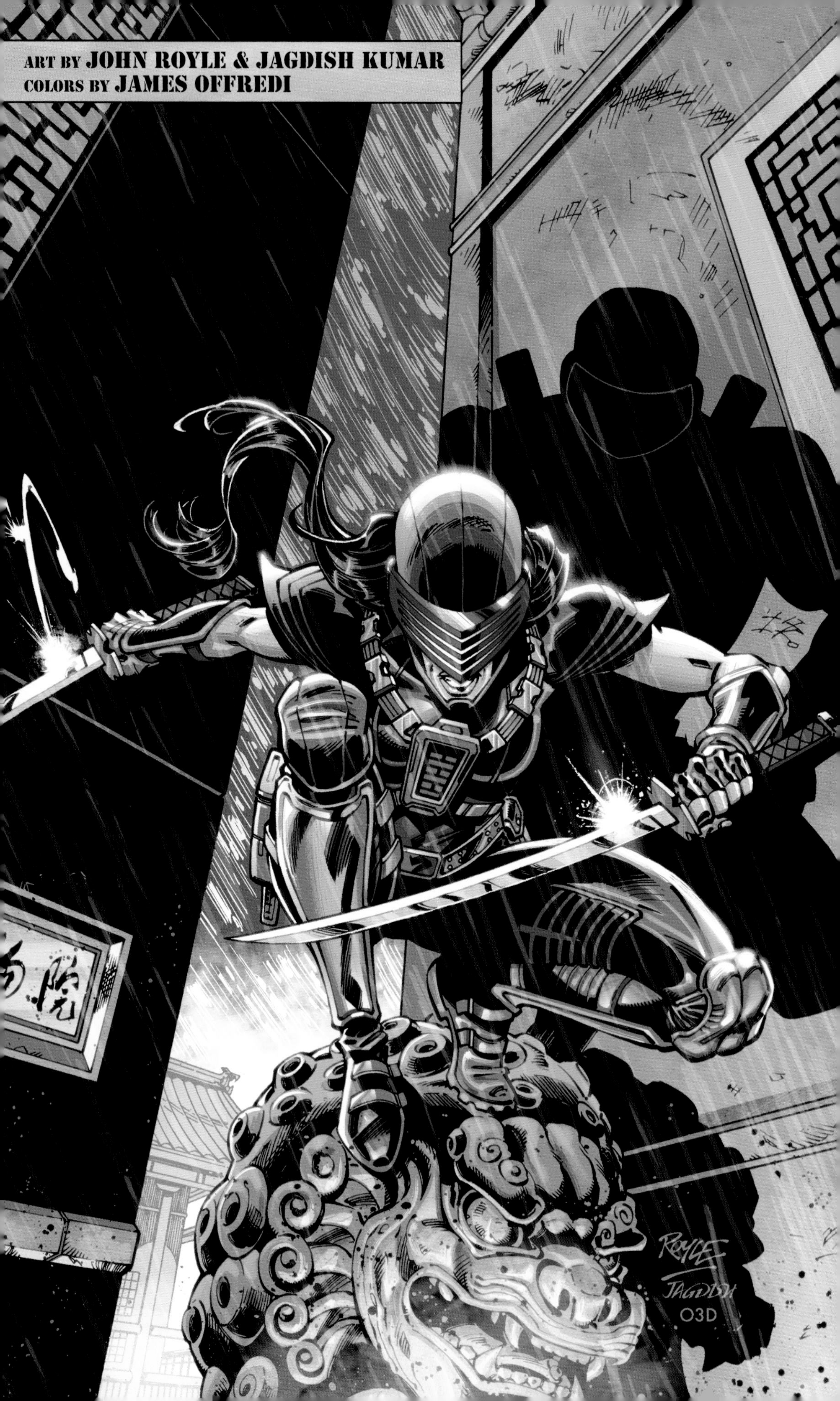
ART BY JOHN ROYLE & JAGDISH KUMAR
COLORS BY JAMES OFFREDI
ROYLE
JAGDISH
O3D

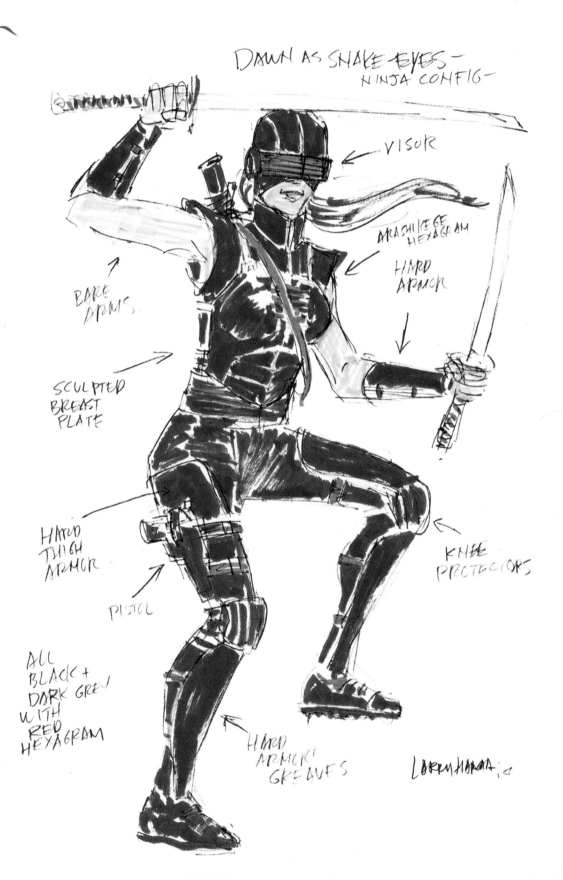

DAWN AS SNAKE-EYES —
— NINJA CONFIG —

VISOR

ARASHIKAGE
HEXAGRAM

HARD
ARMOR

BARE
ARMS.

SCULPTED
BREAST
PLATE

HARD
THIGH
ARMOR

KNEE
PROTECTORS

PISTOL

ALL
BLACK +
DARK GREY
WITH
RED
HEXAGRAM

HARD
ARMOR
GREAVES

LARRY HAMA

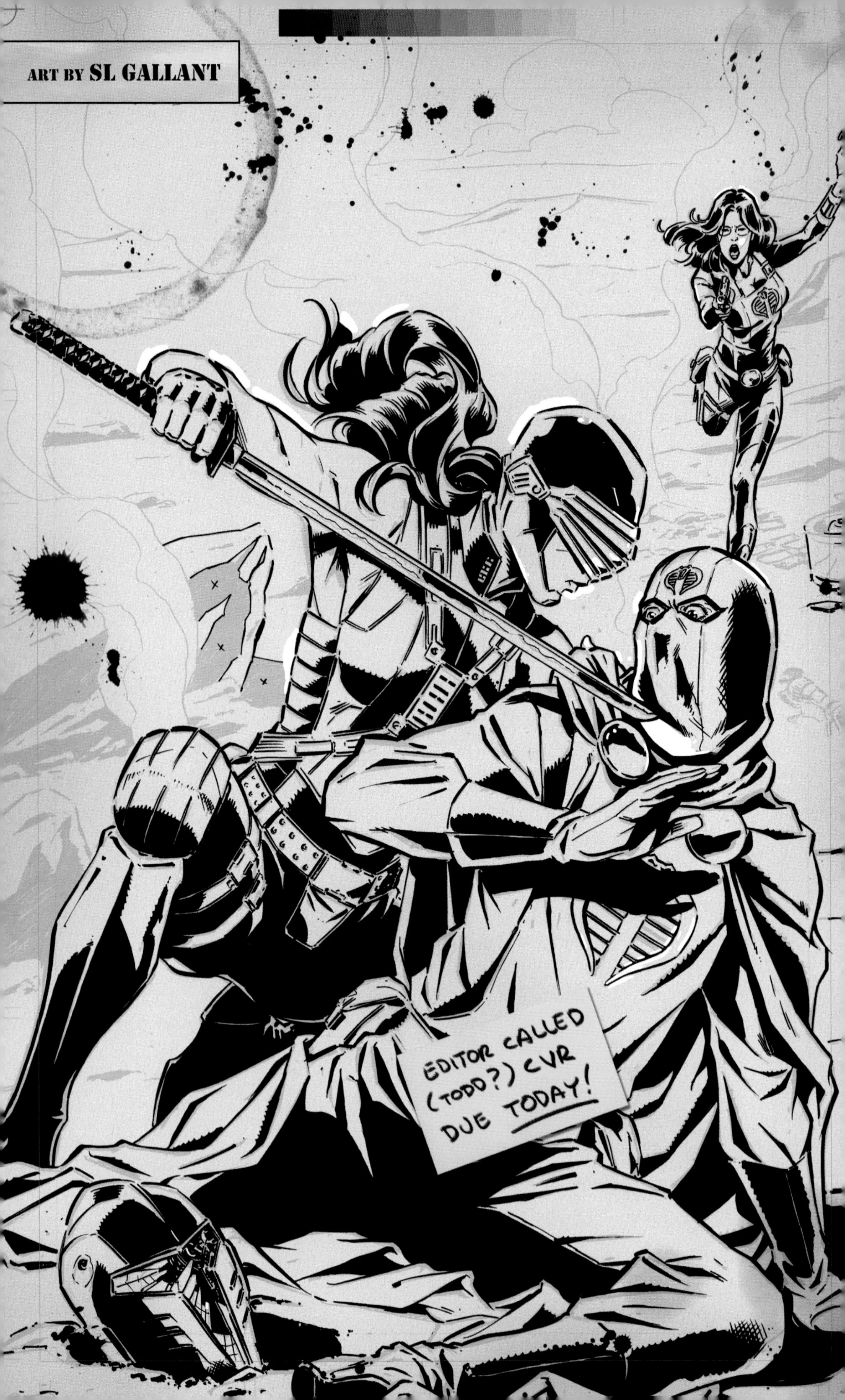
ART BY SL GALLANT
EDITOR CALLED (TODD?) CVR DUE TODAY!

ART BY **JOHN ROYLE & JAGDISH KUMAR**
COLORS BY **JAMES OFFREDI**

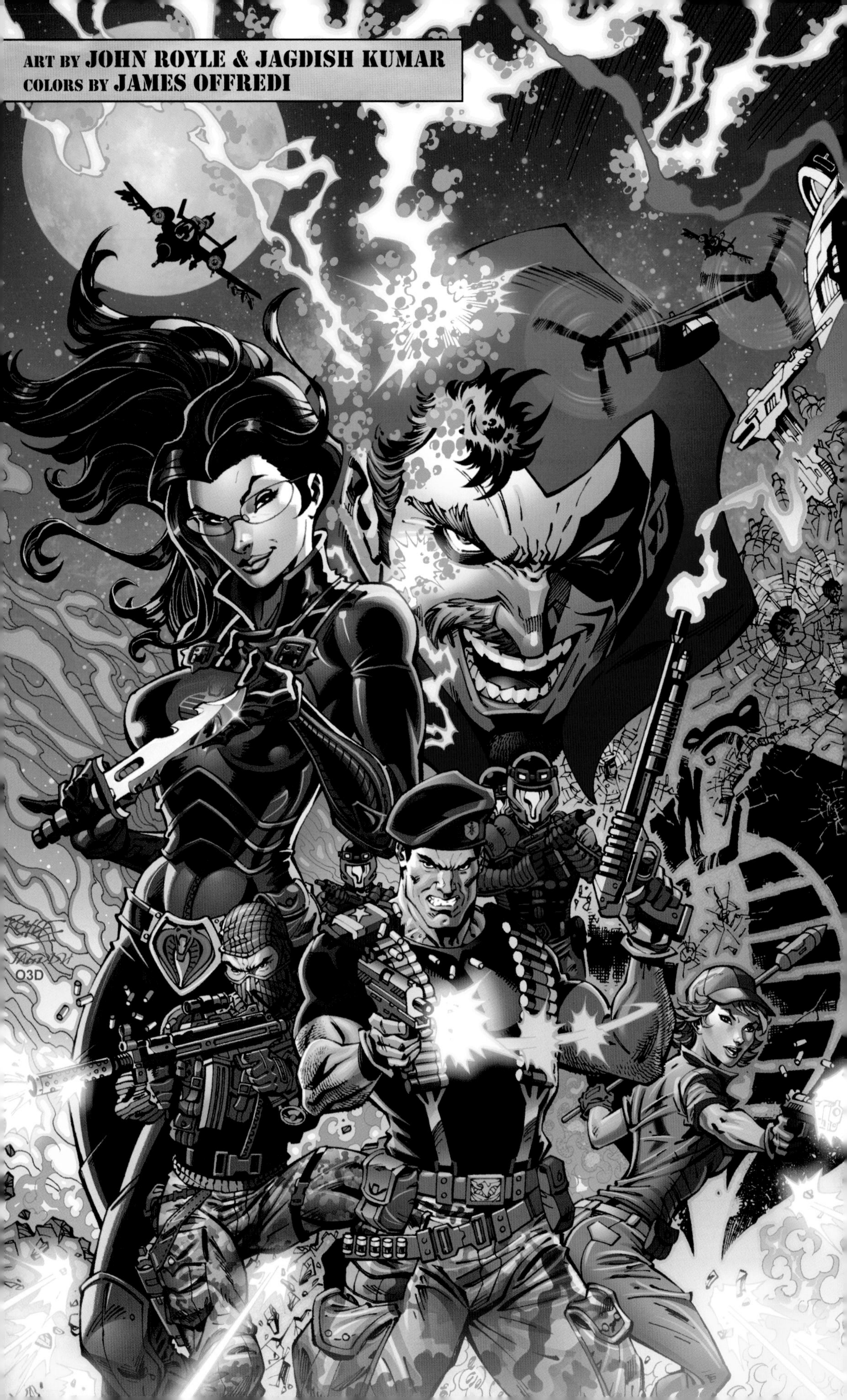

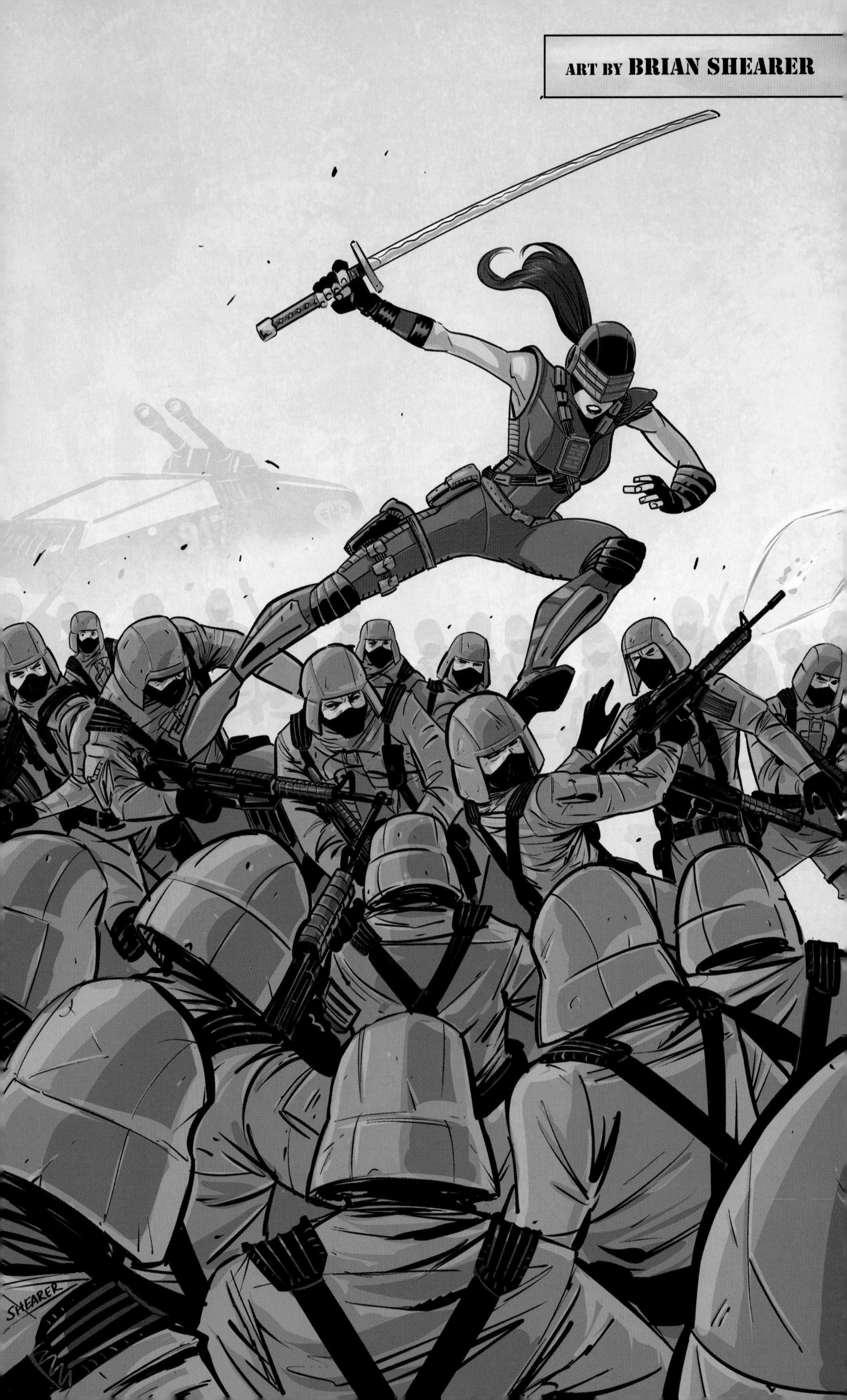
SHEARER

ART BY BRIAN SHEARER

ART BY **MATEUS SANTOLOUCO**

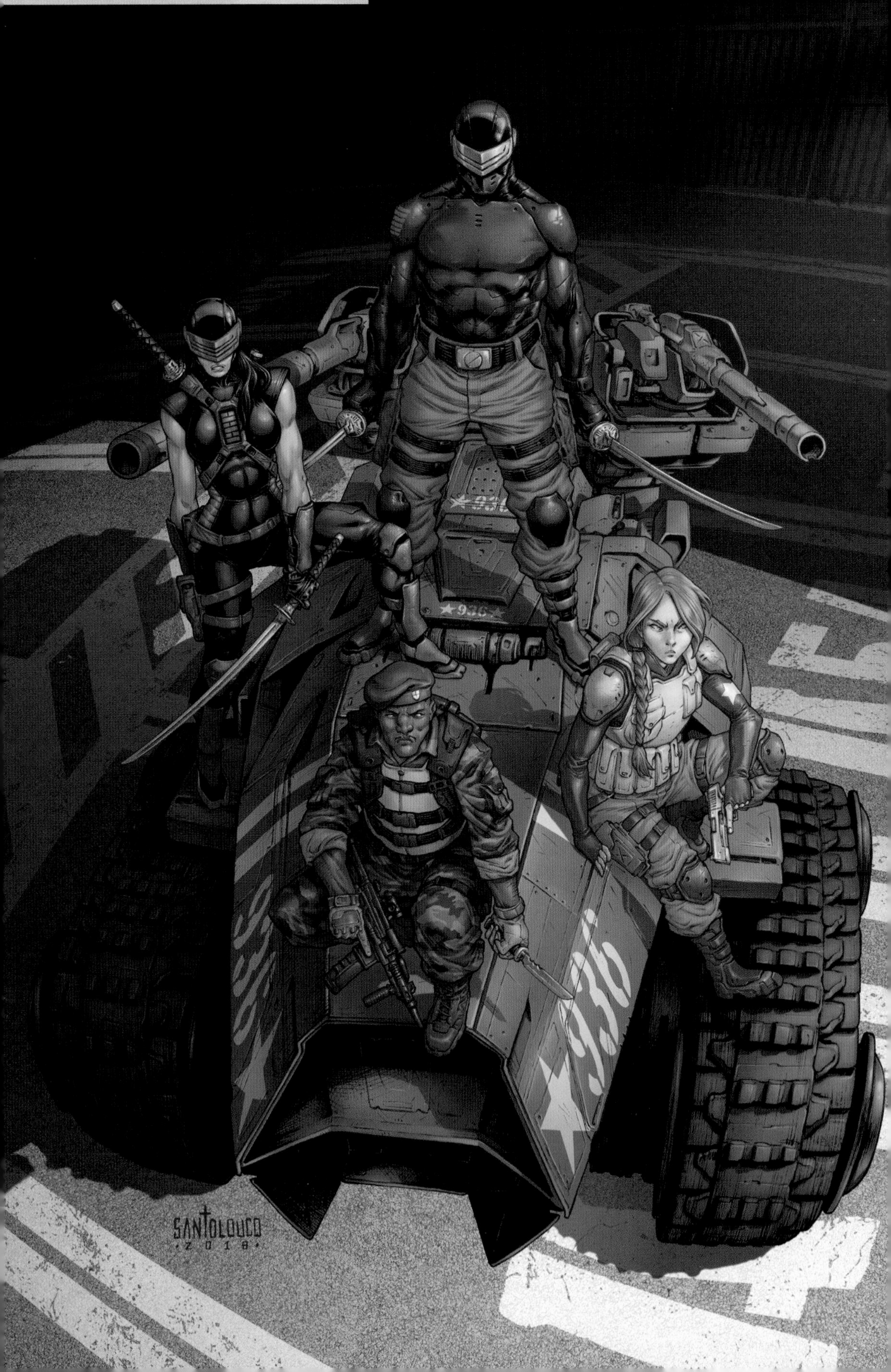
936
SANTOLOUCO
2018

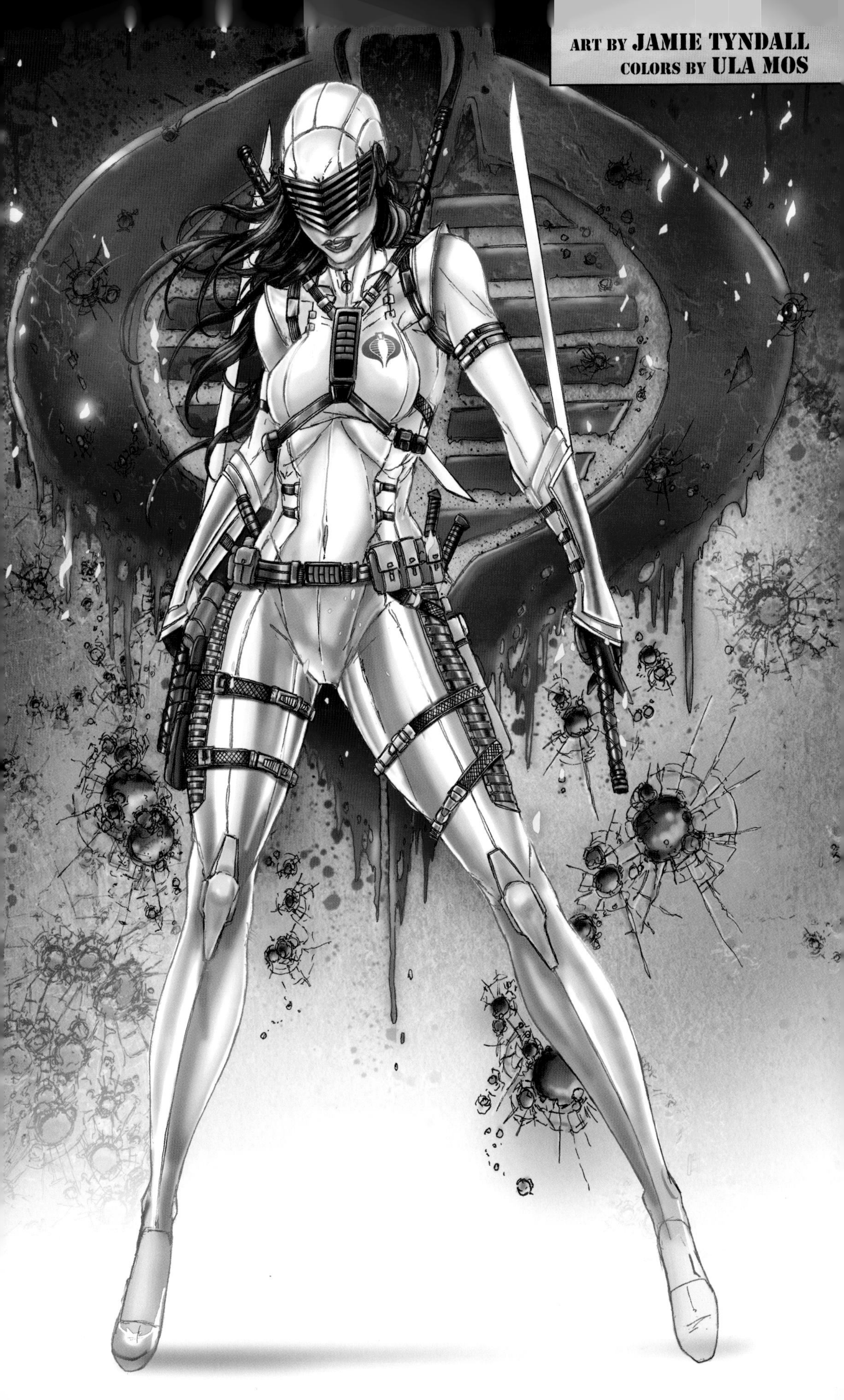

ART BY JAMIE TYNDALL
COLORS BY ULA MOS

ART BY **NATALI SANDERS**

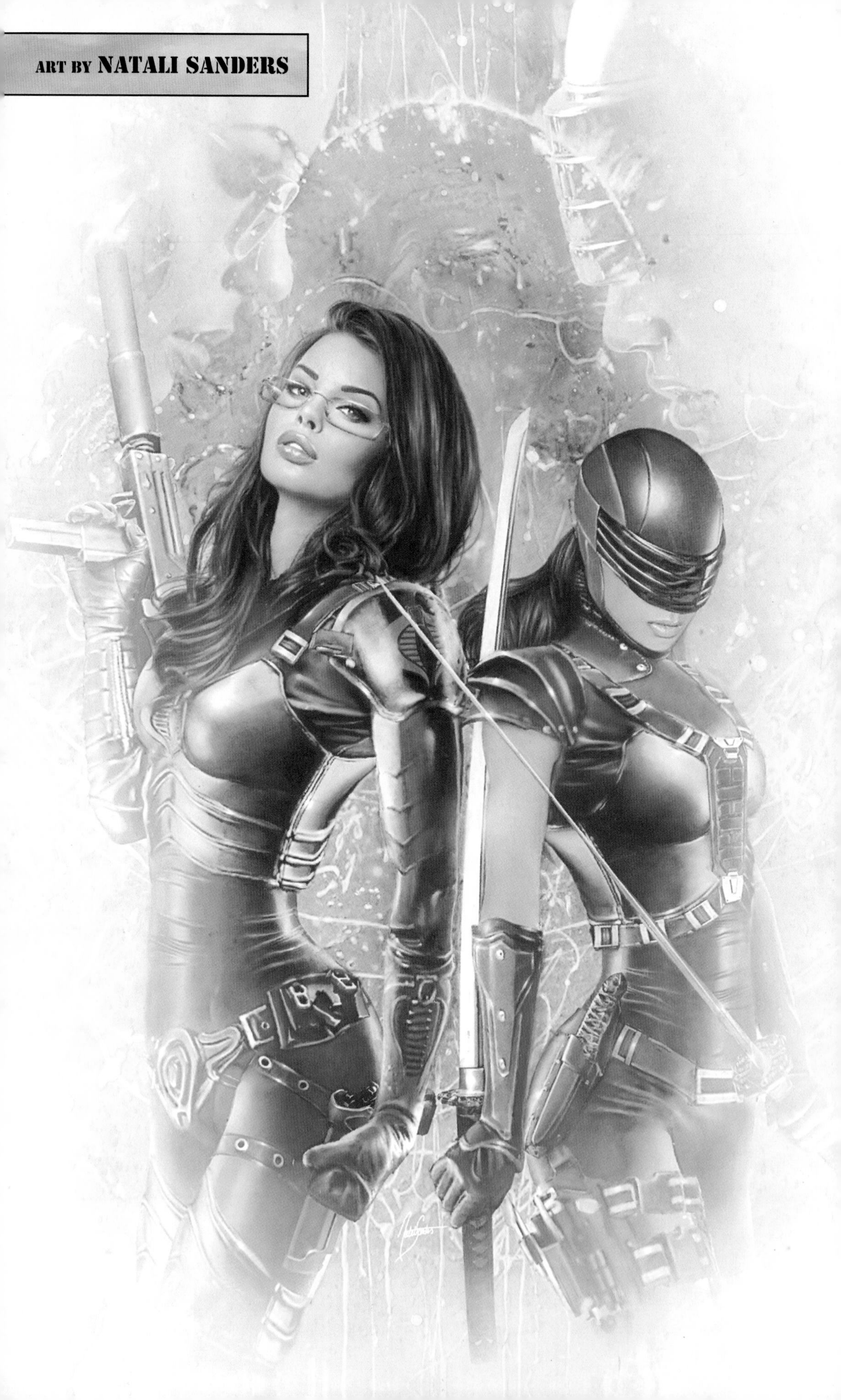

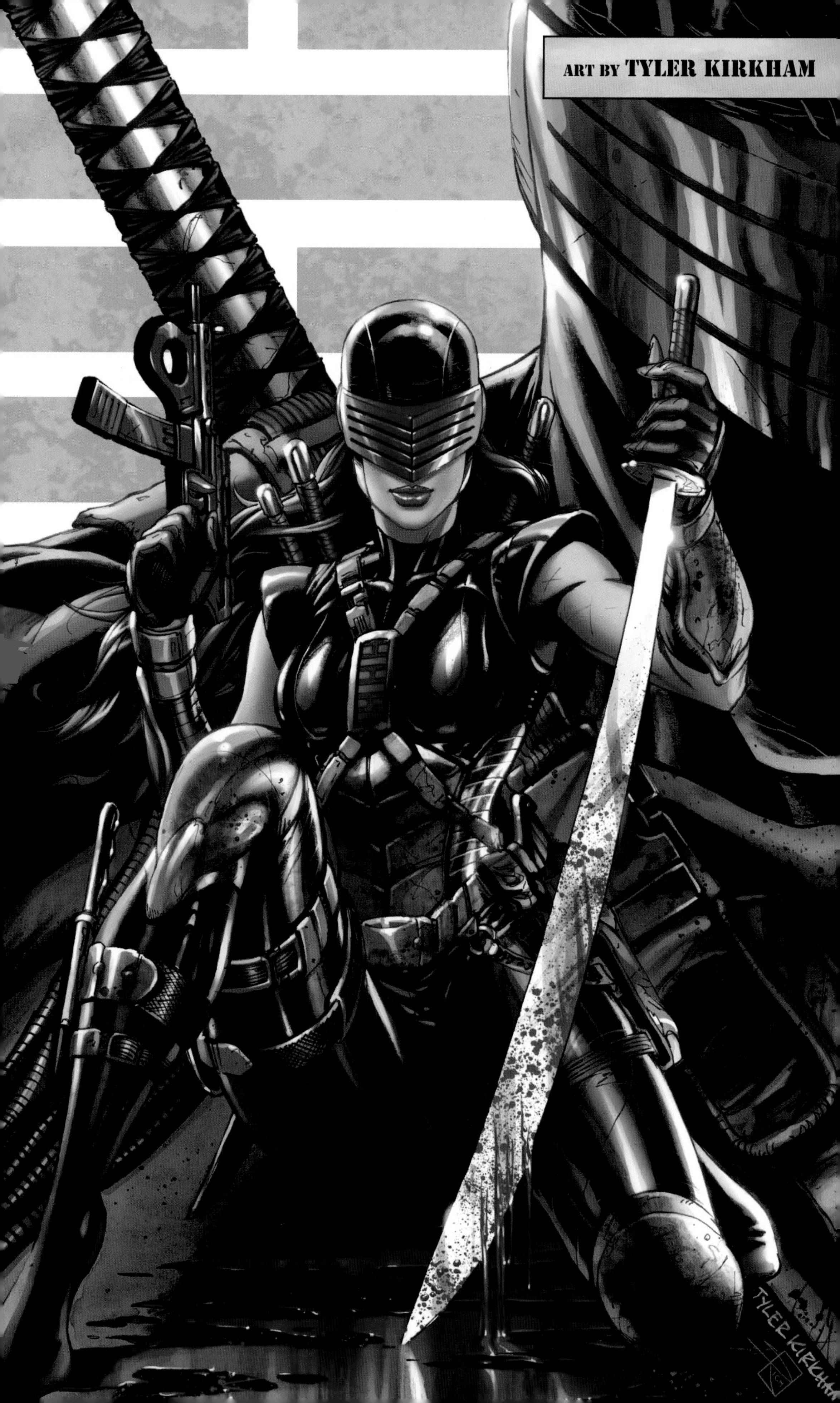
TYLER KIRKHAM
ART BY TYLER KIRKHAM

SNAKE EYES IS DEAD...

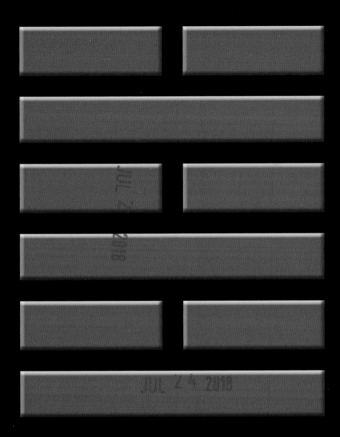

LONG LIVE SNAKE EYES